PRAISE FOR *HOME BEFORE DARK*

WINNER of the Blood Drop Award for Icelandic Crime Novel of the year
SHORTLISTED for The Glass Key Award for Best Nordic Crime Novel

'Eva Bjorg Aegisdottir just gets better and better and this original, clever novel kept me gripped and furiously turning the pages. Stylishly conceived and executed, *Home before Dark* is that rare crime novel: pacy and well-plotted but also driven by well-drawn, believable characters with real depth. Put this at the top of your summer TBR pile' Sarah Pearse

'A complex, increasingly creepy tale of young love, dysfunctional families, long-buried secrets and pen pals who are not what they seem … Its psychological depth and physical shocks recall the work of the great Ruth Rendell' *Sunday Times*

'A chilling, atmospheric mystery with a devilishly unguessable solution. Truly addictive, I inhaled it in a single day' Louise Candlish

'This is psychological thriller writing of a rare order and evidence that any comments about the demise of Scandicrime are greatly exaggerated' *Financial Times*

'A masterclass of psychological suspense from the superstar of Icelandic noir … addictively creepy' *Daily Express*

'*Home Before Dark* will have you checking your doors and windows before you go to bed' *Sunday Mirror*

'Dark, chilling and so atmospheric, I was utterly gripped by this clever, twisty thriller … a must-read' Claire Douglas

'Winter's darkness creates an eerie background for Marsibil's growing instability and her dangerous war on secrets. A page-turning, twisty blend of coming of age themes, family trauma, and well-crafted menace' *Booklist*

'Like an Icelandic winter, *Home before Dark* chilled me to the very core. An utterly gripping read, it kept me guessing till the last shocking twist' Heidi Amsinck

'With sharp twists and explorations of the damaging loyalties that warp those they're meant to protect, the chilling, unrelenting noir novel *Home Before Dark* follows a missing persons case that masks enduring traumas' *Foreword Reviews*

'Eva Björg Ægisdóttir is a masterful storyteller, and the drama she inserts into her novels can leave you breathless' TripFiction

'Addictive' *Crime Monthly*

PRAISE FOR THE FORBIDDEN ICELAND SERIES

WINNER of the CWA John Creasey (New Blood) Dagger
WINNER of the Storytel Award for Best Crime Novel
WINNER of the Blackbird Award for Best Icelandic Crime Novel
WINNER of the Blood Drop Award for Best Icelandic Crime Novel

'She uses complex plots to explore how monsters are made and demonstrate that "evil can lurk behind the most attractive of smiles" … If you have never read Ægisdóttir, now is the time to start' *The Times*

'Fantastic' *Sunday Times*

'So atmospheric' *Heat*

'A canny synthesis of modern Nordic Noir and Golden Age mystery' *Financial Times*

'Your new Nordic Noir obsession' *Vogue*

'So chilling' *Crime Monthly*

'Exciting and harrowing' Ragnar Jónasson

'Chilling and addictive, with a completely unexpected twist …
I loved it' Shari Lapena

'Fans of Nordic Noir will love this' Ann Cleeves

'Emotive, atmospheric and chillingly suspenseful' A.A. Chaudhuri

'This is virtuoso suspense writing' A.J. Finn

'Riveting, exciting, entertaining and packed with intrigue'
Liz Nugent

'A tense, twisty page-turner that you'll have serious trouble
putting down' Catherine Ryan Howard

'Beautifully written … one of the rising stars of Nordic Noir'
Victoria Selman

'Eerie and chilling. I loved every word!' Lesley Kara

'Creepily compelling' Heidi Amsinck

'A masterful writer does it again' Fiction From Afar

'As chilling and atmospheric as an Icelandic winter' Lisa Gray

Home Before Dark

ABOUT THE AUTHOR

Born in Akranes, Eva Björg Ægisdóttir studied for an MSc in Globalisation in Norway before returning to Iceland and deciding to write a novel. Her debut, *The Creak on the Stairs*, was published in 2018, becoming a bestseller in Iceland and going on to win the Blackbird Award and the Storytel Award for Best Crime Novel of the Year. It was published in English by Orenda Books in 2020, and became a number-one bestseller in ebook, shortlisting for Capital Crime's Amazon Publishing Awards in two categories, and winning the CWA John Creasey New Blood Dagger. A TV adaptation of *The Creak on the Stairs*, titled *Elma*, will be available to stream in late 2026.

Girls Who Lie, *Night Shadows*, *You Can't See Me* and *Boys Who Hurt* soon followed suit, shortlisting for the CWA Crime in Translation Dagger, the Capital Crime Awards, and the Petrona Award for Best Scandinavian Crime Novel. *You Can't See Me* won the Storytel Award for Best Crime Novel of the Year in Iceland in 2023. In 2024, Eva won Iceland's prestigious Crime Fiction Award, the Blood Drop, for *Home Before Dark* and was shortlisted for the coveted Glass Key.

The Forbidden Iceland series has established Eva as one of Iceland's bestselling and most distinguished crime writers, and her books are published in seventeen languages with more than a million copies sold. Eva lives in Reykjavík with her husband and three children. Follow Eva on Instagram @evabjorg88 and on Twitter/X @evaaegisdottir and visit www.evabjorgaegisdottir.com.

ABOUT THE TRANSLATOR

Victoria Cribb studied and worked in Reykjavík for a number of years and has translated more than fifty books by Icelandic authors, including Arnaldur Indriðason, Sjón and Yrsa Sigurðardóttir. Many of these works have been nominated for prizes. In 2021 her translation of Eva Björg Ægisdóttir's *The Creak on the Stairs* became the first translated book to win the UK Crime Writer's Association John Creasey (New Blood) Dagger. In 2017 she received the Orðstír honorary translation award for services to Icelandic literature.

The Forbidden Iceland Series

Home Before Dark

Eva Björg Ægisdóttir

Translated from the Icelandic
by Victoria Cribb

ORENDA
BOOKS

Orenda Books
16 Carson Road
West Dulwich
London SE21 8HU
www.orendabooks.co.uk

First published in Iceland as *Heim fyrir myrkur* by Veröld Publishing, Reykjavík 2023
First published in the United Kingdom by Orenda Books, 2025
Copyright © Eva Björg Ægisdóttir, 2023
English translation copyright © Victoria Cribb, 2025

This paperback edition published by Orenda Books, 2026

A catalogue record for this book is available from the British Library.

Hardback ISBN 978-1-916788-60-2
Paperback ISBN 978-1-917764-23-0
eISBN 978-1-916788-61-9

The publication of this translation has been made possible through the financial
support of

Typeset in Minion by Elaine Sharples
Printed and bound by Clays Ltd, Elcograf S.p.A

For sales and distribution, please contact info@orendabooks.co.uk or visit
www.orendabooks.co.uk.

Pronunciation Guide

Icelandic has a couple of letters that don't exist in other European languages and which are not always easy to replicate. The letter ð is generally replaced with a d in English, but we have decided to use the Icelandic letter to remain closer to the original names. Its sound is closest to the voiced *th* in English, as found in *the*n and ba*the*.

The letter *r* is generally rolled hard with the tongue against the roof of the mouth.

In pronouncing Icelandic personal and place names, the emphasis is always placed on the first syllable.

Names which are pronounced more or less as they would be in English, are not included on the list.

Alfreð – AL-freth
Ari – AA-ree
Áslaug – OWS-lohg
Bergur – BAIR-goor
Böðvar – BERTH-var
Borgarfjörður – BORG-ar-FYUR-thoor
Brákarhlíð – BROW-kar-HLEETH
Brú – BROO
Deildartunguhver – DAYL-dar-TOONG-u-kvair
Einar – AY-nar
Eiríksjökull – AY-reeks-YER-koodl
Fjarðaregg – FYAR-thar-egg
Gröf – GRERV
Guðrún – GVOOTH-roon
Gústi – GOOST-ee
Halldóra – HAL-doh-ra
Hallmundarhraun – HADL-moond-ar-HROHN

Helgi Hrafn – HELL-kee HRABN
Höfn í Hornafirði – HUBN ee HORD-na-FIRTH-ee
Hraunfossar – HROHN-foss-ar
Hvítá – KVEET-ow
Hvítársíða (Síða) – KVEET-owr-SEE-tha (SEE-tha)
Ína – EE-na
Ísafjörður – EESS-a-FYUR-thoor
Ívar – EE-var
Jón Ingi – YOHN ING-kee
Jónína (Nína) – YOH-nee-na (NEE-na)
Karvel Kristjánsson – KAR-vel KRIS-tyown-sson
Kleppjárnsreykir (Reykir) – KLEP-yowds-RAY-keer (RAY-keer)
Kristín (Stína) Karvelsdóttir – KRISS-teen (STEE-na) KAR-vels-
DOH-teer
Kristrún – KRIST-roon
Langjökull – LOWNG-yer-koodl
Laxdæla – LAX-dye-la
Maja – MYE-ya
Málfríður Thormóðsdóttir – MOWL-free-thoor THOR-mohths-
DOH-teer
Marsibil (Marsí) – MAR-sib-il (MAR-see)
Mette – METT-uh
Nátthagi – NOWT-ha-yee
Örn – ERDN
Reykholt – RAYK-holt
Reykjavík – RAY-kya-veek
Sætún – SYE-toon
Sigga Steindórs – SIGG-ga STAYN-dohrss
Skeiðará – SKAY-thar-ow
Sólveig (Solla) – SOUL-vayg (SOLL-la)
Torfi Már Sigurðsson – TOR-vee MOWR SIG-oorth-sson
Ytri-Hólar – IT-ree HOLE-ar

Prologue

For many years I've dreamt the same dream: I'm standing in a bathtub in the garden at home and Mum is scrubbing at me with a flannel. The surroundings are covered in snow, the sky is bright with stars, and a cloud of steam is rising from the scalding water to envelop us. 'We've got to get you clean,' Mum keeps muttering, scrubbing at me so hard that my skin turns a fiery red.

A bell jangles in the distance.

I can never work out if this dream is good or bad. I feel all right while it lasts, but when I wake up, a sense of foreboding follows me into the day, and, no matter how often I wash, I can't shake off the feeling that I'm unclean.

I

'There are some people who live in a dream world, and there are some who face reality; and then there are those who turn one into the other.'

—Desiderius Erasmus

1
Marsibil – *Saturday, 12 November 1977*

The letter was on the floor when I got home, a white envelope lying on the dirty tiles. My name was written in block capitals on the front in black ink: MARSIBIL KARVELSDÓTTIR. My heart began to race as I opened the envelope – not neatly with a paper knife, as Dad had taught me, but tearing it messily, greedily open, ripping the contents as I did so. The message inside was handwritten and in some places the ink had run from the letters, like tiny veins.

> *Hello Marsibil,*
> *I've missed you! How are you? I hope you'll forgive me for using your real name this time (ha ha, funny, isn't it?). I felt I had to write to let you know that I'm still here, still just a few words away, if you need me.*
> *Yours in hope.*

A cold sensation crawled like a worm down my back, and my knees felt so weak I wanted to sink to the floor. But I didn't give in to the urge. Instead, I sat down at the kitchen table and stared out of the window for an hour.

The rest of the day I roved around the flat as if on autopilot, checking the locks at half-hour intervals, thinking I heard someone fiddling with the windows, then hiding behind the curtains to watch a man who stood looking up at my flat as his dog squatted on the grass.

I didn't sleep that night.

By the fourth night, as I lay awake, staring into the darkness, I wondered how long it was possible to survive without sleep. I'd heard it was about ten days, but I wasn't sure what would kill you in the end, whether your heart would give up or your body would simply break down. Conk out. Before you reached that stage, you'd experience all the side effects of insomnia – hallucinations, memory loss, the inability to concentrate, sluggish reactions. I had certainly been aware of problems concentrating, but no hallucinations so far.

When Mum rang on the morning of the fourth day, I was counting the leaves on my peace lily. There were seventeen yesterday but now I could only make it fifteen. They wouldn't add up, though I'd counted them three times now.

'Did you see the article?' she asked, her voice husky, as if she'd only just woken up.

'What article?'

'The one about your sister,' Mum said. 'Ten years since Stína went missing, or some rubbish like that. They only write this stuff so people can feed off our grief again.'

The way Mum put it conjured up an image in my mind: me and my family stretched out on a table while a mob fought over pieces of our flesh.

'What does it say?'

I sat down, closing my eyes, which felt hot and sore after all the sleepless nights. Ever since the letter arrived, I'd been short-tempered and jittery, as if constantly expecting someone to jump out and grab me. The nights were the worst because as I lay there, in a waking dream, I kept thinking I could hear noises; a voice whispering in my ear or the crunching of footsteps on the gravel outside my window, though I lived on the third floor. The lack of sleep did strange things to my senses, distorting my hearing. Some sounds receded to a far-off hum, while others seemed amplified. The wind and the hissing of the hot-water pipes felt louder than the people talking to me or music on the radio. My thoughts seemed reduced to unmalleable clay, while my waking dreams were strikingly vivid. I'd always had trouble distinguishing dreams from reality; they had a tendency to blur into one another and become confused. Often, I had the feeling neither could be trusted.

Mum gave a heavy sigh. 'They're raking up Stína's disappearance again. They've put a photo of her on the front page. There's a picture of us in the article too; the one they took in our sitting room just after she went missing, remember?'

I said yes, though I could barely recall it.

Mum sounded close to tears as she groaned: 'How can it be ten years, Marsí?'

'I don't understand it either.'

A long silence. Then a rustling of paper and coughing. 'Are you coming home tomorrow?'

'I'm coming.'

Every year on 17 November, I got into my car and drove home to Nátthagi to commemorate this 'anniversary' that none of us wanted to commemorate. I dreaded the trip for weeks beforehand, inventing countless excuses, but always ended up going.

'Don't set off too late,' Mum said. 'It's safer to drive before dusk. You know how dark it gets out here in the countryside.'

'I know,' I promised. 'I'll be home before dark.'

It was a lie.

After the phone conversation with Mum, I sat at the kitchen table with the letter. I recognised the handwriting, the g's with their long loops and the small r's, and when I closed my eyes, I could picture the very first letter that arrived eleven years ago. If I concentrated, I could smell it, the familiar faint odour of paper and ink, and also of something else. Something alien.

It all started one cold, dreary Thursday. Every Thursday, *The Week* was delivered to our house and my sister and I used to read the magazine together, me hanging over Stína's shoulder as she turned the pages. By the end of 1966, though, Stína had lost interest, so I used to read it alone while she was out with her friends. I read the serials and the comic strips, but what I enjoyed most were the questions sent in by readers for 'the Postman' to answer. On that particular Thursday, a new column caught my eye: 'Penpals'.

I had never given any thought to penpals before or wanted one of my own, but in the last few months I had been feeling increasingly lonely. Ever since Stína started at the senior school in Reykholt she had been spending more time away from home, and I was bored of having no one to talk to.

After some thought, I fetched a sheet of paper and began to compose an advertisement. *Dear* Week, I wrote. *Many thanks for a great magazine. I would like to be penpals with boys or girls aged thirteen to sixteen. I myself am thirteen. My hobbies are…*

Stína came out of her room just as I was wondering what my hobbies were. She posed in front of the mirror in the hall and started combing her shoulder-length, blonde mane. My teenage years were marred by spots and greasy hair, but Stína just seemed to get prettier, developing a womanly figure and prominent cheekbones. What I envied most, though, was her sunny disposition. My mood swings were as unpredictable as the Icelandic weather, while Stína behaved as if the world brought her nothing but joy. Naturally, people were much keener to know a girl with an attitude like that than a sullen, bad-tempered kid like me.

Chewing the end of my pencil, I watched my sister.

In my letters I could be anyone I wanted. I didn't have to be sulky Marsí; I could be more like my sister instead: cheerful, funny, radiant.

I could *be* Stína.

After a moment's reflection, I rubbed out 'thirteen' and wrote 'fifteen' instead. Then I quickly wrote down Stína's interests – art and films – before signing off: *Best wishes, Kristín Karvelsdóttir.*

It was only a trivial little lie, but almost a year later I was still corresponding with my penpal.

He was a boy – Bergur. Or that's what he told me his name was in the regular letters we exchanged over those twelve months. Letters that led us to the decision to finally meet.

He said he was happy to come to me – to make the journey from his place to mine. And that was when it hit home: he would be driving all that way across the country to meet not me, Marsibil, but a sixteen-year-old young woman called Kristín.

And then she was gone.

And I thought he was responsible.

For the next ten years, I remained sure Bergur was involved somehow in Stína's disappearance. But I said nothing. I kept my suspicions to myself. Because if I spoke out, it would be to admit that in some way it might have been my fault. If I'd never told that stupid little lie, Stína would still be with us.

In the immediate aftermath, I had waited, hoping that he would prove me wrong. That he would send an explanation, telling me he'd been prevented from coming or had decided not to meet me after all. But no such message arrived. And in the ten years that had elapsed since Stína vanished, I'd received not a single letter from him.

Until now.

2
Thursday, 17 November 1977

There was a story about the road leading to my house that went as follows:

People who drove the road in the dark sometimes saw a woman standing on the verge, hitching a lift. If they made eye contact with the woman or slowed down, her face would appear in their rear-view mirror a moment later and they'd find her sitting in the back of their car. The shock of it was enough to make them lose control of the wheel and swerve off the road.

Similar stories were told about other roads in the Icelandic countryside. As a rule, it was a man or a woman standing there, and in some versions the figure held a human head under their arm. I'd never spotted the woman myself, despite driving along that route countless times after dusk, but there was no denying that an unusually large number of people had lost their lives on that stretch. I suspected, however, that this had more to do with a combination of poor road maintenance, the lack of streetlights, and the driver's speed or tiredness than a female ghost materialising in their car.

Mum didn't agree.

She was full of terrifying tales like this and believed them implicitly. I had never known anyone as superstitious as her. She had regularly whispered to me that I must be sure to fall asleep before midnight because that's when the evil spirits came out. She used to rap under the table or on wood, saying that ghosts knock twice, so she would always knock three times. Once, she was delighted to find a horseshoe in the hayfield. It was still hanging over the door at home. Mum said it brought good luck, but I had my doubts. Our family had never been lucky.

Before turning to follow the fjord inland, I made a small detour and stopped at the petrol-station shop, where I ate a hot dog and drank a fizzy drink and a cup of weak coffee.

'Hungry?' asked the woman behind the counter, her tongue ticking along her cracked lower lip like the second hand on a clock.

I couldn't stand shop assistants who tried to chat, but I forced myself to smile, then chucked the rest of my coffee in the bin and went into the ladies, where I hunched over the toilet bowl. I retched for a few seconds without bringing anything up, my eyes stinging from the ammonia, then wiped my mouth and flushed the toilet.

The woman I came face to face with in the mirror had a small mouth, thin lips and glassy eyes that gave her face a sickly cast. She horrified me. Insomnia had transformed me, causing my skin to droop like paint that had run.

Rain rattled on the windscreen as I resumed my journey. I pushed a cassette into the car radio and turned up the music to crowd out any brooding thoughts. I had reached such a pitch of exhaustion that I was in an almost constant state of drowsiness – the kind normally experienced just before you fall asleep, except I could never get all the way; I was stuck in limbo, my head heavy, eyelids drooping, thoughts drifting out of control.

As I drove, I kept glancing at the side of the road, imagining a woman's face and wondering how the story had originated. Why would a woman have been standing there, hitching a lift? Where was she going? Or should the question be: who was she fleeing?

The house stood high on a hillside, just outside the small town of Hvítársíða, as if it wanted to set itself apart from the rest to underline its superiority. And it was superior. Most houses in the town were drab, concrete bungalows, built not to catch the eye but to be cheap and functional, but our house, which was called Nátthagi – 'Night Field', was the exception. It was a wooden building, clad in black corrugated iron, with a cellar, an attic, and traditional casement windows. There was a large, six-sided bay window in the middle of the frontage, and the wooden eaves ended in decorative flourishes.

As a child I used to admire it and proudly tell people that I lived in the big black house outside the town, but I avoided inviting the other kids round. From a distance, Nátthagi looked handsome and imposing, but the moment you stepped inside the impression changed. Houses were like people; appearances told only half the story, and I was sure that the other children would sense the same thing I did as soon as they walked in the door.

Not that the furnishings were ugly; the walls were papered in dark patterns and the floors covered with linoleum or carpets in shades of dark brown, orange and emerald green. The furniture was massive, heavy and dark too, and there was a hearth in the sitting room, in which we lit a fire in winter. Nátthagi should have cosy. I should have felt at ease every time I came home. I don't know why I never did.

The garden was different. The plot was bordered by tall poplars, and behind the house a small forest of fir trees climbed up the slope. In summer, I used to lie in the grass, gazing up at the sky with the scent of greenery in my nostrils and the sun on my face, listening to the sighing of the wind in the trees. By the south wall of the house there were flowerbeds where Stína and I had planted chives and tulips, and redcurrant bushes from which we used to pick the berries in autumn and stuff them into our mouths until our stomachs ached.

Nowadays, though, Dad no longer had the willpower to maintain the house, so the black paint was flaking off the corrugated iron and the flowerbeds were nothing but bare earth and withered plants. The only thing my parents had done in the garden in recent years was to plant a laburnum tree in the middle of the lawn. I had never seen it in bloom as my visits were restricted to the winter, but Mum told me that the showers of yellow blossom that covered it in summer reminded her of Stína.

Dad was standing on the steps when I pulled into the drive. He held out his arms and enfolded me in an odour of unwashed hair and sweat. The word 'home' echoed in my head.

Since leaving, I had lived in many places, but none of them had been a *home*. None of them had filled me with the emotion I experienced now as I stood in front of my house, breathing in my father's smell. I knew what the house would smell like inside too; knew there would still be a jar of Grandma's jam in the kitchen cupboard, made decades ago; knew where the floorboards creaked and which windows never shut properly. Sometimes I had the feeling that Nátthagi was the only place that would ever fill me with this sense of belonging.

'Hi, Pipsqueak,' Dad whispered in my ear.

'Dad,' I said.

He looked like he always did; dark eyes set deep under shaggy grey eyebrows. Thin lips, though his smile was wide. But it was a long time since I'd last seen him smile properly. Even now, the corners of his mouth only gave an almost imperceptible upward twitch when he saw me. Worry lines had given him a graver, coarser look. His grief was etched on his face; he was indelibly marked by it, as we all were.

We hugged each other for a long time, our embrace tight and affectionate.

When Dad released his grip, he put his hands on my shoulders and studied me. 'You're getting to be so grown up. How did that happen?'

'It's inevitable, you know that,' I said. 'The years go by and we get wrinkles, grey hair and bad knees.'

'Don't talk nonsense. You'll always be my pretty little pipsqueak.'

I smiled, and Dad let go of my shoulders. 'Well, come in, come in. It's chilly out here and we're letting the cold air inside.'

In the kitchen, Mum was standing over a fiercely bubbling saucepan. There were yellow splashes all around the hob and up the wall, and the smell of curry powder was overpowering.

'Marsí,' she said, in an unusually deep voice, raising her eyes briefly to mine. Mum was never one for cuddles, usually making do with a smile from a safe distance.

She had been an actress before she met Dad, and in 1950 she'd appeared in two plays at the National Theatre – as Lillý in *In Flight* and Isabella in *Vigils*, roles that had brought her to the public eye. But then she had met Dad, one evening in Reykjavík, and they had fallen in love the moment their eyes met across the dance floor. Or so they claimed.

Dad was from a wealthy family who owned and ran an egg farm called Fjarðaregg, here in Borgarfjörður district, and later a poultry slaughterhouse as well. He had moved to Reykjavík in an act of youthful rebellion, and, rather than reading law as his parents had wanted, he'd studied history, refusing to work for the family business. But he hadn't even completed his first term at university, because my mother had got pregnant shortly after they met.

My grandparents couldn't stand Mum. They didn't think she was the right girl for Dad because her family wasn't rich or posh enough; she was only the daughter of a single mother who had struggled to make ends meet and died before her time. But since Mum was pregnant, and she and Dad had decided to get married, his parents had no choice but to accept her. Or Grandma did, anyway. Mum said she barely exchanged a single word with Dad's father, who died while she was still pregnant with Stína. Dad explained that Grandpa had been a stern, difficult man, who had taken out his own unhappiness on other people.

'"I was worst to the one I loved best",' Dad said to me once when I was ten. 'That's a quotation from *Laxdæla Saga*, Marsí, and there's a lot of truth in it.'

I wrinkled my nose. 'Shouldn't it be the other way round? Shouldn't you be nicest to the people you love best?'

'Yes, but sadly we often allow ourselves to show our worst sides to our loved ones.'

I thought about this, then asked: 'Was your daddy nasty to you?'

Dad's smile didn't leave his face but it changed in quality. 'Darling Pipsqueak, there's so much you don't understand.'

I still don't know much about Dad's relationship with his father, but I do know that one day Grandpa woke up, went down to the cellar at Nátthagi, put his shotgun to his head and pulled the trigger. Years later, Stína whispered to me that there had been blood everywhere – up the walls and on the ceiling. Once, the two of us crept down to the cellar, holding hands, to search for traces of that blood. The walls were filthy, not red but brown, as if someone had smeared them with dirt.

'That's blood,' Stína claimed. 'Blood can be brown too. Especially when it's old.'

'You're lying.' I knew that blood was red, not brown.

Later, I went down to the cellar alone, licked my finger and ran it along the wall. My finger left a streak in the grime and I put it in my mouth, trying to work out if it tasted like blood. I couldn't be sure.

After Grandpa died, Grandma was left alone at Nátthagi, grown old before her time. My parents were still living in Reykjavík, and the expectation seemed to be that they should move to Hvítársíða and live with Grandma. But Mum didn't want to move out to the countryside. After all, there weren't many opportunities for an actress in Hvítársíða. The town has a population of about nine hundred people these days, but I remember, when I was in the second year at school, celebrating the one thousandth inhabitant. The population has dwindled since then, mainly because the textile factory closed down and relocated nearer to the coast. Hvítársíða, locally known as Síða, is the biggest settlement in the district, lying in the wide grassy valley halfway between the church estates of Húsafell and Reykholt, on the banks of the Hvítá. Despite its name, the 'White River' is a milky-blue torrent that has its origin in the Langjökull and Eiríksjökull glaciers, which loom over the head of the valley.

Eventually Mum let herself be talked into the move, partly because she loved Dad, partly because she was already pregnant, so her dream of being an actress would have to be shelved for a while anyway. Stína was born in the spring, like the lambs, a year or so after our parents' meeting at that Reykjavík dance hall. She had white hair and big eyes the same pale blue as the waters of the Hvítá.

Grandma only survived another year after Stína was born, and, on her death, Dad inherited both the egg farm and the house. When I came along a year later, Stína hadn't begun to talk yet, but three weeks after my arrival she said her first word: 'Marthí'. It was her version of my name, Marsibil. From then on, I was never called anything but Marsí.

Now, twenty-four years later, my mother was standing in the curry-scented kitchen at Nátthagi, her acting career nothing but a distant memory. Yet she never tired of harking back to it, like some of the newspapers that would print articles from time to time, asking: 'What ever happened to promising actress, Nína Sveins?'

'You're late, Marsí,' Mum said. 'I thought you were going to set off at lunchtime.'

'I got held up.'

'And look at the state of you! Whatever's happened to your hair?' Mum tipped her head on one side and studied me for a moment before coming and running her fingers slowly and assessingly over my scalp. My spine prickled as I felt her nails grazing my skull. Her hand paused at the back of my head and bunched up my hair, as if to check its thickness. Then she smiled faintly. Her smile was as red as her nails, but unlike her nails, which were glossy and immaculate, her lips were dry and the colour had bled into the fine lines around them.

'What?' I asked.

'What's bothering you?'

'Nothing.'

Mum let go of my hair and went back to stirring the curry. 'You can always talk to me, Marsí. You know that.'

'I know.'

'Are you still seeing your therapist?'

'Yes,' I lied. I had stopped seeing my therapist after he said he wanted me to go for 'a more detailed evaluation'. I had nodded, pretending to understand; but I never went back.

'You're just like your dad; not one to wear your heart on your sleeve.'

'Is that something everyone has to do?'

'No, not really. But sometimes it can help to talk about things.'

'Maybe.'

Mum ladled curry into bowls and passed them to me to put on the table.

'Ah, I'm famished,' Dad said once we were all seated, and immediately began shovelling down his food, yellow curry sauce oozing out of the corners of his mouth.

'I can't remember the last time I ate meat in curry sauce,' I remarked.

Mum's curry dish was never the same twice and its contents were anyone's guess. She made it whenever she cleaned out the fridge, and I could still remember encountering a lump of gristle that required endless chewing and gave me an upset stomach afterwards.

'It's chicken,' Mum said. 'We had so much that I decided to use that for a change instead of lamb. I'm sure it'll be just as good.'

'I'm sure it will,' I said, but my stomach heaved. I couldn't stand chicken, however it was cooked, a direct consequence of seeing all those rows of little pink carcases hanging on hooks in the abattoir once too often. I stirred the stew with my fork. It was a strange colour, midway between yellow and brown. I picked out a piece of potato and examined it carefully before putting it in my mouth.

Mum watched me chew. 'You've got so thin, Marsí. Who would have believed it?'

'What do you mean?'

'You were always so soft.'

'Soft?'

'And rounded. You developed womanly curves so young. Already had breasts and hips by the time you were twelve. You'd started your periods by eleven.'

'*Mum.*' I could feel myself blushing. When I started bleeding at eleven yours old, I thought at first that I was dying and confided in Stína, who merely laughed and asked if I was really that stupid.

'Don't be so squeamish,' Mum said. 'All women get periods.'

'I wasn't a woman. I was a child.'

'Sometimes I feel as if you've never been a child,' Mum replied.

'Nonsense, Nína,' Dad intervened. 'I clearly remember Marsí streaking around the place half naked.'

'You never felt the cold,' Mum said. 'Never wanted to wear any clothes.'

'Even at the nursery,' Dad added. 'Once, your mother went to collect you and you'd disappeared, only to be discovered round the back of the house with some boy, both of you stark naked. What was the boy's name again, Nína?'

'That was Árni Jakob. The one who sometimes works at the petrol-station shop. Jonni and Ninna's son.'

'That was it. Remember him, Marsí? He was a year younger than you, wasn't he?'

I nodded, took another mouthful, and racked my brain for a change of subject. Anything. When I tried to swallow, it felt as though something was stuck in my throat.

'He once came round here and the two of you had a bath together,' Mum continued.

'Wasn't he the one that…?' Dad began.

'Yes, exactly. He was the one who did a poo in the bath.'

Mum started laughing helplessly and Dad joined in, both showing curry-yellow teeth.

I took a mouthful of water, trying to clear my throat, but the lump wouldn't shift.

'Are you all right?' Dad asked, as their laughter died away.

I began to gag and got abruptly to my feet. 'Excuse me.'

Outside in the hall I gave way to a fit of violent coughing, but it wasn't enough. The blood rushed to my head as I gagged and coughed in turn.

Dad emerged from the kitchen just as something flew out of my throat: a slimy, ochre lump that landed with a splat on the floor. But I could still feel something at the back of my tongue, so in the end I stuck my fingers down my throat.

And hauled out a long hank of hair.

After dinner, we relaxed in the sitting room. Normally, we'd have watched TV, but as there were no broadcasts on Thursdays, we listened instead to a Danish radio play called *The Three Rogues*, an open bottle of gin on the coffee table in front of us. As always, this annual reunion involved silently drinking together. It's a family tradition we've established over the years.

Before long, Dad got a phone call and had to go over to the egg farm. Ever since I could remember, Dad had been called out at short notice like this in the evenings, often not coming home until everyone else was asleep. I could never understand why the chickens needed him so much this late in the day.

Shortly after that, Mum nodded off with her mouth slightly open, not snoring exactly but breathing loudly. As so often before, I studied her as she slept in her chair. I didn't know quite how I felt as I watched her. As a child I had adored her and hated her, and everything in between, but now my main emotion was pity.

I turned down the radio, topped up my glass and got to my feet.

The house had changed little since I lived here, the same pictures hanging on the walls, the same ornaments on the shelves. My room, too, was exactly as I had left it. On the wall there was a corkboard with photos of actors and singers pinned to it, along with an air ticket from the trip we'd taken to Denmark, two years before Stína went missing. Now I pulled the desk chair over to the wardrobe and reached to the back of the top shelf. The shoebox was still there, full of the letters I had received ten years before.

About two weeks after my advert appeared in *The Week*, I received a letter in reply. It was my job to collect the post every day from the mailbox down by the road, which was how I had planned to intercept any potential replies, and that day I discovered an envelope addressed to Kristín Karvelsdóttir and marked *The Week: Penpals*. I took it up to my room, closed the door behind me and tore it open.

Hello Kristín,

I saw your advertisement in The Week *and thought it sounded interesting, so I decided to write to you in the hope that we could become penpals. A bit about me: I've got a younger brother, I play the piano and I love animals, especially dogs. I'll be seventeen in a week but I hate birthdays (weird, I know!). If you're interested, it would be great to hear more about you.*

Yours in hope,

Bergur

Bergur and I had written to each other every two weeks for nearly a year, so there were about twenty letters in the shoebox. I was glad not to have copies of the ones I wrote him, as they would have revealed how immature I was in those days. Although I'd used Stína's name, the letters had been a mixture of us both. I copied the words she used and repeated her stories. Stína was always so melodramatic; she could never just like something, she had to *adore* it. She adored film stars and singers, teachers and friends, books and songs. At first, I was probably more Stína than me, but as time went on, I started telling Bergur more about myself. About Marsí. But I always polished the text until I came across as exactly who I wanted to be. It was easy: if I wrote something stupid or embarrassing, I simply rubbed it out. Yet I read the letters I received without suspecting for a moment that they too might have been carefully planned and edited, rather than being as impulsive and heartfelt as they seemed.

At first the letters were fairly short; we discussed our interests and hobbies and talked about our lives. But the more letters we wrote, the more personal and intimate they became. My eye fell on sentences like *I feel as if I've never fitted in anywhere* and *I already feel like we know each other so well*. At the time, I had taken the words to heart, but now I blushed to think how gullible I had been. Most teenagers experienced similar feelings, but I'd believed I was unique, that this boy understood me and that our relationship was special. Now I saw something quite different and much darker in his words.

I drained the rest of my glass and continued skimming the pages, though I couldn't actually stop and read them without breaking out in a sweat. The last letter was the hardest. He had brought up the possibility several times of us meeting, saying he'd got his driver's licence and wouldn't mind coming to Síða, but I had ignored his hints. The problem was obvious: I wasn't sixteen-year-old Kristín but just-turned-fourteen Marsibil.

In his last letter, he had written: *I feel like our letters have given us the chance to be sincere and open, and I really want us to meet. I could come to you, if you like, but I have to admit that I haven't been entirely straight with you. I'll explain properly when we meet face to face. There are some things you can't say in a letter.*

Those words had helped me make up my mind: I had agreed to meet my penpal. *Ten p.m., Friday, 17 November, by the bridge over the Hvítá,* I had written, and began counting down the days.

When the seventeenth dawned, I could hardly sit still for nervous excitement. Then … well, I didn't get there in time.

It so happened that Stína had been visiting friends in town that evening and had decided, for reasons known only to her, to come home early. She had left shortly before ten, intending to walk the two and a half kilometres back to our house.

Around midnight on 17 November 1967, Stína's blood-stained anorak was found by the bridge over the Hvítá. Stína herself never came home and was never found. No other clues as to her fate have ever come to light.

I closed my eyes for a moment as the ache in my chest seemed to contract and expand. Then I took out the letter that had dropped through my door a few days previously and compared it to the first letter I'd received from my penpal.

Yours in hope, it said in both. It was a little more mature, but still, unmistakably, the same handwriting.

3
Kristín – *Autumn 1966*

I want to disappear.

People are always disappearing. The world is so big and we are so small, it shouldn't be that difficult to vanish and never be found again.

I want to disappear. The words echo in my head as my name is called, but here in the classroom there is no way out.

I walk with extreme reluctance to the blackboard at the front of the room. I'm not normally shy, but there are so many new faces looking at me that I find myself suddenly overcome with nerves.

The strange faces belong to the kids from Varmaland, Heiðaskóli, Kleppjárnsreykir and other schools in the Borgarfjörður area. Of course, there are familiar faces too from my old school in Síða, but they're in the minority. We've all gathered here at the senior school in Reykholt. In two years, I'll have taken my final exams and will be able to go to art college at last, something I've been dreaming about for what feels like forever. But at this moment I have to read out my Icelandic essay, which, since I scribbled it down in about five minutes flat, is absolutely abysmal.

'Please begin, Kristín,' the teacher says, encouragingly. His name is Thór and he's new at the school – like us. He's also extremely good-looking and quite young, only twenty-four. But, disappointingly, he's married. I've seen his wife. She's stunning – and heavily pregnant. That doesn't prevent the girls in our class from having a crush on him though, especially Málfríður.

'Thanks.' I clear my throat and survey the watching class.

Málfríður knows I didn't do my homework and I can see that she's having trouble suppressing her giggles. Then I meet Guðrún's eye, and she smiles and nods slightly, as if to encourage me, so I take a deep breath and begin.

'You're intolerable,' Málfríður says afterwards, as we leave the classroom. 'Seriously, Stína. You. Are. Intolerable.'

'Why?' I'm finding it hard to suppress a grin. The reading went better than I had dared hope. After the first couple of minutes I got into gear, and it turned out that I knew far more about the subject than I'd thought. Who would have guessed?

'You claim you haven't done the work and don't know anything,' Málfríður says, 'then you manage to rabbit on for hours.'

'I hit my stride.'

'Hit your stride? What are you? … Who are you?' She stares at me, perplexed. 'Even the teacher clapped at the end. Thór literally clapped.'

Málfríður mimes puking, but Gústi, who has come over to join us, pats me on the back. 'I knew she could do it.'

'Stína's always been like that,' Guðrún says. 'Moans and moans beforehand, then does everything perfectly. Not only that, but she paints like Da Vinci and is actually going to study art.'

'Or like Mary Cassatt,' I interject.

'Who?'

'Oh, it doesn't matter.'

'Where are you going to study art?' Gústi asks.

'At Kleppjárnsreykir. It's only a twelve-week course, two evenings a week.' Although I say this casually, I'm brimming with pride.

Halldóra, the art teacher, called me in to see her a few days ago. She teaches here at Reykholt as well as at my old school.

'Do you remember Ívar?' she asked. 'The student who visited us last spring and sat in on some of my lessons?'

'Oh, yes. He was studying to be an art teacher, wasn't he?'

'That's right. Well, they're going to offer various evening courses at Kleppjárnsreykir this autumn,' she said. 'Typewriting, Danish, English, and Ívar's going to teach art. That would be ideal for you.'

'For me?'

Halldóra added that I was a bit young for the course but that she would talk to my parents and was sure they'd agree to my taking part, as it would be a good basis for my further studies.

'She's only been specially invited to take part,' Guðrún says now.

'When do you start?' Gústi asks.

'This evening.'

'Intolerable,' Málfríður repeats, and lies down on the grassy slope beside the school building.

Guðrún and I sit either side of her, while Gústi settles a bit lower down and starts amusing himself by pulling up grass.

'By the way, what are you lot doing this weekend?' he asks.

'There's a party at Snorri's,' Málfríður says. 'Everyone'll be there.'

'Who's everyone?' Guðrún asks, her hands pushed deep into the pockets of her jacket.

'Everyone who matters,' Málfríður says, not looking at her.

They don't get on that well. In fact, they only put up with each other for my sake. It would probably be hard to find two people more different. Málfríður started at our old school in the spring when her father was appointed as the town's vicar. Before that she lived in Reykjavík; she regarded it as a terrible comedown to have to move to the countryside. On her first day, she stood in front of the class wearing a mutinous expression, and when the teacher asked her to tell us about herself, she said her parents had forced her to move to this dump against her will. I was the only one who laughed and was rewarded with a flicker of a smile from Málfríður. We've been friends ever since.

Guðrún, on the other hand, has always lived here, like me, and often says she would never want to live anywhere else. She loves nature and the mountains, and we have countless secret haunts in the countryside around the town, where we used to go when we were younger. We'd take picnics and pretend we were going to live together in the wild, surviving on bilberries and sorrel plants and water from the Hvítá. Sometimes, unbeknownst to our parents, we even ventured all the way upriver to the dramatic Hraunfossar falls in the lava field, where we would sit by Barnafoss and stare into the torrent, picturing the two children who, according to legend, are supposed to have drowned there.

Málfríður is as dark as Guðrún is fair. As tall and slim as Guðrún is small and chubby. And, on top of that, temperamentally they're complete opposites: Guðrún is always cheery, good-natured and smiling, while Málfríður is permanently at odds with the world. She has an acid tongue and likes to take risks, and things are never boring when she's around.

'And who are the people who matter, Málfríður?' I ask now.

'Oh, Gísli and Ómar and…' Málfríður lists the boys she obviously regards as important, and when she runs out of names, she flicks back her hair and says: 'We've *got* to go.'

'What do you two think?' I ask, looking from Guðrún to Gústi. 'Have we *got* to go?'

'Well, if everyone else is going,' Guðrún says.

We smile at each other and I know exactly what she's thinking.

'What about you, Gústi,' Guðrún asks. 'Are you going?'

'Naturally, I shall be in attendance,' Gústi says with mock formality. Like Guðrún, I've known Gústi as far back as I can remember. He often used to walk to school with me and Marsí, always just happening to pop out of his house as we walked by. He's actually our nearest neighbour, as his family's house is just outside town too, about a kilometre and a half from ours.

'Great,' I say.

At that moment a window opens on the first floor of the school building, and a hand bell emerges and rings for us to come in. We don't get up immediately but let the others go ahead, before following along as the last in the line.

Or so we think.

Sólveig appears behind us, carrying a thick tome. She usually finds a deserted spot in the school grounds and reads there alone during break.

'Sólveig,' Málfríður says, in an exaggeratedly gentle voice.

Sólveig smiles but seems suspicious at being addressed like this.

'Are you going to the party?' Málfríður asks.

'What party?'

'The party this weekend. Haven't you heard about it?'

Sólveig shakes her head.

'You should come,' Málfríður says.

'No, I…' Sólveig begins, but Málfríður puts a hand on her shoulder.

'Seriously, it would be great to see you there.' She lowers her voice. 'Böðvar was asking if you were coming.'

Sólveig's eyes light up, pink spots appear on her cheeks and she nods. 'OK. Maybe I will come along.'

Sólveig has been in love with Böðvar for as long as I can remember, and everyone at our old school was aware of her feelings, even the teachers. In fact, I'm pretty sure it's obvious to everyone except Böðvar, who's so absent-minded that he doesn't notice anything unless it's related to engines or cars. His dad repairs cars in their garage at home and Böðvar helps him out. He used to come to school with his hands, and even his face, black with oil.

'Great. Look forward to seeing you there,' Málfríður says, and there's something in her voice that gives me a sinking feeling in the pit of my stomach.

'What was all that about?' I whisper to her once we're inside. 'Why did you invite her?'

'She's always alone, and I just thought she'd enjoy it.'

I fold my arms. 'Really.'

'Yes, really.' Málfríður tucks a hand under my arm. 'See, I can be nice.'

I burst out laughing. 'Yes, sure. You're all right.'

Although Málfríður can be sarcastic and a bit sharp, at heart she's a good person who wouldn't hurt a fly. It's just a pity that more often than not she keeps that side of herself so hidden.

4

Marsibil – *Friday, 18 November 1977*

I didn't exactly fall asleep, but dozed over the letters and passed the whole night drifting in and out of consciousness. At some point I dreamt about Mum. She was standing over me in a white nightie; then, reaching out a hand, she cut a hole in my stomach with a sharp fingernail. 'Lie still, Marsí,' she said. 'Mum will fix you.'

Somewhere a bell was ringing.

I surfaced to hear someone banging on the door.

'Marsí?'

'Yes?' I was still clasping my stomach but loosened my grip when I realised where I was.

Dad opened my door a crack. 'I've got to go out for a bit but I'll be back this evening. Will you still be here?'

'I'll be here,' I said. 'Is Mum home?'

'No, she went out somewhere, but I'm sure she'll be back soon.'

The moment Dad had gone, I lay down again and tried to get more sleep, but when that didn't work, I decided to get up.

By daylight, you could see what a state the house was in; not messy, exactly, but there was a layer of dust on the shelves and the windows were opaque with grime, making it hard to see out. I ran my finger over the white china figurine of a girl with blue hair that used to mean a lot to Stína and me. My finger turned grey.

The bathroom was particularly bad. Mum loved having baths, filling the tub with bubbles until they foamed over the sides, then lying there with her feet propped on the tap, smoking. She never bothered to lock the door, so I got used to going to the loo with Mum lying there. Now there was a brown ring of dirt in the tub, as if it hadn't been cleaned for God knows how long, and there was a strong odour of mouldy towels. I splashed my face with cold water and went into the kitchen.

My stomach was constricting with hunger, so after carefully inspecting the bread for patches of green mould, I made myself some toast. On the kitchen table was a newspaper with a photo of Stína in the top corner of the front page, apparently left out for me to find. I sat down with my toast and coffee and opened it up.

The article about Stína filled a whole page and, as Mum had said, it was accompanied by a photo of our family on the sofa in the sitting room: Mum with her blonde hair in waves, Dad in a dark shirt, and me beside him, looking almost unrecognisable. Mum had dressed me up and done my hair specially for the reporter's visit; with my short bunches, and wearing a polo-neck jumper and pinafore dress, I resembled an overgrown child.

Most readers will be familiar with the name of Kristín Karvelsdóttir, who went missing while walking home from a friend's house on the evening of Friday, 17 November 1967, her bloodstained anorak being found by the bridge over the Hvítá later that night. Kristín's case has attracted more public interest than any other in recent years, apart from the disappearance of Guðmundur and Geirfinnur in 1974.

Kristín's parents, Karvel Kristjánsson and Jónína Helga Sveinsdóttir, own and run the Fjarðaregg poultry farm and slaughterhouse in the Hvítársíða district of Borgarfjörður. Kristín was only sixteen when she vanished. A promising artist, she had been hoping to go to art school abroad. On the evening in question, Kristín had been visiting friends and decided to walk the two and a half kilometres home. She set off shortly before ten p.m., and when she wasn't home by midnight, her parents began to get worried. The police and a group of volunteers conducted a search for Kristín, and before long her anorak was discovered by the road, not far from her home. The coat was stained with blood, believed to be Kristín's, indicating that a struggle had taken place. Even now, ten years later, no trace has ever been found of Kristín Karvelsdóttir.

The article went on to provide a dramatic account of how the little community had been paralysed by shock as the search continued over days and weeks without success.

I couldn't actually recall much about that time, though the morning after was still vivid in my memory; Dad's voice waking me as he sat by my bed: 'How are you feeling, Pipsqueak?'

My head had been heavy and I had felt sick when I sat up, sensing immediately that something was wrong. Dad didn't usually sit on the side of my bed in the mornings like this, and he was still wearing last night's clothes.

'Has something happened?' I asked.

After a brief hesitation, Dad nodded. 'We can't find Stína. She …

she didn't come home yesterday. We've been out looking for her all night.'

I don't remember how I answered or even whether I answered at all, but I do remember that all I could think about was Bergur. Our plan to meet had been all set up, and I'd got myself ready to sneak out without being seen, but somehow I'd fallen asleep and missed my chance.

Dad stroked my hair and I noticed that his eyes were red. 'I'm sure it'll be all right, Marsí love,' he said. 'I'm sure we'll find her.'

If his voice hadn't been so robotic, I might have believed him.

Later that day, having learnt what time Stína had set off home and where her anorak had been found, I joined the dots. I pictured her walking home, only to stop when a car came along and slowed down. Pictured her shielding her eyes against the blinding glare of the headlights, the window being rolled down and a man's face appearing. 'Are you Stína?'

Now, as I stared at the newspaper in front of me, my hand started scratching at the back of my head, I could feel my cheeks coming out in red blotches and my head was echoing with self-recriminations; that spiteful voice telling me it was my fault she had vanished. I was used to it and normally allowed it to go on reverberating in my mind as long as it wanted. I felt I deserved it. When I was younger, I had gone through a period of punishing myself in various inventive ways: clawing at my skin until I bled, tearing out my hair and drinking to excess. I was still full of self-contempt, but these days my drinking was under control and my atonement consisted of being unhappy. It was the least I could do.

In my better moments I managed to convince myself that Stína's disappearance had had nothing to do with me. That someone else had taken her, not my penpal. Just some random stranger who happened to be passing. Deep down, though, I didn't believe in this kind of coincidence. And now, in the letter I received last week, I had the proof. My penpal, the man who had taken Stína, had sent me a new letter after ten years of silence, and it was clear that he knew I had lied about my name. Though I still couldn't work out the purpose of his letter, I wasn't naïve enough to believe that he simply wanted to resume our friendly correspondence.

Judging by the way Stína's door creaked, it was a while since it had last been opened. I had gone inside regularly over the years, lain down on Stína's bed and fantasised that she would be home any minute, but since I'd moved to Reykjavík, it was clear that no one came in here anymore. Now I sat down at her desk and surveyed the room where time had stood still.

Against the wall below the window was a single bed with a patchwork quilt that Mum had made when we were children, and a small, dark-red cushion. There was a dusty china vase on the little stool that served as a bedside table. When Stína was alive, the walls used to be covered with posters of her favourite artists, but Mum had taken them all down and replaced them with a single, framed landscape painting. If you looked closely, though, you could still see the tiny holes made by the drawing pins Stína had used to hang her posters.

After a moment or two, I opened the desk drawer and took out Stína's diary. I'd read it over and over again in the past, so I knew the contents pretty much off by heart. It wasn't very personal, as Stína's talents had lain more in the visual sphere, so the entries mainly recorded the things she had done each day, with little elaboration. The only interesting thing about the diary was that here and there pages had been torn out. I guessed that this had more to do with Stína's perfectionism than anything suspicious.

I put the diary back in the drawer and brought out Stína's sketchbooks. She had drawn countless eyes, some recognisable, others not. Deep-set eyes that resembled Dad's, dark eyes that looked like mine, and Mum's beautifully made-up ones. The last picture in the book had been drawn the day Stína vanished. The eyes had seemed familiar to me when I watched her sketching them, but when I'd asked Stína whose they were, she had shrugged.

'No one in particular,' she'd said, then sighed and closed the sketchpad as if dissatisfied with the drawing. As if she hadn't managed to capture the eyes the way she'd wanted to.

We were alone in the house that day, in Mum's room. Stína spent ever more time trying on Mum's clothes, especially the elegant shirts and skirts Mum had bought at the height of her acting career, and, as we'd been talking, Stína had opened the wardrobe and taken out a jumper made of soft red wool.

'What are you getting all dressed up for?' I asked.

'Why shouldn't I?' she retorted, opening the drawer where Mum kept her silk scarves.

'I thought you were just going round to Málfríður's house?'

'I am. What of it?'

'Nothing.'

I watched Stína hold the jumper against herself in the mirror. The vibrant red enhanced her blonde hair and blue eyes. She looked like an actress. She looked like Mum.

'What are you going to do there?'

'Watch a film,' Stína said, taking off her own jumper, so she was standing in front of me in just her vest.

'What film are you going to watch?'

'There's a Hitchcock on television this evening, about a woman who marries a handsome man, then begins to suspect he's planning to murder her.' Stína pulled on Mum's jumper. 'It's supposed to be amazing.'

I lay back on the bed, imagining the evening ahead. Our parents were expecting guests for dinner, and as usual they were making a big fuss about getting everything ready. I would stay in my room and be careful not to get in anyone's way. Then, when no one was looking, I planned to sneak out.

'You can come along if you like,' Stína said.

'No, it's OK.'

'Seriously,' Stína said. 'It would be better than hanging around here.'

'I'll be fine.'

Stína sat down on the bed. 'Are you quite sure?'

I nodded, though I wanted to say yes. It wasn't often these days that

Stína invited me along to her friends' houses, and our parents' dinner parties tended to be noisy affairs that went on for hours. I considered telling Stína that I had other plans for the evening, but decided to wait. It would be far better to confide in her afterwards. After I'd met *him*.

I felt butterflies fluttering in my stomach and turned over on to my side. 'That jumper really suits you, Stína.'

'Thanks.' She stood up and put on her broad, yellow hairband. Then took a deep breath, her expression unusually serious, as though she was plucking up the courage to say something.

What had she been thinking? I wondered now. Had she sensed that something was going to happen that night?

Normally I tried not to let my mind dwell on those days, but the arrival of the letter had been like a dam breaking, flooding my mind with memories.

I picked up another sketchpad, in which Stína had drawn faces – she had been mainly interested in drawing portraits. I had never understood how she did it. How she could reproduce people's defining features, those little idiosyncrasies that I didn't even notice, didn't even realise were there until they appeared on paper. I paused at a portrait of Mum when she was younger, and marvelled at how Stína had managed to depict the expression that was unique to her. Then I returned the pad to the drawer.

As I did so, my hand encountered a hard object. I clasped it between my fingers and pulled it from the drawer. It was the Kodak Instamatic that Stína had got for Christmas the year before she went missing. The camera was a compact black-and-silver model, and Stína had gone around constantly snapping photos with it, until Dad refused to pay for any more to be developed. It still contained a film that Stína hadn't had a chance to finish, and although I knew it wouldn't achieve anything, I rewound the film, took out the cartridge and slipped it into my pocket before putting the camera back where I had found it.

None of the shops in such a small town as ours could risk specialising in only one area, so the bookshop offered a film-developing service, as well as selling fabric and various other odds and ends.

'It'll be ready tomorrow,' said the man at the counter, handing me a ticket with a number on it.

'Is there no way it could be ready earlier?' I asked. 'You see, I'm leaving town tomorrow morning.' I added that I could pay extra.

He regarded me for a moment. 'You're Nína and Karvel's daughter, aren't you?'

'Yes.'

'I recognised the family resemblance,' he said. 'Marsibil, isn't it?'

'That's right.'

'Well, well.' He took the film with a smile that revealed a gap where his right eye-tooth was missing. 'For a pretty girl like you, anything's possible. Come back in two hours.'

While I was waiting for the photos, I bought a ham-and-cheese sandwich and a bottle of orange from the petrol-station shop, then wandered around the town. In the distance, the Eiríksjökull glacier was brooding under a cloud and the horizon was dominated by the old lava field that covered so much of the landscape. I passed the small white timber church with its red roof and the little graveyard full of wooden crosses, then found myself standing by the school. It was freezing cold, and there was no one in the playground, a gravelled area with swings, a seesaw and a grassy sandpit.

Until Stína went missing, I had always felt safe in this town. When I was a little girl, we kids ran wild, moving in and out of the houses at will, venturing into the surrounding mountains and playing by the river, unmonitored by our parents. We belonged to the town – we were everybody's responsibility, not just our families'. Everywhere there was someone to keep an eye on us, so I grew up trusting other people. Of course, there were a few individuals you had to watch out for: Elli who used to pinch our noses and had once lured a boy into his flat and shown him his dick; Dinna from Vesturgarður, who stank like rancid herring; and the brothers from Höskuldarthúfa, who used to beat up the weaker kids and shout dirty words at the girls. These things were common knowledge and taken for granted. No one tried to change anyone; everything was just the way it was. *Don't go there, come home before dark* and *mind the traffic*: words of warning to six-year-olds who went out in the morning and only came home in the evening when their mothers' voices would carry down the street, calling out one word: *supper*!

After Stína went missing, this changed. For a while, at least. Parents kept their children indoors, no one went out alone after dark, and neighbours eyed each other with suspicion. But in the ten years that had passed since Stína's disappearance, the locals had forgotten their fear. Their dread. No one wanted to believe that there could be anyone bad living in their town. In my case, fear had been drowned out by guilt; that is until the new letter arrived. Now, like a parasite, fear had taken up residence inside me again.

I climbed into one of the tyre swings and rocked back and forth, making the chain squeak.

We used to hang out here in the evenings. In the years following Stína's disappearance, I had grown more sociable and started going out more, mainly because it was better than staying at home. We were typical teenagers – passing around a bottle, smoking cigarettes and playing games. The games were generally based on dares involving something forbidden, which became ever cruder over time: snog each other, touch someone's breast, break a window.

My gaze caught on a broken bottle lying by the wall with a cigarette stub beside it; relics from the night before that told me nothing had changed: new teenagers had come to take our place. Most people believed they mattered, that what they did left some trace behind, but really humans were just like any other living creatures; easily replaced, not indispensable at all. We left nothing behind us that wouldn't be obliterated by time.

Then again.

I went over to the rough wall. After a brief search I found my name, written on the concrete in the handwriting I had adopted when I was fifteen: *Marsí*, with a little heart over the 'i', in just the way Stína used to write hers.

Even after Stína had gone, I was still trying to be her.

Dad's car wasn't in the drive when I got back with the photos I'd had developed, and when I went inside and called out to Mum, there was no reply. But passing the cellar door, I noticed that it was standing ajar. It was usually kept locked as there was a bad smell down there that quickly spread to the rest of the house if it was left open.

A foolish shiver ran down my spine as I descended the first step. The lightbulb clicked on with a buzz that drilled into my ears. 'Hello?' I called, but the cellar seemed to swallow up my voice, muffling it so it could barely be heard.

The cellar evoked the same nightmarish feelings in me as it had when I was young. It was down there that Grandpa had gone with his shotgun, and there that I had been convinced the walls were still stained with his blood.

When nobody answered, I took the few steps back up into the hallway, closed the door and tried the handle again to check it was properly shut.

As soon as I was in the sanctuary of my room, I tore open the envelope of photos.

They had all been taken in the weeks before Stína vanished, a fact that set my heart beating a little faster. The camera had been in Stína's room a long time, but I'd been so sure it would contain no clues about what had happened to her that it had never occurred to me to get the film developed until now. I was surprised my parents hadn't got round to it, though. They knew nothing about my penpal and ought by rights to have been curious, yet as far as I could remember, they'd hardly set foot in Stína's room since she vanished. They must have found it too harrowing.

I flicked quickly through the photos at first, as if expecting to easily spot an important clue. But of course there weren't any. They were mostly snaps of Stína and her friends in a variety of places and poses. Once the excitement had faded slightly, I started going through them again from the beginning, slowly now, carefully scrutinising each picture.

The first photo was of Stína and Málfríður. They were in Stína's room, sitting on her bed, leaning against each other with their legs crossed. Stína was wearing a white T-shirt and high-waisted light-blue jeans. The top of her hair was pinned back, leaving the fringe free and the sides hanging down in waves. Málfríður was in a black vest top and wore an eye-catching necklace. Her dark hair was pulled back in a messy pony-tail and her eyes were ringed with black.

Guðrún must have been behind the camera as she was there in the next photo, sitting on the chair by the desk. She wasn't as dolled up as the others and was smiling, almost shyly, at the camera. With her short hair, make-up-free face and baggy jumper, she looked much more of a child than her friends.

The next photos had been taken outside: Stína in the back of a car; the three friends posing against a wall; then a bunch of young people who seemed unaware of the camera. The snapshot appeared to have been taken at some kind of party or dance. At first, I thought it must be a school dance, but when I inspected the pictures more closely, I saw that these kids were older and had bottles in their hands.

One of the notorious 'country balls', then.

Stína must have gone along without telling our parents. Country balls were held from time to time in a house outside the town. I'd attended a few myself when I was seventeen, eighteen. People used to bring along their own booze, usually *landi* – moonshine – to get around the impossibly strict licensing laws. There would be live music until the early hours, and couples would go out to neck on the rough ground behind the house.

The pictures that came next were very different. First, Stína had taken a photo of herself. Her face filled the entire 10 x 15 cm frame, gravely meeting my gaze. She must have been opposite a window because her face was over-lit, her eyes pale blue, her skin bleached white.

I studied her for a long time. Realised I'd totally forgotten about the scar on her forehead and the small mole under her left eye, standing out against her otherwise flawless skin. The mole was so tiny that you wouldn't notice it at all unless you were close to her.

The next picture showed a rock and a stream that I knew well. The 'Hot Stream', as we used to call it, was a natural hot spring just outside town. You could paddle or wallow in its pleasantly warm water; a popular activity among teenagers, especially in the evenings or at night. Next came a picture of a man – or boy – in the same place, in jeans and jacket, hands in his pockets. He was caught in the act of turning, so his head was slightly blurred. It was impossible to make out his features, though his mouth was open, as though he was speaking. The next photo showed a pair of feet in the steaming water: barefoot Stína in the Hot Stream.

The final picture must have been taken in the wood behind our house. This too was badly out of focus. It showed Stína and a boy in a checked shirt and brown jacket, but the camera had been angled too low, all but cutting off the boy's head. I compared this photo to the blurry one of the figure by the stream. Both had a similar build, so it could have been the same boy, but it was hard to say for sure.

Below me I heard the familiar clunk and swish of the front door opening. I hurried to scoop the pictures into a pile and hide them under my pillow.

'Marsí?' Mum's voice.

'I'm here.'

I heard the clicking of her heels, and she appeared in the doorway, wearing lipstick and far too much eyeshadow. 'What are you doing?'

'Nothing much. Where have you been?'

'I went to see Petra. Her husband died recently; dropped dead during the sheep roundup.' Mum was never more in her element than when some disaster had occurred. Other people's tragedies seemed to perk her up and fill her with energy. Now she smiled. 'Why don't you come down to the kitchen? You mustn't sit alone up here. It's like you're a teenager again, always moping in your room.'

'I wasn't always moping in my room.'

'You know, I used to worry there was something wrong,' Mum said over her shoulder as I followed her down the stairs to the kitchen. 'It was so hard to get close to you.'

'I don't remember that.'

'Don't you?' Mum took out the bottle of gin from last night and filled two glasses. 'You've always had a bad memory, Marsí.'

'That's not true.' I took the glass she held out to me.

'Always remembering things that never happened.' Mum chuckled and shook her glass, sending the clear liquid swirling up the sides. 'Like when you were convinced we'd been to a funfair and you'd gone on one of the rides. It turned out you'd seen it in a film.'

Mum was right. I had insisted I'd been on that stupid ride.

'You're a dreamer,' Mum continued. 'That's what comes of reading so much as a child. You become immersed in other worlds, and confuse what really happened with what you *wanted* to happen.'

I protested, but the fact was I could remember several occasions when I had muddled up dreams and reality. Things I had believed to be memories had turned out to have no basis in truth. For example, I could have sworn that Stína had taken dancing lessons, that I'd been on a ferry and that Dad used to play the guitar. They were trivial details of no importance, but it still frustrated me that I couldn't distinguish fact from imagination. Because if I couldn't tell them apart, which of my memories could I trust?

And then there were things I could recall, but wasn't so sure were real. I didn't dare ask my parents about them. Some were troubling and, true or not, they'd had an impact on my life. One was particularly disturbing. I must have been very young, probably no more than two or three, which was in itself a sign that the memory was almost certainly false. Yet I had a vivid image of Mum's face looking at me teasingly. 'If you don't come out of your room, I'll tickle you,' she threatened.

As I remember it, I was both surprised and excited, because usually it was Dad who played with us. Mum didn't like games, Stína and I both knew that, and didn't expect them of her. So I stood there without moving, wanting Mum to tickle me but unsure if she was serious. When I didn't budge, Mum pounced on me and began to tickle me under the arms. I laughed and tried to push her away. She tickled differently from Dad. Her fingers were bonier, her nails sharper, boring into my skin, and the sensation quickly became unpleasant. I begged her to stop, but Mum just laughed.

'Too late,' she said, and kept at it unmercifully until I fell on the floor.

She pursued me, continuing with the tickling until I started struggling in earnest.

'You should have obeyed,' Mum whispered, her face so close to mine that I could smell her sour breath. She was smiling, but there was something distinctly unpleasant about her smile.

Mum continued tickling me under the arms and thighs, pinching and poking at me with her sharp nails. I tried to speak but couldn't get out a word; I felt trapped, unable to breathe. My stomach twisted and I lost control and started lashing out. One of the blows hit Mum, and she grabbed my hand and pinned it in a cruel grip down by my knee.

'You should have obeyed me, Marsí. I warned you that I'd tickle you if you didn't.'

That was when I felt something leaking into my knickers, then trickling hot and wet down my thighs.

Mum stopped abruptly and rose to her feet, pushing her hair back from her face. She looked at me in disgust. 'Only babies wet themselves.' Then she walked off, leaving me lying on the floor.

This scene regularly flashed into my mind, but I determinedly pushed it away. It was so unbelievable that I was sure I must have dreamt it. Even so, I once hit a boyfriend who tried to tickle me. An involuntary reaction, I tried to explain. I never saw him again.

After Stína disappeared, I started having nightmares, and in many of them Mum took on monstrous forms. She would chase us sisters along narrow passageways or around the cellar. In my dreams, I was constantly trying to escape.

'How is Petra?' I asked now, not that I was interested in the answer.

'Oh, she's all right, poor thing. Her old man left her enough money, so she's thinking of buying a summer cabin up north. Her family's from there.'

'Oh, really?'

'I'd like to go on holiday.' Mum sighed, poured herself a refill, and began to examine herself in the mirror.

'Mum?'

'What?' She ran a finger along one eyebrow, then wiped some invisible dust off her cheekbone.

'Do you think Stína had a boyfriend – you know, around the time she disappeared?'

Mum's eyes met mine in the mirror. 'Why do you say that?'

'I was just wondering if she'd recently met someone.' We had discovered after she went missing that Stína had been going out with Málfríður's older brother, but that their relationship had been over by then.

'Oh, Marsí. Don't start brooding on all that again.'

'But you must wonder?'

'No, I don't.' And Mum brushed past me as she left the kitchen, making her way towards the bathroom, where she started running a bath.

'Did she go out a lot in the evenings?' I asked, leaning in the bathroom doorway.

'How am I supposed to know that?'

'You were – are – her mother.'

'Stína was a big girl by then and I didn't go sticking my nose into everything she did.'

'But do you think she might have done?'

Mum poured something from a bottle into the bath and the scent of lavender filled the room. 'I don't know, Marsí. I just don't want to think about it anymore. It makes me so tired.'

'But—'

'*Don't*, I said.' Mum glared at me. Then her expression softened. 'Why all these endless questions?'

'Sorry.'

Mum sighed, closed her eyes and rubbed her forehead, as though in sudden desperation. 'When are you going back to town?'

'Tomorrow, for sure. But I've been invited somewhere this evening,' I lied.

She didn't ask where, just nodded and drew a deep breath before closing the bathroom door, shutting me out.

5
Kristín – *Autumn 1966*

Marsí's in the kitchen eating a piece of toast when I get home.

'You've got to see this,' she says, pointing to something in *The Week*.

It's a reader's question from two girls who are both madly in love with a boy they saw on the bus but don't know how to get in touch with him.

'God, they're crazy. What on earth do they think *The Week* can do about it?'

'Maybe advertise for information about him,' Marsí suggests.

'Like he'd know that two girls had fallen in love with him after seeing him once on the bus.'

'Do you believe in that?' Marsí asks.

'In what?'

'Love at first sight,' she says. 'Dad says that's how it was with him and Mum. That he only had to look at her once to know that she was the right woman.'

'I know,' I say, glancing towards the bedroom where Mum's asleep.

When I was younger, I used to love hearing the story of how our parents met at a Reykjavík dance. Listening to Dad describe how everything and everyone else vanished into a sort of mist and he only had eyes for Mum. But yesterday Dad didn't come home until late, and I heard them quarrelling in their bedroom until the early hours. Perhaps that's why the story about how my parents met no longer moves me the way it once did.

'It's so childish of those girls,' I say, pushing the magazine back to Marsí.

'I suppose so,' Marsí says.

She's got brown hair like Dad, a round face and a small mouth, which she's always twisting into grimaces when she's not gnawing at her lips. But it's her eyes that are her most striking feature. They remind me of a bird of prey: staring, flickering watchfully to and fro. Nothing ever gets past my sister.

'What?' Marsí asks now, without looking up from the paper.

'Nothing,' I say.

'Are you going out this evening?'

'I'm going to that art class. Why do you want to know?'

'No reason.' Marsí closes the paper, gets up and leaves the kitchen, and a moment or two later I see her out of the window, stalking up the slope to the wood.

Marsí can be so strange. Most people say we could hardly be more different. As a rule, she's quiet, but when she does say something, it's generally short and to the point. At school, she seems untouchable, uninterested in anyone or anything, but I know better. I know her as well as I know myself, and when we're alone she can be quite different: warm, funny and interesting.

I take her plate, throw away the rest of the toast and wash it up.

Marsí and I have always been close. If that's changed, it's my fault. Recently, I've been finding it hard to spend much time at home in the evenings. I've never particularly liked our house, Nátthagi. It's unlike other houses; situated on the outskirts of the town, black, imposing, forbidding, even. Sometimes I feel as if the house has isolated us from the rest of the town, made us different.

Dad inherited it from his parents and promised Grandma he would never sell. He's kept his word, but although the promise might have seemed easy to make at the time, I've noticed that neither of my parents enjoy being here. Inanimate objects have a way of tying you down without your realising it, and lately the feeling has been growing in me that if I don't leave home soon, I'll end up like my parents, trapped in this house. That it will come to own me, just as it has claimed them.

I know it sounds like nonsense, but I sometimes wonder what would have happened if my parents had sold the house and chosen a new home for themselves. I can't help feeling that our lives would have been very different.

Later that afternoon, Dad gives me a lift to Kleppjárnsreykir, more commonly known as Reykir. The evening classes aren't taught in the modern school buildings but in a house called, for obvious reasons, the Old Doctor's House. It's used for teaching nowadays, but it's clear from the cramped rooms and narrow corridors that it wasn't originally built for that purpose. I get there early, and it takes me a while to locate the toilet, which is in a small room at the end of a corridor. While I'm washing my hands, I look in the little mirror and notice the black circles under my eyes. On recent nights I've been waking up after only a few hours' sleep, unsure what has disturbed me. When I drop off again, my sleep is fitful and I start awake at the slightest noise. As a child, I used to be afraid of the dark, and my old fear seems to be rearing its head again.

When I emerge from the toilet, I nearly walk straight into Ívar, the art teacher. He's quite different from how I remembered: younger and better-looking, with honey-coloured hair and a suntan. He's holding a folder, and I notice that his fingers are stained with paint, just like mine.

Ívar came to observe some of Halldóra's art lessons back in the spring, walking around and watching what we were doing. We had a chat about realism in art and whether paintings should have to reflect reality at all, which we both agreed was unnecessary. 'Art should reflect the soul and our emotions,' he had said. 'It should be much bigger and more profound than reality. In fact, art should be a unique expression of the artist's view of the world.'

'Oh, hi,' he says now. 'Nice to see you here.'

'I'm really keen to get started,' I say.

'It's Kristín, isn't it?' he asks.

'Yes, but everyone calls me Stína,' I say.

'Do they?'

His question takes me aback. From his expression, he seems to think Stína is a peculiar shortening of Kristín. Yet most Kristíns in the country are known as Stína.

'I've always been called Stína,' I say.

'I see,' he replies. 'I think Kristín's such a pretty name.'

'My sister's called Marsibil and I've always preferred that,' I confide. 'It's so unusual.'

'My grandmother was called Kristín,' Ívar says, and I feel like I've offended him somehow.

He looks at his watch, says the class is about to start and ushers me ahead of him into the room, where I take a seat towards the front.

Once everyone has taken their places, Ívar surveys the seven students sitting before him. Most of them are much older than me, and although a few faces are familiar, I don't know anyone well enough to speak to.

'Some people say you can't teach art,' Ívar begins. 'And I agree in a way. Talent is innate, but it needs to be cultivated and watered if it's to grow and thrive.' His gaze alights on me briefly, to my embarrassment. 'The history of art is intrinsically linked to the history of mankind. Movements and trends at any given time are part of our history, from Stone Age Man to Da Vinci or Van Gogh. But I'm going to start with Newton.'

'Newton?' someone asks, after a puzzled silence. 'But he wasn't—'

'An artist?' Ívar says. 'Quite right. But in 1666 Newton discovered that sunlight consisted of colours, and in the following decade he identified the colours of the spectrum. Can anyone tell me what these are?'

I stick up my hand and reel off the seven colours. Ívar rewards me with a smile that makes my stomach flip and I feel myself turning bright red.

6
Marsibil – Friday, *18 November 1977*

Síða had only one bar, which, like the bookshop, served more than one role: during the day, it was a café and restaurant, offering lunch and dinner menus of fish, chips, soups and sandwiches. As long as you didn't mind the floor being sticky with spilt alcohol, Café Hvítá wasn't a bad place.

I was starving but couldn't face hanging around at home, feeling unwelcome, so I had come into town and taken a seat at the back of the café, in the corner by the window. A waitress came over to me. She was wearing a black top that revealed her midriff, though that probably wasn't the intention. I recognised her but couldn't recall her name. She didn't smile as she took my order: deep-fried fish, chips and vodka. Then she stalked away.

The gin Mum had given me earlier had worn off and my thoughts were crowding so thick and fast into my mind that I couldn't catch hold of them. The photos of Stína showed that she had been going out a lot in the weeks before her disappearance and spending time with at least one, if not two, boys. She'd had a whole life outside our home with her friends – but without me. It shouldn't have come as a surprise, and yet I felt a twinge of pain in my gut at the realisation.

The fact I didn't recognise the boys – or boy – in the blurry pictures didn't necessarily mean they weren't known to me. It could have been Elvar, the guy she had been going out with earlier that year, but after several close examinations, I was now fairly sure that the headless boy in the last picture was someone else.

'Your food,' the waitress said, slapping down a plate piled with fish and chips that I suddenly didn't want.

'I also ordered—'

'It's coming.' She spun on her heel and returned with the vodka, plonking it on the table without a word. As she did so, her name came back to me: 'Sunny Solla'. A nickname she'd acquired because she never cracked a smile.

After she'd gone, I heard a voice say: 'Someone's having a bad day.'

A man was sitting at a table on the other side of the restaurant, eating a plate of chips.

'I'm fine, thanks,' I replied curtly.

'I meant her.' He nodded in the direction of Solla.

She was looking over, so instead of answering, I hastily dropped my eyes and ate a chip.

'I recognise you,' the man went on.

'Do you?' I didn't recognise *him*. He had tousled dark hair and thick stubble. The sleeves of his checked shirt were rolled up and I couldn't tell if his arms were dirty or just covered in hair, freckles and moles.

'Maybe you've just got that kind of face,' he added.

'What kind of face?'

'Familiar.'

Mum once said I had a hard face. I'd always known I was unlovable and off-putting, but I hadn't noticed the harshness of my expression until she pointed it out to me. Afterwards, I stood in front of the mirror for a long time, wondering what lent my features this impression. Was it my dark eyebrows or the sullen cast of my mouth? Or my contemptuously turned-up nose? Was the innate harshness of my features the reason why I sometimes rubbed people up the wrong way without having done anything to deserve it?

'So, what is there to do in this town?' the man asked, after a short silence.

'Not a lot. It's not really a town that offers anything but long walks,' I said, and took a sip of my drink. Then, remembering what my therapist had said about making more of an effort to show an interest in other people, I asked: 'What are you doing here?'

'Just taking a look around.'

'Why?'

'Because I'm writing something set in this town.'

'What kind of thing?'

'If you want to know more, let me buy you another drink.'

My glass was nearly empty, though I couldn't remember taking more than a sip. I wanted another drink, but this wasn't the kind of town where you got to know people over fish and chips, so I was wary. 'You want to buy me a drink? Why?'

He burst out laughing. 'Because I'm bored out of my mind. Because the only alternative is going back to the guesthouse and being in bed before ten. Come on, do you need any more reasons?'

'There's no guesthouse in this town.'

'Well, farm accommodation, then. I got a room with the people at Brú.'

He stood up, though I hadn't accepted his offer, and shortly afterwards returned bearing two drinks and took the seat opposite me without so much as a by-your-leave.

'What's this?' I asked, examining the brown liquid in the glass.

'Bourbon. Don't tell me you've never drunk whisky before?'

'I'm not much of a drinker.'

'Why do I get the feeling you're lying?'

I shrugged.

He pushed the glass closer to me. 'You look like you need a pick-me-up.'

I took a mouthful and grimaced.

He laughed. 'So, why are you sitting here with such a long face?' he asked.

'Is it that obvious?'

'Yep.'

'Bad associations, I suppose.'

'You're from around here, then?' He glanced out of the window as two older women walked past.

One of them looked familiar and after a moment or two I realised she used to teach at my school. When our eyes met through the glass, she hurriedly averted her gaze and whispered something to her friend, who shot me a glance.

'That's right,' I said, and took another sip of bourbon. It didn't taste as bad this time.

'Have the people here always been this unfriendly?'

'Who says they're unfriendly?'

'The waitress sighed aloud when I asked for ketchup, like it was a terrible imposition. And earlier, when I went to the petrol station, everyone stared at me like I came from another planet.'

'I don't suppose many people come through unless they have business here.' I'd got glances at the petrol station too, though for different reasons.

'Watch,' he whispered, then gave Solla a sign for another drink. She heaved an exaggerated sigh and told us to wait.

We both giggled.

'Why base a story here?' I asked.

He shrugged. 'Maybe because this town is so bleak, it would make a good setting for a terrible tragedy.'

'Like what?' My neck was burning now and my fingers tightened convulsively on my glass.

'I don't know. I was hoping you could tell me some stories.'

I studied him for a moment, suddenly feeling that I'd been recognised, picked out. From time to time, back when I still went out partying, I used to be drawn aside and asked to tell the story of what had happened to Stína. People seemed to believe I was in possession of information that had never come out. As if I knew what had happened but didn't want to tell.

Some years ago, I was at a student party in Reykjavík, where I studied literature at the university for a year and a half before dropping out. I had been drinking *landi* and, unable to see straight, had stumbled into the toilets and sat down in one of the cubicles, wondering if I was going to puke, before eventually emerging and splashing cold water on my face. When I looked up, there was a girl standing beside me. She attended some of the same lectures as me and we'd talked a few times.

'Where are you from again?' she asked, as though we'd been in the middle of a conversation.

'The west. Hvítársíða in Borgarfjörður.'

'Oh, right, the town where that girl vanished,' she said, so disingenuously that I was sure she had rehearsed the whole thing beforehand. She began putting on lipstick without waiting for an answer. 'Did you know her?'

I shook my head. 'She was older than me.'

'Oh, OK.' She smacked her lips together and smiled. 'I heard that everyone in the town knew what had happened to her. That it was hushed up.'

'Who by?'

'The police. Her family.'

'I don't think so.'

'They're supposed to be weird, aren't they – the family? Especially the mother.'

I mumbled something that could have been assent.

'I heard,' the girl continued, lowering her voice, 'that her parents started behaving strangely after she went missing. Not like people in mourning, if you know what I mean.'

I just shrugged.

I'd heard comments like this before, broken-off sentences (*but if she was seen going home…*) or jokes (*isn't she just round at your place?*); comments that provoked embarrassed laughter, glances and whispering. A few weeks after Stína's disappearance, people more or less stopped coming round to our house and Mum's trips to the shops became shorter. No chatting by the milk cooler anymore; no one stopping us for a friendly word as we walked around town. One day everyone had stood by us, the next it was as if it was us against them.

I never knew why or how it had started. The change wasn't sudden, it came about so gradually that at first I simply thought people didn't know what to say to us. Long afterwards I realised that right from the beginning they had been watching us, trying to interpret our behaviour and coming up with theories about us, based on how we acted. The fact that Dad was never seen crying, that Mum never took part in the search, that I started going out partying and staying away from home, it was all grist to their mill. If we smiled too much, laughed too loud or did anything that was considered inappropriate for a grieving family, the rumours would start doing the rounds. I don't know if they reached my parents' ears but I got to hear them when I was out on the town. They were whispered to me on a blast of booze-soured breath, and I was held to account for any number of things to which I had no answers.

'I don't know any stories,' I said now to the man, swirling the drink that had arrived at the table, in spite of my protests that I didn't want another.

'Oh, I find that hard to believe. In a town like this there are bound to be stories.' He smiled, and his smile was friendly, as if he had no idea that most of the stories were about my family.

'So you want gossip?' I leant forwards, as impulsive as I'd been as a child. 'The waitress is called Sólveig, known as "Sunny Solla". I heard she used to sleep with older men when she was a teenager. The story goes that she always stayed behind after her maths lessons and slept with the teacher to get higher marks. She was fifteen, he was fifty.'

'Oof.'

'But I don't suppose you're after stories like that, are you?'

'Well, it's interesting. Maybe even a bit dodgy.'

'Looking back, I suppose so. But at the time everyone just thought she was a terrible slut.'

'What happened to the teacher?'

'Haven't a clue. He's probably still working at the school.'

'Tell me more.'

But before I could continue plying him with tales, I felt a tap on my shoulder.

'I thought it was you.'

It was Lilla, an old classmate of mine. We'd been briefly inseparable when we were nine. Although our friendship had cooled, the small size of our class meant that we were all constantly thrown together, every time one of us had a birthday or there was a school dance or during the Ash Wednesday fancy-dress parades. There were only six girls in the class and no one was allowed to be left out, however badly we got on. Which was typical of this town. All the inhabitants were bound together by the fact of living here. We had to put up with one another, whatever happened. We were trapped, like wriggling fish in the same net.

'Hi, Lilla,' I said.

My companion the author rose to his feet and offered Lilla his chair.

'If you remember any more stories, I'll be here,' he said, raising his glass in a toast.

'Stories? What stories?' Lilla asked when he had gone, but I just shook my head as though I had no idea what he was on about.

Lilla and I exchanged some inconsequential chitchat. Or, rather, she talked and I listened. Lilla's voice seemed to come from a long way off as she told me who had married who, how many children they had now, and how Tommi, her boyfriend, was almost certainly going to propose to her at Christmas. When Lilla paused briefly to take a sip of her soft drink, I managed to slip in a question.

'Talking of boyfriends – do you remember if Stína had one? When she disappeared, I mean?'

Lilla blinked at me for several seconds before smiling awkwardly. I'd never discussed Stína with my classmates, so there was little wonder she was surprised. In the old days, I used to storm out of the room whenever the subject came up.

'Well, I remember the vicar's son fancied her,' she said.

'I know about him, but she split up with him a while before she vanished,' I said, a little irritably. It still upset me that Stína had never confided in me about Elvar. 'I was thinking of someone else. I've come across a photo of Stína with another boy, you see.'

'What did he look like?'

'You can't see his face in the picture but I don't think it was Elvar.'

'I could ask my brother: they were in the same class.'

I nodded and mumbled a 'thanks', swilling the remains of my drink around the glass for a moment. Then I knocked it back in one go, to a look of astonishment from Lilla.

I put the glass back on the table with a noisy clunk and, before I could stop myself, I had blurted out the question that had been going round and round in my head:

'Do you think Stína could be alive?'

Lilla was silent for a long moment.

'Maybe,' she said warily. 'Your sister was unpredictable, Marsí. I remember thinking it would be typical of her just to leave.'

'Typical of her? How do you mean?'

'Wasn't she always talking about studying at art school abroad? It was like this town was too small for Stína. Like she couldn't wait to get away.'

'So you *do* think she could still be alive?' I said. 'That nothing bad happened to her?'

'Well, I don't know…'

'No one would have wanted to hurt Stína. She was so nice.'

Lilla opened her mouth, then closed it again.

I frowned at this. 'What?' I demanded.

'Nothing.' She smiled and leant towards me. 'Look, Marsí, I expect it was all a terrible accident. I think it's time to put it behind you.'

I nodded and for a moment or two I even believed Lilla. Stína must have died in an accident. The whole thing had been a mistake. But another part of my mind objected: if Stína had died in an accident, her body would have been found, not just her anorak.

'Oh, Marsí, love.' Lilla took my hand in hers, and I realised that tears were trickling down my cheeks. 'Isn't it ten years this November? That must be tough.'

I nodded and said hoarsely: 'Yeah, quite tough.'

Lilla was one of those tactile girls who was always touching you, rubbing your back or wanting to hold your hand. Normally I couldn't stand the physical contact, but now I felt the need to wallow in her kindness like a puppy, so I let my hand rest in hers.

Much later, when she said goodbye, more people had gathered at the bar and the music had been turned up. I squinted at the clock that hung over the bar, but the numbers danced before my eyes and I had no idea what time it was, only that it must be getting late. There was a bunch of kids outside who looked far too young to be admitted. They couldn't have been more than fifteen or sixteen, hardly out of secondary school.

I scanned the room but couldn't see the author, so I made my way rather unsteadily to the bar and ordered another drink. In recent years I had drastically cut down my intake, but I could sense myself sliding back into my bad old ways tonight. For years I used to go out boozing every weekend and sometimes during the week too. Alcohol had numbed my feelings and I became increasingly dependent on this numbness. I used to sleep around too. A new boy almost every weekend, sometimes several. My first weekend at university in Reykjavík, I went to a party where I screwed a guy in the toilet to the accompaniment of insistent banging on the door from the people waiting outside. Afterwards, we walked out, me ashamed, him exultant. Later that same night, I had sex in a car with another boy, a mate of the toilet guy. Before the term was over I had slept with so many men that I'd lost track, and at one party a girl informed me that everyone was talking about what a slut I was. I shrugged and claimed not to give a shit, but afterwards I locked myself in the loo and cried.

In spite of my tough exterior, I was sensitive and because I didn't get the attention I wanted at home, I went looking for it elsewhere: at school, from my friends and later from the opposite sex. My therapist didn't put it exactly in these words, but was essentially saying I would have to learn to love myself before I could love anyone else.

And I tried. I really did.

I quit the booze for a while and went for long walks along the Reykjavík shoreline, gazing out to sea. I stopped bothering with make-up in the mornings. Stopped talking to people outside work. Stopped doing anything, really. By the end I couldn't cope with any kind of social contact at all. I dreaded going out to the shop, turning up to work, even answering the phone. Communicating with other people became an ordeal that filled me with anxiety and misery.

Yet I still had a desperate need for acceptance. Sometimes I caught myself making such pathetic attempts to please other people that it left a bad taste in my mouth. Why should I care if the sales assistant didn't smile at me? Why, before going to sleep, did I waste time obsessively trying to interpret the possible undertone in the voice of the man who had opened a door for me? Some nights I would lie there, mentally reviewing my day, wondering what people had thought about me in this or that situation. I brooded over stupid things, trivial incidents from childhood, like the time I shook the hand of the man in the shop instead of giving him the money he was holding out his hand for.

Now, sitting in this old bar, I didn't know what I was doing anymore, only that I was downing drinks, feeling that I'd come full circle. Where was the beginning, middle and end of a person?

'There you are.'

The author had materialised at my side, though it took me several seconds to register the fact. He was still wearing that superior smirk, like he knew better than everyone else.

The evening was suddenly looking up.

'Were you trying to find me?' I asked, my voice sounding odd and unlike me.

'Maybe,' he said. 'Did you want me to find you?'

I shrugged, feigning indifference.

'To be honest, I was hoping you hadn't left,' he admitted.

I didn't answer because just then, out of the corner of my eye, I caught sight of a familiar figure propping up the bar. Gústi was our neighbour growing up, went to the same school as us and was a friend to us both. He was the only person in Síða who I missed more than I liked to admit, and now there he was, talking to a girl, so close that they could have been kissing. I leant sideways to get a better view and almost fell off my chair.

'Whoa, everything OK?' The author grabbed me.

'Yeah, you?' I shot back.

He laughed. 'I'm just fine.'

'What's your name?'

'Einar, nice to meet you.' He held out his hand and I took it. Then he tightened his grip, pulled me close and whispered in my ear: 'Do you remember any more stories now?'

'Maybe,' I said.

I had a momentary close-up of the brown flecks in his moss-green eyes, as if his irises had been out in the sun too long and developed freckles.

Einar smiled. 'I was going to offer to buy you a drink, but I see you're already sorted. And to be brutally honest, I think you've had enough.' So saying, he took my glass and drained it in one go.

'I've got an idea for a story,' I said. 'You can write about a girl and a boy who meet in a bar and the boy tells the girl she's pissed, then steals her drink. Guess how it ends?'

'Not well?' he said, after a beat.

I stood up.

'Where are you going?'

'Home.'

I made a dash for the ladies.

It was dimly lit, the wood so deeply impregnated with urine that it stank. I sank down, not caring about the filthy seat, and closed my eyes. I didn't want to go home in this state. I would have to give at least the appearance of being in control of my faculties, but for that I'd probably need a bit of time to sober up.

Sometime later – I wasn't sure how long – my eyes opened. They took a while to focus, but when they did I was staring at the wall, in the corner under the sink, where someone had scribbled something. It took another moment for the words to register in my mind:

Stína lives.

I reeled out of the toilet, cheeks burning, heart pounding. It wasn't my sister's writing, so it must be a joke. Someone trying to be funny. Yet there was nothing funny about my body's response. My heart was now racing uncontrollably and my head was swimming with dizziness.

Einar was waiting for me outside the toilet. He seized my arm in an attempt to stop me running past. 'Let me take you home.'

'I don't need anyone to take me,' I protested, tearing myself loose.

I *was* horribly drunk.

The floor was moving in waves. I was having trouble keeping my balance and kept veering off to the side and cannoning into people. On my way out, I tripped and before I knew it the ground was rushing towards me.

I heard someone calling out and felt a searing pain in the palms of my hands.

'Hey, is everything OK?'

When I could focus again I discovered that I was looking up into the familiar eyes of Guðrún, Stína's childhood friend.

She bent down. 'Marsí, I thought I recognised you but I wasn't sure at first.'

'Guðrún,' I groaned, grateful to see a friendly face. And even more grateful when Gústi appeared beside her.

Gústi lived on the outskirts of town, and although it was a bit of a way between our houses, he had been our nearest neighbour. Back when Stína and I used to walk to school, he would generally walk with us.

I took the hand he held out and with his help struggled to my feet.

'I can take her home,' said Einar, joining us.

'No.' I shook my head.

Gústi's gaze swung from me to Einar and back again. 'Was this man…? Why don't you come back inside with me and sit down for a bit?'

'She needs to go home,' Einar said.

Gústi, who was still holding my arm, glared at him. 'What? Are you offering to take her?'

'Actually, I agree,' Guðrún said, stroking my hair. 'She needs to go home.'

'I can take her,' Einar repeated.

'No, I think Marsí needs a lift,' Gústi said. 'And you don't look like you're in any fit state to drive. Is that OK, Marsí? Shall I give you a lift home?'

I nodded, said goodbye to Guðrún, and let Gústi lead me away.

When I glanced over my shoulder, I saw that Einar was still standing there, watching us. I tried to send him an apologetic smile but I probably looked like I was going to throw up because he didn't return it, just shook his head and turned away.

7
Kristín – *Autumn 1966*

On Friday evening I tell my parents I'm going round to Guðrún's and Guðrún tells her mother she's going round to my place. Only Málfríður doesn't need to lie. Her parents aren't bothered about where she goes in the evening, so long as she's back by morning.

Málfríður has three older brothers, and I get the feeling the vicar and his wife have given up the struggle when it comes to discipline.

They may have tried with the oldest boy, but by the time the fourth child came along and turned out to be an insolent, wilful girl, they admitted defeat. And Málfríður knows how to play on her parents' guilt about forcing her to move from the city to the countryside. As a result, she gets away with murder.

'Come in,' the vicar says when Guðrún and I arrive. 'Málfríður's upstairs in her room.'

'Thanks.' I take off my jacket.

'Pretty blouse,' he says.

It *is* pretty; white, with large buttons and a low neckline, but it seems odd and creepy that he should comment on it. Málfríður's dad is different from the other fathers I know; he notices everything, like if you're wearing new shoes or change your hairstyle. And he's always smiling. I never know quite how to take his remarks, so usually I just smile politely and thank him. But it makes me so self-conscious about my appearance that when I go round to Málfríður's I often deliberately avoid wearing anything new or in any way eye-catching.

This evening, though, I spent ages getting ready, blow-drying my hair and painting my eyes with white eyeshadow and thick black eyeliner. It's not that different from painting on a canvas, if you stop to think about it. Both involve shading and carefully blending your colours. Drawing portraits, especially eyes, is what I find most satisfying. Eyes can convey so much if you get them right. It's Mona Lisa's eyes that smile, not her lips, and in Vermeer's portrait of the girl with the pearl earring, it's her eyes that draw your attention.

Some eyes are so charged with meaning that they seem to conceal whole stories behind them.

There's a sofa upstairs, currently occupied by two of Málfríður's brothers. The middle brother is called Elvar and he's the best-looking of the lot. He's like a painting – not that perfection in art has ever really appealed to me. His features are completely symmetrical, like the guidelines you draw on a page before sketching a face. Everything is perfectly aligned: the angular jaw, the soft lips and straight nose. He has dark hair, olive skin and eyes as brown as earth.

From the moment Elvar moved here he became the number one

topic of conversation among the women of the town. He's a year older than me, only sixteen, but even Mum asked if I'd seen the gorgeous new boy. Elvar seems immune to the attention, though, and as far as I know he hasn't got together with any of the local girls. Málfríður says he had a girlfriend in Reykjavík and that they sometimes still talk on the phone, which explains a lot.

When I say hello, neither of the brothers look up, though Elvar returns my greeting.

'Are you coming out with us this evening?' I venture.

Elvar shrugs and says he doesn't know if he can be bothered.

'You should come.'

'Should I? We'll see,' he says, then looks up and meets my eye for the first time. My stomach does a somersault and I can sense rather than see Guðrún grinning.

'I'm coming,' Málfríður calls from her bedroom.

When she emerges, my jaw drops. 'What have you done?'

'It's OK, isn't it?' Málfríður runs her fingers along the fringe she has cut herself. 'It's not crooked?'

'Mum's going to have a fit,' her youngest brother remarks. 'You look like that woman at the shop.'

'Oh, shut up,' Málfríður snaps.

No one would want to look like Ninna from the shop, but I can see what her brother means. There is a certain similarity there now that Málfríður's fringe is so brutally short.

'It looks great,' I reassure her.

'Yes, wild,' Guðrún agrees.

Málfríður smiles. 'This evening is going to be wild.'

There's an odd smell at Snorri's house – maybe something's cooking? – and there are bottles of vodka, rum and gin on the table. Snorri's fiddling with the record player. The music is so deafening that we have to shout to make ourselves heard.

Gústi is there already. He greets us and pours me a glass.

He says something I can't hear, but before he can repeat it, a Beatles song starts playing and Málfríður whoops. Snorri grabs her by the hand and whirls her round the floor until she collides with a small side table. The vase on it rocks back and forth and we all hold our breath until it recovers its balance, after which there's a roar of laughter.

I take a seat on the sofa, sip my drink, though it tastes awful, and lean back against the cushions.

'Everything OK?' Guðrún asks.

'Yeah, sure,' I say, aware that I sound irritated. Elvar hasn't turned up and I doubt he will now.

Later that evening I go into the bathroom and tidy my hair. My cheeks are flushed and my eyes glazed from the alcohol. I'm not used to knocking it back this hard; it's because I'm feeling agitated. I bite my lips and rub them vigorously with water to restore some colour to them before going back out there.

Outside the door I bump into someone who is standing there waiting.

'Sorry—' I begin, then break off when I realise it's him. Elvar has finally arrived. All my irritation evaporates in an instant.

'Hi, Stína,' he says. 'Everything OK?'

'Yes, sorry. I'm fine.'

Elvar smiles. 'Could I maybe…?'

'What?'

'Get past.'

'Oh, yes, of course. Sorry.' I step aside, then linger in the hallway for a while after he's gone into the bathroom. Why do I always have to behave like such an idiot around him?

Before I have a chance to think about the answer to this, there's a knock at the front door. Since I'm in the hall, I open it and find Sólveig standing outside. For a moment or two, I gape at her, speechless. She's wearing one of the most ridiculous dresses I've ever seen, and has put her hair up in a perfect bun.

'I've come for the party,' she says.

'Right, come in.' I make way for her and we enter the sitting room together.

'This is Sólveig,' I tell Snorri. 'We invited her.'

'Hi, Sólveig,' Snorri says. 'Take a pew.'

Sólveig takes the only free spot on the sofa, beside Snorri. I sit down next to Málfríður, who jabs me so hard with her elbow that I hiss at her to stop it.

'Let me fetch you a drink.' Málfríður jumps up and goes into the kitchen. After a moment or two she calls to Snorri to come and help her. While they are in the kitchen, Elvar reappears and takes the free place beside me.

'So you decided to come, after all,' I remark.

'Well, you told me I should.'

I smile, then see that Málfríður has returned with a drink that she hands to Sólveig.

Sólveig peers into the glass and sniffs at it dubiously. 'What is this?'

'Just drink it,' Málfríður says. 'Don't be a drag.'

Clearly eager not to be a drag, Sólveig takes a great gulp, chokes and starts coughing.

Snorri strokes her back. 'There, there,' he says soothingly. 'Nice dress, by the way.'

Sólveig looks at him, wipes her mouth and thanks him for the compliment. 'Is Böðvar here?'

'No, but he should be any minute,' Málfríður lies.

'That stuff any good?' Elvar asks, nodding at my glass.

'It's all right,' I say.

'I'm not much of a drinker myself.'

'Nor am I. Want a taste?'

I hand him the glass, and he knocks it back, then shudders. 'No one could describe that as good.'

I laugh. 'Well, the effects are nice, at any rate.'

'Yes.' He leans back and I copy him. They're playing a song I love, and the rest of the room seems to fade into the background, as if we're alone together.

After a little while, Elvar turns his head to me. 'Want to grab some fresh air?' he asks.

I nod, and we slip out of the room just as Snorri hauls Sólveig to her feet for a dance.

8
Marsibil – *Friday, 18 November 1977*

It wasn't the first time I had been 'rescued' by Gústi. That was probably when I fell off my bike outside his house and he came running out with a plaster and a chocolate biscuit. After Stína went missing, he took me under his wing and was the person who drove me home at the end of the evening or handed me a glass of water when I'd had too much to drink. I always knew it was because I was Stína's little sister. He was her friend, so he felt he had a duty to look after me. I would often catch his eye when I was out partying and find him frowning at me, as though he'd taken on the role of big brother now that Stína was no longer there.

As a teenager, Gústi had been tall, gangling and not much to look at. He had mousy-blond hair, pallid skin and acne. He used to be heavily into the Beatles and grew his hair in a mop top like them. One time, he brought round his entire record collection and we listened to it together in the sitting room, while he translated the English and explained the lyrics to me. These days, Gústi was hunkier, and his skin was clear and had developed a bit of colour; but the most striking change of all was his short hair.

He led me away from the pub, past the teenage kids hanging around outside, who yelled after us, and along the street to where his car was parked.

'There we go,' he said reassuringly as he helped me into the passenger seat and fastened the seatbelt. This was typical of him; only Gústi would bother with a seatbelt. I smiled to myself when I glimpsed the Beatles T-shirt under his jacket.

'You don't have to do this,' I said. The world was still spinning, though the cold air had revived me a little.

'I was about to head home anyway. And I didn't like the look of that guy who wanted you to go with him. Do you know him?'

'Only since this evening.'

'Well, I've never seen him before, and you never know what men like that have in mind. Or rather, I can just imagine what he had in mind.'

I turned to Gústi. 'Why do you always do this?'

'What?'

'Bother about me.'

'Well, because I want to. I care about you, Marsí.'

'You care about me.' I leant back in my seat with a low laugh.

'Honestly.'

'Yeah, yeah.'

I used to care about Gústi too. For a while I thought we might stay in touch after I moved away. I gave him the phone number of my digs and told him to ring me, but the phone remained stubbornly silent and the only person who ever called was my mother. If Gústi had cared about me, he'd have called at least once after I moved away.

There was silence in the car as we drove out of town. Only a few minutes left and we'd be outside my house. The sky was unusually bright with stars, and through the passenger window I could make out the distant glacier, a darker shape looming on the horizon. The fenceposts marking the fields flashed by in the headlights.

Then I saw it.

'Stop,' I shouted.

Gústi slammed on the brakes. 'Are you going to be sick?'

I didn't answer but scrabbled to open the door the moment the car came to a halt.

'Marsí?'

Gústi got out after me but, ignoring him, I broke into a run, stumbling, weaving erratically back the way we'd come, scanning the side of the road. I'd caught a glimpse of something as we drove past. Something red.

After I'd gone a few more steps I spotted it. The skin prickled on my arms and my heart began to pound. The red thing by the side of the road was an item of clothing. An anorak, just like Stína's.

'What are you doing, Marsí?' Gústi caught up with me, panting slightly.

I turned to him and said in a shaky voice: 'This isn't funny.'

'What isn't funny, Marsí?'

'That,' I said, pointing to the coat. 'Who put that anorak there?'

Gústi walked to the side of the road and peered around. Then he turned back to me. 'There's no anorak there, Marsí. Where do you say you saw it?'

I went over to him and strained my eyes in the gloom. There was nothing to see but gravel, withered grass and a barbed-wire fence set back from the road. No clothing, let alone a red anorak.

'Are you OK, Marsí?'

Gústi's voice was so full of pity that I couldn't bear it. I knew what he was thinking, but this had nothing to do with Stína. I wasn't hallucinating or imagining things now, even though her red anorak had been found here. But it would sound even weirder if I tried to deny it, so I retraced my steps to the car in silence and didn't say a word for the remainder of the journey.

'Do you want me to come in with you?' Gústi asked, when we reached my house.

'There's no need.'

'Marsí,' he said, before I could get out. 'If you're going to be here for a few days, maybe we could go for a coffee?'

'I'm leaving tomorrow.'

'You can't wait to get away from here,' Gústi teased, but his smile was strained. 'If you change your mind, you know where I am: just a few steps away, if you need me.'

'I know,' I said, and climbed out of his car.

I stood outside the house until it was out of sight.

Reluctant to go in straight away, I gazed up at the sky, which remained stubbornly clear, despite the forecast of snow.

The evening Stína vanished we had the first snowfall of the winter, and it didn't let up for several days. It was a heavy fall, the big flakes settling in a thick white quilt over the landscape and hampering the progress of the search parties. She could be anywhere, they said, buried under a drift.

Then the wind had picked up, filling the air with flying snow and blinding the volunteers. Everyone had predicted that Stína would be found as soon as the storm subsided, as soon as the snow melted, so when the rain came a week later, the searchers combed the area again, holding their breath. Now she would turn up, they said. But all their efforts were in vain.

I gave up waiting for the snow, went inside and quietly slipped off my shoes. The house stank of cigarettes and there was a candle still burning in the sitting room. A bottle stood open on the coffee table. I poured the dregs into a glass.

Our family photo albums were kept on the bottom shelf of the cupboard. I sat down with one on my lap and started turning the pages filled with old black-and-white snapshots of me and Stína. I paused at the ones I was particularly fond of: the two of us at Christmas, or helping the farmer at Ytri-Hólar rake the hay. The oldest photos were from before I was born, of Stína as a baby. I studied her, a newborn in the cradle we'd later been given for our dolls. The cradle was still down in the cellar, two of the dolls lying entwined inside, looking pretty battered these days. I felt a sudden impulse to go down and rescue them.

Stína loved playing with dolls. In fact, she loved everything that was girly: dresses and jewellery and make-up. Even in the photo of her as a newborn baby her face was unmistakably feminine. With some babies it was impossible to tell their sex unless they were kitted out in pink or blue, but in Stína's case there was no question.

I stroked the picture with my finger. One corner was bent, and when I touched it, I noticed that there was something tucked in behind it. Another photo. I prised it out and saw that it was of a baby too, dressed in a knitted romper suit.

At first I assumed it was Stína, but when I compared the photos I saw that this baby was nothing like her, with its dark eyebrows and eyes, not so different from mine. I examined it for a while, sure that it was neither me nor Stína. Perhaps it was a photo of Dad as a newborn, because somehow I was sure that this baby was a boy.

I put the picture back, deciding to ask Mum about it in the morning.

Up in my room, I took out the letter I had received several days ago and reread it. The terror it had evoked was fading now and I had even begun to make light of it, telling myself it was harmless. It might not be from my penpal at all, just from someone playing a trick on me. I couldn't remember ever confiding in anyone about my penpal, but that didn't mean I hadn't. There were all those evenings and weekends that were just blanks, all those gaps in my memory, as though someone had gone crazy with an eraser and rubbed out chunks of my life.

The letter wasn't unfriendly or menacing; quite the reverse, in fact.

…still just a few words away if you need me.

I stared at this blearily for a few seconds before I realised what it was that had troubled me about Gústi's parting words. He had said he was 'just a few steps away' if I needed him.

His choice of words was so similar to the letter that for a moment I was sure they must have been a figment of my imagination, like the anorak.

9
Saturday, 19 November 1977

I must have been about six years old.

Mum came in, holding a baby. 'Look,' she said. 'This is your little brother.'

Stína ran over to her and kissed the child on the head. 'Oh, Mum, he's so sweet,' she cried.

But when I approached, the little boy began to scream. Mum and Stína both looked at me accusingly, as though it was my fault. Mum held him tighter and Stína cupped his head with a protective hand.

Then I was older, perhaps nine, and Mum was carrying my brother, who was still no bigger than before. 'Out of the way,' she said, and went into the bathroom. She perched on the edge of the tub, and I watched as she carefully lowered the baby into the water.

'What are you doing?' I asked in sudden alarm.

'We've got to get him clean,' Mum said, without taking her eyes off the baby.

Stína was sitting beside her, watching. The little boy began to make high chuckling noises and splashed with his arms and legs. Mum kissed him on the forehead, then without warning she let him go. He sank below the surface at once, his arms flailing.

I rushed forwards to help him but Mum stopped me, grabbing me by the shoulder. 'We've got to get him clean, Marsí.'

My heart pounding frantically, I tried to move. But nothing happened. My legs wouldn't obey. I watched helplessly as my little brother's movements gradually ceased and his wide-open eyes closed.

I woke to find myself in Stína's bed. I had crawled under her duvet and was clutching a yellow cushion that still smelt of her, although I must have been imagining it. Smells couldn't last for ten years.

The terror I had experienced in my dream slowly ebbed away, but an ominous feeling persisted as I got out of bed and went down to the kitchen to make myself some coffee.

Dad was sitting there with a newspaper and I took the chair facing him.

'Won't you have something to eat?' he asked.

'I'm not hungry.'

'You should eat.' Dad raised his eyebrows. 'You've got so thin. Your mother's worried about you.'

'She needn't be.'

Abandoning the subject, Dad turned the page of his newspaper and carried on reading. I drank my coffee, leaning back against the wall, and closed my eyes. The events of yesterday evening were coming back to me: the conversation with Lilla, the author and Gústi. The red anorak that hadn't been there.

When I opened my eyes again, Dad had gone and it was Mum sitting across from me. I was mystified as to how this had happened. I felt as if I'd only blinked and a transformation had taken place. Dad in front of me reading the paper – *blink* – Mum in his place and the radio on.

'How did you sleep, love?' Mum was drinking orange juice and eating a cracker. She must have been the only person in the world who dunked crackers in her juice.

'Well,' I said. 'And you?'

'Oh, I had a bad dream. I get such awful nightmares.'

'What about?'

'About...' Mum paused to think. 'Now you ask, I can't actually remember. Running away from something. But of course that's common, isn't it? That feeling of being paralysed, unable to move.'

'Yes.'

'You know, at one time I used to keep a dream diary. I was so convinced dreams were messages that we ought to take seriously.'

'But you don't believe that anymore?'

Mum sucked her cracker, then dunked it in her orange juice again. 'I do believe dreams can contain important messages.'

'What kind of messages?'

'Well, the usual ones about being chased, they mean you're trying to run away from a problem. Losing your teeth means losing friends, and if your mouth bleeds, that means losing a loved one. Then there are the ravens, of course.' Mum's voice deepened. 'Ravens symbolise betrayal. Death. Dreaming about ravens is never a good omen.'

I didn't dream about ravens: I dreamt about hens – hens, bathtubs and babies – but I didn't want to know what this meant, so I didn't ask. Dreams almost always seemed to signify something bad, and the last thing I wanted was for Mum to start trying to psychoanalyse me.

'At other times, dreams just reflect our subconscious fears,' Mum went on. 'When I was acting, I used to have constant nightmares about forgetting my lines, though I never did; I was always word-perfect.'

As Mum talked, she grew animated, and her cracker, temporarily forgotten, dissolved in her juice.

I had listened to her talk about her years in the theatre so often that after a while I tuned out. It was always the same stories, the same anecdotes. But as I watched her eyes sparkling, it occurred to me that the only times I ever saw her look truly happy were when she was reminiscing about her acting career.

Mum had never wanted children. That was one of the recriminations she used to fling at Dad when they were having a row.

Recriminations about sacrifices and living in a dump and the meaninglessness of her existence. I didn't really understand them then but I did now: Mum had sacrificed everything for us girls – we were the meaningless existence.

'I'm telling you, Marsí,' Mum was saying, 'he wasn't that charming in real life.'

'Who?'

'Styrkár Hansen. He may have looked like Marlon Brando but, between you and me, his breath stank.' Mum leant forwards confidingly over the table. 'And as if that wasn't bad enough, he couldn't keep his hands to himself, if you know what I—'

'I found a photo last night,' I interrupted, suddenly recalling the snapshot of the baby.

'What of?'

'Of a baby.' I left the room, dug out the picture and brought it back to show my mother.

'Where did you find this?' Mum's smile vanished and she re-tied her dressing gown more tightly around her.

'In one of the albums, behind a picture of Stína as a baby. Who is it?'

Before she could answer, there was a knock at the door; two heavy raps. Mum's eyes widened and I wondered if she really believed that ghosts knocked twice, as the superstition would have it.

We both went out into the hall. Through the mottled glass, we could see the shape of a figure in dark clothes. We exchanged looks and it was a moment before either of us moved. Mum got to the door first and opened it.

On the doorstep stood Torfi, the local police inspector, a grave expression on his face. My thoughts immediately flew to Dad. Where was he? Had something happened to him?

'Hello, Nína,' Torfi said. His eyes moved to me. 'And Marsibil. Could I come in for a minute?'

'What...? Has something happened?' Mum asked, stepping aside to let him in.

'Well...' Torfi began and Mum clutched her heart theatrically.

'Nothing like that, Nína,' he said, laying a reassuring hand on her shoulder. 'This morning a young woman was found lying by the road not far from here. She was dead when we arrived at the scene. It was Ninna from the shop who found her, but sadly by then it was too late.'

Mum gasped, and her hand moved from her heart to her mouth. 'Really, Torfi? Who is she? Someone we know?'

'Her name was Mette. She was from Denmark and she'd been working on a farm near here – at Gröf.'

'Mette. I don't know her.'

'No, I didn't think you would.'

'What happened to her?'

'Well, that's the question. Nothing untoward, I don't think, but it's too early to be sure.'

'How terrible,' Mum said.

'The reason I'm here is that we found something beside the body.' Torfi's gaze shifted to me again. 'A note.'

'A note? I don't understand…' Mum looked from me to Torfi and back again.

'The envelope was addressed to you,' Torfi said, his eyes never leaving my face. 'To Marsibil.'

10
Kristín – *Autumn 1966*

Elvar and I go and stand in the lee of the house, round the corner where no one can see us. Now that autumn is here, it's properly dark outside and the air is chilly, even out of the wind. I accept Elvar's jacket, though I'm not cold. He takes out two cigarettes, puts them in his mouth and lights them, then hands one to me. Putting it in my mouth after it has just been between his lips sends a frisson of heat through my body. We don't say a word. Elvar leans his back against the wall and gazes upwards.

'Do you ever wonder what's out there?' he asks.

I raise my eyes to the star-studded sky. 'Like aliens, you mean?'

'Well, life of some kind. The idea that we might not be alone.'

'No, not really,' I say truthfully. Then I regret not having made up some response, because for a moment there's complete silence. 'Do you miss living in Reykjavík?' I ask hurriedly.

'Yes,' he says, without hesitation. 'I didn't want to leave.'

His answer makes me sorry I asked. I know he has a girlfriend in the city but I don't dare ask if it's her he's missing. 'What do you miss most?' I ask instead.

'The cars, probably.'

'The cars?'

'Yes. I love watching them drive around the streets all day.' He smiles. 'I'm going to buy myself a Mustang as soon as I get my licence.'

I laugh.

'What?' he asks.

'That wasn't the answer I was expecting.'

'What answer were you expecting?' He turns to face me, still leaning his shoulder against the wall.

'Málfríður said you had a girlfriend. I thought maybe you were missing her.' I turn towards him and his beauty almost robs me of words. His face is so perfect that I yearn to draw it. I imagine the dark pencil I'd use for his eyes and their surrounds, and how satisfying it would be to delineate his lips.

'I did miss her,' he says.

'Did miss her? In the past tense?'

'In the past tense.'

'I'd like to draw you,' I say without thinking.

'What?'

'You've got such a beautiful face.' I run my finger along his eyebrow and down the line of his jaw. 'Such straight lines. But—'

Before I can finish, he leans forwards and starts kissing me.

Unlike with the other boys I've kissed, there's no hesitation, no questions or insecurity. He just kisses me purposefully as though perfectly aware that I want it, and *oh my God* how I want it. Dropping my cigarette, I put my arms round his neck and run my hands through his hair.

Suddenly he moves away, his gaze directed over my shoulder, at the street. 'Who's that?'

I turn my head and see a figure not far off, standing there motionless.

'I have no idea and I really don't care,' I say, pulling him back towards me.

I don't think there can be anything more wonderful in the world than kissing, feeling someone's heat, their tongue, the softness. I press myself against him, wanting to feel his body, and he spins me round, pushes me back against the wall and kisses me so hungrily that it feels as if we can never be close enough. But a sudden outbreak of shouting forces us to break off. Peering round the corner, we see Sólveig burst out of the front door.

I can hardly believe my eyes: Sólveig is stark naked. She is running our way.

Elvar tightens his arms around me, as though afraid she's heading for us, but she streaks past without giving us a glance.

'What's going on?' I ask Málfríður, who has come outside with the others to watch.

'We dared her to run round the house naked. Told her it was a tradition.'

'You're joking?'

At that moment Sólveig reappears round the far corner of the house and everyone cheers. Snorri hands her a drink and she knocks it back like a pro.

'Where are her clothes?' I ask.

'They're inside, but—'

Leaving Elvar, I hurry into the house and find her dress and tights. When I re-emerge, Sólveig is sitting on the step, her back to the wall. She's so woozy now that I'm afraid she's going to black out any minute.

'Sólveig, put your clothes on,' I say, trying to help her. But it's hopeless; Sólveig doesn't move.

'Bravo, Solla,' Málfríður says.

I look daggers at her, and Málfríður bursts out laughing, apparently not giving a damn that Solla is about to pass out drunk on the steps in the cold with no clothes on.

'Can't you at least fetch a blanket?' I snap.

'I'll get one,' Elvar says, heading inside.

He comes back a moment later with a woollen blanket from the sofa. We wrap it around Sólveig.

'Where's Gústi?' I ask. 'Didn't he come by car?'

'He left earlier; didn't you see him?' Guðrún asks, peering around. She's swaying so badly she can hardly stand upright and is mumbling as if her mouth is full.

I shake my head, then realise that the motionless figure Elvar spotted while we were kissing must have been Gústi.

'There he is,' Guðrún slurs, and I see Gústi coming back along the road. 'Where were you?' she asks.

'I just went for a walk. Did I miss something?' Gústi asks, then he catches sight of Sólveig and his eyes widen.

'How are we going to get her home?' I ask.

'I've got a car,' Gústi says.

'Right. You take her arms and Stína her legs.' Málfríður cracks up again.

'We should ring her parents,' Guðrún suggests.

'I don't know. It might not be such a good idea for her dad to collect her in this state.' I turn back to Sólveig and give her a shake. 'Come on, Sólveig, wake up.'

'I'll bring the car over here,' Gústi says.

'OK.' I give Sólveig another little shake, but there's no response.

In the end, we do more or less as Málfríður suggested: Elvar takes her legs and Gústi her arms, and together we lug her over to the car and deposit her in the back seat. When Elvar goes to get in, however, Gústi stops him.

'I think it's best if Stína comes along.'

'I'll come too,' Elvar says.

'There's no room in the back.'

Gústi is right; Sólveig is sprawled across the seat, but for a moment or two Elvar looks undecided.

'It's all right,' I say. 'We'll talk later, OK?'

Elvar nods and as we drive away, I see him heading home, looking rather dejected.

'I didn't know you two were…' Gústi begins.

'We aren't,' I reply.

'Aren't you?'

'I don't think so,' I say, leaning back in the passenger seat. Elvar must be so used to kissing girls at parties that I don't have a clue whether he wants anything more.

'You deserve better,' Gústi says.

I look at him in surprise. 'Why do you say that?' I don't think I've ever heard him say a bad word about anyone before.

'Just…' He shrugs. 'It's true.'

Before I can respond, we're pulling up in front of Sólveig's house. With difficulty, we drag her out of the back and cart her over to the house, where we lay her down on the steps. I ring the doorbell, then we race back to the car and Gústi accelerates away down the street.

On the way home, we don't say another word about Elvar, though I'm longing to ask Gústi what he meant. I'm just not sure I want to hear the answer.

11
Marsibil – *Saturday, 19 November 1977*

Above the entrance was a large sign saying: *POLICE*.

I had only twice been beyond reception: once on a school trip, then again shortly after Stína went missing. The school trip was exciting; we were fed biscuits and orange squash, and given a talk by a friendly policeman.

The visit following Stína's disappearance was less fun.

I had sat at a table and answered the questions about Stína put to me by Torfi: whether she had ever talked about leaving home, what I had been doing that evening, where my parents had been. I had answered in a low mumble, so he had kept having to ask me to repeat myself and speak louder.

Now Torfi was sitting behind his desk, regarding me like an old acquaintance. 'You're a big girl now, Marsibil.'

'You certainly know how to talk to women,' I responded drily, sitting down on a chair with a green cover.

Torfi smiled faintly. 'How are you?'

'Surviving.'

'Good, good.' He clasped his hands on the desk. 'I asked you to come in because I wanted you to read the note that was found on Mette's body. You say you didn't know her?'

'No, not at all.'

'How strange. Do you have any idea why she should have been carrying a note for you?'

'Absolutely none.'

'No? Well, there you have it.'

That took me straight back to the days when Torfi was investigating Stína's disappearance: the repeated refrain of 'there you have it'.

'How did she die?' I asked.

'Of exposure, presumably. She had been meeting friends in town. They played board games until fairly late, then went to the bar, and after that she decided to walk home. She was staying at Gröf. It's not that far but still quite a long walk that late at night.'

The farm at Gröf used to be home to a couple called Dilla and Jóndi, who kept horses. When Stína and I were young we used to go there with Dad, and Jóndi would lead the horses round in a circle with us perched on their backs.

'Jóndi's son Anton took over the farm two years ago,' Torfi continued. 'He has three daughters and his wife's pregnant again. They employed Mette to help with the children and housework. She arrived in August.'

'How old was she?'

'Nineteen.'

'I didn't know her,' I repeated.

'No. But this note was lying beside her.' Torfi opened a drawer in his desk, took out a large envelope and removed from it a smaller envelope with my name on the front and a sheet of paper.

'Go ahead, read it, but please don't touch it.'

I obeyed.

DARLING MARSÍ
WE'VE KNOWN EACH OTHER SO LONG
THAT IT WOULD BE A PITY IF IT HAD TO END LIKE THIS.
WARMEST WISHES

I read the lines several times, trying to concentrate through the throbbing in my head. Unlike the earlier letters, it was written in clumsy block capitals, but it had to be from the same person. Who else would write me a letter? The capitals gave me the feeling I'd provoked someone to anger; that they were shouting at me, though the words weren't in themselves unfriendly.

Torfi was watching me narrowly as I read, which made me extremely self-conscious about my reactions. I tried to give the impression of being perplexed rather than afraid. Tried to disguise my shock.

'Can you explain this to me?' he asked.

I shook my head.

'Were you expecting a letter?'

'No.'

'And you didn't know Mette at all? You didn't meet her yesterday, for instance, when you were at the bar?'

It was a small town, all right. I shook my head again.

'I don't believe Mette wrote the note. Her Icelandic wasn't good enough, although she spoke a bit.' Torfi sighed. 'I was just wondering … could she have been bringing you the note from somebody else?'

'Unlikely,' I said, my mind going back to the bar. Had she been there yesterday evening?

'It occurred to me that someone might have asked her to deliver it.'

'It's possible.'

'But you have no idea who that might have been?'

'No,' I said, wondering suddenly if the note could be from the stranger who had struck up a conversation with me.

'It's obviously someone you know.'

'What?'

Torfi pointed to the first line of the letter. '"We've known each other so long", he read out. 'So someone you know, in other words. Can't you think of anyone?'

I shook my head. Again.

Torfi's eyes were boring into me, as though he'd like to open up my brain and pull out my thoughts to examine them.

Well, he wouldn't find anything there because I had no answers. I couldn't understand what the note meant and I hadn't a clue who could have written it. Perhaps I should confess to Torfi about my penpal, but the story was so long and convoluted, and, besides, it was far too late in the day to tell it now. I should have come clean ten years ago. If only I had come forwards then, Stína might have been found and I wouldn't be receiving letters like this all these years later.

If only was a game I'd been playing for many years, yet now, presented with a chance to make amends, all I did was sit there in silence, staring down at my hands.

Torfi nodded when I asked if I could go.

I wanted to go back to the bar and drink until the voices in my head fell silent. But the more I thought about the note, the angrier I became; and that anger drowned out my fear, though it would probably have been more sensible to be afraid. Because the message could be interpreted as a threat: *It would be a pity if it had to end like this* suggested some kind of reckoning. I just didn't know what kind.

'Marsibil,' Dad called out when I got home.

He and Mum were in the sitting room and looked as if they'd been in the middle of a conversation. Mum turned her face to the window, but he rose to his feet.

'I'm going to lie down,' I said, hurrying up to my room and locking myself in.

Dad knocked on the door. 'Your mother told me what happened. What's going on? Did you know that girl?'

'No. It was just a misunderstanding.'

'Marsibil, can you open the door?'

'I'm in bed. I slept badly.'

There was silence for a moment, then I heard his footsteps retreating.

I took out the box of letters with shaking hands, wondering what on earth to do. I began searching through them again, rereading and examining each phrase. But if I'd been hoping for a revelation, for a lightbulb moment, I was wrong. They contained any number of details but nothing I could rely on.

One option was to trace the letters. The first thing I had done after Stína went missing and Bergur stopped writing was to look up the address I'd been sending the letters to – I'd had that much sense, at least. It had turned out to be just outside the town of Höfn í Hornafirði, in the south-east of the country. I had found the phone number too and rung it, only to learn that no one called Bergur lived there. The couple who answered had only recently moved in, but the woman assured me that the family who lived there before them hadn't included any Bergur either. The discovery had been like a punch in the gut. I had racked my brains in an effort to work out all the tricks someone could have used to send the letters to me and to receive mine at a different address, but the mystery was beyond me.

I could go further; I could drive all the way around the country to Höfn. It wouldn't be as big a deal nowadays, since a couple of years back they had finally bridged the Skeiðará rivers and completed the Ring Road around Iceland. I could visit the address in the letters and demand information about everyone who had lived there or had access to the house. But I had a hunch that the answers were to be found here, in Síða. After all, the most recent note had turned up here without a postmark or stamp, so it stood to reason that the person who wrote it must be here too.

'Marsí.' This time it was Mum's voice outside my door. 'You can't just hide away in your room. Weren't you planning to go home today?'

'I'm coming,' I said, stuffing the letters back in the box and hiding it under my bed.

When I emerged, I found Mum on her own. She had put on red

lipstick and was doing her hair. The house was full of the fragrant smells of baking and cinnamon.

'What was that note about?' she asked.

'Nothing,' I said. 'It was just … the note wasn't to me, after all.'

'Oh?'

'No,' I said. 'What are you baking?'

'I'm going to take some cinnamon buns over to Gröf. They must be terribly upset after what's happened.'

'Isn't it a bit soon?'

'Of course not. This is exactly when they need help. I don't suppose Gudda will have had time to cook anything. They must be starving.'

Mum arranged the buns carefully in a pretty basket, then pulled on her coat. She was in her element – the tragedy had provided her with an important role to play. I pictured her turning up at the couple's farmhouse and sharing her experiences with them. They could talk about what it was like to lose a child, though of course Mette hadn't actually been their child.

I sat down with a bun that Mum had left for me and broke off a piece.

When Stína vanished, my parents had reacted in very different ways. I don't remember them crying, but perhaps that was because the circumstances of Stína's disappearance had been very different. We had been so sure she would come back. Or at least we had tried to convince ourselves we were.

Mum hadn't taken part in the search but stayed at home in case Stína turned up while Dad was out looking. He went out with the search parties at first. Then, when they eventually gave up, he started spending ever more time at work or in his shed, collecting evidence about the case and persevering with the search alone.

My main memory is of a profound, suffocating silence, and that every time I asked a question, Dad would shush me. 'Not now, Marsí. Your mum can't take it.'

When I looked back, that period seemed simultaneously endless and oddly compressed. First the search and the waiting, then the silence and the grieving. I had gone out every day to intercept the post, hoping against hope that there would be a letter from my penpal, explaining that he hadn't been able to come that day. Every time the letter wasn't there, I was overwhelmed anew with guilt and self-recriminations.

Then, all of a sudden, a year had passed. A year of the silent house, a year without Stína. A year that seemed to blur into one day and, at the same time, to have lasted for a thousand years.

Mum came home with rosy cheeks and shining eyes. I was still sitting at the kitchen table. I'd finished my bun and must have dozed off because I could have sworn hardly any time had passed. She sat down beside me with what she called tea, but which was really just hot water with milk and sugar, and started to tell me about her visit.

'The poor couple were so upset,' she said. 'Anton was just staring emptily into space; he could hardly string his words together. And Gudda just cried and cried.'

'Did they have any idea why Mette would have decided to walk all the way home in the middle of the night?' I asked.

'No, it came as a total surprise to them. She'd been out playing board games with some kids she'd met through the church choir: Fríða, the daughter of Ingimundur, who owns the bookshop, and Ína, Alfreð's daughter. Anton and Gudda hadn't a clue what she was doing at the bar, as the girl didn't drink. Apparently she was very religious.'

Ína was Gústi's younger sister, so perhaps Gústi had known Mette. Perhaps he'd bumped into her after giving me a lift home.

'Did they know what time Mette left the bar?' I asked, then realised that the answer wouldn't tell me much. I hadn't a clue what time I had got home myself. I'd been so drunk and out of it that for all I knew I could have had a long chat with Mette and forgotten all about it.

'What time?' Mum asked. 'How are they supposed to know that? All they know is that the girl was found just before eight this morning by Ninna from the shop as she was on her way to work. She was just lying there by the road, as if she'd given up halfway home. Poor girl. At least she was found, though; they can console themselves with that.'

It was a certain consolation, I thought, as I watched Mum warming her hands on her teacup. The sparkle had gone out in her eyes and her cheeks had faded to their usual colour. She seemed deflated and I knew that sooner or later she would have to go for the inevitable nap.

After our chat, Mum decided to have a bath while I went over to the sitting-room window and contemplated the garden shed. I didn't know what time Dad would be home but I was itching to sneak a look inside to see if the paperwork he had kept about Stína's disappearance was still there.

I was greeted by a bitter wind when I stepped outside. Like the house, the garden had been neglected in recent years. The flowerbeds were so choked with weeds that you could hardly make out the shape of them anymore, and in the corner the rhubarb lay flattened and rotting.

The shed was in the far right-hand corner. On the left-hand side, Dad had built a hencoop. Not content with being surrounded by chickens all day at the egg farm and slaughterhouse, he had recently acquired five hens to keep in the garden. They were all inside their house now, apart from one, which was roaming around the run. These weren't white like the chickens at the farm but brown Icelandic hens, descended from the stock brought over by the original settlers in the Viking Age. They were beautiful birds and Dad was very attached to them.

I couldn't understand how he could discriminate between these pet hens and the white ones at the egg farm, which existed in a pecking throng, crushed so tightly together that the weakest were often trampled underfoot. Stína and I used to avoid going to the farm with him, having seen too many hens lying on the floor with open wounds, being pecked at by the others. All the blood on the white feathers and those staring eyes, flickering around in desperate hope of escape. In contrast, these hens had a spacious run, and Dad talked to them as though they were his children: 'There, there, Spotty, you've been such a crosspatch lately. Is Sunny giving you a hard time?'

I went over to the fence and watched the lone hen. She froze for a moment, staring back at me, then returned to her circling, head moving rhythmically back and forth until she paused and began to peck at something on the ground that, on closer inspection, appeared to be a strip of meat. My stomach shrank and I hurried away to the shed.

The door creaked open and I was met by the musty odour of rotten timber. Apart from that the shed was in fairly good condition; it was reasonably warm inside and the lights came on immediately. There was a desk and a chair, an easel and some tools. A few canvases were propped against the wall: old paintings by Stína, portraits of us family members, as well as famous actors and singers. There was even a painting of Twiggy, in which Stína had taken great care over depicting her huge eyes with their conspicuously long, black lower lashes.

I had expected the papers relating to Stína's case to be spread out over the desk as they always used to be, but the desk top was clear apart from a few pens and mugs. Perhaps Dad had given up the search and no longer sat poring over documents about her disappearance. The thought made me sad. I'd always hoped that something would come of Dad's private investigations – something that had nothing to do with me or my penpal. I doubted he had thrown the paperwork away, though, and, sure enough, when I opened the desk drawer, I saw that it was still there: folders, exercise books and papers, all with my sister's name on them.

The wind was gathering strength, sending chill draughts through gaps in the planking, and in the run outside I could hear the hen flapping her wings. I opened the file and started reading.

Police Report written 20 November 1967
Author: Torfi Már Sigurðsson

Description of the Incident:
At 00:32 hours I received a telephone call from the father of Kristín Karvelsdóttir, saying that his daughter had not come home from her friend's house. The father had rung her friend,

*domiciled at no. 2 Sunnusíða, and the family reported that
Kristín had set off home just before 22:00 hours. The distance
between the two houses is approximately two and a half kilometres.*

*At around 01.00 hours I arrived at Nátthagi, the home of the
girl's parents, Karvel and Jónína. Kristín's father and I drove
along the route his daughter was supposed to have taken and
when we failed to find any sign of her, we took the decision to
walk the route with torches. At around 01:30 hours we found an
anorak near the road, half buried by snow, about a kilometre
from Nátthagi. Kristín's parents confirmed that the anorak was
hers. The garment was stained with what appeared to be blood,
so it was sent for analysis. The weather had been fine during the
early part of the night. Between 22:00 and 23:00 it began to snow
and the snowfall grew heavier as the night went on. After finding
the anorak, we called out search parties but their efforts proved
unsuccessful.*

During the following days volunteers had combed gullies and
ditches, as well as the nearby mountains and hills, and the entire
Hallmundarhraun lava field with its caves and fissures, though it must
have been impossible to search them all. The banks of the Hvítá were
also walked, though everyone knew that if Stína had ended up in the
river, she would have been swept downstream to the sea. No one
pointed this out, though. Everyone behaved as if they believed she
would be found, and visitors were constantly tramping in and out of
our house. But, although I learnt these details later, I couldn't actually
remember being there myself. At the time I felt oddly detached from
it all, as if it wasn't really happening, and when I tried to dredge up
the memories later, they slipped through my fingers like grains of sand.

I went on looking through the papers and saw that there were more
police reports, containing interviews with Stína's friends: Guðrún and
Málfríður and her family – her two brothers and the vicar and his
wife. But before I could read them, I heard a car pulling into the drive,
so I hastily replaced them in the drawer.

When I came out of the shed, I saw Gústi standing at the front door, talking to Mum. He had always been a favourite of hers; she had constantly praised him in Stína's hearing, telling her how clever and nice he was. Stína used to turn a deaf ear, clearly uninterested.

'It's always so good to see you, Gústi dear. Won't you come in?' I heard Mum say.

'I just wanted to check on Marsí.'

'I'm fine,' I called, and they both looked round.

'Oh, there you are,' Mum said.

Gústi had his hands in his pockets and was looking troubled. 'Hi, Marsí. I just wanted to check if you were all right.'

'I'm fine,' I repeated, but could hear how hollow my voice sounded, even to my own ears. The truth was that a feeling of dread had been slowly but surely growing inside me over the last few days, initially triggered by the letter sent to my flat and now made worse by this second note. I sensed that somebody was lurking out there, watching me and awaiting their chance.

'Won't you come in?' Mum asked again. 'Have some coffee? It must have been a shock to hear about that poor girl.'

'I, er…' His eyes were still fixed on mine. 'I thought maybe me and Marsí could go for a drive. If you'd like, I mean?'

After a brief hesitation, I nodded.

'Are you sure you won't come in?' Mum repeated. 'I think I've got a raisin sponge cake in the freezer.'

'Maybe next time.' Gústi forced out a smile for Mum.

'All right, just as you like, dear,' Mum said, the disappointment plain in her voice.

'Thanks, Nína.' Gústi looked back at me. 'Are you ready now, or…?'

Making up my mind then and there, I told Gústi to hang on and darted indoors.

In my room I shoved everything in a bag: the letters, both old and new, and the photos. I couldn't do this on my own, and if there was anyone I could trust in this town, it was Gústi.

My penpal had taken Stína and had now sent me two new letters. The danger wasn't imaginary; it was real. I could disappear just like

Stína, but if that happened at least there would be one person who knew the truth.

I used to have a crush on Gústi, in that desperate, all-consuming way that teenage girls have crushes. I dreamt about him, wrote his name in my school exercise books and blushed whenever he spoke to me. Over time, the effects had diminished, to be replaced by something more like friendship. One evening, after I had decided to move away, I asked him to come with me to Reykjavík.

'It'll be like a new start,' I'd said. 'No one will know us there.'

Gústi had smiled, a little sadly. 'But I don't want to leave, Marsí,' he'd said. 'I don't want to make a new start. I like knowing everyone here.'

In the end that was the big difference between us. Despite our mutual affection, we were fundamentally different: for him, this life was enough; for me, it would never be enough.

Gústi slowed down once we were outside the town and we dawdled along the road, alone in the world. The sun shone on the dazzlingly white glacier and the sky was blue. We were close to the Hraunfossar falls, where the clear water cascaded down through the lava field with a roar. In different circumstances, maybe I could have been happy here and felt it was enough for me, as Gústi did.

'Why did you come round?' I asked.

'To see if you were all right,' Gústi repeated. 'When I heard about that girl, I thought at first it was you. I didn't remember seeing you go inside the house and thought maybe you'd wandered off somewhere.'

'I wasn't that drunk.'

Gústi didn't say anything in response, but the expression on his face spoke for him.

'What?' I said.

'Well, you were in a pretty bad state.'

'Not bad enough to wander off.'

Again, Gústi tactfully didn't comment on this, just said: 'All the same, I was worried about you. Especially after that anorak business.'

That anorak business.

The anorak had been plain to see, until it wasn't. The vision had frightened me. How could I have seen something so clearly if it wasn't real?

We drove on for a while in silence as I tried to gather my thoughts. Where should I begin? How was I to explain everything?

'There's something I need to tell you,' I said, feeling suddenly like a seven-year-old. *Shall I tell you a secret?*

'What?'

'I don't know how...' I sighed. My mouth was dry and my heart was racing.

'We've got all the time in the world,' Gústi said, after a pause in which I had added nothing. 'We could stop here, if that would help.'

He pulled over to the side of the road and switched off the engine.

Somehow this made it worse, but I closed my eyes, drew a deep breath and started talking.

I began falteringly, but then it all came pouring out. I told Gústi that I had put an advertisement in *The Week* in Stína's name and how that had led to my correspondence with a boy called Bergur. In his letters he had come across as funny and interesting, and writing to each other gave us the freedom to be ourselves. With every letter we'd got to know each other a little better, become a little more intimate.

'We'd been writing to each other for nearly a year before we decided to meet,' I said. 'The time and date we had agreed on was ... It was that evening – the evening Stína vanished.'

Gústi didn't say a word but a frown of concern had formed on his face as I was talking.

'Can we get out for a minute?' I asked. Suddenly I was finding it hard to go on and felt short of breath, as though I'd been running.

We got out of the car and started walking along the well-trodden path that skirted the cliffs near the falls, heading away from the countless clear-blue cascades to where the river was quieter and the roar more muted. The low-growing birch scrub was bare of leaves, and the endless lava field seemed bleak and forbidding without the carpet of green moss that softened its jagged edges in summer.

'You were saying that you'd decided to meet up,' Gústi prompted. 'How old was he, by the way?'

'When we first started writing to each other, he said he was sixteen, and of course he thought I was fifteen. By the time we agreed to meet, he was seventeen and had passed his driving test. I didn't see anything wrong with meeting him alone. We'd been exchanging letters for months. I thought I knew him.'

'Why didn't you tell him your real name when you first started writing?'

I shrugged. I didn't know why I'd lied. My behaviour as an adolescent had rarely been rational or carefully considered.

'So, what happened that evening?' Gústi asked. 'Did you meet him?'

'No, I didn't get that far,' I said.

After Stína left to go to Málfríður's house, I went into her room and opened her wardrobe. I nicked her bra and a brown jumper with a diamond pattern, put rings in my ears and made up my face with a little eyeshadow and blusher.

When I looked in the mirror, though, I hardly recognised myself, so in the end I removed the earrings and wiped off the eyeshadow. I tried stuffing socks into the bra, then took them out again, afraid he might be able to feel them. Then I thought about what that meant. Was I really going to let him put his hands inside my shirt? Were we going to kiss?

When I looked back in the mirror, my cheeks were scarlet.

Meanwhile my parents had turned up the volume of the music and raised their voices to be heard over the noise. Their guests were a couple who regularly came over for dinner and often stayed late. I wasn't worried they'd notice my absence.

By half past nine I was ready and crept out of Stína's room. I decided to leave by the back door and had almost reached the kitchen when I heard Dad's voice.

'Marsí, where are you going?' he called.

'Just getting something to drink,' I lied.

I saw at once that Dad wasn't as drunk as the others and swore under my breath. In the kitchen, I poured myself a glass of water, hoping Dad would get distracted and forget about me. On the table beside the sink was a large collection of bottles and glasses. I'd never touched alcohol before but I picked up one of the glasses and quickly tipped its contents down my throat. People said drinking calmed their nerves, and I was certainly feeling anxious. I waited for a while, to see if it worked. Perhaps it did, because I felt more relaxed. Or perhaps it was just relief, because I could hear all the adults chatting loudly in the sitting room.

A laundry led off the kitchen and from there it was possible to go outside via the back door. I was just crossing over to the laundry door when, without warning, Dad reappeared.

'All right, Pipsqueak? Are we being too noisy?'

'No, not at all.' I was suddenly anxious again. What if Bergur arrived and I wasn't there? What if he left without us meeting?

Dad narrowed his eyes. 'You're very dressed up. Are you going out somewhere?'

'No, I'm going to bed in a minute.' I faked a yawn, then started walking slowly upstairs, my heart going like the clappers.

'All right, love. Night, night.' Dad was still watching, so I went all the way up, closed the door of my room, sat down on the bed and waited.

And that was the last thing I remembered.

'What do you mean that's the last thing you remember?' Gústi asked.

We had halted on the riverbank; the distant roar of the waterfalls was somehow soothing.

'I remember going into my room with Dad watching from downstairs, then I don't remember anything else until I woke up next morning in my pyjamas, with no idea how I had changed into them.'

Gústi stared at me, bemused.

'I must have flaked out,' I explained. 'I must have gone up to my room, stretched out on my bed and fallen sound asleep. I woke up next day with a splitting headache.'

I had often wondered how I could have passed out like that when I was so excited about meeting my penpal at last. It crossed my mind that there might have been something in the glass I drank out of by the kitchen sink. It can't just have been that I'd never touched booze before since I really didn't have that much of it. I remember feeling strange as soon as I sat down on my bed. A bit dizzy, then pleasantly numb, before I presumably dropped off.

'Where had you been planning to meet?' Gústi asked.

I gazed down into the churning water. 'By the bridge over the river. On the road Stína was walking home along at exactly the same time.' I glanced up at him. 'Don't you understand? It should have been me who vanished; my anorak that was found covered with blood. It should have been me, not Stína.'

For a while, Gústi didn't say anything. He stared down at the river, his hands in his pockets, his expression unreadable. I lowered myself on to the wet rocks, indifferent to the damp seeping through my trousers.

After a short interval, Gústi sat down beside me. 'That's quite a lot to take in, Marsí.'

'I know.'

'What did the police say about your penpal? Didn't they believe you? Didn't they investigate him?'

I was conscious of the shame spreading through my body. 'I never told anyone,' I muttered.

'What do you mean?'

'I never told anyone about my penpal, OK? I tried to get hold of him myself, only to discover that he'd lied about everything. It was the wrong address: there was no Bergur living there, just an old couple who knew nothing about anyone called Bergur or any letters. Maybe I should have done more to try and track him down, but I was so ashamed of myself. I've been living with that shame for the last ten years. Telling myself that *if only* I'd said something, Stína might be alive now. The police could have traced the letters, discovered who had written them and found Stína, but I … I never said a word.'

I felt I ought to be crying, now that I'd finally unburdened myself, but instead I just gazed unseeingly at the water, feeling as cold and numb as the glacial torrent. No tears, no howling.

'I tried to convince myself that he hadn't come to meet me,' I said. 'That someone else had taken Stína. But deep down I knew it was all my fault.'

'But that's perfectly possible, Marsí,' Gústi said. 'Why are you so sure it was your penpal?'

'Because it must have been him,' I insisted. 'Anything else would be too big a coincidence. And now…' I paused, preparing myself for the next part of my story. 'I've been sent more letters. New ones. From him, I think. The first came only a few days before I got here.'

I took the letter out of my bag and handed it to Gústi.

He took it gingerly, almost scared to handle it. 'Does he admit that he took her? Is this a confession?'

'No, no,' I said. 'Read it, and you'll see.'

He opened it and scanned the page, then frowned. 'What does he want? Does this mean he knows now that you were pretending to be Stína?'

'Apparently. And there's more,' I went on. 'The girl who was found this morning – beside her, there was a note addressed to me.'

Gústi gaped at me. 'What do you mean? I don't understand…'

'Neither do I.'

'What did it say?'

'I haven't got it, the police kept it,' I explained, then repeated, more or less, the contents of the note. They were imprinted on my memory, had been echoing in my head ever since I read them: *It's a pity it should end like this.*

'Bloody hell, Marsí.' Gústi rubbed his forehead, regarding me with a mixture of disbelief and horror. 'What the hell does it all mean?'

'Two things,' Gústi said, once we were sitting in the car again.

We had walked most of the way back in silence. I could almost hear his brain cells whirring away beside me. There was a deep furrow between his brows, as always when he was preoccupied, and although I was longing to know what was going through his mind, I didn't say a word.

It was a relief that he turned to me and spoke as soon as we had got in the car.

'Yes?' I replied.

'I'm not sure there's necessarily a connection – between your penpal and your sister's disappearance, I mean. I think your penpal's definitely a suspicious character and I haven't a clue why he would suddenly send you a letter now, all these years later, or how the other note ended up with the girl, but I'm not convinced he took Stína.'

'For one thing, we know Stína left Málfríður's house early, and I'm pretty sure she was going to meet someone. I've been wondering about her disappearance all these years, Marsí, and I'm convinced that Stína had arranged a rendezvous that evening. She left Málfríður's halfway through the film, and she had a reason for doing that, I'm sure of it.'

'Maybe,' I said. 'What's the other thing?'

'The other thing is that if it *was* your penpal, he was under the impression that he was meeting the girl he'd been corresponding with. He couldn't be sure who you might have told about the two of you. Most people would assume that a teenage girl would talk to her friends and confide in them if she was going to meet a boy. In which case the police could easily have tracked down his address or traced him somehow. So I can hardly believe he would have taken that kind of risk – doing something to Stína when it could so easily be traced back to him.' Seeing my expression, Gústi added: 'Sorry, Marsí, but it's true. A boy who kidnaps a girl he's been writing to for months would surely realise how many incriminating clues he'd left behind.'

'Then he was lucky that I didn't say a word to anyone,' I said flatly and began to chew a lock of my hair.

'Marsí,' Gústi said kindly. 'I find it far more likely that the person who took Stína was someone who knew her, not your penpal.'

I considered this new angle. Was it possible that I had been wrong all this time? But although the idea was tempting, the most recent letters seemed to prove otherwise.

When I pointed this out to Gústi, he shrugged. 'There's nothing threatening in that letter, if you stop to think about it.'

'No, I suppose not. But what about the note that was found on Mette's body?'

'Maybe someone asked her to deliver it. And there was nothing directly threatening in that one either, was there?'

I sighed and suddenly didn't feel like arguing about it anymore. Instead, I took out the photos I'd had developed and handed them to Gústi.

'I found a film in Stína's room and had it developed.'

Gústi picked up the pictures carefully and flicked through them, passing quickly over the ones where Málfríður and Guðrún were posing, then lingering on the close-up of Stína's face.

'I'd almost forgotten how beautiful she was,' he said, his voice a little husky.

'I know,' I replied, trying to ignore the twinge in my stomach.

He went on looking through the photos until he came to the one by the Hot Stream.

'Do you recognise the boy?' I asked.

Gústi studied the photo. 'I'm not quite sure. I feel as if I do. Ten years ago, I'd probably have twigged immediately, but now … I don't know. There's something familiar about him. Maybe it's that Elvar she was seeing for a while.'

'Málfríður's brother?'

'Yeah.'

'What about the headless guy in the last picture? Do you recognise him?'

Gústi examined the photo for a long time, apparently giving it a lot of thought, before shaking his head. 'No, I can't work out who it could be.'

He flicked through the pictures again before returning them to the envelope and handing them back to me. 'What do you have in mind, Marsí? What do you think we should do about all this? Do you want to go to the police?'

Our eyes met, and I shook my head. 'No. No, I want to find him myself. I want to find out who took Stína.'

'So why are you telling me all this?'

'Because I need help. Because I'm scared.' I swallowed. 'I want to find out who snatched Stína before he comes for me.'

Gústi reached out and laid his hand over mine. 'Where shall we begin?'

I smiled gratefully but had no idea how to answer.

Where were we supposed to begin?

We could begin by trying to trace the penpal who had suddenly started sending me letters again, but I had no idea how to do that. There was no trail to follow. The letters hadn't provided any clues about their sender.

'What if we start with a clean slate – make no assumptions?' Gústi grinned, despite the gravity of the situation, and withdrew his hand. 'In detective novels they're always being careful not to jump to conclusions but to examine all the evidence and work on the basis of that.'

'Detective novels,' I echoed. 'Which authors do you read?'

'Ian Fleming, Agatha Christie and loads of others. I'll lend you some.'

'Thanks, but I think I've got enough on my plate right now trying to solve my own mystery.'

'OK, so what have we got then?' Gústi replied in a businesslike tone. 'You said you'd checked your penpal's address and there were no leads there.'

'No. Not unless we make the journey to Höfn í Hornafirði.'

'We can do that, if you like.'

'But I got that note from him last night,' I pointed out. 'Surely that indicates that he must be here, in town?'

Gústi nodded thoughtfully. 'If it was definitely from him. Maybe we should examine everything we've got relating to Stína and the letters first.'

'The police are holding on to the most recent one, so—'

'No,' Gústi interrupted. 'I meant the letters he sent you ten years ago. You've kept them, haven't you?'

'Yes.'

'Right. Then we should read them. Maybe there's something of interest there; clues, for example.'

'I don't think so.'

'Let me be the judge of that.'

'I'd rather not.'

'Why, are they secret declarations of love or something?' Gústi wrinkled his brow, then added: 'It's not *your* letters we'd be reading – though I'd give anything to see into the mind of the fourteen-year-old Marsibil…'

'No, thanks.' I coughed. 'I've reread his letters and, believe me, there's nothing there. Besides, he almost certainly lied about everything. The letters are full of information but I have no idea if any of it is true. And, in all honesty, I don't see how it will help us to know that he played the piano as a child, had a dog and hated snow.'

'OK, maybe not. But what's that?' He pointed at the notebook I had taken out of the bag.

'Stína's diary. I've read it and there's nothing in there about a secret lover or anything like that, though pages have been torn out here and there. Anyway, she'd never have risked writing anything that private in the diary because we both knew that Mum read it.'

'Really? Then what about documents relating to her case? Police reports and so on?'

'I can get hold of them,' I said.

'Shouldn't we start there, then?'

'But…' I vacillated. I still wasn't sure there was anything to be gained from going through the official paperwork.

Gústi took charge. 'We'll start there,' he said decisively.

'All right,' I said. 'Though I still think it was my penpal who took Stína, not someone who knew her.'

'Who knows?' Gústi said. 'We could be talking about the same man.'

'How do you mean?'

'Maybe your penpal was somebody who knew Stína.'

A shiver ran through me. I had never really stopped to think that my penpal could have been someone from our neighbourhood. Someone we knew well.

Mum was cleaning the house with the music turned up full blast. That was a rare sight. She didn't notice me until I was standing right beside her.

She jumped and clutched at her heart. 'Oh my God, Marsí. Are you trying to kill me?'

'Sorry.'

She got down from the chair she was standing on and wiped her sweaty forehead with her sleeve. 'It's filthy in here, don't you think? You don't notice until you start dusting. Look at this cloth, look how dirty it is.' She almost shoved the cloth in my face: it was black with grime.

'So I see,' I said, recoiling.

She looked at me for a moment, her eyes glittering with adrenaline. Then abruptly licked her finger and rubbed at my cheek.

'What are you doing? I'm not five years old,' I protested, wiping off my mother's spit.

Mum continued to study me. 'Did I ever tell you that I wanted a boy when I was pregnant with you? Even when Stína was born, what I really wanted was a son.'

I felt almost as though an apology was in order but I bit my tongue. The truth was that I'd always known it had been a disappointment to my mother that it was Stína who vanished, not me. I was always difficult. The baby who wouldn't sleep, the disobedient, peevish child, the sulky teenager. When I was a kid I went through a phase of experimenting with swearing, saying 'damn' and 'bloody' and 'hell'. Once I asked if it was bloody chicken for supper again, and Mum slapped my face.

'Why didn't you have more children, then?' I asked her now.

Mum gathered her hair up in an elastic band that she had pulled off her wrist. 'I wanted to but your father didn't. He probably thought I wasn't the maternal type. I wasn't a proper little homemaker like his mother.' She laughed and took a drink from a glass that was on the table. Something alcoholic, I guessed. She had obviously been drinking for a while already.

'What was she like?'

'Oh, your typical mother, always washing your father's underpants and making sure he ate enough. She even cut his toenails before he went to bed. I asked him to stop her, but he said he put up with it for her sake as she loved pampering him.'

'What was *your* mother like?' I knew little about my maternal grandparents, apart from the fact that my grandfather had never been in the picture and my grandmother had died when Mum was in her teens.

'Oh, all these endless questions, Marsí. You're starting to sound like your sister.' Mum gave an exaggerated sigh. 'You know I don't like talking about it. I had a difficult childhood, but so what? I'm not going to brood on it or ask for anyone's sympathy. I made something of myself, didn't I? Have I shown you the pictures I found?'

She paused for another sip of her drink, then went into the laundry and came back with a bunch of pictures and cuttings from magazines. A youthful version of my mother beamed out from all of them, beautiful and blooming with health.

I couldn't get away for what felt like ages.

Mum had abandoned the cleaning and gone to put her feet up with a book that I knew she wouldn't read, and Dad wasn't home yet, so I took the opportunity to slip out to the shed. It was dark outside now and, for once, the hencoop was quiet as I walked across the garden.

Inside the shed, I hurried over to the desk and opened the top drawer, but when I reached in to take out the papers, I came up empty-handed. I opened all the drawers and groped around in them but found nothing except a few tiny pellets that I suspected were mouse droppings.

All the documents relating to my sister's case that had been there earlier in the day had vanished.

12
Kristín – *Autumn 1966*

'I heard she got into so much trouble,' Málfríður says on Monday morning.

'Who?' I'm doodling in my notebook, which is full of eyes, painstakingly sketching in all the fine details; the streaks in the whites, the colour gradations in the irises. If Málfríður was watching it might dawn on her that the eye I'm colouring in now is exactly like her brother's.

'Sólveig,' Guðrún says. She doesn't sound gleeful, like Málfríður.

'Who would have guessed that Solla had it in her?' Málfríður giggled.

I look up from my notebook and scan the room for Sólveig, but she's nowhere to be seen. She wasn't in her classes this morning either.

'Where is she, anyway?' I ask.

'I expect Sunny Solla is recovering at home after her big adventure,' Málfríður says.

'You should have seen her,' Snorri says later. He's standing outside the school, showing off to a group of kids. 'The ground shook as she ran and all her bits wobbled.'

He follows this up with a mime of running around like a giant troll.

Everyone laughs, and I join in, despite a queasy feeling in the pit of my stomach. Elvar has draped his arm over my shoulders. Gústi is standing across from me. He's the only person who isn't laughing, and our eyes meet for an instant before Elvar pulls me against him.

Ever since we left Sólveig behind on the steps of her house I've been picturing her parents' reaction. I've always been scared of her father, who's a big, heavily built man. I can't imagine how he reacted to the discovery that his daughter had been deposited, naked and drunk, on his doorstep, but something tells me he won't have been pleased.

'Are you free this evening?' Elvar whispers in my ear.

I nod and dismiss the image of Sólveig.

Sólveig doesn't show her face again at school until the following Monday, and then she's anything but the 'sunny' Solla of Málfríður's nickname. On closer inspection, I notice a yellow discolouration around one of her eyes, as if from a fading bruise.

'What on earth happened to her?' Guðrún whispers.

'Maybe she fell over,' I say, though I suspect the bruise has a very different origin.

'Maybe.'

Several days later we're summoned to the headmaster's study. Örn is an amiable man, with a round face and a bald head, but today his normally kind eyes are as sharp and penetrating as his namesake, the eagle's.

'Come in, girls,' he says, holding his study door open to admit us.

Sólveig is already in there, sitting on one of the chairs, with her parents behind her – her father even bigger and more imposing than I remembered, her mother a small woman who doesn't deign to look at us.

Sólveig's face is puffy from weeping, her eyes small and red, and every now and then she lets out a sob.

'Right, do you know why you're here?' Örn asks sternly.

None of us says a word.

'Then let me explain,' Örn says. 'Sólveig's parents got in touch to tell me that several days ago she was invited to a party at a private house, where she was given an alcoholic drink that we suspect may have contained something that—'

'Just a minute,' Málfríður interrupts hotly, and I tense up. 'We didn't spike her drink, if that's what you think.'

Örn opens his mouth to reply but Sólveig's father gets in first.

'We found our daughter abandoned outside our house, stark naked, badly chilled and extremely unwell.' His voice is low but so icy that I can feel the skin prickling on my arms. 'Sólveig has never touched alcohol before. She's a good girl who has no interest in that sort of thing, unlike you slu—'

'That's enough.' Örn holds up a hand.

I haven't been able to bring myself to look Sólveig's father in the face so far, but now that I do, I shiver. I've never seen anything like the hatred in his eyes, and he's staring straight at me, not at Málfríður or Guðrún. He's glaring at *me* as if I'm the most despicable creature he's ever set eyes on.

I keep my gaze lowered to the floor for the rest of the meeting, until we have to shake Sólveig's hand, one after the other, and make our apologies.

As I take her hand, I glance up and meet her eye. What I see there is not what I was expecting at all. She's not angry or accusing; she's afraid.

Once, Dad cornered a mouse in the cellar. It was so petrified that it couldn't move when Dad picked it up; it just sat there, frozen, awaiting its fate. In this moment, Sólveig reminds me of that mouse, and I wonder what can have filled her with such terror.

13
Marsibil – *Saturday, 19 November 1977*

It was the second time in two days that something had vanished into thin air; first the anorak, now the documents relating to Stína's case. My eyes were dry and stinging, so I closed them and tried to think logically. I clearly remembered holding the police reports in my hands and leafing through them. Surely my mind wasn't playing tricks on me?

So, who could have removed them?

Mum had fallen asleep over her book, which gave me some breathing space to search the house before Dad came home. I turned off the music, then immediately regretted it. Our house wasn't one of those quiet buildings; its timber frame emitted a constant creaking. When I was younger, I used almost to jump out of my skin at the sudden squeaks and cracks from the ceiling or roof. Over time, I had grown more accustomed to these noises, though I never particularly liked them. Despite having lived here for eighteen years, I never felt at ease when alone in the house. I thought it might have had something to do with the story of my grandfather in the cellar, but perhaps the discomfort had always been there. In some paradoxical way, although it was my home, I never felt it truly belonged to us. It didn't feel like a house anyone could own.

Shaking off my unease, I focused on trying to work out where the papers could be. The kitchen was an unlikely hiding place, but I opened all the drawers anyway and peered into the cupboards. Nothing. The laundry received the same treatment, but the papers were nowhere to be found. Of course, my parents' bedroom was the most likely place, but I didn't know how to explain my presence if Mum woke up. Deciding to risk it anyway, I tiptoed in and hurriedly went through the wardrobe and bedside table, Mum snoring gently all the while, then peered under the bed. All I found there was a pair of lace knickers and a bowl containing some ancient, malodorous leftovers, but no bundle of documents.

I could only think of one other place; the place where Dad spent the bulk of his time: his office at Fjarðaregg.

I arrived at the farm and was a little surprised to find Alda there on a Saturday. She was the mother of Stína's best friend, Guðrún, and had worked there for many years. Like her daughter, she was short and plump, her round face marked with dimples, but her light-blonde hair was mostly grey now. She greeted me warmly and after a bit of chitchat I got a chance to ask if Dad was around.

'No,' she replied. 'He dropped by this morning but I haven't seen him since.'

'Oh.' I cast around for an excuse. 'Dad left his hat in the office and he asked me to fetch it.'

'Really?' Alda seemed confused. 'I could have sworn he was wearing it when I saw him leave this morning. And didn't you say you were looking for him?'

'Yes, but he asked me to fetch his hat.' Seeing that Alda was looking at me oddly, I hastily changed the subject. 'How's it going, by the way?'

'Everything's pottering along as usual.' Her face brightened. 'Would you like to see the new facilities, since you're here?'

I dithered. The last thing I wanted was a tour of the egg-laying shed, let alone the slaughterhouse. On the other hand, everything had been renovated a couple of years ago, so the facilities should be in a better state than the last time I was here. Besides, Alda's expression didn't really leave me any room to refuse.

The egg-laying shed was a big barn-like space containing countless cages and an open area with channels for the feed. Every cage housed five hens and had a chute below it to carry away the newly laid eggs. The noise was deafening, and the stench of ammonia was powerful enough to make my eyes sting.

'We need to get on with culling all the ones on this side.' Alda had to raise her voice to be heard over the racket. She pointed to an area with a large number of birds clustered together. 'They'll be sixteen months old next week, which means their time is up.'

I stared down at the hens, which were packed in so tight they could barely move.

'There's not much space,' Alda continued, a little apologetically. 'So many of them have reached the cut-off age and have to be separated off from the others.'

Hardly any of the wretched birds had a full set of feathers. On most, the pink skin shone through the quills and in places there were large bare patches. The feathers themselves were torn and shredded from where they'd been pecked by the other birds. I couldn't tear my gaze away from one particular hen which had an ugly wound on one of the bald patches on her head. There was a crust of dried blood around it but it still appeared to be oozing. Another hen lay motionless on the floor. I thought she was dead until I looked at her head and noticed that her eyes were still moving. She blinked weakly every now and then.

'Are they all right?'

'Well … like I said, their time's up.' Alda didn't linger but walked on briskly, beckoning me to follow her over to the slaughterhouse.

I imagined that this destination would come as a relief to the hens, finally putting them out of their misery. Their eyes were staring and empty, their lives almost at an end after sixteen months spent shut in the same shed, among the same hens. What kind of life was that?

I thought of Dad's Icelandic hens, which led such a spoilt existence in our garden; allowed to go outside in the fresh air, with plenty of room to roam, their glossy plumage a testimony to their wellbeing. They hadn't an inkling of how lucky they were.

The slaughterhouse was next door. Unlike the laying shed, dead silence prevailed here. As we entered, we had an overview of the white-and-chrome interior. Rows of small pink carcases hung by one leg from steel hooks. In this position, their legs looked uncannily human: thighs, calves and stumps where their feet had been hacked off at the ankle. Without the feathers, their slimy skin gleamed. They reminded me of newborn babies.

I felt sick.

'Actually, I need to get going,' I said, swallowing my nausea.

'Now?' Alda stopped. 'Really?'

'Yes, I—'

'You look awfully pale. Have something to drink. Shall I fetch you a glass of water?'

'No, thanks. I just want to check if Dad's hat's in the office, then I must dash.'

'Oh, well.' Alda said goodbye, looking a little disappointed.

I had to restrain myself from breaking into a run. Once I was outside, I bent over and retched, but nothing came up.

In Dad's office, I opened the first cupboard I saw and immediately spotted the files from the shed. They had been crammed on to a shelf with no attempt to hide them. So I hadn't imagined them. I was in too much of a hurry to consider the implications of the fact that Dad had removed them from the shed and stashed them away here. Or to wonder how he knew I had been looking at them and why he didn't want me to read them.

I took the bundle of papers and stuffed them under my coat.

'Did you find the hat?' Alda called after me, as I was hurrying back to my car.

'Yup, found it,' I replied, not looking round.

As I drove away, I could see her standing there with her hands on her hips, staring after me with a puzzled frown.

On the way home I drove past Café Hvítá in the hope of seeing the writer again. I parked, got out and peered in through the windows. He had entered my thoughts several times during the day, mainly because it was unusual to see new faces in town. I was suspicious about the way he had struck up a conversation with me, and had then apparently hung around waiting for me at the bar later in the evening. Could he have got talking to Mette after I left?

'Who are you spying on?' asked a voice before I could get a proper glimpse inside.

It was Lilla, wearing a blue dress and dark-blue jacket today. I said hello, trying to recall our conversation the previous evening. I vaguely remembered talking about Stína and hoped I hadn't said anything too personal or revealing.

'You were on pretty good form yesterday,' she remarked.

'Thanks; you too.'

Lilla immediately went into gossip mode, lowering her voice confidentially. 'It's so terrible about that girl, deciding to walk home and dying of exposure like that. Did you see her at the bar? The Danish girl?'

I said I hadn't. Then it dawned on me that I didn't actually know what Mette looked like. Besides, I had been in no fit state to notice anything.

'All very strange, don't you think? My boyfriend's got a mate in the police, and he reckons there might have been foul play involved. I don't know exactly what that means but it does sound odd, doesn't it?'

'Yes, I suppose so,' I said. 'What makes him think that?'

'I haven't a clue. Maybe she had injuries or something.'

'What kind of injuries?'

'Well, I don't know any more than that.' Lilla glanced at her watch, as if she was in a hurry. She had always loved delivering the kind of news that made people gasp and clamour for more; throwing her audience a few crumbs, just to give them the taste, then leaving without saying too much.

'By the way, I talked to my brother earlier,' Lilla added. 'He said your sister had been asking some odd questions in the days before she vanished. About prostitution, he said.'

'What are you talking about?'

'You asked me to ask my brother if Stína had been seeing someone at the time she went missing. He wasn't aware of anyone, apart from Elvar, which isn't news.'

'No,' I said.

Lilla continued animatedly: 'But he remembered that he'd been in a class with Stína not long before that, and she'd started asking questions about prostitution in Iceland and whether even teenage girls could be on the game.'

'How strange,' I said.

'Yes, don't you think so?' Lilla's eyes were fixed on me, eagerly waiting for a reaction.

'I suppose so,' I said, wondering what Lilla was thinking. I could just imagine the gossip she would now start spreading about Stína and prostitution, and how the story would grow in the telling, from an innocent question by a sixteen-year-old girl to goodness knows what dark insinuations.

'It must rake up painful memories...' Lilla prompted, before I had a chance to play down the significance of Stína's question.

'What?'

'Oh, I mean, the fact there's been another death on that road. I know it's not the same, but still. You must be shaken.'

'Er ... yes. A bit, maybe.'

Lilla waited a moment or two, in case I was prepared to open up further. When I didn't, she said goodbye, adding that I was welcome to come round for coffee whenever I liked. We both knew it would never happen.

Before going home, I scanned the café again for the author, but if he was still in town, he wasn't in there.

I could see Dad silhouetted in the sitting-room window when I got home. He appeared to be looking out, but when I waved, he didn't wave back, and when I went into the sitting room, it was empty.

On entering the kitchen, however, I found him standing by the sink with the tap turned on full. Hearing me, he turned it off and banged down a glass in the sink.

'Still here, Marsí?' He sounded oddly short of breath.

'Still here,' I said, wondering where he had been all day, given that he hadn't been at the egg farm. And why he'd removed the documents from the shed and taken them to his office.

'Good, good.' He smiled and wiped his forehead with his sleeve. 'Listen, I was just going out to feed the hens. Have you said hello to them yet?'

'Briefly, yes.'

'There's a bit of meat from last week in the fridge that I was going to take out to them. Why don't you come and help?'

Dad fetched the dish of leftovers and beckoned me to follow him.

The hens cracked open their eyes when we opened the door of their house, and the instant they spotted Dad, they came out to greet us, clucking eagerly.

'Yes, my dears,' Dad said in a gentle voice. 'Did I keep you waiting? Aren't they beautiful, Marsí?'

'Yes, sure.'

'Did you know they're actually quite clever?' Dad said, and I saw his eyes softening with affection. 'Icelandic settlement hens like these are rare nowadays, but I managed to get hold of a few through a friend of mine out west. This one here's Dotty, and that one's my favourite, Bossy – you can see where she gets her name. And here's my pet, Wavy.'

Dad prattled on like this as he took the scraps of meat and threw them on the ground. The chickens fell on them, fighting over the best bits by shoving each other aggressively out of the way, though there was more than enough to go round. The meat was a pale colour and I found myself staring at the small bones that were mixed up in it.

'Dad,' I said. 'What kind of meat is that?'

'Oh, just leftovers from the farm. Cooked, of course. We don't want these poor loves to get ill.'

'Is it chicken?'

There was a moment's silence.

'Marsí, they're not bothered what sort of meat it is. It's a good source of protein.'

I didn't answer but turned my head away, wondering for a moment or two whether I was going to be sick.

After we had finished feeding the hens, Dad went in to take a shower. The phone rang while I was in the kitchen splashing cold water on my face. I dried myself, then went into the other room to answer it.

'Are you hungry? Dad wants to invite you round for supper. It's fine if you're busy, though. We can always meet up afterwards.' Gústi said all this in such a rush that I couldn't help smiling.

'Well, there's no supper on offer here.' I glanced towards the bedroom, where my mother hadn't stirred. Dad had finished his shower but was still in the bathroom, from which issued the sulphurous reek of the geothermal water supply. 'What time should I come round?'

14
Kristín – *Autumn 1966*

Our parents were informed of what had come to light in the headmaster's study, with the result that I'm now grounded for a week. I'm not allowed out in the evenings, except to attend my art classes, and although I should be sad, to be honest I'm quite glad to have an excuse to stay at home and work on my pictures.

Before one of the classes, I bump into Ívar in the corridor and he invites me to go for a coffee with him. I hesitate before saying yes and feel as if I'm doing something forbidden as I walk by his side to the canteen. But he chats away and gives me such friendly looks that I can't help feeling flattered by his interest. He's a really good teacher and his work is unlike anything I've seen before. His human figures are oddly elongated. Indistinct, nebulous, like reflections in water. Murky, somehow. One day I got a glimpse of his sketchpad; one of the pictures struck me as quite disturbing. It showed a figure floating against a dark sky, its mouth wide open. A ghostly image that seemed incompatible somehow with Ívar's easy-going manner.

'I have to warn you about the coffee,' he says, placing two mugs on the table. 'If I had one wish it would probably be that the coffee here was drinkable.'

'Mine would be that I could sing,' I say without thinking.

'One wish, and you tell me you'd like to be able to sing?' He raises his eyebrows. 'You mustn't be greedy, Kristín.'

'What do you mean?' I ask, noticing that he has called me Kristín again, although I've told him everyone calls me Stína.

'Well, you're obviously a very talented artist, and I'd have thought that would be enough for you. Your portraits are exceptional, Kristín. I've never seen anything like them, though you're still so young.'

Feeling myself blushing, I say lightly: 'Thanks. But in spite of that I've always dreamt of being able to sing.'

'OK, so to hell with world peace, ending all famine or becoming a millionaire – all you want is a good singing voice?'

I sigh. 'When you put it like that…'

'No, it's a good answer.'

'Just think how amazing it would be. Getting up on stage, just me and the microphone, and as soon as I open my mouth, everyone stops to listen and watch.'

'For three whole minutes,' Ívar says mockingly.

'Like it's any better to wish for decent coffee.'

'Well, it would be high on my list, at any rate.'

'And you have the cheek to criticise my wish,' I say, taking a sip from my mug. The coffee truly is vile. It tastes of earth or something else unidentifiable. I push the mug away with a shudder.

'What did I tell you?' Ívar says.

After the class, he stops me and asks if I'm in a hurry to go home. I shake my head, explaining that Dad's not due to pick me up for another quarter of an hour.

'The thing is, I found something in my room the other day that might be of interest to you,' he says mysteriously, beckoning me to follow him.

I hesitate before following him, wondering how it will look if anyone sees us, but we don't meet a soul and Ívar doesn't seem in the least concerned.

Accommodation is in short supply in the countryside, so a number of the teachers live on site in term time. Ívar's room, which is at the end of the corridor, turns out to be small and rather spartan. There's a window with four panes, a single bed and a small table beside it. A chest containing three drawers, and a jacket hanging on a peg. That's it. No personal items on display, apart from a book and a pair of glasses on the bedside table. I pause nervously in the doorway, watching him crouch down to retrieve a shoebox from under the bed. Then I take two steps into the room, taking care to leave the door open.

'I found this concealed under some loose floorboards under the bed.' He hands me the shoebox and tells me to open it.

The box contains several envelopes, a photo and a brooch decorated with a gilt rose. I take out the brooch and hold it up to examine it. It's a fine piece of work and the rose is delicately moulded. I have the sense that this piece was once precious to its owner.

'Whose is it?' I ask.

'Search me. It appears to date from 1943, judging by the year written on the back of the photo. Since you're into portraits, it occurred to me that you might find it interesting.'

From the bottom of the box he lifts out some sheets of paper with drawings of faces on them. They're small pencil sketches, yet incredibly intricate and well executed. Whoever did them had a genuine talent for portraiture. Although I don't recognise the people in the pictures, they exhibit distinctive traits that are hard to capture unless you really know what you're doing.

'Wow.' Forgetting my shyness, I sit down on the bed, and pick up the drawings one by one, carefully laying them aside after I've scrutinised them. There are quite a few, and a landscape as well. In contrast to the faces, this is composed of soft pencil strokes, blended together to form a whole.

'Hold it like this,' Ívar says, lifting my hand until the picture is level with the window. I draw in a sharp breath at his touch, then suddenly I understand what it is he wants me to see.

'It's the view from here,' I exclaim. There it is: the mountain outside the window, the river running down its slopes and the steam rising from the hot springs nearby. I lower my hand and look at Ívar. 'What was here in 1943?'

'I asked around and apparently it was a workhouse for teenage girls. But it was only in existence for a relatively short time – less than a year.'

'Right, I vaguely remember hearing something about that,' I say. 'Weren't the girls involved in the "situation"?'

'Yes, exactly,' Ívar says, sitting down on the bed beside me. For an instant I stiffen, wondering what he's going to do, but he continues talking quite normally. 'They were girls who'd been with soldiers from the occupying forces during the war.'

The 'situation' was the euphemism they used at the time to refer to relationships between Icelandic women and foreign soldiers.

He takes a photo from the box and hands it to me. It shows a teenage girl with short hair, in a buttoned-up coat. In front of her are two little boys who can't be more than two or three years old.

'Is she the one who drew the pictures? Was she at the workhouse?'

'Presumably.'

'You should try and find her,' I say. 'I bet she'd like to have her belongings back.'

'I've thought about it.' He gathers up the drawings and returns them to the box.

'But?'

'I just … I wonder why she left them behind.'

'Oh.'

'She could have forgotten the box, but…' He breaks off. 'But I don't think these are the kind of things someone would forget. Do you?'

'You mean something might have happened to her?' I ask. 'She might have been forced to leave them behind?'

'Possibly. But that's only speculation, of course,' he says. 'I don't have any evidence.'

'How old do you think she was?' I ask, studying the photo.

'Your age. Maybe younger.'

I imagine the girl having to leave the workhouse in a hurry. Perhaps there was an accident or she was prevented from going back to her room to fetch her things. Or maybe she was thrown out. Whatever happened to her, as I was studying her drawings I had felt a strange sense of connection between us.

15
Marsibil – *Saturday, 19 November 1977*

I'd dropped the idea of going back to Reykjavík today, but I hadn't thought to pack a change of clothes, so I went back into Stína's room in search of something clean to wear. A lot of the things in her wardrobe were hopelessly out of fashion – multicoloured tops, skirts and polo necks – but in the end I found a simple black jumper with long sleeves. It gave off a faint smell of mothballs, so I sprayed myself with some perfume I found on the dressing table, though that smelt a bit odd too. So now, not only did I exude a combination of stale perfume and camphor but when I ran my hands through my hair, I noticed to my dismay how thin it had become. In just a few days, it had lost almost half its volume. In the end, I pulled it back in a clip and hoped no one would notice.

Gústi still lived in the same house on the outskirts of the town. His mother had died very suddenly of a heart attack a few years ago, so now the family was reduced to Gústi, his father, Alfreð, and his younger sister, Ína.

I knocked on the door and Gústi opened it immediately. He'd changed his clothes and combed his hair to one side.

'Hi,' he said, and I felt a bit self-conscious all of a sudden. I'd often been round to Gústi's with Stína when we were younger and knew his family well, but I no longer knew what was expected of me.

But the appearance of Alfreð, clad in an apron, a smear of gravy on his forehead, immediately put me at my ease.

'Marsí,' he said, giving me a hug. 'It's so good to see you. Gústi told me he'd run into you. I haven't seen you for such a long time. How are you? Aren't you bored out of your mind in Reykjavík?'

I told him about the various jobs I'd had in the city, including the one I'd most recently started – working for a printer, and he asked me questions and made me taste the gravy he was making. Luckily, they weren't having chicken this evening but a leg of lamb.

'Who would have thought that cooking could be so much fun?' Alfreð exclaimed. 'I never did any until Hildur died, as it's women's work and all that, but I find I thoroughly enjoy it. I've even started growing herbs in the garden.'

'He's a great cook,' Gústi confirmed.

'Thank you, my boy. I do my best.'

'Are you still teaching literature?' I asked.

'Indeed, yes. Icelandic literature, as ever.' He opened the oven, releasing a cloud of steam. 'Right, this is just about ready. Gústi, call Ína, will you?'

The table had already been laid, and I noticed they'd got out the Sunday service. It was all so nice, and as we tucked in, I had to suppress a moan of pleasure.

'This is absolutely delicious,' I said.

'This is nothing, you should taste Dad's rack of lamb. Peas?' Ína pushed the bowl in my direction and I shovelled several spoonfuls on to my plate.

'So, what brings you to town?' Alfreð asked. 'Just a flying visit?'

'Yes.' I hesitated. 'Though I may stay on a bit.'

'Aha.' Alfreð was waiting for an explanation so I took a mouthful of lamb to give myself an excuse not to answer.

'There's not much happening here,' Ína said.

'What do you mean? It's all happening here,' Gústi teased, but the moment he had spoken, the atmosphere changed.

'Of course, it's terrible,' Alfreð said. 'Absolutely tragic.'

'You knew her, didn't you, Ína?' I asked.

Ína took a mouthful of Coke, then nodded. 'We were in the choir together.'

'She hadn't been in the country long,' Gústi said. 'Only a few months, so no one can have known her that well.'

'Were you with her yesterday evening?' I asked Ína.

'Uhuh.'

'It's terrible,' Alfreð said again. 'People just don't realise how dangerous it is to walk home when the weather's that cold. I remember, back when your mother and I first set up home together, hearing about a case of a man dying of exposure in the mountains. He'd been visiting the neighbouring farm, had a drop or two to drink, then decided to walk home. His bones were found the following spring, the wrong side of a crag on the mountainside above the farm. He'd so nearly made it home, but it's all too easy to lose your sense of direction in a blizzard.'

'But there was no blizzard last night, and Mette didn't drink,' I pointed out.

Ína frowned. 'Mette *did* drink.'

'Did she?'

'The couple at Gröf didn't know,' Ína said. 'They genuinely believed Mette was a Christian teetotaller, but, take it from me, Mette was drinking last night.'

'So, she'd been drinking and decided to walk home. Why didn't she get a lift with someone?' I asked. 'It must be at least four kilometres to Gröf. That's almost an hour's walk.'

'Maybe she wanted to sober up before she got home,' Ína said.

'She wanted to hide it,' I said, thinking aloud. That seemed plausible. Mette was an au pair, and the couple at Gröf had probably chosen her on the basis of some boxes she'd ticked. Doesn't drink: check. Believes in God: check.

'Anyway,' Alfreð said. 'Let's talk about something more cheerful. Like Christmas. Will you be spending it with your parents, Marsí?'

For the rest of the meal we avoided the subject of Mette, and for a while I was able to forget the real purpose of my visit. But once we'd cleared up and Alfreð had settled in front of the TV to watch the news, I fetched the bag of papers and Gústi and I went to his room.

I'd been in here a few times when we were younger. Then it had been cluttered with all kinds of stuff, like model aeroplanes and cars, and the walls had been covered in posters. Now there was only a bed, a desk and a bookcase. It was only when I sat down on the bed that I noticed a poster of the Beatles, half hidden behind the door.

Gústi was twenty-eight and still lived at home, but I hadn't found that at all strange until now, as, surveying his room, I realised it belonged not to a boy but to a grown man.

Gústi seemed to read my thoughts. 'I expect I'd have moved out long ago if Mum hadn't died,' he said, taking the office chair facing me. 'But after that it felt hard to leave Dad and Ína alone in the house, especially since he often works late.'

'How old is Ína again?'

'Nineteen.' He smiled. 'At this rate I wouldn't be surprised if she moved out before me.'

I returned the smile, but I was too preoccupied by the letters to be able to focus on anything else for long.

'Why do you suppose Mette even wanted to come here?'

'I don't know. A desire to travel probably; to experience something new.'

Perhaps our town seemed exotic to some people, I reflected. 'Did you see her talking to anyone at the bar?'

'Like who?'

I shrugged. 'Anyone.'

'You think someone gave her that note at the bar?'

'It crossed my mind.'

'I don't remember seeing her talking to anyone in particular, apart from maybe Ína and her mates.'

'But you did see her last night?'

'Briefly. I didn't stay long. I had to drive home a friend who'd overdone it a bit.' He grinned. 'Seriously, though, if we assume the person who gave Mette the note was at the bar, it must have been someone we know, not a stranger.'

'I realise that,' I said, reluctantly. I'd always thought of my penpal as a stranger; as someone who had never met me, didn't know who I was and lived on the other side of the country. The idea that he might have been someone I knew was deeply unsettling. I had told him *everything*.

'What was the name of that bloke you were talking to last night?' Gústi asked. 'The one who was so keen to walk you home.'

'I … I'm not sure I can remember,' I admitted. 'Hang on … Einar, that was it. He's a writer.'

'What did he want?'

'To chat.' I shrugged. 'Apparently he's writing a book that's set here.'

Gústi waited for more, but I shook my head. I didn't know anything about the man. Perhaps I should have been more on my guard – asked him more questions about himself.

'He was the only person I didn't recognise at the bar,' Gústi said. 'But if this Einar didn't write the note, there's every chance that your penpal is someone who knew your sister.'

'In that case, why answer an advert for a penpal? Why not just talk to Stína directly?'

'Maybe it was someone who didn't know her to talk to.'

'No,' I said. 'No, impossible. The address wasn't here in town. I posted my letters to the east of Iceland.'

'He could have had some connection to Síða.'

'I don't know.' It struck me as highly unlikely that the person who wrote the letters could have had any link to our town if he lived on the other side of the country. I couldn't remember anyone our age who would fit that description. Then again, the person who wrote the letters could have been any age.

I buried my face in my hands. 'This is hopeless.'

'Hey,' Gústi rolled his office chair over to the bed and pulled my hands down from my face. 'Let's start by looking into Stína's case and put your penpal on ice for now. There are still plenty of unanswered questions about Stína's disappearance, and I have a hunch that if we can get answers to those, they might lead us to your penpal.'

'I'm not so sure about that.'

'No, but…' Gústi paused. 'Stína left Málfríður's early that evening for a reason. Maybe she bumped into your penpal by chance or maybe she met somebody else – somebody she'd arranged to meet. I'm just saying that we don't know anything yet, so we should avoid making any assumptions at this stage.'

'You and your detective novels,' I said, still unconvinced. Nevertheless, I opened the bag containing Stína's files. 'Right, here's the paperwork. Everything Dad's collected over the years. I've had a quick look through, but haven't read them properly.'

It was a sizeable bundle of papers, mostly typed reports that Dad had been given by the police. At the bottom of the pile, though, I found a small notebook in which he had scribbled down some names and times, in no recognisable order, their significance difficult for anyone but him to grasp.

That evening Stína had left home before supper and Dad had noted down a very precise time: 18:15. Guðrún and Stína had gone round to Málfríður's house, intending to watch a film on TV. Málfríður's parents had invited the girls to eat with them, then Stína had left halfway through the film, a bit before ten p.m. I noticed that 22:00 was another precise time Dad had noted on the first page. After that came 22:25, which I couldn't link to any specific event. As Stína had never been found, it was impossible to say exactly when she had vanished, but the timeframe wasn't that wide, if we assumed that she'd walked straight from Málfríður's house to the place where her anorak was found.

Gústi picked up Dad's notebook and leafed through it. 'He's written quite a lot in here.'

'Dad's been poring over this for years,' I said. 'After Stína went missing, he was obsessed with finding her. He was out every evening and every weekend. While Mum…' I didn't finish the sentence but Gústi nodded. He knew what Mum was like. 'If I can find some answers, it might help them.'

'Maybe.'

'Or maybe not,' I said.

Gústi pointed to the book. 'There are some names here.'

I skimmed the list: Málfríður and Guðrún were at the top. I knew Stína's childhood friend Guðrún well, of course, and had always liked her. I'd met her mother Alda at the egg farm earlier this afternoon. Her father had died when she was young.

I knew Málfríður less well. She had moved to the town a year and a half before Stína vanished, when her father took over from the old vicar. Her mother hadn't gone out to work, but then she'd her hands full with four kids, three of them boys. Stína and Málfríður had quickly become close friends. Stína used to invite her round to our house, and they would lie in her room for hours, listening to music and gossiping. Unlike the times when Guðrún came round, I wasn't invited to join them. They preferred to meet at Málfríður's house, though, and it didn't take a genius to guess why. Unsurprisingly, Dad had written down the names of Málfríður's three brothers: Elvar, Páll and Sigthór.

The brothers had attracted a lot of attention when they first arrived in town, especially the two youngest. The eldest was away at college for much of the time. Páll was closest in age to Málfríður, born in January to her December, while Elvar was a year older and Sigthór three years older than him. The brothers used to go around in the latest fashions, grew their hair long, smoked and drank, and gave the impression of regarding us country kids as desperately uncool. The local girls were mad about them and tried to outdo each other in comparing them to famous actors and singers.

Stína was no exception. She had suddenly started making a lot more effort over her appearance. At the time, I simply assumed she was trying to catch the brothers' eyes. It hadn't occurred to me that she had succeeded.

But the relationship with Elvar was over by the time of her disappearance, and he and his brother Páll had been at home that evening. Their parents had confirmed their alibi, though I wondered whether they would have noticed if one of the boys had sneaked out.

When there were so many people in the house, would anyone realise if one was missing? And it shouldn't be forgotten that family members would lie without hesitation to protect one another. I didn't doubt that my parents would have lied to protect us. The fact that Málfríður's father, Thormóður, was a vicar didn't change that fact.

The only hitch was Guðrún. She would never have lied for Málfríður's family.

'I don't know if we'll learn anything useful from this,' I said, putting the notebook aside. 'There's nothing new here. We won't get any further on the basis of this evidence than Dad did.'

I picked up a folded sheet of paper. When I opened it out, I saw that it was a map of the town. Dad had drawn circles around Málfríður's house and the place where Stína's anorak had been found. The two points were about a kilometre and a half apart. One more kilometre and Stína would have been home. Twelve minutes' walk that had been the difference between life and death.

'What have you got there?' I asked Gústi, who was absorbed in reading.

'A report.' He handed me the page he had finished and started reading the next.

The typed report had a number of columns at the top. In one of them was written: *Interview with Málfríður Thormóðsdóttir* and, underneath: *Nature of the Case: Missing person.*

I hated seeing Stína's case set out as a form-filling exercise like this but I read on in spite of that.

According to Málfríður, Kristín arrived at her house with Guðrún Hafsteinsdóttir shortly before suppertime. They went up to her room and chatted until Málfríður's mother called them to come down and eat. After supper, the girls went back up to Málfríður's room. Málfríður said they had chatted about all sorts of things and that she hadn't noticed anything unusual about Kristín's behaviour. The plan had been to watch a film that was being shown on television. Shortly before 22:00 Kristín announced that she had to leave but didn't explain why. Málfríður

*and Guðrún finished watching the film and Guðrún was col-
lected by her mother when the film was over. When asked if
Kristín had a boyfriend, Málfríður said not that she was aware;
and if she had, she'd kept it very quiet.*

The next page had the same layout, except this time the interview
was with Guðrún.

*According to Guðrún, she and Kristín arrived at Málfríður's
house at around 18:00. The girls chatted in Málfríður's room
before supper, then ate with the family. Afterwards, they went
back up to Málfríður's room. When the film started, they
watched it in the sitting room with two of Málfríður's brothers,
Elvar and Páll. Guðrún said that Kristín went to the bathroom
and was away for a while, and when she returned, she announced that she had to leave. Guðrún didn't know why, but
assumed she just wanted to go home. Kristín had been feeling
uncomfortable on account of Elvar, Málfríður's older brother,
since, according to Guðrún, Kristín and Elvar had been going
out with each other until a few weeks previously. After Kristín
left, Málfríður and Guðrún finished watching the film alone as
both brothers had gone to their rooms when Kristín left and
Guðrún hadn't seen them again that evening. Guðrún wasn't
sure if everyone had been at home; she assumed they had but
couldn't say so with complete confidence.*

'They could have gone out,' I said to Gústi when I'd finished reading
the reports. 'Either of the brothers could have gone after Stína.'

'Exactly what I was thinking,' Gústi replied. 'And, of course, Elvar
had been seeing Stína for a while.'

'When did they break up?'

'Like Guðrún says in that report – a few weeks earlier.'

'Do you think he could have written the letters?'

Gústi sighed. 'I have no idea. I didn't know him that well.'

'Weren't you friends?'

'Nope. The brothers were way too cool. They regarded us country kids as losers.'

'Which I suppose we are.'

'Perhaps. Depends who you ask.' Gústi put his feet up on the bed and the office chair squeaked as he leant back.

I laid aside the papers and asked Gústi the question that had been put to me at the time: 'Did you notice anything different about Stína's behaviour in the weeks before her disappearance?'

'Well … she changed after Málfríður joined her class.' But then Gústi immediately backtracked: 'Oh, I'm probably making too much of it, though.'

'No, I know what you mean.'

During the year before she vanished, Stína had been out practically every evening with Málfríður. The previous summer I had hardly seen her at all, except briefly during the day. She slept late and came home after I'd gone to bed in the evenings. She was still Stína, but a more distant Stína. A Stína I rarely encountered.

'We didn't exactly hang out with the same people,' Gústi continued. 'I reckon she found me a bit square and boring compared to Málfríður's brothers.'

'I find that hard to believe. I always thought you were very cool.'

'Thanks, Marsí. It means a lot to me to hear that at least the younger girls thought I was cool.'

'I didn't say the other girls thought so. Only me.' I gave his feet a shove. 'Anyway, I got the impression Stína had calmed down a bit that autumn. She'd stopped going out as much in the evenings and I think she was seeing less of Málfríður.'

'True,' Gústi said. 'But … but I still had the feeling something was weighing on her.'

'Why do you say that?'

'She just … oh, it was just a feeling I had.'

I waited, but Gústi didn't elaborate, so in the end I said:

'I need to talk to Guðrún and Málfríður. Maybe they know more. Where do they live now?'

'That shouldn't be a problem as they both still live here. Málfríður married Ari, who's involved in politics now, and lives just outside town. Guðrún's single and doesn't have any children. These days she lives with her mother in the red house opposite the Co-op.'

'You keep tabs on everyone.'

'It's impossible not to in this town.'

Gústi was right. Everyone knew everything about everyone else here, and gossip spread among the inhabitants faster than the seasonal flu.

'Like you say, everyone knows everything about everyone,' I said aloud. 'If Stína had a boyfriend, it stands to reason somebody must have known about it. I find it hard to believe that the secret wouldn't have got out in the last ten years, so perhaps she was doing something else entirely.'

'I don't know. Maybe she'd only just started seeing him. Or maybe he had a reason to want to keep it quiet.'

'You mean he was married?'

'It's possible.'

'Then his wife would know he'd been out that evening, wouldn't she?'

'He could have told her he was going out for some other reason,' Gústi said. 'Anyway, plenty of people are willing to cover up for their spouses.'

'Even if he was an adulterous shit?'

'Even then.'

I sighed and felt a sudden compulsion to pick at my skin or tear out my hair. My hand rose of its own accord to the back of my head, and I scratched at my scalp but controlled the impulse to do any more than give my hair a gentle tug.

'There must be something more here,' I said.

Gústi watched me leafing pointlessly through the papers.

I was filled with despair. I had all the police files and my father's notes, yet I was no closer to solving the mystery. My naïve hope that I'd find some answers seemed to be slipping away, and I felt suddenly overwhelmed by the old sense of guilt.

When I looked up, I saw that Gústi was watching me. Meeting my eye, he smiled, and there was such affection in his expression that my heart seemed to stop, then rush up to my head and resume its beating there.

'What?' I asked, instantly conscious that I hadn't washed my hair since Thursday. That I probably still stank of last night's booze, stale perfume and mothballs.

'You remind me of her,' Gústi said. 'You have the same expression when you're pissed off.'

I could feel myself blushing and hoped he wouldn't notice. We'd switched on the lamp in the corner to illuminate the papers but apart from that the room was in semi-darkness.

'It's funny. I never thought you were alike at the time, with you being dark and Stína so fair, but now ... now I can almost see her – if I screw up my eyes.' Gústi made a frame with his fingers and squinted at me through it.

'I should go home,' I said.

'Yes. Of course.' Gústi got to his feet. 'Do you want me to give you a lift? Or, no, you drove here, didn't you?'

I nodded and we went out.

Alfreð was sitting at the kitchen table, the ceiling light casting a yellowish glow on the papers scattered in front of him. His pupils' homework, I guessed.

'What's up, kids? Are you leaving, Marsibil?' He glanced at the clock on the wall and suppressed a yawn. 'Yes, it's getting late.'

'Nearly midnight,' Gústi said. 'Have you been sitting here working all this time?'

'The exciting life we teachers lead, eh? Whole evenings spent marking tests.'

'Remind me never to become a teacher,' Gústi said.

'Where are you teaching now?' I asked.

When we were younger, before Gústi's mother, Hildur, died, his father had worked at a school in the countryside and only come home at weekends. That must have changed when he unexpectedly found himself a single parent.

'I've just started work over at Reykir.'

'Exciting.'

'Yes, I like it there.' Alfreð stood up. 'You know, Mette came to the school several times to help out.'

'What with?' I asked.

'Danish. Thorvaldur, the Danish teacher, had the idea of inviting her along to his classes to talk to the kids. He thought it might make them more receptive to speaking the language.'

'Stína went to classes at Reykir for a while too,' I said, thinking aloud.

'Oh, did she?'

'She took evening classes in art.'

'So she did,' Alfreð said. 'Your sister was pretty talented.'

I nodded, but on the way home I started wondering if I could have found a common denominator. Stína and Mette had both gone to the college at Reykir. Could they both have encountered the same person there? Lilla had hinted, darkly, that Mette's death might not have been an accident, and now I couldn't get the thought out of my head.

The jangling of the bell was cut off the moment I surfaced. When I opened my eyes, I was sitting up in bed, my duvet flung aside, and had my feet on the floor.

Downstairs I could hear the repeated banging of a door. I guessed immediately that it was the cellar door. If it was left unlocked, it tended to be sucked open by the draught. I waited for a while, listening, in the hope that someone else would go downstairs and deal with it, but when the banging didn't stop, I forced myself out of bed.

As I'd suspected, the cellar door was open, but when I went to close it I heard a sound. A thud. It wouldn't be the first time I thought I'd heard noises coming from down there: footsteps, moaning, and even, on occasion, I had woken up gasping at the sound of a shot ringing out, but as this mostly happened at night, or when I was alone at home, I knew the noises were imaginary. My grandfather wasn't lying in wait for me down there with a gun in his hands, and his blood no longer covered the cellar walls. When I had these nightmares, I used to crawl into Stína's bed with her; and, even after she had gone, I often used to take refuge in her room and lie down at the foot of her bed, imagining that her legs were tangling with mine.

Now, dismissing my fear, I switched on the light.

The bulb buzzed for a few moments before lighting up the gloom at the bottom of the stairs. I descended with firm steps and was halfway down when the buzzing began again, only to end with a small bang, then everything was plunged into blackness. I was instantly seized with terror – paralysing, suffocating and completely irrational.

I strained my ears, but all I could hear was my own frantic breathing. I tried to slow it down, but the panting continued, rapid, shallow.

It was not mine.

Then I heard a voice, a mumbling from somewhere in the impenetrable gloom.

The hairs on my arms prickled and I told myself to go into reverse, to make a run for it. But my body betrayed me; my legs wouldn't obey.

I was dreaming.

That had to be the explanation. I'd come home, fallen asleep on the sofa, and now I was dreaming. That's why I couldn't move or utter a word. What's why I was hearing things that couldn't be real.

I'd experienced it before, this state between sleep and waking, my dreams merging with reality, nightmares continuing after I was awake, in which I saw figures and sensed their presence, but couldn't move. Right now I was having one of those nightmares.

'Marsí.' It was Dad's voice.

'Dad,' I tried to croak.

I heard him fiddling with the light switch. 'Damn it, has the bulb gone? Is there someone there?'

'Dad,' I said again. Something like an electric shock seemed to zing through my body. I blinked and suddenly I could move.

'Hey, easy there, Marsí,' he said as I fled up the stairs. I couldn't move my legs fast enough and almost fell into Dad's arms on the top step.

'There's somebody down there,' I whimpered.

I expected Dad to tell me not to be silly, as he used to when Stína and I had been terrified of the cellar as little girls. He used to say that the only monsters down there were a few spiders and we were much bigger than them.

But Dad didn't say anything of the kind. Instead, he fetched a torch and shone it down the stairs. I stood at the top and watched as he started cautiously descending. The feeble torch beam flickered over the walls, a few boxes, the concrete floor, then came to a halt at a spot on the floor.

I leaped back in shock.

In the centre of the beam's circle were human toes.

Dad moved the beam upwards and a face appeared. I gasped. I thought it couldn't be human, just a doll or mannequin. In the torchlight the face appeared oddly white, the eyes wide open, the head completely hairless.

Then I realised.

Mum was standing stock still in the middle of the cellar in her nightie. Her eyes were open but she couldn't see us.

'Go up to your room, Marsí,' Dad said, but I didn't obey. Instead, I watched as Dad took Mum gently by the arm and led her up the steps.

After they had gone upstairs and I'd heard their bedroom door close, I remained standing there for a long moment. Then I closed the cellar door, went to my room, got back into bed and lay there, sleepless, until morning.

16
Kristín – *Winter 1966*

'You seem tired,' Elvar said between kisses.

Maybe because I *am* tired. I've had trouble sleeping lately, and what happened last night is guaranteed to make the problem even worse.

For several nights in a row now, in the early hours, I've heard the sounds of someone moving around: running water, the clinking of glasses and once even the front door opening. But the noise that woke me last night was different: someone was fiddling with the handle of my bedroom door. I waited calmly but, although it was unlocked, the door didn't open. The handle was pushed up and down a few times, then nothing more. No one knocked or came in.

I held my breath, wondering whether I should get up, but Dad says it's dangerous to wake sleepwalkers, though he's never explained why. I sat there for a while, listening, and when there were no more disturbances, I lay down again and tried to go back to sleep. When I woke up this morning, the door of my room was wide open and on the floor beside my bed was something that looked like … earth? Or sand? I don't know what it was, but I'm quite sure it wasn't there when I went to bed yesterday evening.

Mum's doing better, though, and before I came round to Elvar's, she insisted on making me up with her eyeshadow. She danced around me, showing me all these clothes she'd acquired during her years in the theatre. When I was younger, I used to feel like a doll Mum liked to play with. She would spend hours making me pretty and combing my hair. At one time I enjoyed the attention, but now it makes me uncomfortable and I don't know why I let her do it. Perhaps because it's so long since I last saw her looking happy.

'I slept badly,' I say now.

'Oh, poor you.' Elvar kisses my closed eyelids. I should enjoy it but all I want is to go home.

Elvar and I have been seeing each other for several weeks. At first I was mad about him, but now I'm not so sure. I haven't said anything to my friends, though, as they wouldn't understand, especially Málfríður. In their opinion, Elvar and I are perfect together. And, on the surface, everything does look perfect. In spite of Gústi's warnings, there's nothing wrong with Elvar. He's good, thoughtful and kind.

Yet something isn't right.

Our conversations are often stilted, and there are times when it seems like we have nothing to talk about, which is a completely new experience for me. Normally I prattle on non-stop. At least, Gústi and I have always been able to talk about everything under the sun without any awkwardness or uncomfortable silences.

Perhaps it's unfair to compare them, though.

Gústi and I have known each other for years, but I have no desire to kiss him. Doesn't a relationship require both: the desire to kiss and the ability to talk to each other?

I fake a yawn. 'I should probably go home and catch up on some sleep.'

At that moment the door bursts open. 'The bloody bitch,' Málfríður snarls.

'Who?' I sit up, tidying my hair, but Málfríður isn't interested in what we've been up to.

'Guðrún,' she says, her jaw working furiously.

'What has she done?'

'It was her who told tales. Who told them I'd given Solla the drink and probably spiked it.'

'No, she would never—'

'She *did*,' Málfríður hisses. 'Sometimes you think you know people but then…' She clenches her fists, her knuckles whitening.

'You needn't be so angry. I'm sure Guðrún didn't do it deliberately.'

'That's typical of you, Stína.' Málfríður shakes her head. 'You're always defending her. Don't you understand that she ruins everything? You can't trust her at all. She … she … she'll live to regret this.'

'Oh, Málfríður, calm down,' I say.

'I don't know why you always insist on letting her tag along. She's so stupid and annoying and—'

'Cut it out, Málfríður. Don't talk about her like that,' I say sharply. I know they're very different characters, but I can't let Málfríður get away with slagging Guðrún off like this.

Málfríður stares at me for a moment, then turns on her heel. The door slams so hard behind her that the wall shakes.

I instantly wish I'd held my tongue. 'Oh, maybe I shouldn't have said anything.'

Elvar strokes my cheek. 'Málfríður's just got a short fuse. Don't take it to heart.'

'What did she mean when she said Guðrún would regret it?' I ask.

'I'm sure she won't do anything.'

'No, but…' I don't for a minute believe that Málfríður will go through with her threat. Until, that is, I catch the look of concern on Elvar's face. 'Do you really think she might do something to get back at Guðrún?'

'I'll talk to her.'

'But what could she do?'

'Well…'

'What? What could she do?' I repeat.

'It's just … There was an incident at our school in Reykjavík.'

'What kind of incident?'

'I promised not to tell anyone.'

'Elvar,' I insist, 'what happened?'

'It's one of the reasons why we had to move. You see, Málfríður fell out with a girl at school, and she can be…'

'Can be what?' I prompt, when Elvar hesitates too long.

'She can be a bit hot-headed.'

'What did she do to the girl?'

'Well … they had a fight.' Elvar grimaces. 'Oh, I promised not to talk about it. Don't say anything to Málfríður, she'll go nuts if she knows I told you.'

'But Guðrún would never get into a fight,' I say. The idea is laughable.

'It wasn't exactly a fight,' Elvar says reluctantly. 'More like, Málfríður went for the girl. She was a year younger, quite small for her age.' He sighs. 'She was in hospital for weeks.'

A cold feeling goes through me.

'But Málfríður has changed,' Elvar adds hastily. 'She's not like that anymore, so I don't think you should worry.'

'You "don't think",' I repeat.

'I'm sure.' Elvar smiles, but his smile isn't as reassuring as he thinks.

17
Marsibil – *Sunday, 20 November 1977*

Dad was sitting in the kitchen when I emerged from my room this morning. There was a coffee mug and a newspaper on the table. Exactly the image that came to mind whenever I thought of him.

I took a seat opposite him with my coffee.

'Last night...' I began.

'Oh, Marsí,' he said, without looking up from his newspaper. 'There's no need to talk about it.'

'Isn't there?'

Dad raised his eyes to me then, smiled and, changing the subject, asked: 'Are you going home today?'

'I suppose so.'

'You've got work tomorrow, haven't you?'

I made an indeterminate noise in reply, because I'd started to wonder if I was in fact going home today. There were still things I had to do, questions I needed answered.

Dad seemed satisfied, though, and returned to reading the paper. We drank our coffee in silence.

Dad had never been willing to discuss Mum's nocturnal wanderings and clearly nothing had changed. He wanted us to play it down, in case Mum got upset. Stína had explained to me that sleepwalkers didn't remember anything about it afterwards, so it was best not to mention it.

Mum used to walk in her sleep when Stína and I were small. Sometimes nothing would happen for months, then we would wake up one day to find the contents of the hall cupboard emptied out on to the floor or the kitchen utensils strewn around the house.

The times when I was most scared in my childhood was when I woke to find her in my room, standing there, swaying like a sapling in the wind, staring at something that no one but her could see, just as she had last night.

The red house was one of the most attractive buildings on the road that ran through the middle of Síða and passed for a town centre. The other buildings along the road included Café Hvítá, the Co-op, the police station, the clothes shop and the hardware shop. The red house had decorative trim and handsome timber cladding like an old Danish merchant's house. The cladding was well maintained, its colour vibrantly red whatever the time of year.

It was also known as the 'Official's House', as it had originally been built for a local district official. As far back as I could remember, though, it had been home to an elderly couple called Silla and Doddi, who had been as much of a fixture in the town centre as the house itself. He used to saunter around the streets in a top hat, carrying a cane, while she sat on a bench outside with her knitting. I wondered what had happened to Silla and Doddi, since it seemed that Guðrún and her mother had now moved in.

It was past nine o'clock on Sunday morning, and after the commotion in the night with my mother I hadn't been able to get back to sleep. I was in the middle of a yawn when Alda came to the door.

'Marsibil. Nice to see you again.' I thought she was looking at me a little oddly, no doubt still puzzled by my strange behaviour yesterday.

'Likewise,' I said. 'Is Guðrún home?'

'She's upstairs. Come in, come in. No need to take your shoes off. I was going to mop the floor anyway ... Guðrún!'

I followed Alda inside and, after a brief interval, Guðrún came downstairs. Her whole face split into a grin and she hugged me tight.

Once we were in the sitting room and Alda had gone to busy herself in the kitchen, Guðrún leant forwards and said in a low voice: 'How are you feeling after the other night?'

'Oh, that.' It had escaped my memory that Guðrún had been at the bar on Friday night. 'Fine.'

'Good. You know, for a moment when I saw you there, I mistook you for your sister, and my heart nearly stopped. You look so like her now. And that jumper, it looks familiar too.'

'I borrowed it.' For some reason I felt myself reddening. I had pinched yet another garment from Stína's wardrobe, this time a jumper with red, orange and brown stripes.

Guðrún gave her infectious laugh and it came back to me that she'd always reacted to slightly awkward situations by laughing. It invariably eased any embarrassment as it was impossible not to laugh with her.

'Right, girls.' Alda came in with a tray of biscuits and marzipan pieces. She placed the tray on the table, then returned with coffee in delicate china cups. Just as she was about to sit down with us, there was another knock at the door and she excused herself.

This was my chance for a private talk with Guðrún, but she got in first.

'How's life in Reykjavík? What are you up to these days?'

'I've just started a new job, actually. At a printer's.'

'Oh, how exciting,' she said, and sipped genteelly from her coffee cup. She was wearing a skirt and blouse and seemed much more ladylike than the Guðrún I remembered so well. She had never been obsessed with her appearance the way Stína had. Had never bothered to doll herself up, style her hair or put on make-up. I'd always liked that about her.

'I was hoping we could talk about…' I began, '…about Stína.'

Guðrún's face grew sad. 'I can hardly believe it's been ten years. It feels like it happened yesterday.'

'I know.' I put down my cup and it rattled on the saucer. 'Look, I recently came across some police reports about it. And I suppose I just wanted to … well, I don't really know what it is I want. I suppose I'm making another attempt to find her.'

'Oh, Marsí. I do understand, but…' Guðrún looked as if she wanted to say more but she stopped herself and asked instead what I wanted to know.

'Could you go over that last evening for me? The night she disappeared.'

'Yes, I can do that.' Guðrún settled more comfortably on the sofa. 'We were round at Málfríður's. The plan was to watch a film, and her parents had invited us to supper first. In the middle of the film, your sister suddenly stood up and said she had to go.'

'Didn't you find that strange?'

'If I'm honest, no. Your sister was always a bit unpredictable like that.'

'How do you mean?'

'Oh, nothing serious,' Guðrún said. 'But she used to do that sometimes – head off without any warning, claiming she had to be somewhere else. She hardly ever explained why, if you asked; just smiled secretively. But, you know, I'm not even sure she did need to leave that evening; I think she was just bored. Or maybe she was feeling uncomfortable.'

'Why?'

'Because of Elvar,' Guðrún said. 'They'd been going out with each other for ages but they'd split up. There was definitely a tense atmosphere between them that evening, and I could see that she was uncomfortable. I don't think anyone else noticed, but I knew her so well.'

'I know.'

'Málfríður's dad may have embarrassed her too.'

'Really? In what way?'

'Oh, I don't want to imply anything, but he kept paying her special attention, you know what I mean? During supper he kept pushing food her way and saying she was too thin and should eat more. He said, "Boys like having something to grab hold of," and laughed. It made us cringe. His wife smiled but the atmosphere was … awkward.'

'Do you think he was flirting with her?'

'Oh, no. God, no. He was just behaving the way lots of men do around young girls. Of course, I don't need to tell you, your sister was very pretty, and even some of the teachers at school made a favourite out of her, teasing her and lavishing praise on her. Nothing major, just … she always got more attention than the rest of us.'

'So, you don't believe Stína had planned to leave early? That she'd arranged to meet someone?'

Guðrún deliberated for a moment or two. 'Well, we'd arranged to watch the film together, so I wasn't aware of any other plans she might have had. But what do I know? Maybe she was going to meet someone.'

'Did everyone else stay at home after Stína left?'

'Well, I didn't see anyone leave except her.' Guðrún put her head on one side. 'I understand that you're looking for explanations, Marsí, but I don't believe any member of Málfríður's family hurt your sister.'

'But you said Málfríður's brothers had been watching TV with you, then left the room after Stína went.'

'When did I say that?'

'In the police report.'

'Oh, I … I'd forgotten that. No, they didn't watch the entire film with us, but I didn't notice anyone else leave the house…' Guðrún was chewing her thumbnail. Then, apparently struck by a thought, she jerked it out of her mouth.

'What?' I asked.

'Oh, I don't know. Now that I stop to think about it, I don't remember seeing them go to their rooms, not Elvar, anyway. Not definitely. Stína left, then I went to the toilet and when I came back, the boys had both gone.'

'But you said in the report that they'd gone to their rooms.'

'I heard music coming from Elvar's room, so I just assumed they had,' she said.

'Assumed they had,' I repeated, the brothers' alibi crumbling before my eyes. 'Why did Elvar and Stína break up?'

'No one could understand it. They were the perfect couple and your sister was mad about him at first, but then she suddenly lost interest. That was typical of her. Anything new was exciting, but she quickly got bored of things when they became familiar.'

This description of Stína wasn't entirely unfair. She'd been like that with the toys we'd been given as children, chucking aside the old ones as soon as we got something new. But toys were one thing, people another.

'Was Elvar upset when they broke up?'

'He was very upset. Like I said, there was a tense atmosphere between them that evening and Elvar kept staring at her. She may not have noticed, but I did.'

'What about Málfríður's parents? Were they both at home? Would they have noticed if anyone had gone out?'

'Well, I think so. I can't believe they wouldn't have. After the film was over, her mother saw me to the door. I don't remember seeing her father, but I don't think he'd gone anywhere. Their car was in the drive. And I thought I could smell cigar smoke coming from his study downstairs.'

'Cigar smoke.' It was coming home to me that neither Málfríður's parents nor her brothers had solid alibis.

'Marsí, don't do this to yourself,' Guðrún said, pushing the tray of treats towards me. 'I know it all sounds very … well, suspicious, but I'm positive the police did a thorough job at the time.'

'Did they?'

'Of course they did. But I do understand.' Guðrún smiled. 'Oh, how I miss her.'

'What do you think happened?'

'I don't know, Marsí. I mean, there was often a lot of drama around your sister.'

'Was there?'

'She may have had the face of an angel but she had this … effect on people.'

'How do you mean?'

'Like they wanted to eat her up. When Málfríður first joined our class, it was like she wanted to own Stína.'

'Own her?' I laughed, but Guðrún wasn't smiling.

'She wanted to spend every minute of the day with her, and it was always Stína this and Stína that. Like she was obsessed by her. And your sister was the same. She changed after Málfríður joined our class.'

'In what way?'

'Málfríður was … Oh, I don't want to be bitchy about her, but she came from Reykjavík, you see? She was used to different things.'

'Like what?'

'You know, partying and drinking and so on. She used to skive off lessons and smoke in the playground. She was a bit wild and thought it was cool not to give a damn.'

'Do you still keep in touch?'

'God, no.' Then, realising how this sounded, Guðrún added: 'It's not that I've got anything against her, but she just … We're too different.'

'Do you think Stína would have been more likely to confide in her than in you?'

Guðrún's lips tightened. 'I sometimes got the feeling that she and Málfríður were hiding something from me. They were always catching each other's eye and grinning, but when I asked what was so funny, they just shrugged. But there was definitely something going on … Your sister had become very unpredictable and I didn't always know what she was thinking anymore.' A faraway look had come into Guðrún's eyes. 'I was always so afraid of losing her. It's odd to say it, but at the time the thought of no longer being her friend felt like … like losing a limb.' She laughed. 'But I'm sure it was only a phase and that we'd have gone back to being the way we were, if … if…'

'And was it?'

'What?'

'Like losing a limb?'

Guðrún seemed to think about it. 'In some ways, yes. I miss her terribly but … Oh, it's awful to say it.'

'What?'

Guðrún looked apologetic. 'In some ways I was freer after she'd gone. It wasn't until afterwards that I realised how dependent I had been on her. That wasn't her fault, of course. Far from it. It was mine. I was always hanging around with her, I never even considered doing anything different or trying anything new. I just wish I'd realised it earlier and still got to keep her with me. I miss her so much.'

'Me too.'

'She was such fun.' Guðrún put a piece of marzipan in her mouth. 'I don't think I've ever laughed so much with anyone else. Somehow everything seemed possible. We had all these plans about what we were going to do together.'

In the hall I heard Alda say goodbye to whoever it was that had been keeping her at the door all this time.

Guðrún sighed. 'Sometimes I like to imagine that she just upped and left; that she'd had enough. That she's abroad somewhere, painting pictures like she always wanted to.'

'I'd kill her,' I blurted out, and Guðrún's eyes widened. 'No, I mean, it's a nice idea and all that, but if Stína was alive and hadn't told me…'

'I understand, Marsí. I know exactly what you mean.'

'Sorry about that, Marsibil.' Alda came back into the sitting room. 'I do apologise for my rudeness. That was Ingibjörg from next door. I thought I'd never get rid of her.'

'That's perfectly OK,' I said. 'Guðrún and I have been having a good catch-up.'

'I'm so glad. Would you like some more coffee?'

'No, thanks. I need to make a move, actually.' I rose to my feet. 'Thanks for the chat, Guðrún. It was nice to see you.'

'My pleasure.'

They both accompanied me to the door, then after I'd said goodbye, Guðrún came out on to the steps.

'Marsí,' she said in a low voice. 'I do understand that you want answers but … it doesn't do any good to dwell too much on the past. It won't change anything, if you know what I mean?'

I nodded, though I strongly disagreed. Guðrún could have no idea of the guilt that had been festering inside me ever since Stína vanished. For me, getting answers could change everything.

18

As it was bright and sunny outside in spite of the cold, I left the car behind and walked along the street, thinking back over my conversation with Guðrún.

I had always envied her and Stína's friendship; it had been so straightforward. For me, finding and keeping friends had always been a strain, whereas their relationship, in contrast, had seemed easy. Guðrún was like a third sister at our house; it was as common to see her drinking cocoa in the kitchen as it was to see Stína or me. But after Málfríður's arrival at the school, Guðrún had become an increasingly rare visitor. Málfríður was wilder and more exciting than dependable old Guðrún.

I halted in front of a shop window to stare at a china doll on display. Its black pupils gleamed in the sun, and I had a vision of my sister playing with Málfríður like a shiny new toy. Tossing aside the old, pretending she couldn't see it anymore. But surely Stína wouldn't have discarded her faithful childhood friend like an old toy? Stína wasn't like that.

'Marsibil, wasn't it?'

Without warning, the man I'd met at the bar was there beside me, clad in a light-weight jacket as though it was summer, not a freezing November day. Einar was even more handsome than I'd remembered, with his speckled eyes and dark hair.

'Yes,' I said.

'Hello again. Did you get home all right?'

'I got home.'

'Good.' He smiled, and I could tell that he had noticed my flushed cheeks. 'Have you got time for a quick coffee?'

My own, and Gústi's, doubts about this man came crowding into my head. Yet I found myself nodding and smiling back at him, my cheeks on fire now, and following him into Café Hvítá.

We fetched some filter coffee and took a table at the back, in the same place as last time. At another table I saw two girls who used to be in my class. They waved at me diffidently, and I gave them a brief on-off smile, having long ago given up any pretence of politeness. I had no interest in empty chatter about the old days or what we were all up to now.

'Friends of yours?' he asked.

'Once upon a time.'

'How fleeting are the things of this earth,' he said, quoting a famous line.

'Aren't you the poet?' I retorted.

He sipped his coffee, watching me over the rim of his cup. 'Actually, that's what I wanted to talk to you about.'

'Oh?'

'I'm afraid I lied to you.' He put down his cup. 'Or not exactly lied. Let's just say I omitted to tell the truth.'

'Is there a difference?'

'Absolutely. I didn't lie deliberately, I just failed to correct your assumptions.'

'Which were?'

'That I was an author – writing a book.'

'But you said yourself that you were writing one.'

'Aha.' He aimed his forefinger at me as if I'd hit the nail on the head. 'True. But I'm not writing a book. You arrived at that conclusion all on your own.'

'What then?'

'I'm writing an article.'

'You're a journalist?'

'Guilty as charged, I'm afraid.' He seemed anything but contrite as he watched me with teasing eyes.

'OK. What's the article about?' I asked. 'A sensational exposé of life in a country town?'

'Something like that,' he said, and I got the feeling there was more he wasn't telling me.

'No, really, what are you writing about?'

There was a brief pause before he answered, his face suddenly serious. 'I'm writing about your sister, Marsibil.'

The protective barriers immediately went up, and I shrank back from the table. 'What are you writing about her?'

'About her disappearance.'

'Why? It's already been done to death.'

'Yes,' he agreed. 'But I think there's more that hasn't come out.'

'Like what?'

'Do you want to know?'

I waited.

'All right. Like the fact the police refused back-up from Reykjavík to help them with the search,' he said. 'Like the fact that no forensic team was ever brought in.'

'Sure, they were.' I distinctly remembered the police visiting our house. Remembered them going into my sister's room while we waited outside, Dad pacing the floor, Mum exclaiming in anguish.

'Were they really? Was it a proper forensic team from Reykjavík or just the local police?'

'Is there a difference?' I asked. I tried to sound dismissive, but I couldn't help thinking about the camera, and its roll of undeveloped film that had been left undiscovered for years. Would a 'proper forensic team from Reykjavík', as he called them, have missed that?

'Yes, there's a difference.' He was still being very serious, no hint of a smile or that teasing glint in his eyes. 'To be honest, I've been thinking about Kristín's case for ten years. I was in my early twenties when she vanished; I remember hearing about it on the news. Since then, she's never been far from my thoughts. I've been wanting to take a closer look at her story for ages. Because it's an unusual case, Marsí. Very unusual. I know people are forever going missing in Iceland, but it's rare for the person to be a teenage girl on her way home. And I've always found it odd that no evidence was found at the time or has ever turned up since, apart from her anorak. And then there's the business of the local police's reluctance to accept help. Even now, I've tried repeatedly to get them to talk to me but they refuse to comment.'

He must have been able to hear the crashing of my heart; it felt as though it was about to break its way out through my ribcage.

He leant towards me. 'It's like they're hiding something.'

'Who's *they*?'

'People in a position of authority.'

I almost burst out laughing. 'So you think Stína was spirited away by someone in the police and they've been trying to hush it up? That's quite the conspiracy theory. Will you be putting it in your article?'

'I don't know. But I was hoping you'd want to be quoted in it. What do you remember about the evening she went missing?'

For a moment or two I wasn't sure how to react, then I determinedly pushed my chair away from the table. 'I have to go.'

He didn't seem surprised, just sat back and took a leisurely sip of his coffee. 'It's getting to be a habit.'

'What is?'

'Walking off like this.'

I growled at him like a wounded animal. 'I'm so sick of people like you.'

'People like me? What am I like?'

'People who think they know Stína and own some part of her. Who behave as if they have a right to feel that she matters to them.'

'Don't you want her to matter to people?'

'Yes, but...' I heaved a deep breath. 'But for you Stína's disappearance is just a sensational mystery, something you can write about for your paper. Vultures like you don't really give a damn about her. You never knew her. And you're not interested in knowing her better, just in digging up new material.'

I said the last words with a shudder, thinking about all the articles I'd read, all the conversations I'd had in which people had referred to Stína like a character in a book, as if her disappearance was just an intriguing puzzle to solve. I had to bite back the urge to scream at them. I wanted to tell them that Stína was so much more than a name in the papers; that she had been my sister, sometimes a tease, sometimes annoying, but mostly nice and kind. I wanted to tell them about how, when I was five and crying my eyes out because I didn't get a bicycle for my birthday, Stína had drawn a picture of a bicycle for me and I had torn it to shreds, then afterwards we had laughed so hard that we had both wet ourselves. I longed for people to understand what I'd lost. But I knew it was hopeless.

'I'm aware that I didn't know her,' Einar said.

'No, you didn't,' I retorted. 'Look, for most people life just went on as normal after Stína vanished, but not for me. For me, it stopped. It just ... stopped.'

Einar stared at me and, in place of the smug expression he usually wore, his eyes were full of pity. Which was infinitely worse.

'Oh, stop it,' I snapped. 'Stop looking at me like you're sorry for me. Like you understand me. You don't understand a thing.'

'Sorry. I don't know how else I'm supposed to look.'

'No, right. So stop it. Write your article. I don't care. But I'm not helping you.'

All I could hear was the blood throbbing in my head as I walked the short distance from the café to my car. Words kept spinning round and round in my brain, appearing before my mind's eye in little clouds: 'prostitution', 'police', 'authority', 'toy'. The girl I was hearing people describe wasn't the Stína I had known, and I felt increasingly disorientated, no longer sure which Stína was real.

Once in the car, I closed my eyes and tried to calm down, but for some reason images from the egg farm kept appearing before my mind's eye: the hen lying on the floor, more dead than alive, blood oozing from her open wound. The pink carcasses in the slaughterhouse.

I opened my eyes, then rolled down the window and shook out the hairs I had unconsciously plucked from my head. I no longer had the self-discipline to limit myself to tugging gently.

When I got home, instead of heading indoors, I walked round the back of the house to the hencoop. The hens were all inside, so I squeezed into their little house and crouched there for a while, watching them sitting on their nests. They opened their eyes a crack when I came in but otherwise appeared undisturbed by my presence. They were used to my father's visits and knew they had nothing to fear. I wanted to tell them to stop being so self-satisfied. I wanted to go to the egg farm, collect up all the birds that were waiting to be slaughtered and install them here instead.

Mum was up and about when I went inside sometime later. 'Where have you been?' she asked. She was sitting at the kitchen table, chopping up an apple with a small penknife.

'I dropped by Café Hvítá.'

'Alone?' Mum said it with a slight shudder in her voice, as if the worst fate that could befall a person was to go to a café alone.

'I met a friend.'

'Oh. How nice.' I saw that she didn't believe me. She knew I didn't have any friends.

'Yes, we had a blast.'

Mum studied me, then speared a piece of apple with the knife and put it in her mouth. 'I don't understand you, Marsí. Haven't you got a job to go to in Reykjavík?'

'I've taken some holiday.'

'What for?' Mum chewed with her mouth closed, her dry lips moving up and down.

'Don't you want me here?'

'Of course, I do. I'm just trying to understand what's going on.' She speared another piece of apple and raised it to her mouth, the blade of the knife almost brushing her lips.

'There's nothing going on. I just needed a holiday.'

'Do you promise me there's nothing going on?'

I shook my head, adopting an innocent expression. 'Can I make a phone call?'

'Who to?'

'To work,' I lied.

'Go ahead,' Mum said, and seemed to believe it, even though it was Sunday. But then she stopped me as I turned to leave the room. 'I'm worried about you, Marsí. Are you sure everything's all right?'

'Everything's fine.'

'You seem so stiff.'

'I'm fine,' I insisted.

I dialled Málfríður's number. She lived on a farm some way out of town, so it made sense to ring ahead. If she was willing, we could arrange a time to meet and I wouldn't have a wasted journey.

The husband answered after several rings and handed the receiver to Málfríður. She sounded disarmingly friendly, quite different from how I'd expected. The farm was about twenty minutes' drive away, and she agreed to meet me there the following day. She said she got up early, so I was welcome whenever it suited me.

After I'd hung up, Mum said again that I seemed very stiff and insisted that I have a nice hot bath. She filled the tub for me, putting all kinds of bubbles in it.

'You need to relax, Marsí,' she said, humming a tune as she dug out a towel – one of the soft ones that were kept for guests. Perhaps I was now a guest in Mum's eyes.

'Where's Dad?' I asked.

'At work. Always at work. The chickens don't take the weekends off.' Her voice was soothing, almost singsong, as though lulling a child to sleep.

She forbade me to lock the bathroom door and promised she wouldn't disturb me, but as soon as I had lowered myself into the hot water, she brought me a glass of gin.

I took it and steadily sipped at it, as my muscles relaxed in the heat and the steam made the whole room slightly misty. The discussions I'd had during the day were still circulating in my head, but somehow I was able to distance myself from them. The disorientation from earlier seemed to fade away, as a pleasant numbness spread through my body and my eyelids grew heavy.

I woke with a jerk to discover that Mum was sitting on the toilet seat, watching me. The bathwater was cold and I had a headache.

'What time is it?' I asked.

'Late,' she said.

I was too tired to protest when she helped me out of the bath and dried me like she used to when I was a little girl, rubbing so hard that my skin turned scarlet.

Once I'd dressed again, I wandered into the living room, where Dad was on the sofa, reading a book. I dropped down beside him.

'Hi, Pipsqueak,' he said. 'Still here?'

'I'm still here. I've taken a few more days off work.'

'That's good. It's so nice to have you with us at last.' Although his words were warm, Dad's voice sounded oddly hollow, and he was looking at the book as he spoke, not at me.

'I was telling Marsí that she ought to stay on,' Mum said, coming into the room. She was holding a drink, I noticed. They both were.

'What time is it?' I asked again.

'Nearly suppertime,' Mum said.

A whole day had passed without my knowing exactly what I had spent it on. I was briefly filled with a sense of futility, unable to grasp where the time had gone. How could it have run away from me like this when I had work to do?

After Mum had gone back to the kitchen, Dad finally raised his eyes from his book. 'Are you all right, Pipsqueak? You look so sad.'

'I miss Stína.'

Dad stopped smiling and averted his gaze. 'Me too,' he said quietly.

That night I didn't get a wink of sleep. I just lay there wide awake, listening to the noises in the house. I felt oddly like a prisoner – like I would never be able to leave. Like I'd become part of the house.

In the end, I gave up trying to sleep and went downstairs to sit on the sofa. The darkness was so unrelieved that I could barely see the hand in front of my face.

'I'm not scared,' I whispered into the blackness. 'I'm not scared.' Then I looked out of the paler square of window, at the dark silhouette of the laburnum tree, its bare branches swaying in the wind. It felt as though the tree was waving at me, as though it wanted to tell me something.

After a short deliberation, I got up and went towards the cellar door. I stood in front of it, holding the handle, and counted to three before opening it. Dad must have changed the bulb because the light clicked on immediately.

There was a strong smell of mildew down there and the usual unsettling feelings I had whenever I opened this door started to creep over me. But determinedly pushing away my fear, I considered where to begin. The shelves were full of old junk: toys that had belonged to us sisters, schoolwork and craft projects. Children's clothes and little pairs of shoes. Then there were all the things left behind by my paternal grandparents: bits of furniture and knick-knacks that had ended up down here after Grandma died.

I started rooting around in this stuff at random. Picking up objects, moving them from one pile to another, sifting through boxes and rummaging in corners.

It felt like I had been doing it for hours. Now and then I would be shocked awake by my head nodding, or by the sound of a shot or weeping; my dreams bleeding over into reality. 'It isn't real,' I whispered to no one in particular.

I thought about how Dad used to forbid us to come down here because it was so filthy. We used to sneak down anyway, as his prohibition only made the prospect all the more exciting. Was that where it had originated: my impulse always to do the risky, the forbidden thing?

I wondered now how Dad could bear to live in the house where his father had shot himself. It had never even occurred to me before to consider this. Most people would probably have sold the place the first chance they got, but not Dad. He chose to go on living in the house and bring up a family there. What did that say about him?

In a corner, under my father's fishing tackle, I found a bag, knotted at the top. I guessed it would contain rubbish, but I opened it anyway and drew out a pair of Stína's gym shoes. Hadn't she been wearing this very pair when she left home that evening? I couldn't be sure. Perhaps I was groping for clues. Closing my eyes, I tried to picture her, but couldn't remember if it had been these specific shoes or another pair. They seemed almost unused, no grit under the soles, as if they'd been washed. Stína must have been wearing something else.

I put them back, knotted the bag closed again and replaced it under the tangle of fishing rods in the corner. Then I went upstairs, lay down on the sofa and stared up at the ceiling.

There's something rotten in this house, I thought. *Something rotten, thriving and spreading through the walls and under the floorboards.*

A rot that was contagious, that had infected all of us who lived here.

19
Kristín – *Winter 1966*

'What's up?' Ívar asks.

I've had Dad drop me off early at Reykir, hoping I'd get a chance to speak to Ívar, since this is the last lesson of the course. I like talking to him as he seems genuinely interested in what I have to say. And even though he's older than me, I feel there's a connection between us that I can't explain. A connection not just to do with our shared interest in art but something else. Something more.

We're in the canteen, drinking the terrible coffee, but this time I can't think of anything to say. Málfríður's outburst is still troubling me.

The atmosphere at school was tense today and I found myself constantly caught in the crossfire between Málfríður and Guðrún. In the end, I couldn't take it anymore and went home with Gústi. Yet in spite of his efforts to amuse me, it's like I can't enjoy anything anymore. Gústi seemed to guess how I was feeling, and instead of asking what was wrong or persisting in his attempts to make me laugh, he just walked most of the way with me in a silence that wasn't awkward or strained, but was comfortable somehow. When we reached his house, he asked me to wait while he ran in and fetched a book. 'I usually read this when I'm down. Not that I'm saying you're down, but, you know, if you need something to cheer you up. Or not exactly cheer you up, but … Oh, just read it.' The book he handed me was *The Little Prince*. Gústi assured me it wasn't a children's book. 'It's about what matters most in life … Well, it's about love.' And he turned red.

'Nothing's up,' I tell Ívar now.

'No?'

'It's only that…' I bite my bottom lip, trying to fight back the urge to tell him everything. 'Oh, just problems with my friends.'

'Well, I'm not going to pretend to have much experience when it comes to friendships between girls, but I do know a bit about other kinds of problem, so if you want to talk, I'm here. Have you tried writing it down?' When I stare at Ívar in puzzlement, he explains: 'When something's bothering me, I often write it down and usually discover that it seems less insurmountable on paper than it did in my head.'

'Really?'

'Yes. Honestly, you should try it. I know it sounds strange but I promise you it works.'

'I don't know,' I say. 'What if your best friends have fallen out and you're stuck in the middle?'

'In that case, I'd have thought it would be best to let them work things out for themselves. Tell them that you're not going to get involved or take sides. After all, it's their business, not yours.'

'Yes, but…' I say. 'The thing is, one of my friends can be a bit … Well, I'm scared about what she might be capable of.'

'What she might be capable of?' He studies me for a moment, then nods. 'I see. Are you scared of this friend?'

'Not exactly, but she can be a bit hot-headed.' I lower my voice, though there's no need, and relay what Elvar told me about the girl in Reykjavík who Málfríður had put in hospital.

'I see. And you want to be friends with a girl like that, do you?'

'Well … she is a lot of fun.'

'Fun can be OK in the short term,' he says. 'But I've discovered that there are a lot of other things that matter more in the long run, like being dependable and honest.'

'I suppose so,' I say, and look down, but I can feel his searching gaze on me.

'You said you know her brother well?' he asks, after a moment's silence.

'Yes.' I can feel my cheeks burning and regret having mentioned Elvar.

He cottons on immediately. 'So, he's your boyfriend?'

I nod, look down into my cup then raise my eyes. To my surprise, Ívar laughs when he sees my expression.

'Sorry,' he says. 'Look, my advice would be to decide which of these girls is worth having in your life. It's not normal to be frightened of your friends, and if you really believe this girl is capable of doing something that bad, then I'm not sure she's very good company for you. Even if you are going out with her brother.'

'But how—' I begin, and Ívar puts his hand over mine and smiles.

'Stína, you're young, clever and you've got a bright future ahead of you. I'm confident that with your talents you're going to do something out of the ordinary. Don't worry too much. Things have a way of working themselves out, and people you don't need in your life have a way of disappearing of their own accord, as if by magic.'

'Disappearing?'

'Oh, I've put it badly. I mean that some people stick around, others don't; and that's OK. The people who matter are the ones who stick around, and I believe you just have to trust that this happens for a reason.'

'Yes, maybe.'

'On the other hand, it can take time to work out who's worth knowing, and sometimes you have to actively seek them out.' He smiles teasingly. 'Do you see what I mean?'

'I think so,' I say.

'Good,' he replies. 'Because I've got a job for you.'

'Oh?'

'This is our last lesson.'

'I know,' I say sadly.

'Come up to my room after the class this evening and take the shoebox away with you. There's more in it – a photo, letters and so on – that you might find useful.'

'Useful for what?'

'For tracing the girl. I think you should track her down and return the box to her,' he says. 'I don't have much free time myself, but I reckon a project like this could help to distract you from your friend worries.'

'Thanks,' I say, experiencing a little thrill of anticipation.

'My pleasure.' He smiles, then adds: 'Anyway, you'll need something to occupy your time once I'm gone.'

'Are you leaving?'

'Yes, I'm going home. This is our last class, remember?'

'But … but couldn't you stay on a bit longer?' My heart misses a beat and I'm filled with despair. I don't want him to go.

'It's all right, Stína. I actually want to go home.'

'Oh.'

He smiles. 'Don't be sad. Find the girl and return her box of belongings to her. I'm sure your friend troubles will solve themselves.'

I nod and manage somehow to hold back my tears. Then I give him the picture I've been working on at home over the last few days.

It's different from anything else I've done and has more in common with Ívar's own work. Not that I've been copying him, more that he's inspired me. Him, and all the stuff that's been going on at home.

Ívar takes the picture and examines it. The painting is of our garden at home, not so much a faithful rendition of it as an impression of the feelings it awakens in me. The trees are strangely elongated, their branches tangled, the sky dark. In the middle of the picture a human figure is standing, indistinct in the gloom.

'Wow,' Ívar says. 'This is one of the best things you've done.'

'I want you to have it,' I say.

'But I can't…'

'Yes, please accept it,' I say, forcing a smile.

The truth is that since finishing the picture I can hardly bring myself to look at it.

20
Marsibil – *Monday, 21 November 1977*

The drive was just a long pot-holed track, and the farm itself resembled many others in the district: white house, red roof, and a few other buildings in the same style. All was quiet, no people or animals to be seen. It reminded me of the derelict farm at the head of the fjord that had been abandoned at the turn of the century. The crunching of gravel under my feet seemed magnified in the stillness as I walked up to the house. I was prepared to find nobody at home but then I spotted a shadow in the kitchen window. Someone was watching me, though there was a delay before the door was opened.

Málfríður was wearing flared jeans and a knitted polo-neck jersey. Her dark hair had been blow-dried back from her face and she had white eyeshadow in the corners of her eyes. Clearly, she'd dressed up for my visit, but the make-up and trendy clothes couldn't conceal her tiredness. There were deep circles under her reddish eyes and when she invited me to come inside, I got a glimpse of unusually yellow teeth. Málfríður wasn't yet thirty but looked older.

'Let's use the sitting room,' she said. 'Would you like coffee?'

I accepted the offer and took a seat on a black leather sofa that smelt of freshly slaughtered calf.

The room was smartly furnished, but the winter sun shining through the window lit up a thick layer of dust on the shelves. My gaze caught on the pale-grey china figurine of a girl feeding hens on the top shelf. There was another of two children, a boy and girl, kissing. I remembered the same kind of figurines at home. Then I became aware of a noise and noticed a small boy sitting in the corner of the room, staring at me. He scowled, projecting his lower lip, his eyes hidden by a tangle of dark hair. He was wearing nothing but a vest and underpants.

'Hi,' I said tentatively, but the little boy didn't react.

'Back to bed, Loftur,' Málfríður ordered sharply, returning with two mugs. The child stood up and ran out of the room. 'He's ill and supposed to be resting,' Málfríður explained. 'Do you have children?'

I said no, I didn't, and Málfríður examined my face for a moment, a small, inscrutable smile on her lips.

Then she sniffed lightly, picked up her mug, and came straight to the point of my visit. 'What did you want to know about Stína?'

Despite the hospitable offer of coffee, her tone was much cooler than it had been on the phone. I wondered if she was one of those women who put on a show for their husband, acting the sweet, kind, rosy-cheeked wife who pandered to him, only to transform into a very different person as soon as his back was turned. Hadn't somebody said he was a politician?

'You and Stína were quite close that autumn,' I began.

'Yeah, sure we were. My family had moved to town the year before and Stína was the first friend I made. She was all right, not a boring prude like most of the country girls.'

Feeling like a prude myself, I carefully put down my mug. 'What sort of things did you two get up to?'

'What did we get up to?' she repeated.

'For kicks.'

'Just the usual. Hung out in the evenings, talking about boys, pinched booze from our parents' drinks cabinets, listened to records.'

'Had you both started drinking that first year at school in Reykholt?'

'Of course. Everyone was drinking by then, some people long before.' This was accompanied by a condescending smile, as if I was being naïve. Then she narrowed her eyes and leant back slightly. 'So, are you trying to find out what happened to her? I suppose I can understand that. It must be torture not to have any answers. For her just to vanish like that.'

I didn't like her, I decided, but I was careful not to let it show. 'What do you think happened?'

'She was always talking about going away somewhere to study art. Moving abroad, meeting some tall, dark handsome guy.' She gave a shout of laughter. 'I wouldn't be surprised if she'd staged the whole thing, left the country and is sitting on a beach somewhere as we speak, all tanned, blonde and beautiful, while I'm mouldering away here.'

There was a true bitterness in her voice that made it clear she was discontented with her lot. Many women her age would have been delighted to have a husband, a child and a farmhouse, but perhaps Málfríður had envisaged a very different future for herself.

'I can hear you, Loftur!' she screeched suddenly. 'I told you to get back in bed.'

She stood up abruptly and left the room.

She returned after a short interval, but instead of sitting down again, she glanced over at the dark cabinet in the corner and whispered to me in a tone like a child suggesting stealing from her father's wallet: 'Shall we have something stronger?' Without waiting for an answer, she opened the cabinet, took out a bottle and poured a generous splash into both our coffee mugs.

'So you believe Stína left the country?' I said, returning to where we had left off. 'Did she say anything to give you that idea?'

'She was always talking about travelling.' Málfríður took two greedy mouthfuls of coffee, then closed her eyes. 'Always letting herself dream.'

'What about her anorak?'

'I've always assumed she'd staged the whole thing,' Málfríður said, looking as if she found the idea rather exciting.

I gulped my coffee awkwardly and the alcohol burned my throat. 'Staged it?' I gasped.

'Yes. Of course you'll remember how badly Stína and your dad had been getting on back then. In the last few days before she went missing, they'd been at each other's throats continually.'

'Are you sure?' I couldn't remember any rows, but then I'd been distracted by my own bit of intrigue at the time.

'I'm positive,' Málfríður replied. 'Stína said she couldn't stand him.'

'Dad?'

'Uhuh. She was furious with him.'

'When did she tell you that?'

'A few days before she disappeared,' Málfríður said, inspecting one of her nails. 'Or at least, that's how I remember it. Maybe it was a couple of weeks before – not long, anyway.'

'Do you know what they were fighting about?'

'She didn't say exactly. Something he'd done, I think. Something that really pissed her off. Or maybe it was something he did to her, I'm not sure. When I asked her, she said it didn't matter; but I knew she was lying. It mattered a lot. She said she wanted to go away, but she meant it differently from before, you know? Like she *had* to go, rather than just wanted to.'

'Like she was running away from something?' I asked.

'Like she couldn't face staying here any longer.'

I took a more careful sip of my fortified coffee and considered this. If Stína had been angry with Dad, she might conceivably have made a foolish decision, something that had led to her disappearing. But I couldn't imagine what she could have been so angry about. We never had rows with Dad. Yes, he could be strict and he wouldn't let Stína go out when she was supposed to be doing her homework, but he never did anything to us. I remember being spanked a few times when I was small and Mum slapping my face for swearing, but Stína usually avoided any sort of punishment. She was rarely told off and didn't argue with our parents, whereas I was the difficult one and got blamed for everything imaginable. If the biscuits disappeared from the drawer or a glass got broken, our parents' automatic reaction would be: "*Marsí!*" And they were generally right.

'Do you think she might have confided in someone else about this?'

'No, I don't,' Málfríður said bluntly.

It was obvious I wasn't going to get any further with this line of inquiry, so I tried changing tack: 'Do you think anyone had it in for Stína? Would have wanted to hurt her, I mean?'

'I can think of a few people.' Málfríður smiled. 'Your sister was no angel. There was the business with Sunny Solla, for example.'

'I knew about that,' I said.

Ignoring this, Málfríður grew animated and embarked on the story. 'Sólveig Inga Jónsdóttir, her name was. We called her Sunny Solla because she hardly ever cracked a smile her whole time at school. Stína and I used to wonder if she actually had any smile muscles in her cheeks. And God knows, it wasn't like she didn't have cheeks. Anyway, one day we invited her along to a party. To cheer her up, you understand. She was in love with this boy called Böðvar, and we wanted to help her. This guy we knew had his parents' house to himself that evening, so a few of us kids met up there. I didn't expect Solla to turn up, but she did, wearing this ridiculous dress like she was on her way to a ten-year-old's birthday party. But Böðvar didn't come, and she was so gutted that we wanted to cheer her up, so we gave her a drink.'

'Of alcohol?'

'Yes, just a little one. I don't quite know what happened but suddenly she was pissed out of her mind. Maybe she'd never touched booze before, but, whatever the reason, it didn't have a good effect on her. Or it did – depending on your point of view. She ended up stripping off and running round the house starkers. I don't think I've ever seen anything so funny in my whole life. Then she passed out, naked, and it was impossible to move her. We took a photo, just for a laugh. Eventually, though, we managed to shove her into a car and drive her home. It was only a bit of friendly fun, but then her parents got involved and I think Solla must have claimed that we spiked her drink, which was a total lie.'

'Spiked it with what?'

'Something that got her smashed out of her mind, then made her black out. She claimed we'd used her. That it was all our fault. I swear we didn't put anything in her drink, but her parents went ballistic.' Málfríður shuddered. But then she broke into a smile so spiteful that it reminded me of a picture of the witch in Hansel and Gretel.

'I see.'

'God, I haven't thought about Sunny Solla for years,' Málfríður sighed. 'And no one can deny that the name suited her even better after that.'

I drank my coffee to hide my distaste, almost choking again on the strong spirits.

'Was Stína seeing any boys?' I continued.

'Define "seeing".'

'Did she have a boyfriend when she disappeared? I know she'd broken up with Elvar a few weeks before.'

'No.'

'So she wasn't going out with anyone?'

'Mm, no, I wouldn't say going out with.' Málfríður splashed more brandy into her now empty mug. 'She was playing the field.'

'Was she seeing several boys, then?'

'She was stringing several along, let's say.'

'Who?'

'She was such flirt, your sister. But she was mainly interested in the older guys.'

'Anyone in particular?'

'Maybe.'

'But she did go out with your brother?'

'Oh, that was nothing,' Málfríður said, waving a hand dismissively.

'Elvar wasn't seriously interested in her, and they were only together for a few months. Besides, I reckon he had bigger ambitions than shagging a sixteen-year-old country girl.' She took a mouthful of brandy and sighed with pleasure.

This conversation was severely testing my patience, but I bit my lip and decided to steer it in a slightly different direction. I took out the photos and asked if she recognised the boy in them.

'That's Elvar,' she said immediately, pointing to the picture of the boy by the stream. Then she took the photo of Stína with the headless boy from me. 'But I don't know who that is.'

'Are you sure it's not Elvar too?'

'Yes, I'm sure,' Málfríður said, handing back the pictures. She seemed suddenly resentful, as though Stína had betrayed her.

'You're not alike,' Málfríður remarked out of the blue, her eyes running over my face.

'No.'

'Everyone thought Stína was so beautiful. People like her can get away with murder.'

'She was very beautiful,' I agreed, though I didn't like Málfríður's insinuation that Stína had got some kind of special treatment.

'I suppose so. At least, a lot of boys fancied her. And Stína flirted with them all – including that friend of hers who always followed her everywhere like a faithful dog.'

'Gústi?'

'That's the one. He wouldn't leave her alone. And she led him on, letting him believe there could be something more.'

I felt a slight pang at her words, though I was sure they were a gross exaggeration, like most of what Málfríður had been saying. I didn't like the way she denigrated Stína. And I was reminded of what Guðrún had said about Málfríður being obsessed with my sister. Maybe she was, but she still seemed prepared to insult her. It seemed that Málfríður was the type who wouldn't hesitate to slag off other people behind their backs.

'Was there ever any more to it?'

'I don't think so,' Málfríður said.

I decided to change the subject again. 'Stína took evening classes at Reykir for a while. Do you remember?'

'Uhuh. Like I said, she had all sorts of opportunities that weren't on offer to the rest of us.'

'She was studying art,' I said.

'She never stopped yakking on about that place.' Málfríður sat back in her seat.

'About anyone in particular?'

'No, nothing like that. It was about the building. About the doctor's house or whatever it was. You know the evening classes were held there, don't you? Stína became obsessed with the building. She decided to do a project about it.'

'What kind of project?' I asked.

'I have to admit I didn't really listen, but I think she was planning to talk to someone to find out about the history of the place.'

Before I could ask any more questions, Málfríður heaved a sigh and her eyes became dreamy and unfocused. 'That was such a fun time. I miss being young and carefree, with no responsibilities.' She shot a glance in the direction of the hallway into which her little son had disappeared.

'You two certainly had your share of fun.'

'Oh, yes. We were out partying every weekend that summer.'

'I don't remember that.'

Málfríður smirked. 'We were so cunning – much cleverer than our parents realised. My God, the things we got away with.'

'Like what?'

'Like lying about where we'd been. I used to say I was with Stína and she'd tell her parents she was with me, and no one ever discovered the truth.'

'So where were you?'

She leant forwards again. 'Wherever we wanted to be. Parties at people's houses, country balls … She really let her hair down that summer, maybe because Guðrún wasn't there to nanny her. If you only knew how long Stína could stay awake and how much booze she could put away.'

'Stína?' I said, disbelievingly.

'Your sister was terrible.'

I stared at Málfríður sceptically, unsure whether to believe her. She seemed like someone who played fast and loose with the truth. A memory came back to me of Málfríður going through my mother's wardrobe while my parents were out. I'd seen her take out a beautiful shawl that Mum loved and bury her nose in it. Several days later Mum had turned the whole house upside down hunting for it, but the shawl was never seen again.

'What do you mean by that – "terrible"?'

'Oh, you know.' Málfríður yawned hugely without bothering to cover her mouth, looked at her watch, then announced that she had an awful lot to do.

Taking the hint, I stood up. 'My parents were afraid she was mixed up in bad company before she went missing. Do you know if that was true?'

Málfríður put on a look of fake sympathy. 'Oh, darling, don't look at me like that: it wasn't *me* who was the bad company.'

21

Gústi was sitting drinking orange juice with Mum when I got home. She was dunking her biscuit in her juice as usual.

'I tried to ring,' he said apologetically. Or accusingly. Or both.

I joined them at the table and Mum fetched a glass for me. 'Gústi was just telling me that you're both looking into what happened to Stína.'

'Did he say that?' I glared at Gústi, who dropped his eyes.

'No, I just said we'd discussed it,' he muttered.

Mum sat down on the bench again, close to Gústi. 'I said I thought you should drop it. It's put too much of a strain on all of us. Just look at your father. He's like a shadow of his former self. And he's hardly ever home, as if he can't face being in this house.'

I wanted to point out that he'd hardly ever been home before either, but I stopped myself. 'I thought Dad was doing his own investigations,' I said.

Mum refilled Gústi's glass. 'You love your children so much. No one ever warns you what it's like before you have them. You love your children more than anything else in the world, so if something happens to them, it's so much more devastating than you could ever imagine.'

She looked close to tears, and Gústi placed a comforting hand over hers. She smiled gratefully. I didn't know where to put myself. I tried to work out whether Mum was drunk, but I couldn't tell.

When I suggested going for a walk, Gústi agreed, and Mum raised her eyebrows, as if going for a walk together held some deeper significance.

'Please, for my sake, stop speculating about this,' she said, before we left. 'I couldn't bear it if…'

'But what if we find her?'

Mum looked grave. 'Marsí, you won't find her. Believe me.'

'Why not?'

'She's gone, I can sense it,' Mum said, pressing a hand to her heart.

I'd never put much faith in my mother's psychic powers. If anything, I felt closer to Stína now than I had in a long time. Sensed that she was somewhere nearby, waiting for me to find her. But of course I didn't tell Mum that, I just assured her that we'd stop looking.

Gústi and I went out into the garden and walked up to the little wood. The air was still and it was milder than it had been for the last few days, though the mountainsides were white with snow. I felt guilty about not having talked to Gústi yesterday, but it wasn't like I'd promised him that we would do this together. Although I had asked him for help, ultimately it was my journey, my sister. Added to which, the fact that Gústi had been crazy about Stína had been preying on my mind.

Perhaps I'd always known, deep down. Gústi was forever hanging around Stína. In fact, he would be the perfect candidate for the theory he himself had come up with about who might have sent the letters: someone who had wanted to get closer to Stína but didn't know how. Furtively studying Gústi's kindly face now, though, I found it hard to believe him capable of anything bad.

'How are you feeling, Marsí?' he asked. 'You look tired.'

'I couldn't sleep.'

'I tried ringing.'

'I wasn't home.'

'No. Your mother didn't know where you were.'

'I was looking into a couple of things,' I said.

We stood there without speaking for a while, listening to the wood. Despite the still weather, the fir trees were never quiet. They seemed to keep up a constant whispering among themselves.

'Did you find out anything new?' Gústi asked, and I thought he sounded hurt.

'Possibly. Was Stína…' I wondered how to phrase it. 'Was she a bad influence?'

'A bad influence?' Gústi laughed, only to break off when he saw my expression. 'Oh, Marsí, don't be ridiculous.'

'But the picture Málfríður painted of Stína was so different from the one I knew. I felt the person she was describing wasn't my sister but a complete stranger.'

'Ah, so you've talked to her, have you?' Gústi sighed. 'I wouldn't pay too much attention to what Málfríður says. She has a tendency to bend the truth for her own purposes. Málfríður's been in a bit of trouble in recent years. For one thing, she was caught going from doctor to doctor in several different towns to get hold of pills.'

'But Málfríður spent so much time with Stína before her disappearance,' I pointed out. 'Perhaps Stína *had* changed and I'd just failed to notice.'

'No, Marsí, I don't believe that. Though to tell the truth, I was worried about Stína spending so much time in her company. Málfríður wasn't a good influence. I never liked her.'

'I heard what they did to Solla.'

'That was bad. I helped Stína carry her home.'

'I don't believe Stína would have done a thing like that.'

'No,' Gústi said. 'Neither do I. But Stína let Málfríður get away with the most unbelievable stuff. She was always making excuses for her. I never understood their friendship.'

'What about Elvar?'

'What about him?'

'Do you think he could have done something to her?' I asked, adding, before Gústi could answer: 'Guðrún couldn't swear to seeing both brothers at home later that evening. They went to their rooms when Stína left and she didn't see them after that.'

'So you've talked to her as well?' Gústi said. 'I suppose the police must have looked into their alibis at the time.' He didn't sound sure.

'Did they?' I said. 'Would they really have subjected the vicar and his family to a proper grilling?'

Gústi was silent at that. Up to now, I hadn't given much thought to Málfríður's father's position, but now I wondered if it could have been significant; if it could have influenced the police's handling of the case. I couldn't shake off the journalist's words: that someone in a position of authority might have interfered with the investigation. Was his suggestion really so far-fetched?

Gústi ran his hands through his hair. 'I've always been confident that the police did everything in their power. There was such a big operation in the days after she went missing. The search parties and all that.'

'I know,' I said.

I was beginning to feel chilled now and gave a sniff. Gústi was watching me with those grey-blue eyes of his, and there was something in his gaze that made me forget about the cold.

When he spoke again, his voice was a little husky. 'You're so like her.'

'You've already said that,' I retorted.

'I know. Sorry, I just … When I glance at you quickly like that, I sometimes feel like Stína's come back.'

He probably meant this as a compliment, but I didn't take it that way. I wanted Gústi to like me for myself, not because I reminded him of Stína.

His face grew serious. 'Marsí, I'm worried about you. Those letters you've been getting … I've been thinking and I reckon we should talk to the police. If it's the same man who took Stína…'

He didn't need to finish the sentence. It was a thought I kept trying to push away: if it was the same man as had taken Stína, I might be in danger myself. The crazy thing was that a tiny part of me actually wanted him to come for me. Because at least then I would finally get the answers I craved.

'I'll be careful,' I said.

Gústi nodded, clearly unconvinced. The thought that he cared about me made it hard for me to suppress a smile as we walked back to the house.

After he had gone home, though, I felt like a liar. I'd deliberately omitted to tell him what Málfríður had said about Stína rowing with Dad, though I didn't know why I wanted to keep that secret. It wasn't like Dad would have done anything to hurt Stína, yet I felt an instinctive need to protect him.

'When did Stína start going to evening classes at Reykir?' I asked Mum, when I was back inside.

She groaned in exasperation. 'Oh, Marsí, can't you let it go? Haven't we had enough? Didn't we just agree that you would leave it alone?'

'I just couldn't remember what she was doing there.'

'She was taking art classes or something,' Mum said.

I paused, staring at her.

'Did she and Dad quarrel shortly before she went missing?'

'*Marsí.*' Mum looked at me with a scandalised expression. 'What?'

'This really is the limit. You come here and start asking questions that…' She massaged her temples as though the mere thought had given her a headache, then announced that she was going for a rest.

Clearly, I wouldn't get any answers from Mum, but I might be able to get them from someone else.

It was late and the drive to Reykir would take a good forty minutes.

It was too late to set off now, but I could go early tomorrow morning. Not that I knew exactly what I intended to do when I got to the school or whether the same teachers would be working there ten years on, but I found it interesting that Mette had helped out there as a language assistant. The school was the only obvious link between Mette and Stína that I'd found.

Then there was Stína's project that Málfríður had mentioned. Perhaps I could find out more about that at the school as well.

There was Elvar, too, but I could go and see him any time, though I hadn't a clue what to ask him without sounding like I was accusing him of something.

Then again, I thought, I didn't really care how I sounded.

22
Kristín – *Winter 1966*

In addition to the drawings, photograph and brooch, the contents of the shoebox include several envelopes. Once I'm home, I open the envelopes and discover that they contain half-finished letters from the girl to her mother. Only a few lines, yet her desperation shines through them. *I feel I need to explain myself*, she writes, followed by broken-off sentences: *I woke up to find him… It wasn't supposed to happen, but…*

At the bottom she had written: *Dear Mama, I hope you can forgive me. I'll come back home and help you as soon as I can.*

She had never sent the letters.

What on earth had happened to her? What was she trying and failing to tell her mother?

I search and search again through the letters and drawings for clues to her identity, but I can't find anything. How am I supposed to trace the girl when I have nothing to go on but this?

I replace the lid of the shoebox and hide it at the bottom of my chest of drawers.

'Mum,' I ask the following day. 'Did you know that Reykir used to be a workhouse for delinquent girls?'

Mum is in the middle of hanging up the washing and is taking such a long time to peg out a sheet that I can't see her face.

'Mum?'

'What, Stína? Can't you see I'm busy?' She bends down and goes on hanging up the washing.

'But I—'

'Go and find your sister,' Mum interrupts. 'You two never do anything together these days. And I'm worried about Marsí. She's become so … withdrawn.'

Mum's right. I should probably be more concerned about my sister than a stranger who may not even be alive.

When I open the door to Marsí's room, she's sitting at her desk, writing. She jumps and covers the paper with her arm.

'What are you doing?' I ask.

'Nothing.'

'Are you hiding something?' It's meant as a joke, but Marsí reacts badly.

'Can't you just leave me alone?' she snaps.

This is unlike Marsí. She can be rude and stroppy, but never with me. We've always been friends, though lately I've been so preoccupied with my own problems that we've hardly spent any time together.

'Sorry, Marsí. I only meant to ask if you wanted to do something.'

'Do something?'

'Yes.' I smile. 'I was looking at the latest issue of *The Week* and there's a feature showing you how to do your make-up like Twiggy.'

'So?'

'Twiggy's only the most popular model in the world at the moment. I read it in *The Week*. She's only seventeen but apparently she earns fifty thousand krónur a week! Can you beat that?' I put my hands together imploringly. 'Please, please, let me do your make-up…'

'OK,' Marsí says grudgingly. 'But don't go over the top. I look nothing like Twiggy.'

'I know, I know. Though I think it would suit you to thicken the lashes under your eyes,' I say. 'And you'd look good with short hair.'

'Forget it,' Marsí says, but she gets up anyway. I notice that she slips whatever she was writing into the drawer of her desk.

She follows me into my room and closes her eyes obediently while I apply the pale-blue shadow to her lids. When she opens them again, her dark eyes are illuminated.

'Perfect!' I exclaim.

Marsí examines herself in the mirror. 'I look like a clown.'

'No, you don't.' I'm a little hurt, as in my opinion I've done a beautiful job. Pretending not to mind, I ask casually: 'By the way, what were you up to in your room? Are you writing something?'

Marsí sighs. 'Do you have to stick your nose into everything?'

'What?'

'You just … you don't always have to know everything.'

'I was only asking.'

Marsí examines herself in the mirror again, then says: 'I look ridiculous. I'm going to wash it off.'

I tell Marsí to do as she likes, and start tidying away my make-up.

At school, Guðrún is a chastened figure these days. She's begged Málfríður over and over again to forgive her, but Málfríður won't listen to any excuses, so Guðrún has found herself a new group to hang around with. I still catch her stealing glances at us, though.

'How could I have been so stupid?' Guðrún says after school, hiding her face in her hands.

'You didn't do anything wrong,' I assure her.

'I shouldn't have said anything.'

'You only told the truth.'

'Did I? I'm not sure Málfríður spiked her drink. Why on earth did I have to give them that impression?'

I, on the other hand, am fairly confident that Málfríður *did* spike Solla's drink, though I don't say this to Guðrún. 'It'll be all right,' I comfort her instead. 'She just needs a little time.'

'I suppose so,' Guðrún says.

'It'll be all right,' I repeat, hoping I sound convincing.

Guðrún looks at me for a moment. 'You seem tired. Is everything OK?'

'Oh, yes,' I say. 'It's just been difficult to get any sleep lately.'

Guðrún immediately guesses what I'm referring to, as she's the only person I've confided in.

'What does she actually get up to in the night?' Guðrún asks.

'It depends,' I say. 'Mostly nothing in particular. She just wanders around. But sometimes she goes outside. Dad's terrified she'll hurt herself. And sometimes I wake up to find her in my room.'

'Doing what?' Guðrún gasps.

'It depends. Usually she just stands there.'

'Can't you tell her to go away?'

'Dad doesn't want us to wake her,' I say, without elaborating.

'What does she say about it the next morning?' Guðrún asks. 'She must be terribly embarrassed.'

I pick at my thumbnail for a moment. Then decide to tell the truth: 'She doesn't know she does it. The next day she wakes up and it's like nothing has happened.'

23
Marsibil – *Tuesday, 22 November 1977*

I didn't sleep a wink last night and couldn't drag myself out of bed until late this morning. When I finally got up, I drove into town and parked in front of the church.

It was small and pretty, with white walls and a red roof, built at the beginning of the century. Elvar worked there with his father, and although I was interested in talking to both men, I wanted to catch them separately, so I waited outside.

It was pouring with rain. The drops rattled on the windscreen and no other sound could be heard over the monotonous drumming. The effect was oddly soothing, drowning out my thoughts. I closed my eyes, just for a moment, to rest them from the dry stinging that only seemed to get worse with every day that passed. One sleepless night was all right, but recently I had reached a whole new level of tiredness; tiredness that had become such an indelible part of me that I felt, if I didn't stay alert, my body might simply give up the struggle and conk out.

The shrill jangling of a bell shocked me awake. I flicked my eyes open with a gasp. I looked at my watch: half an hour had passed without my noticing. I cursed my stupidity. Elvar could have left for all I knew. Just as I was wondering if I should stay or go, I saw a man come out of the church and lock the door behind him. He put up his hood, stuck his hands in his pockets and set off down the street.

I waited until he was a discreet distance away, then turned the key in the ignition and followed him to his house.

I had remembered Elvar being handsome, but when he answered the door I was knocked sideways by his beauty. His features were both delicate and clear-cut: straight nose, angular jaw, yet soft lips. His dark eyes turned down in an unusual way and his chocolate-brown hair was thick, wavy and slightly damp from the rain.

'Hi,' I said breathlessly.

'Hi.' He waited, his eyebrows raised enquiringly. 'Are you looking for someone?'

I swallowed, then managed to introduce myself.

'Marsibil, of course,' he said. 'Stína's sister. I should have realised, but I don't think we've ever been formally introduced, have we?'

'No, probably not.' Stína had kept her boyfriend away from me, Mum and Dad the whole time they were together. We'd only found out they were dating after she vanished.

After that, there was another awkward silence before I was able to blurt out why I was there.

Elvar raised his eyebrows in surprise but he invited me in. I had got drenched during the short walk from the car to the house as my jacket wasn't waterproof. I took it off in the hall, only to regret it as my wet T-shirt clung to my skin, making me shiver. We sat down at the kitchen table, on chilly plastic chairs, and it was an effort to stop my teeth from chattering.

'I saw the article the other day. The one about her disappearance.'

Elvar's voice had a bright, pure quality, as if it had barely changed since he was in his teens.

'They regularly rake it up,' I said.

'That must be tough.' He looked at me and I experienced an almost uncontrollable impulse to confide in him. Elvar would make a good vicar. For a moment there I had nearly forgotten that he might be the person who had taken Stína.

'Yes.' I shrugged. 'I suppose.'

He nodded and I felt he understood me.

'I think about her often.'

'Do you?'

'We only knew each other a short time but she made a big impression on me.'

'What kind of impression?'

Elvar thought about this for a few moments. 'I'd never been in love before I met Stína. She was my first heartbreak, if I can put it like that.'

I pushed away a feeling that was almost of envy. If a boy like Elvar had wanted me when I was in my teens, I'd never have messed around with letters, never have become obsessed with the attention I was getting from my penpal, or planned to risk meeting up with a stranger.

'Heartbreak?' I shook off my regrets and sat up a little straighter. 'I thought *you* broke up with her.'

'Me? No, quite the reverse: it was Stína who chose to end things.'

'Why?' I asked, thinking back over what Málfríður had said. She'd made it sound as if Elvar wasn't serious about Stína.

'She didn't give any reason.'

'How long were you together?'

'Nearly a year.' Elvar smiled. 'Quite a long time at that age.'

It certainly was. Yet in all those months Stína had never once mentioned him to me.

'She often talked about you,' Elvar added, when I had been silent for an unnaturally long time.

'She did?'

'She was worried about you.'

'About me?' I echoed. 'Why?'

'Because of the goings-on at night.'

If Stína had confided in him about Mum's sleepwalking, they must have been close. I was overtaken by a sudden fit of shivering and hugged myself in an attempt to stop it.

'There was no need,' I said. 'Stína didn't have to worry about me.'

'All the same, she did. That's what comes of being an older sibling, I suppose. I got the impression Stína felt a strong sense of responsibility where you were concerned. She felt she had to look after you.'

I let out an explosive laugh that sounded like a hiccup, and felt myself blushing. 'She didn't need to,' I muttered. Then I drew myself up again. 'Were you angry when she broke up with you?'

'Not angry, just very upset. I shut myself in my room for days and wouldn't talk to anyone.'

'What was it like having to see her again when she came round to visit your sister that evening?'

'Difficult. I can't deny it.' Elvar's gaze had become evasive and wary, I thought. He seemed to have a ready answer to any question I could throw at him.

'Did you notice when she left?' I asked.

'Yes, and I was convinced she'd left because of me. So I went into my room to listen to music.'

'Alone?'

He nodded. 'Marsí,' he said, although I had introduced myself as Marsibil. 'I didn't do anything to her, if that's what you think.'

Our eyes met and we held each other's gaze. My T-shirt was still stuck to my skin but I was no longer shivering.

'You're like her, did you know that?' Elvar smiled. 'There's a look of her about your mouth. The same ... lips.'

I felt suddenly short of breath and experienced a heady, floating sensation, but at that moment the door opened and a child's high voice called from the hall.

'Hello, I'm home.'

'I'm in here,' Elvar said, without taking his eyes off me.

A few seconds later a small girl appeared in the doorway. She was no more than seven years old. Her cheeks were ruddy from the cold rain and her wet hair hung down in rats' tails.

'Who's that, Daddy?' she asked, staring at me.

'My friend Marsibil.'

I smiled at the little girl, who looked back at me doubtfully.

'Go and get yourself dry, Stína,' Elvar said. 'I'm going to show Marsibil out.'

I almost buckled at the knees as I stood up. I was sure I must have misheard. The girl couldn't really be called Stína.

'We lost my daughter's mother to illness three years ago, so it's just the two of us now,' Elvar explained.

'Is her name…?'

'Yes, she's called Kristín, like your sister,' Elvar said. Then, seeing my face, he added: 'After my late wife's mother, though I have to admit I've always been rather fond of the name. Just as I was fond of Stína, Marsí. That hasn't changed.'

I thanked him and hurried out of the door, still a little weak at the knees.

At home, Mum was still asleep and Dad was out. I poured myself a glass of rum and took it into the sitting room. I drank until I was feeling fairly cheerful, then got into the bath and thought about Elvar's soft lips.

A bell was ringing insistently somewhere nearby.

I awoke to a banging on the door. Dad was shouting, and the door was shaking under his hammering, as if he was beginning to despair. 'Marsí, are you in there?'

'Coming.' My voice was hoarse, my mouth parched.

The bathwater had gone cold again, I was shivering and my eyes ached so much that I switched the light off. I went out wrapped in a towel, and came face to face with Dad.

'Are you all right?' he asked.

I shrugged. 'I'm fine.'

'You didn't answer when I knocked. I thought something had happened.'

'I was just tired. I must have fallen asleep.' My hair was soaking and the water was dripping on to the floor, forming a small puddle at my feet.

'But I was knocking for several minutes. What on earth's going on, Marsí?'

Something in Dad's eyes – a spark of fear – made me suddenly sure that he didn't want to hear the answer to this question. He wanted me to say everything was fine, that *I* was fine. He wanted me to go back to Reykjavík and leave him and Mum in peace.

I cleared my throat. 'What were you and Stína quarrelling about shortly before she went missing?'

'Marsí,' Dad said, after a moment's shocked silence. 'You've got to stop this.'

'Why?'

'Your mother will only get worse if you persist in going on like this.' I'd seldom seen Dad so stern. 'Why can't you just…'

'Why don't you two want me to look for her?'

'Don't do this.' Dad heaved a deep breath. 'You've got to … got to stop.'

'Anyone would think you both had something to hide,' I mumbled.

'What did you say?'

'Nothing.' I hurried to my room before he could ask any more questions, and got into bed, still shivering, and pulled the duvet over my head.

Why did I suddenly get the feeling my parents were concealing something from me? The idea only increased my curiosity about the nature of Dad and Stína's quarrel. Was it actually conceivable that my sister could have staged her own disappearance, leaving her anorak as a decoy, as Málfríður had suggested? Could she be alive somewhere, all these years later?

Part of me was happy at the idea, but my strongest emotion was anger. I wasn't sure I would ever be able to forgive her if she did turn out to be alive.

Not long afterwards I drifted off to sleep. For once, I dreamt about Dad. Dreamt he came and sat on my bed, stroked my cheek and gazed at me with staring, deep-set eyes, but every time he opened his mouth to speak, I heard the croaking of a raven.

24
Kristín – *Winter 1967*

I'm at the library, taking out a thick volume on the Second World War, when I bump into my art teacher, Halldóra. On the spur of the moment, I decide to ask if she knows anything else about the girls' workhouse that was once run in the Old Doctor's House.

She tells me she only knows a little about it but is happy to share what she recalls. 'Reykir was set up for girls who had been caught fraternising with soldiers from the occupation force,' she explains, as I walk beside her back to her classroom. 'Mainly teenage girls from Reykjavík who had slept with British or American soldiers. They were sent here to work, in the same way that juvenile delinquents are sent to work in the countryside nowadays.' Halldóra smiles and shakes her head. 'As if the countryside and a bit of fresh air could solve all the world's problems.'

'What work were they expected to do?'

'This and that. Household chores, probably, and various kinds of handiwork like sewing. But why are you asking? Where does this interest come from?'

'When I was going to evening classes at Reykir, I came across something I think must have belonged to one of the girls who'd been staying there. Nothing very exciting, just a few pictures and letters. But I'd like to return them to her.'

'You should talk to Jón. He's a historian. In fact, he was one of the people involved in setting up the workhouse.'

'Where does this Jón live?'

Halldóra gives me directions and I decide to go and see him as soon as I've finished school this afternoon.

Jón's house looks new, which is unusual in this town. It was built a few years ago and at the time I remember Dad saying that a man from the city was building it for himself and his family.

The moment the door opens, my heart sinks. It's the woman I met in the headmaster's study back in the autumn – Solla's mother. She glares at me and I'm struck dumb by the realisation.

'Who is it?' I hear a voice calling from inside the house, and my fear intensifies. I don't want to face Solla's father again, but next minute he's there in the doorway, as massive and powerful as I remembered.

Somehow I manage to stammer out my reason for being there: that I was wondering if he could tell me something about the workhouse run at Reykir during the war because I've found something that belonged to one of the girls and would like to return it to her. Did he know anyone who could help me?

'Why should I help you?' he asks.

I begin to back away from the door. My cheeks are hot and I keep having to blink back tears. Then I turn and start walking rapidly away from the house. He calls after me – some name or other that I'm too panicked to take in. As soon as I reach the pavement, I break into a run.

My heart is beating so fast that I don't notice the car beside me until I hear Gústi's voice.

'Stína, is everything OK?' he calls out of the window.

I stop, trying to pretend everything is all right, though a moment ago I was running as if my life depended on it and I can't stop panting. 'Yes, I just … I'm in a hurry.'

'Want a lift?'

I don't reply, but after a moment I get in the car beside Gústi, doing my best to get my breathing under control.

'Where were you going?'

I hesitate. I can't tell him I was on my way home because I was running in the opposite direction, so I answer that I'm going to the egg farm.

'Were you planning to run all the way?' Gústi asks, surprised.

I shrug. 'It's not that far,' I mutter, but I can feel my cheeks burning and, from his puzzled frown, Gústi obviously doesn't believe me. He doesn't ask any more questions, though.

By the time we reach the egg farm, my heart is beating normally again. I thank Gústi, tell him there's no need to wait, and go in search of Dad.

At first it appears no one's there, which is unusual. As a rule, there are always some members of staff around, as if the chickens were babies that required constant care. The employees are probably on their lunch or smoking break. I open the door of the laying shed to be greeted by the powerful reek and deafening squawking of thousands of chickens. The air is full of a fine dust that irritates the throat and eyes if you spend too long in there. Dad is nowhere to be seen.

I stare at the wretched hens in their cages, packed so tight they can barely move. In one of the cages, they're pecking at something on the floor. When I step closer, I see that one of the hens is lying down, apparently dead. Then I notice her eyes flickering and realise she's not dead, only injured. Yet the other hens have already begun to eat her alive.

'I'll deal with that.'

I jump at the sound of Guðrún's voice. 'Guðrún, what are you doing here?'

'I came with Mum,' she says, reaching into the cage to lift out the injured hen. Then, with a quick, practised movement, she wrings the poor creature's neck. There's a faint snapping of tiny bones, then it's over.

'Couldn't she have been saved?' I ask, though I know it was the only thing to do in the circumstances. Suffering animals should be put out of their misery; anything else would be inhumane. And anyway, these chickens don't get to live that long before they are sent to the slaughterhouse.

'She never stood a chance,' Guðrún says, beckoning me to come outside, where she puts the hen in a sack, then washes her hands in a big steel sink.

Guðrún's mother works for Fjarðaregg, and Guðrún often spends time here with her. Alda takes care of the accounts, and Dad says that without her the business would have gone under long ago. When Guðrún has finished washing her hands, she tells me to come with her to the little kitchen at the back, where she hands me a glass of water. I drink it down, then try unsuccessfully to smother a yawn.

'Did you sleep badly?' Guðrún asks.

'Yes.' I've told her what's going on at home, so I don't need to explain the reason for my disturbed night.

'Can nothing be done? Like taking her to a doctor or something?'

'No,' I say. 'We just … we don't discuss it in the daytime. Just act like nothing's happened.'

Guðrún is regarding me sympathetically but I know she doesn't understand. I don't understand it myself. Don't understand why we can't all just sit down together and thrash out the problem. I've hardly had an uninterrupted night's sleep for weeks now.

After a little while, I say: 'I'm going to find Dad.'

'He's not here, I don't think,' Guðrún says.

'Yes, he is, I saw his car.' I glance out of the window to make sure. Yes, it's there in the car park, as I'd thought.

'But he … I think he's busy.'

'Which is it?' I ask, raising my eyebrows. 'Is he busy or isn't he here?' She doesn't reply, so I turn to go. 'See you later, Guðrún.'

Guðrún touches my arm and opens her mouth, but no words come out.

'Is everything OK?' I ask. 'Did you want to tell me something?'

She turns crimson and nods. 'It's just such a long time since we've had a proper chat.'

'What do you mean? We're always chatting. I only want a quick word with Dad, then I'll come back. Maybe we can do something together, OK?'

I leave the kitchen and head in the direction of Dad's office, and I find that Guðrún is following me. I turn. 'What is it? Did you want something else?'

'No, but your father asked me to make sure no one disturbed him.'

'I'm not going to disturb him; I just want a quick word.' I laugh. 'You needn't be afraid of my dad, Guðrún. If he's annoyed, I'll tell him you tried to stop me.'

When I reach his office door I open it cautiously, in case he's on the phone or in a meeting.

I stiffen when I see them. My father has his arms round Alda, and they're so preoccupied they don't even notice me. Their embrace looks tight and intimate – too intimate.

I close the door at once and stand there, rooted to the spot. There's a loud buzzing in my ears and my heart is racing.

'What...?' Guðrún says behind me. 'What did you see?'

I turn slowly and stare at her.

It's then that the truth sinks in: this is why my father is always at work. This is why he's out every evening.

The red flush has drained from Guðrún's face, leaving her cheeks grey.

'You knew,' I say, suddenly realising. 'That's why you didn't want me to go in there.'

'No, I...' Tears spring into Guðrún's eyes but she can't lie. She's never been a good liar. She knew exactly what my father was doing in there.

She's known about it all this time and kept it secret from me.

25
Marsibil – *Wednesday, 23 November 1977*

The school at Reykir was relatively new, built in the early 1960s for children aged seven to twelve. Its creation had the knock-on effect of undermining attendance at our school in Síða, as kids living in the countryside around Reykir started going there instead.

The clouds of steam rising from the ground here and there – the 'smoke' from which 'Reykir' took its name – were even more conspicuous in the cold. The land the school was built on was very geothermally active; the famous hot spring at Deildartunguhver was practically in the schoolyard, and this natural hot water was used to heat a number of greenhouses, where my family used to go at weekends to buy fruit and vegetables.

Beside the schoolhouse there was a massive new structure covered in scaffolding. I remembered hearing something about fundraising for a gymnasium: clearly, it had been successful. A crowd of kids were kicking a ball around the playground, most of them lightly dressed in spite of the cold.

Hugging my coat around me, I surveyed the various buildings that were dotted about the grounds according to no obvious plan. One stood out from the rest, as it was clearly older, with a pronounced gable, and stood several storeys high, including two under the eaves and a basement below ground level. The Old Doctor's House had, as the name implied, once been a doctor's surgery but now contained classrooms and offices.

Inside I was met by a strong smell of meatballs and boiled potatoes, and an apron-clad woman with greying hair, mopping the floor.

'Excuse me, is the school secretary around?'

'No,' the cleaner replied and sniffed. 'What do you want her for?'

'I'm trying to find information about people who attended some evening classes that were held here ten years ago,' I explained.

'Evening classes,' she repeated. Close up, I couldn't help noticing the long dark hairs on her upper lip.

'Or if there's anyone else I could talk to…'

'I think Sigga used to teach evening classes.'

'Is she around?'

'Sigga Steindórs. I saw her just now,' the woman said, gesturing towards the canteen.

There were no pupils about, just a few members of staff having their lunch. After I had stood there for a while, trying to work out which of the three women could be Sigga Steindórs, one of them looked up and asked what I wanted. When I said Sigga's name, a grave-faced woman in her fifties said: 'That's me.' I noticed that she had mixed together peas, potatoes and gravy in a dog's dinner on her plate.

'Who did you say you were?' she asked, wiping her mouth with a paper napkin.

'Marsibil. My sister attended evening classes here ten years ago. I don't know if you're aware, but…' I coughed. 'She went missing a short time afterwards.'

'I remember your sister.' The woman got up and beckoned me to accompany her into the kitchen, where she put her plate in a pile and poured herself a coffee. She offered me a cup too, and suggested we sit down to talk in the canteen.

We took our cups to a table at a discreet distance from her colleagues, and she gave me a small smile as we sat down.

'What can I help you with, Marsibil?'

'I'm looking for my sister. I mean, I'm not actually looking for her, but doing a bit of a private investigation into what happened to her. Or what could have happened.' Despite my attempts to rehearse it on the way here, my explanation had come out all wrong.

'I see,' Sigga said. 'Stína was studying art, if I remember. It was a fairly new addition to our evening courses at the time, and most of the other students were much older than her. But I gather Stína was very promising. Reykholt School offered only limited art classes, which was why Halldóra, the art teacher there at the time, was keen for your sister to be accepted here. If it was like any of our other courses, it would have been held twice a week for twelve weeks. I think it was well attended, by local standards. People came here from all over the surrounding countryside, if memory serves.'

'Do you know if Stína was working on a project connected to the school?'

'A project? No, I'm afraid I couldn't tell you that,' Sigga replied. 'The young man who was teaching the course would know, I suppose, but I'm afraid I can't remember his name. You could ask Halldóra. She's bound to remember him. And might know about a project.'

'Actually, I don't think Stína's project was about art; I think it related to the building itself.'

'Which building?'

'This one. The Old Doctor's House.'

'Oh. No, I know nothing about that,' Sigga said. 'Perhaps they were supposed to paint a picture of the house or something. Talk to Halldóra. I believe she's still teaching at Síða School.'

It was so cold when I went back outside that the steam rising from the ground had thickened into a mist that spread out over the landscape, wreathing it in an eerie whiteness. I was momentarily distracted by the phenomenon, reflecting on how different a world this was from the tame environs of the city. I had grown up with the sense that the earth under my feet was alive. That the landscape all around me was thrumming with energy. Jets of steam shooting up from hot springs, icy waterfalls roaring down from mountainsides and lava fields. Every time I left the house as a child I was told to beware of nature, of the rocks, rivers and hot springs. The idea that the land could snatch me away was still vivid in my mind, particularly when I returned to the countryside from Reykjavík. And the fear wasn't unfounded. There were endless stories of children who had fallen into mountain torrents or scalding springs. Of people who went out and were never seen again, like Stína. If it hadn't been for her bloodstained anorak, it would have been very easy to blame nature for her disappearance. It would have been almost commonplace. Tragic but not unexpected, since everyone knew how cruel Iceland's landscape could be. It was so much worse to think that the cruelty could lie in ourselves, in our fellow men.

As I drove home, I wrenched my thoughts away from the elements and back to the job in hand, trying to plot my next steps. But I kept being distracted by the thought of a drink. The problem was that restaurants didn't serve alcohol on Wednesdays and I had no desire to drink alone at home. Being at home sent my thoughts off at strange tangents, gave me bizarre dreams and seemed to make time slip through my grasp.

Halldóra might be able to tell me more about Stína's interest in the Old Doctor's House, but school was over for the day, so it would probably be better to talk to her tomorrow. I resolved to stop off at Café Hvítá and drink something soft.

I was served by Sunny Solla again.

'Chips,' I said. 'And Coke.'

She brought my order promptly and slammed it down on the table without a word.

Just as I was tucking into a mouthful of chips, someone appeared next to my table. I looked up to see the journalist, standing there with an ironic smile on his face.

I took a swig of Coke. 'Anyone would think you're following me,' I said, looking down at my plate.

He laughed so loudly that the men at the next table glanced round.

'No, Marsíbil, I'm not following you.' And without asking if I minded, he pulled out a chair and sat down at my table. He even took the liberty of stealing one of my chips.

Although I pretended to have no time to talk to him, in truth I was grateful for the company. I was tired and bored. But above all I wanted to take a risk. I didn't trust him, but perhaps spending some time in his company would be a quicker way to find out the truth than trying slowly and painstakingly to piece together the information I had gleaned so far. In addition, it was a novelty for me to inspire someone's interest to this degree and, despite my doubts about him, I was conscious of a growing desire to please him. It was similar to the feeling I got whenever someone found out who my sister was and I was briefly the centre of attention. A situation I both revelled in and couldn't bear.

'What do you want, then?' I asked. 'What are you planning to write about in this article of yours?'

'Tell me about your family,' he replied, stealing another of my chips.

'What do you want to know about them?'

'Where are your parents from?'

'Dad's from here. His name's Karvel. His parents started the egg farm and he expanded it and added a slaughterhouse. Today he's the biggest egg producer in the west of Iceland.'

'Oh, I'm well aware of that. Do you ever visit the farm?'

'Often,' I said.

'Why are you looking like that?'

I had shuddered without realising it. 'Because I don't like going there. It's just … I don't know how to explain but I've never been able to eat chicken. Seeing all the hens crowded together like that, then their carcases hanging from hooks in the building next door.'

'I understand. I worked in a fish factory as a teenager and couldn't eat fish the whole time I was there.' He shivered as well. 'Where's your mother from?'

'Reykjavík. From a poor family. I think she has brothers but we've never met them. Her mother died when she was quite young; she'd been ill a long time so Mum was forced to grow up fast. Her brothers were sent to a children's home but she was old enough by then that people didn't feel guilty about leaving her to fend for herself.'

'She became an actress, didn't she?'

'Mum was in the theatre for a while, yes. She acted in a few plays that made a splash. But her career was over almost before it began because she met Dad, got pregnant and moved out here.'

'And how did she feel about that – giving it all up?'

I shrugged. 'I reckon it must have been hard for her. She'd made quite a name for herself nationally. Enough to make me and my sister popular when we started school. At least for a while.'

'She was very glamorous…' He pinched another chip, and I pushed the plate over to him. Somehow I'd lost my appetite.

'She was…'

'What was your home life like? How did you and your sister get on?'

'Are you going to put any of this in your article?' I asked.

'Not if you don't want me to,' he said. 'I'm just trying to get a better picture of your family.'

'So you can write something sensational,' I said cynically. 'Hadn't I better tell you something sensational then, like that we were constantly quarrelling, that Mum and Dad were messing about with the occult or selling drugs from our house? Something to sell papers.

Something to give people the impression it was our fault Stína went missing. Because that's what they want to believe, isn't it?'

Showing no sign of being offended by my sarcastic tone, Einar wiped his mouth with a napkin and got to his feet. 'Come on,' he said, 'let's go for a walk. You can show me the best hiking trails around here.'

I looked out of the window. 'It's started raining.'

'I've got a bottle.' He grinned. 'And a drop of rain never hurt anyone, did it?'

I rolled my eyes but didn't need any more persuading.

Before leaving, I went to the ladies. And while I was in there, I spotted again the graffiti on the wall in the corner. *Stína lives.* I ran my fingers over Stína's name. Who had written that and why? Did people really believe she was still alive?

Einar and I walked briskly along the main street, not slowing until we had turned off it on to a rough track. If we continued in this direction, we'd soon reach the foot of the mountain, but we strolled along at a more leisurely pace now, passing the bottle back and forth. The egg farm was clearly visible from here, and I could almost hear the clucking and squawking of the hens. I realised I was knocking back the spirits far too hard but told myself that my normal rules about drinking didn't count here in the countryside. Here, merely existing was a strain; so, in the circumstances, I shouldn't place overly strict demands on myself.

'The egg farm and slaughterhouse are important businesses for the town, aren't they?' Einar remarked, his eyes on the farm buildings. 'How many people work there?'

'Not as many as you might think. Nearly thirty in total, I believe.'

'Which isn't that negligible in a community this small,' Einar pointed out.

'What are you insinuating?' I immediately wondered if he was implying that Dad might have been the person in authority who obstructed the investigation; as if the threat of losing jobs in the town could have had an influence on the outcome of the case.

'I'm not insinuating anything, Marsí. Only that thirty jobs is quite a lot in a town of only a thousand people.'

'I suppose so.'

'Did you ever work there yourself?'

'No, never.'

'But you'll inherit it, won't you? When the time comes.'

'I'd sell it.' We'd reached a small stream and I halted. Dusk was falling and it would soon be pitch-black out here. 'Is it true what you said about the police?' I asked. 'That they didn't carry out a proper investigation?'

Einar nodded and handed the bottle back to me. 'I've got a friend with contacts in the force. He heard it from the horse's mouth – the police here refused any assistance from Reykjavík.'

'Who would have been responsible for taking that decision?'

'The local inspector, presumably.'

I pictured Torfi. He'd always been a good mate of Dad's. They used to go hiking in the mountains together before Stína's disappearance. Once, when I was about six, he had bought me some barley sugars when we met by chance at the shop. I hid them from Stína because I didn't want to share them.

'What?' Einar asked, but I shook my head, so he continued: 'I'm not necessarily saying he had anything to do with your sister's disappearance, I'm just wondering what was behind the decision not to carry out a more rigorous investigation.'

'I presume you've been talking to plenty of people. You've been here a few days. What are they saying?' I asked.

Einar opened his mouth, then closed it again.

'What?' I asked. 'I just want to know the gossip…'

'Well…' He seemed to be thinking what to say. 'I gather your sister had been talking a lot about moving away. She wanted to study abroad, didn't she?'

I nodded, a little reluctantly. Stína had certainly talked about going away to art college. But my parents weren't keen on the idea and I had almost torn all my hair out at the thought of losing her. But then I recalled my conversation with Málfríður – she'd said Stína was desperate to get away from here.

'What of it?' I tried to affect a scoffing tone.

'If you want my theory, I believe there was an accident that evening that somebody wanted to cover up.'

'And you think a member of my family was responsible for that accident.'

'I didn't say that.' Einar took the bottle back from me. 'Where were you that evening?'

'I was at home with my parents.'

'Do you remember if they were both there the whole time?'

'Yes,' I lied.

Einar frowned. 'Because, according to the reports I've read, you were asleep that evening and your mother didn't remember anything either. She claimed she went to bed early.'

'What reports have you seen?'

'We journalists have our methods.'

'This is bullshit,' I said.

It was clear what Einar was implying; he didn't need to put it into words: he suspected my father. I held out my hand for the bottle and took a long swig.

'I want to go home,' I said, and Einar didn't object, just walked silently at my side back to town.

In the end, we got no further than the church. The rain had eased and a crowd was gathered outside. I was startled to see my parents among them. Excusing myself to Einar, I went over to join them.

'What's going on?' I asked.

'Mette's memorial service,' Mum whispered. 'I told you about it.'

She hadn't, but I knew better than to argue with her.

Clearly, I had missed the church service, but now there was to be a procession along the main street, following Mette's route, to light candles at the spot where she had been found. The vicar, Málfríður's father, was at the head of the procession. Elvar was assisting him. For a moment our eyes met and I thought he smiled.

Mum pointed out the couple from Gröf. The woman's face was puffy from weeping; her husband appeared to be trying to hold back his tears. The group moved off and I let myself be carried along with them.

When we reached our destination, candles were lit and lined up along the road. The flames flickered despite the windless air. I put my candle down beside all the rest and closed my eyes as the vicar recited a prayer, my thoughts dwelling not on Mette but on Stína. I felt I'd failed her all over again. I would never find her; I was too pathetic, too weak and muddled.

When I opened my eyes again, I noticed a couple I didn't recognise, leaning against each other. The woman was holding a large photo of a girl who must be Mette, and I realised this was the first time I'd seen what she looked like. She was pretty: brown hair, a beautiful smile, her face oddly familiar.

I was back in my car, just about to drive away, when Inspector Torfi tapped on the driver's window. I rolled it down hoping to goodness he wouldn't smell the alcohol on my breath.

'Marsibil. I need another word with you,' he said. 'Could you come by the police station tomorrow?'

'What for?'

'Just come by. It's only a minor matter.'

Realising he had no intention of telling me any more at present, I simply nodded.

'You should get a lift home with your parents,' he muttered in an undertone, before walking off.

Obediently, I got out again, put the car keys in my pocket and hurried after my parents, aware of Torfi's eyes following me.

They didn't question why I was coming with them rather than using my own car. Maybe they could smell the alcohol too. Maybe they didn't care.

I sat in the back and watched the dark countryside roll by, feeling like a little kid again, but without Stína at my side.

'Why didn't we move away?' I said quietly, and I wasn't sure whether I was asking myself or them.

'Where to?' Mum asked.

'Away from here.'

'Why should we have done that? We've got so much here, Marsí,' Dad said. 'The chickens. The farm. The house. You know I promised my parents I'd never sell it.'

I fell silent again. But Einar's words were still rolling around in my head. 'Why didn't a police forensics team come and search the house after Stína vanished?' I asked suddenly, thinking about the camera and the film that no one had thought to get developed.

'What do you mean?'

'No forensics team came round to examine the house. Why not?'

'Oh, Marsí,' Mum sighed.

'What are you trying to say, Marsibil?' Dad hardly ever called me Marsibil. Feeling like a naughty child, I lowered my eyes.

'I'm looking for Stína.'

'I want you to stop digging around,' he said sharply. 'Do you understand?'

'But I—'

'Promise me, Marsibil. Promise me you'll stop.' When I didn't answer, he thundered: 'Promise me!'

'I promise,' I said.

Dad's voice softened. 'Are you still seeing someone?'

'Like who?' I asked, though I knew perfectly well that he meant a therapist.

'I know you stopped going to see your therapist,' Dad said. 'I haven't been charged for any appointments for months now.'

'So what? I don't understand why I have to go.'

Dad didn't answer at first. Then he said in a low voice, sounding almost ashamed. 'You should go home, Marsí. Being here isn't doing you any good.'

'What do you mean?'

'It's not that I don't want you here. You just … you've started…' He couldn't bring himself to finish the sentence.

The anger was building up inside me. I could feel it.

'It's not making you happy, love, being here,' Mum chimed in.

'Why don't you two want me to look into it anymore?' I shot back. 'Why don't you want to find Stína?' I was choked with tears now, my words slurring. The alcohol had gone to my head and the walk had done nothing to sober me up.

When we got home, I went straight to my room. I expected to hear a knock at my door, but they didn't come after me and a little while later I heard the door of their bedroom closing.

26
Kristín – *Spring 1967*

'You've had a bit too much to drink, Stína,' Guðrún says. 'Shall I ask Gústi to give us a lift home?'

'Stop it, Guðrún.' Málfríður gives her a shove. 'Do you have to be such a bore all the time?'

I take another mouthful, just to be deliberately provocative. Guðrún and I haven't discussed what happened last week, and I haven't said a word to Dad either.

After all, what can I say?

I don't want Mum to know that Dad's cheating on her, because she wouldn't be able to bear it. Dad hasn't only betrayed Mum, he's betrayed me and Marsí too, but that's not the worst part. The worst part is that I don't want to lose him and I'm afraid of saying something that might prompt him to leave us; leave me and Marsí alone with Mum.

'Drink it.' Málfríður pushes the glass at Guðrún, who obeys, too afraid not to.

Málfríður hasn't mentioned the fact that Guðrún told tales about us, though the atmosphere between them is still strained. I'm forever putting out fires, but this time I almost want Málfríður to give Guðrún an earful because I'm too much of a coward to do it myself.

Desperate to please us, Guðrún takes a sip of whatever Málfríður hands her. She's begged me to forgive her a million times, but I've been ignoring her at school as far as possible. When she trails around after us, I no longer make any effort to include her in the conversation.

I've given up defending her. Given up putting out the fires.

Elvar has one arm around me and I drink whatever he passes me. I'm done with being careful and well behaved. I don't care that he's started coming on strong. Perhaps I'll go home with him this evening. Perhaps we won't even go home, just use one of the bedrooms in this house.

I no longer give a damn about what happens.

When I go to take another swig from the bottle, I discover that it's empty, so I head into the kitchen to fetch a new one. I have to force my way through a crowd of kids, some much older than us. I don't know when they arrived at the party.

In the kitchen some of the guests are sitting on the table, smoking. The air is so thick and grey that it's hard to make out their faces. I fill my glass, drink it down, then refill it twice.

'Stína.'

Gústi's face suddenly appears through the grey haze.

'What?'

'Would you like … Shall I give you a lift home?'

'No. Why?'

'You don't seem to be having much fun and…' He hesitates. 'And you seem quite drunk.'

I force myself to smile. 'I'm having a fantastic time, actually. So what if I'm drunk?'

I don't give Gústi a chance to reply but walk out with two full glasses and resume my place beside Elvar.

'Cheers,' I say, handing Guðrún one of the glasses. 'To friendship.'

'What's this?' she asks.

'Just drink it,' I say.

She raises the glass reluctantly to her lips and grimaces, but she obeys.

I lean back my head, close my eyes and let the alcohol slide down my throat. I don't get up until Málfríður hauls me to my feet because there's a good song playing and she wants us to dance. Then Elvar's there. He grabs me, thrusts me against him and kisses me in front of everyone. I don't care, I tell myself, and when the song's over, I take his hand.

'Come on,' I say, and pull him into the nearest bedroom.

Once upon a time I thought I'd lose my virginity to my husband and that it would be a magical experience. Guðrún and I used to talk about saving ourselves for Mr Right.

Elvar isn't Mr Right, but he's there. Too tired to think straight, I go through the motions, taking my clothes off, kissing him, not really understanding what I'm doing.

Even so, he stops at the last minute. 'Are you sure?' he asks.

I don't answer, just pull him closer and shut my eyes.

It's getting light again when I stir. I start pulling on my clothes. Elvar is lying beside me. I give him a push.

The guests have thinned out now; there are only a few older boys left. It's way past going-home time and I'm surprised no one has come to fetch us. There's no sign of Málfríður, but Guðrún is asleep on one of the sofas.

'Don't you want to wake your friend up?' Elvar asks.

I stand there for a few moments, looking down at her.

Guðrún doesn't usually drink much. Last night was probably the first time she's ever got properly legless. She's a sorry sight, lying there on the sofa with her top all stretched out and a stain on the front where she's spilt something.

For a second or two I feel sorry for her, then I remember what she was hiding from me and my heart hardens.

'No,' I say, shaking my head. 'Let's just go.'

'Are you sure?'

'Quite sure.'

27
Marsibil – *Thursday, 24 November 1977*

I left home early next morning, deciding that nine was a reasonable time for me to turn up at the police station.

'Marsibil, good morning,' Torfi said, far too cheerfully in the circumstances.

We went into his office, where he picked up a bowl containing squares of chocolate filled with raisins, and offered me some. I shook my head and watched as he ate a piece.

'Right,' he said, sucking the chocolate. 'How are you?'

'Fine.'

'Good. I see you've decided to stay on in town for longer than originally planned?'

'I'm going home after the weekend.'

'Ah. Do you have a job in Reykjavík?'

I said yes, but didn't elaborate, keen not to prolong the conversation. I had no interest in sitting here, making small talk with Torfi over a bowl of chocolate. There had to be another reason for my presence here.

'I expect you're wondering why I asked you to come in,' Torfi said, seeming to read my mind. 'The thing is, we've received the report from Reykjavík – the report on Mette, that is. They haven't done a post-mortem, but the doctor there says he can see signs of pressure marks on her throat.'

I could feel myself going cold all over.

'You were at the bar that evening. A note with your name on it was found on her body. And now it appears that she was strangled that night.'

Facts, rather than questions, yet it seemed that Torfi wanted an answer from me.

'I didn't know her.'

'I am aware of that. And yet there's this connection. Have you no idea who the note could be from?'

'No. I haven't a clue.'

But I could tell that Torfi didn't believe me.

'Did you see her in the bar that evening?'

'You've already asked me that. I don't even know what she looked like. I never met her.'

Torfi brought out a photograph and placed it on the table. 'This is her. This is Mette.'

I stared at the girl from the photo I'd seen the previous night. I had a better look at her this time. Her hair was reddish rather than dark, as I had thought when I'd seen the picture the unknown woman had been carrying at the procession. Then it dawned on me – I now knew where I recognised her from.

'No,' I lied. 'I've never seen her before.'

Torfi grunted and took the picture back, giving me a hard stare. Again, I could tell that he didn't believe me, and this time his instincts were correct: I had seen her before. She was the girl who had been talking to Gústi at the bar that night.

Halldóra was in the middle of teaching an art lesson when I arrived, so I sat down on a chair outside in the corridor and waited. Since I'd been at school here, they had added a new wing to the building, in a burst of optimism after the population of the town had increased for several years in a row. Those responsible for the extension couldn't have known that things would only go downhill after that.

As the kids started to stream out of the room, I knocked and went in. Halldóra didn't look up from the canvas she was working on, so for a while I just stood there and watched. She had short dark hair and long slim fingers, stained a patchwork of colours, though principally black. Her shirt was flamboyant and so were the large gold hoops in her ears. Halldóra had taken a special interest in me when I'd first had art lessons with her, no doubt assuming I'd demonstrate the same flair as Stína, but the scales had soon fallen from her eyes.

'Yes?' she said, without taking her eyes off her painting.

I said hello, then trotted out the usual introduction: that I was Marsibil, Stína's sister, and could we have a word.

A few seconds passed before she looked up. I detected a faint smile on her face. 'What can I do for you, Marsibil?'

'Well, it was about the evening classes Stína was taking at Reykir.'

'What about them?'

'I heard that Stína had become interested in the Old Doctor's House, where the course was held. That she'd been doing some kind of project related to the house. Do you remember who taught the classes at the time?'

'Yes, that would have been Ívar, who came up from Reykjavík to teach them. But I can tell you about Stína's interest in the house, if you like. I remember that she came to see me, asking questions about it.'

I felt a little rush of anticipation. A small step forwards. 'Yes, please. That would be great.'

'Well, I don't know if she was working on a project in a formal way, but you know the Doctor's House was once used as a reform school for young girls who'd been fraternising with soldiers?' I nodded. 'Well, I think I'm right in saying that about fourteen or fifteen girls were accommodated there for nearly a year. To be honest, in practice, it was a sort of workhouse. Stína became interested in it because she'd found something she believed once belonged to one of those girls. She was hoping to return it to her.'

Moving closer, I put my fingers on the edge of her desk. 'Do you have any idea what it was?'

'Pictures and letters, I think she said. I suggested she talk to Jón Ingi, the historian who wrote all those books about the Second World War. He was involved in setting up the workhouse at the time.'

'Do you know if she spoke to him?'

'I'm afraid I don't. That's all I can tell you about it.'

She stood up and I thought it was my sign to leave. So I thanked her and was turning to go, but Halldóra stopped me.

'Wait there a minute. I have something you might like to take with you.'

I frowned, unsure what she meant.

'It's a painting Stína did during her evening classes. Ívar gave it to me. I've always meant to pass it on to your family. But, well, I'm terribly ashamed to admit it, but I never got round to it after … after what happened, you know.'

She disappeared into a back room and re-emerged with a canvas.

'Your sister had genuine talent,' Halldóra said, a note of regret in her voice. 'It's such a pity we never got to see how it would have developed.'

I nodded but all my attention was fixed on the painting. It showed a girl standing in a garden, possibly our garden, with a faraway look in her eyes, almost as if she wasn't really present. The whole picture was painted in dark shades and the long, thin poplars seemed to be bending over the girl.

'That's you, isn't it?' Halldóra said. 'Stína's captured you pretty well. But then she was very good at faces and expressions. I always had the feeling that this was so much more than a painting, as if Stína was telling a story with it.'

I took the canvas, too shaken to utter a word.

'But I can never work out what the story is,' Halldóra continued. 'I suppose that's the beauty of the work. That we can all put our own interpretation on it.'

28
Kristín – *Summer 1967*

Some secrets consume you from within. They gnaw away at your stomach until you twist and writhe, then crawl up into your head, where they eat up all your happiness and enjoyment of life.

'Do you remember when we used to play the cloud game?' I say one day towards the end of the summer.

Marsí and I are in the garden because Mum asked us to weed the flowerbeds, but, instead of working, I'm lying on my back, gazing up at the sky. The clouds scud by, in all their multitude of forms. I used to be able to see castles, faces and animals in them, but now all I can see are fluffy white puffs of vapour.

My imagination has deserted me.

I don't feel myself anymore. I haven't drawn anything all summer or made any attempt to trace the girl, as I'd promised Ívar I would. Instead, I've spent the holidays with Málfríður, Elvar and a bunch of other kids, most of them older than me. Guðrún went away for the summer, and during her absence my resentment towards her has faded, while my anger with Dad has festered and grown. I can hardly bear to look at him, hardly bear to be in the same house as him. But the worst part is seeing Mum, who has been unusually jolly this summer, as if she can sense the tension in the household and is constantly trying to cheer us up.

'I remember,' Marsí says, pulling up chickweed.

She's been standoffish and uninterested whenever I've spoken to her recently. I've tried to chat to her but she rebuffs all my efforts, answering in monosyllables and asking no questions in return.

'How are you getting on, Pipsqueak?'

The sound of Dad's voice shocks me upright. At the sight of me, he stops dead.

'Are you here too, Stína? I didn't see you.'

I don't reply but our gazes lock until he lowers his.

Recently, Dad has been looking at me differently, studying me furtively when he thinks I don't notice, and there's something in his expression that makes me uneasy. Although I haven't said a word, I'm guessing he suspects that I know about his affair. His eyes betray guilt but also uncertainty, as if he can't gauge how much I know.

I lie down again and watch a raven floating overhead, a black dot against the white sky, as Dad's footsteps recede.

After a moment or two, Marsí leaps up and runs off.

Curious, I follow her at a distance, and round the corner of the house just in time to see her greeting the postman down by the mailbox. I pause, unobserved, and watch. She hurriedly flicks through the bundle of envelopes and newspapers, extracts one envelope and crams it in her pocket, then takes the rest of the post indoors.

I might not be able to solve all my own problems, but here at least is a possible explanation for Marsí's behaviour: she's got a secret too.

And her secret is sending her letters.

29

Marsibil – *Thursday, 24 November 1977*

Gústi was outside the Co-op when I emerged after buying myself a bottle of orange. Instead of going in himself, he strolled along the road with me, heading away from his car, and I gave him an update on my investigations, telling him what I knew about Stína's interest in the girls from Reykir. However, I kept to myself the knowledge that Mette had been strangled and that I had seen him talking to her at the bar that evening.

But all of a sudden my suspicions seemed petty. When I looked at Gústi, all I wanted was to be with him. I didn't want to say or do anything to jeopardise our friendship.

'Had you heard about those girls?' I asked. 'Did Stína discuss them with you?'

'No, though I was aware that they'd been there. My mother met one of them.' Gústi shoved his hands in the pockets of his jacket. It was freezing, the wind was bitter, and he only had a thin jacket on. 'Mum was from Ísafjörður, as you know. Her cousin married a woman from Reykjavík, and a few years later she confided in Mum that she'd done a stint at Reykir. According to her, it was a grim place.'

'Really?'

'Yes. Though the worst part was going home afterwards.'

I wrinkled my brow. 'She didn't want to go home?'

'No. Because of the shame. People judged them. The girls found the whole thing so humiliating.'

'But they were so young,' I said, finishing my orange.

'She begged Mum not to tell anyone. She was terrified someone in Ísafjörður would find out, and said she couldn't bear the thought. So Mum didn't say a word until years later, after the woman had died.' Gústi paused. 'She killed herself. Her name was Brynja. Mum said she'd never got over what happened.'

'Stína was going to see some historian called Jón to ask him about it.'

'Well, that's Jón Ingi, obviously.'

'Who's he?'

'The one who wrote all those books.'

'Oh, right,' I said, pretending to know what books he was referring to.

On the way home, my thoughts dwelt not on Jón Ingi but on the girls and the shame and humiliation they had felt. Shame that was so devastating, it caused a woman to take her own life many years later. I wondered what had happened to the other girls, whether they were still alive and what they now thought about their experience. Whether they all had a similar overpowering sense of shame.

And then the thought occurred to me that Stína might have come across something in her investigations that wouldn't stand the light of day. She was organised, unlike me, so it stood to reason that she must have made a note somewhere of the information she had gathered. But it wouldn't necessarily have occurred to anyone to connect it to her disappearance. If they had come across some notes about those girls, it would have looked like a school project, irrelevant to the investigation.

But it probably hadn't even crossed anyone's mind to go through Stína's school books.

Mum pulled up in the drive at the same time as I did. She had on her brown coat, the one with fur at the collar and cuffs, that made her look like a Russian aristocrat.

'Give me a hand, Marsí,' she said, opening the boot.

'Where have you been?'

'Out and about. I went to the shops to have a look at some fabric. I'm thinking of making new curtains. I haven't sewn anything for years, but I think it's time. Help me with this.'

I took a bag in each hand and Mum followed me, carrying two bolts of material, one green, the other cream with a green floral pattern.

'I was thinking of using the dark green in the bedrooms and the flowery one in the sitting room,' she said when we were inside. 'They're so stylish, don't you think? Awfully smart. Ólína told me the colour is all the rage these days.'

'It is very pretty.'

Mum grabbed my hand and pressed it to the fabric. 'Feel how soft it is. This is quality stuff, Marsí. It should be, considering how much it cost.'

'You two have decided to make some changes, then.'

'Oh, your father never wants to change anything, but it's high time we did.'

Mum was still stroking the material, running her fingers lightly up and down it. Then she went over to the window and held a length of it up, measuring it for size.

She seemed so relaxed, in such a good mood, I decided to probe her a little. 'Did you know that teenage girls from Reykjavík were once locked up in the Old Doctor's House at Reykir as a punishment for getting involved with soldiers?'

'I've heard about it.' Mum put the curtain material back on the table. 'Stick the bags in the kitchen, will you, love?'

I did as she asked. 'Do you know anyone who was there?' I continued as she came into the kitchen after me.

Mum opened the fridge and started unpacking the shopping bags with clumsy haste, banging the milk bottles down on the shelves. 'That was long before I moved here, Marsí.'

'Well, do you know anyone who could have been working there at the time? Apparently Stína was very interested in the subject.'

She slammed the fridge shut, suddenly exasperated. 'Oh, Marsí. Please leave it alone. I beg you. I understand that you want to know … but it does nothing but open old wounds.'

'I'll help,' I said, hurrying over and taking a jar of pickled gherkins out of the shopping bag just as Mum swung round. We collided and the jar fell on the floor and smashed. The liquid went everywhere, releasing a pungent stench of vinegar.

'Oh, *Marsí*.'

'Sorry, I…' I went to fetch a cloth, but Mum got there first, then she was down on her knees, scrubbing furiously at the floor.

'Marsí, why do you always have to … to ruin everything?' she muttered, so quietly I could hardly hear her.

'Sorry, I'll deal with the broken glass,' I said, but Mum struck my hand away and started grabbing recklessly at the pieces herself.

She gasped. A shard had cut deep into her palm and blood was running down her arm.

'I'm sorry, I'm sorry!' I blathered. 'Where are the plasters? Put it under the tap—'

'Oh, leave it, Marsí!' Mum chucked the pieces of glass in the bin, then carried on scrubbing at the floor as if nothing had happened.

A moment later she straightened up and wiped her forehead with the back of her hand, leaving a streak of blood there.

'How much longer are you planning to stay?' she asked.

'I'll leave on Monday.'

Mum seemed pleased to hear this and went back to wiping the floor with the cloth, which was now bright red.

It was the subject I'd raised that had caused Mum to do a 180° turn, from excitedly showing me the new curtain material to this. Perhaps she was right and it was a bad idea to rake up the whole Stína business. I was picking at old wounds and could feel my own pain and grief welling up again.

The trouble was that the wounds had never closed properly. For ten years they had continued to weep, and the only way I could see of healing them was to rip them open first, regardless of the pain.

Instead of going up to my bedroom, I went into Stína's room and closed the door quietly behind me. I wasn't afraid of Mum coming in. Even if she did, I had a perfect right to be in here, but I was sure the thought of a drink would hold more allure for her at this moment than another difficult conversation with me.

In her relationships with Stína and me, Mum had always gone out of her way to avoid anything difficult, any confrontations or rows. Every time she sensed the storm clouds gathering, she would grow short of breath, mutter something inaudible, and shut herself in the bathroom or her bedroom. She preferred to wallow in other families' dramas – they were at a safe distance from her own life, so she could be a spectator rather than a participant.

My mother wasn't just fragile; she had broken long ago, and I sometimes felt as if the pieces were strewn all over the house.

I heard the telltale clink of glass and the click of a record being put on the stereo in the sitting room. I remembered Mum dressing up in her old costumes from her theatre days, Dad at work, and Stína and me restlessly searching for some way of occupying ourselves. Usually we would go and play outside when the music became too deafening. Yet it was a carefree life, in spite of that. We didn't miss out on anything, because we had each other. Now that I thought back, though, I was aware of an ache in my chest that I hadn't noticed before. At the time I used to find Mum tiring to deal with and looked up to Dad instead.

My daddy.

I had always been Daddy's girl – his Pipsqueak. I loved it when he used my nickname; it made me feel special. Stína was Mum's favourite because they were so alike: dreamers and artists. Beautiful, radiant. But Dad was mine. As a little girl, I used to crawl on to his lap and always insisted on sitting next to him at mealtimes. I forgave him everything: his absences, his reserve, and sided with him whenever he and Mum quarrelled. Now I wondered whether the affinity between us might have had different roots. Did we have the same darkness inside us? Was that why I was closer to Dad?

After Stína disappeared, my relationship with Dad changed. He still called me his Pipsqueak, but the old warmth had gone from his voice; the affection wasn't there in his eyes when he looked at me. All the endearments he came out with seemed unaccountably flat and perfunctory, as though he no longer meant them the way he had before.

It was Stína who had vanished, yet I seemed to become invisible too, even though I went on living in that house. Stína took me with her when she disappeared, or a small part of me, at least. Who knows? Perhaps, if I could find her, I would get it back.

Stína's school satchel was at the end of the bed, her old exercise books still inside it. Her name was written on the front of them in elegant joined-up writing. The first book I took out was for geography. In it, Stína had made notes about maps, coordinates and scales, but there was no mention of Reykir. Next, I skimmed through a history book but drew a blank here too. There was a piece on Snorri Sturluson and the Old Icelandic Eddic poems, but nothing about the Second World War. I went through every single notebook in her satchel without finding anything relating to Reykir or the girls who were sent there, just the standard homework exercises from her last term at school.

I put the satchel down and surveyed the room. Music was booming up the stairs now. Something stirred in the depths of my memory. In an attempt to recapture it, I closed my eyes and tried to relive the evening that Stína had gone missing, when I had sat in here waiting for my chance to go out and meet Bergur.

What had they been playing then? It couldn't have been this same song, could it?

A chill spread through my nerves and flesh, as though someone had opened a window and let in the cold. Yet the bedroom window was tightly shut. I pulled on one of Stína's warm jumpers and decided to look through her bookcase to see if there was anything related to Reykir there.

It was full of books, figurines and pictures. A china clown smiled down at me from the top shelf with its white-painted eyes and red lips. I bent down and scanned the book titles. We used to read a lot as kids. Series about girls mostly: the Katy books, the Hanne books, the Mette Marit books. I had also zipped through the Enid Blyton series, reading and rereading my favourite adventures.

I ran my finger along the shelf, pausing at a book that stood out from the rest; a history book about the Second World War. I didn't remember seeing it before, and when I removed it from the shelf, I saw a school library label on the spine. Inside, there was a borrowing label with a list of names and dates, Stína's at the bottom, beside the date stamp: 23 April 1967.

As I flicked through the pages, a scrap of paper that had been trapped between them fell out. Not paper, I realised when I picked it up, but a black-and-white photo. It showed a young girl standing in front of a house with two little boys. The girl had short, curly hair and was wearing a buttoned-up coat.

This must be the girl Stína was looking for, the girl she had mentioned to Halldóra. I hadn't a clue where she could have come across the photo or why she had wanted to trace the girl, but my heart started beating faster. A connection at last; a new piece of evidence about Stína that no one else had discovered.

Turning the picture over, I saw that there was a date written on the back: *1943*. I tried to imagine what the girl would look like as a grown woman, but the old snapshot was too small for me to make out her features in any detail.

But below the date was the name of a farm – or perhaps a street. It was in different ink, and with a jolt I realised it was in my sister's handwriting:

Sætún.

30
Kristín – *Autumn 1967*

When school resumes in the autumn, everything seems to become clearer at last. Just this academic year, I think to myself, then I can leave this place. After one lesson I stare at the blank page in front of me, then write the number 1 in the top left-hand corner. It's time I confronted the problems that have been weighing on me all summer. Ívar said problems seem more manageable if you write them down, and although I have little faith in the idea, I make a list.

> *Dad's affair*
> *Relationship with Elvar*
> *Friendship with Guðrún*
> *Marsí*
> *The girl in the photo*

As I sit there contemplating the last item, I feel a twinge of guilt over Ívar. I've spent a lot of time thinking about him. I even painted his portrait from memory, taking days to get his features right, particularly his eyes. But I've hardly given a moment's thought to the girl who left behind the shoebox, put off at the first hurdle by Jón Ingi's hostile reception.

Dad's affair is not really something I can sort out myself. But at least I can end things with Elvar. It's been dragging on far too long, though I don't have any feelings left for him.

It's so typical of me to dodge conflict and unpleasantness like this; to try to keep everyone happy. I don't want to be like that anymore.

I slip the list into my pocket and, oddly enough, it works. Now that my problems have been committed to paper, it seems I've bought myself a temporary respite from the thoughts that have been circling round and round in my head, day in, day out.

When I get home, I open my sketchbook for the first time in months and embark on a new portrait. Using my imagination, I draw the girl in the photo as she might look today. If she's still alive, she'd be around forty now, so I add small lines around her eyes and mouth and make her face thinner. When I've finished, I study the drawing, my heart pattering. The woman looks familiar.

'Stína.' At the sound of Mum's voice, I hurriedly close the sketchpad. 'What?'

'I'm just popping out. I won't be long.'

'All right,' I say.

The moment she's gone, I seize the opportunity to sneak into Marsí's room. I've been biding my time, waiting for a chance to read the letter she got the other day, but it's easier said than done, because she's always home. And if she's not here, Mum is. But now, at last, I'm alone and free to search through her things.

Marsí's room has undergone a transformation recently. She's removed all her toys – the cute teddy bears and dolls – and now there's almost nothing on display apart from the writing materials on her desk and a corkboard with some pictures pinned to it. I know she's much too clever to keep anything important in the desk but, to be on the safe side, I check through the drawers.

Nothing.

There's nothing under the bed either, except dust that makes me sneeze. I turn my attention to her wardrobe next, carefully pushing the clothes aside. When I've searched every last inch of it, I glance around, puzzled.

She can't have thrown the letter away after reading it. So where can it be?

Then my gaze catches on the picture above her bed. It's slightly crooked. I straighten it and only then does it occur to me to peer behind the frame. There it is: an envelope that Marsí has fixed under one of the clips that holds the picture in place. Carefully I prise the envelope free, making a mental note of exactly how it was fixed there, so I can replace it undetected.

It immediately becomes apparent, however, that this is not the letter Marsí received but one she is planning to send; a letter to a boy.

So that's why Marsí has been so dreamy and distracted lately. She's been writing to a boy called Bergur and what I have in my hand is a half-finished letter in Marsí's handwriting. *Darling Bergur*, she begins, and I am briefly astonished by the intimacy of the greeting. Marsí never says *darling*; she can't even read romantic books or stories. She can't bear anything soppy or sentimental.

Overcoming, with an effort, the temptation to read the rest, I replace the picture behind the frame, just as I found it.

31
Marsibil – *Friday, 25 November 1977*

There was a street in Reykjavík called Sætún, but then there were bound to be similarly named streets and farms all over the country. Most Icelandic farm- and street names were endlessly repeated; there were any number ending in -*tún*, -*hóll*, -*gröf*, -*ból* and -*brekka*, so the name Sætún gave me little to work with.

The next morning I hung around at home, feeling utterly sapped of energy after the events of the previous days, and couldn't get properly into gear until the afternoon. Then I went back into Stína's bedroom and systematically leafed through all the books on her shelves, without finding any other photos or letters concealed between their pages. Then I carefully returned them to the shelves in the same order, as if Stína might come back at some later date and accuse me of poking around in her things.

Just before supper I rang Guðrún, hoping she might be able to enlighten me about Stína's research into Reykir and tell me whether she'd uncovered anything of interest. Besides, I had no desire to hang around at home this evening feeling unwelcome. I had to get out of the house.

Guðrún picked up immediately and agreed to meet me at Café Hvítá after supper.

Mum was asleep in the wine-red armchair when I left. The sitting-room window was open, the old curtains flapping in the draught, and Mum kept shivering. She would twitch, lie still for a while, then twitch again.

I closed the window, then spread a blanket over her and tucked her in. 'Sweet dreams, Mum,' I whispered, pausing briefly to study her face.

Life hadn't treated her kindly. Her skin was no longer smooth; yet she was still beautiful. People were always talking about parents' boundless, unconditional love for their children, but they rarely mentioned that the feeling was mutual. I loved my parents regardless of all their flaws. My memories of Mum were mixed, yet I had clung to the good ones, warmed all these years by the thought of them. Little things, like the packed lunches Mum used to make us, the carefully chopped-up pieces of fruit and parcels of sandwiches. The way she used to sit by the bath when Stína and I were small and allow us to daub her with bubbles, giving her a beard and hat of foam. All the times she had let us try on her clothes and jewellery, turning up the music and dancing around the sitting room with us. I did my best to block out the bad memories with these happy ones, and most of the time I succeeded.

Mum smiled in her sleep, pulled the blanket more tightly around herself and murmured something.

'What's that, Mum?' I whispered.

Her eyes were still shut, she was sound asleep, her mouth slightly open. I was about to leave when she started murmuring again, the words a little more distinct than before, and this time I heard what she said.

There was no mistaking it.

I backed away and almost ran out to my car. Only then did I release the breath I hadn't been conscious I was holding. I must have imagined it – that was the only rational explanation. Because in her sleep, Mum had whispered the refrain from my recurring dream:

We've got to get you clean.

Outside the school was a throng of noisy, dressed-up teenagers. There was obviously some event going on – a school disco or something. Then it dawned on me that it must be the Christmas dance. I had completely forgotten the approach of Advent, despite the Christmas lights already decorating the town.

As I drove round the back of the school I noticed a bunch of kids standing in a huddle, in the shadows beyond the streetlights, passing around a hipflask. That took me back; accepting the flask and taking the biggest possible swig in the shortest possible time. Making an effort to appear exaggeratedly sober when I went back indoors, hoping none of the teachers would detect the smell of spirits. And later in the evening, sitting in a car with some older guys, one of them kissing me and running his hand over my short hair.

Mum cut off all my hair one day, giving me a boyish crop, a style that didn't suit me at all as it only made my face appear even rounder. My features weren't feminine enough to carry it off and for a long time afterwards no boy had given me a second look. That evening, sitting in the car, the older guy had squeezed my breast and said it was like kissing a boy. They had all laughed but it had made me determined to prove to them that I was a girl.

Later that night, Dad had collected me from a house where I had no business to be. A few days later I had my first session with a therapist and didn't open my mouth once. I let him do all the talking while I stared fixedly at the floor, counting down the minutes until I could leave.

'What do you dream about, Marsibil?' the therapist had asked, as though that had any relevance at all.

In contrast to the rowdy teenagers outside the school, things were quiet at Café Hvítá. While I was waiting for Guðrún, I took out the old photo of the girl and tried to imagine where she might be today. What kind of life could someone look forward to after being socially ostracised and sent to an institution for promiscuous girls? Had they been 'cured'? Had the society that repudiated them subsequently welcomed them back with open arms and given them a second chance? As if they had been sent to a sanatorium to recover from TB?

When Guðrún arrived, she ordered herself a soft drink and a plate of chips, saying she wasn't into alcohol; she'd experimented as a teenager and decided it wasn't for her. But when I returned from the ladies, I noticed that my drink was halfway down the glass.

'I suddenly felt like one,' Guðrún admitted ruefully. 'I've ordered another for you. For both of us.'

'Oh, OK. Why don't you just take this one?'

'Thanks.' Guðrún took my glass, rather shyly. 'I just felt like something stronger.'

'Any particular reason?'

'Plenty.' Guðrún laughed. 'No, to be honest, your sister has been on my mind so much since you came back, and raking it all up has made me angry. But it's my mother too. She wants me to do something more interesting with my life. Get an education, I don't know.'

'Isn't that the dream?'

'For some people, maybe.' Guðrún ran her finger round the lip of her glass. 'But I've always been content here and can't see why I would want to be anywhere else. Everything I know is here. Everything I want.'

'I understand.' I did, though I didn't share the feeling.

'Life is so strange, Marsí,' Guðrún continued. 'You can make all the right decisions, do all the things you're supposed to, yet in spite of that everything can go wrong. People treat you badly, however much you've done for them. You keep giving and giving, you're always there, yet people still think it's OK to treat you like dirt.' Guðrún sighed. 'I'm so sick of being taken for granted.'

'By your mother, you mean?'

'Yes. She nags me constantly. Granny too. They're always on at me either to go abroad or to find a husband and have a baby. But I don't know what my mother would do without me there. I mean, I do literally everything around the house: the hoovering, the cleaning, the shopping, and my hands are aching from all the Christmas cards I've spent the evenings writing recently.'

'Our parents don't always know what's best for us.'

'Exactly.' The drinks arrived and Guðrún raised one of the glasses. 'Cheers to that.'

'Cheers.'

'And I bet I end up exactly like them.' Guðrún laughed.

'Maybe. But they mean well.'

I hesitated a moment, deciding whether or not to share something similarly personal. It seemed a good opportunity. I turned my glass around and around, and without looking at Guðrún said, in a low voice:

'Did you know I was in therapy for years? I started going after Stína went missing, or about a year afterwards. I'd been having nightmares. I was becoming just like my mother too. Maybe I *am* just like her in some ways. We're both a bit messed up.'

'Oh, Marsí, that's not true. Neither of you are messed up,' she said. 'Anyway, I always thought your mother was wonderful. Everybody did.'

'Really?'

'Yes, of course. Didn't you realise? She was always so glamorous. Such fun.' Guðrún made a face. 'You should have grown up with my mother. She was over thirty when she had me, and even then I was an accident. Mum was under the impression that she couldn't have children, but then along I came, the miracle child. And when Dad died it was like I was the only thing she had left. Can you imagine what a burden that is? Being the person somebody else lives for?'

'You must have been given everything you wanted, though,' I said.

'I *was* given everything. Every single thing I could think of. When I was four, I had to have two teeth pulled out because she was always slipping me sweets. I'm horribly fat now because I was allowed to eat everything I wanted – always. Mum loves me so much that it'll probably kill me one day.'

'You're not horribly fat.'

'Yes, I am!' Guðrún squealed, then she began to laugh, jerky, hiccupping laughter, like a broken toy. 'But it's all right, I don't care. I'm just content where I am. But … sometimes I burn with shame when I remember your sister. You see, we used to dream about all the things we would do together. About the future. I bet she'd be turning in her grave if she could see me now.'

'In her grave?'

'Oh, sorry, Marsí. It's just a turn of phrase – you know what I mean. Wherever she is. She would be horrified that I've done nothing with my life.'

'Cheers to that,' I said, and we drank again. I put my glass down and stared at her. 'But *do* you think she's lying in a grave somewhere?'

Guðrún thought about it for a moment. 'No. No, I don't think so. I believe she's alive.'

'Are you serious?'

'Yes. You know, I picture her coming home one day. Just turning up in town and laughing her head off at the lot of us.'

'You're crazy,' I said, but I was aware of a warm feeling in my stomach. Perhaps it could happen. Perhaps Stína would just pop up one day, all tanned and beautiful. It was a comforting thought.

'I know about a party,' Guðrún said.

It was quite a lot later. We were fairly drunk by now. We'd both cried, collapsed in fits of hysterics and visited the ladies together, where Guðrún had put lipstick on me and plaited what was left of my hair. I hadn't even asked her about Reykir yet: I was completely useless as an amateur detective.

'Party.' I giggled. I couldn't remember the last time I'd been to a party.

'Yes, let's go,' Guðrún said.

'OK.' By this point, I was up for anything.

'Do you mind if I give you a hug?' Guðrún asked. 'I'm so glad you're here, Marsí. I feel like your sister's come back. With you around, I don't miss her quite so much.'

'Same here. I feel almost like we're little girls again.'

We hugged each other tightly, affectionately, and I felt as if things were looking up.

On the way out, Guðrún tripped over the threshold and, before I knew what was happening, she had gone down heavily on the tarmac. She didn't get up immediately, just lay there, her whole body shaking.

I bent down unsteadily to see if she had hurt herself. There was blood on the pavement, and when I saw her face I gasped: she'd split her upper lip, and it was already swelling up, the blood trickling down her chin.

'Oh my God, Guðrún, are you all right?' I asked, crouching down beside her.

She sat up and only then did I notice that she wasn't crying, she was laughing so much the tears were pouring down her cheeks.

'I haven't had *tho* much fun in year*th*,' she lisped, and wiped her bloodied lip on the sleeve of her coat.

'What *are* you doing?' We both looked up at the sound of Gústi's voice.

Guðrún started shaking with laughter again, but I straightened up and brushed the dirt from my trousers.

'How come you always pop up wherever I go?' I asked.

'I come here every weekend, Marsí,' Gústi said drily. 'If anything, it's you who's suddenly started turning up at all my haunts.'

'*Th*top it.' Guðrún gave Gústi a nudge, making him look round. 'Mar*thí* and I are going to a party.'

'You're covered in blood, Guðrún. Come on, I'll give you a lift home.'

'*Th*top being *tho* boring. I don't want to go home.'

'The fall seems to have knocked your esses out of you,' I joked, and, holding out a hand, heaved her to her feet. 'Come on, let's get a lift with Gústi.'

Guðrún sighed. 'OK, OK.'

We got into Gústi's car and he drove us to Guðrún's house.

He offered to help her to the door, and I watched them making their slow way to the house, Guðrún hanging round Gústi's neck, almost pulling him off balance. I heard her telling him how much she loved him, and Gústi laughing. She gave him a long hug in parting, and when he returned to the car I saw there was a smear of blood on his jacket.

'Right,' he said.

'Can we go somewhere?' I asked.

I was in no mood to head straight home. I'd been in my chrysalis too long, afraid to hatch out. Work was my only social life, but I didn't think you could even call it that, as all I did was grace my colleagues with my presence at the office. I never went to cafés with them or to staff get-togethers. I had convinced myself that I didn't need the company of other people, and my years in Reykjavík seemed to have passed in a blur, each one indistinguishable from the last.

In contrast, my last week here had been so packed with incident that it felt as if it had lasted for years. Difficult and painful though it was to be back in Síða, at least I was alive. An active participant in life.

But at the same time, I was disappointed in myself. I had become immersed in this new life instead of concentrating on Stína. My decision to stay on longer was supposed to be about investigating what had happened to her, about finding answers, but instead here I was, getting plastered out of my skull and having fun on my own account. I wasn't here for Stína but for myself. As if I couldn't tear myself away from this town or who I was when I was here. Finally, I had people to turn to. I was popular. I had Gústi and Guðrún, and they were my friends. This was followed immediately by the worrying thought that I was cheating: they weren't my friends at all; they were Stína's and I'd stepped into her life and taken her friends as well. Was I still, at heart, that sulky little crosspatch Marsí who envied her big sister? Hadn't I changed at all in the ten years that had passed since Stína vanished?

For weeks – no, months – before she went missing, I'd been at odds with everyone, including Stína. I was angry with her for being out all the time, for having an exciting life outside the home that I was excluded from. We'd always been close, but now we'd started fighting. Or, rather, I fought; Stína just shook her head. She seemed instinctively to understand the source of my resentment and to feel sorry for me.

Perhaps it wasn't my penpal who was the enemy but myself.

'Where do you want to go?' Gústi asked.

'I just don't feel like going home yet,' I replied.

'It's late, Marsí.'

I gazed into the darkness. The wind had dropped towards evening, the sky was overcast and there was a cold, fresh hint of snow in the air.

I turned to Gústi. 'I know where we can go.'

32
Kristín – *September 1967*

'You've been in my room.'

I jump at the sound of Marsí's voice. She's standing in my bedroom, and I wonder how she managed to creep up on me so soundlessly.

'No, I haven't,' I say untruthfully.

'Don't lie.'

'I'm not lying.'

Her gaze is so fierce. When did Marsí become ferocious like this?

Although she's wearing a T-shirt and loose trousers, I can tell that she's lost a lot of weight; she's nothing but skin and bone these days. Her face has changed too. Her eyes, which have always been quite dark and piercing, seem to have grown even darker and sunk deeper into her head, and there are violet shadows underneath them.

'No, right.' She smiles, but it's a spiteful smile; an expression quite unlike Marsí. 'You never lie. You're so perfect.'

'I never said that. Why are you being like this?'

'Like what?'

'So … so angry?' I long to get through to her, to find the Marsí I know behind those deep, dark eyes. In a softer voice, I continue: 'You know you can talk to me, Marsí. Is there something you want to tell me?'

For a moment I think she's going to relent and unburden herself, but instead she emits an exasperated sigh.

'You can never leave anything alone, can you?'

'Marsí, I'm not trying to be mean. I just care about you.'

'Since when did you care about me? Why are you suddenly asking me now what the matter is?'

'I've always cared about you.'

'Liar,' Marsí hisses, and turns away, but not before I've caught the glitter of tears in her eyes.

The sleepwalking has got a lot worse and I keep being woken by noises outside my room during the night. This morning, I woke up to discover that it was freezing in the house and when I left my room, I saw that the front door was wide open, swinging back and forth in the breeze. There were dirty footprints across the floor.

How is it possible to walk in your sleep without being aware of the fact?

It's taking its toll on Mum, who looks perpetually tired and drawn, and usually goes for a rest in the afternoons. Dad hardly shows his face at home, except at night when he has to be there to limit the damage. The only person who seems completely unaware of anything is Marsí. This morning, I asked her how she'd slept, and she just shrugged and said well. Marsí has always been a deep sleeper.

I miss the way she used to crawl into my bed and cuddle up to me when we were younger. Since our recent quarrel, there have been days when the house has felt like a minefield, but in spite of that I've decided to stay at home to show Marsí that I have no intention of running away. Not anymore. After a few days, she stopped getting up and leaving the kitchen table every time I sat down. And today we even laughed together over the readers' letters in *The Week*, before she went upstairs and locked herself in her room.

Now I'm reading in the sitting room. No one has mentioned the dirt on the floor and suddenly I've had enough – I can't bear to spend a moment longer in the house. I stand up, put on my jacket and shoes, and leave without saying goodbye.

I set off without a thought of where I'm going until I find myself standing outside Guðrún's house. I haven't seen her since she got home after the summer holidays. She's not expecting me, but I need her. I've felt so alone these last few weeks. I've been struggling to bear the weight of all my problems on my own, desperately missing the old days when I could confide in Guðrún about everything, big or small, and share the problem with her. Without her, I feel like only half a person. I've never been so lonely in my life.

Guðrún comes to the door, and for a long moment we just stand there, eyeing each other.

'I thought you might like to do something,' I venture at last.

Guðrún is still staring at me, as though unsure how to react. Then she shrugs. 'Yes, sure, count me in.'

'Oh, Guðrún,' I say, welling up.

'Oh, Stína,' Guðrún says, and hugs me tight.

When we eventually release each other, we're both tearful. Then we start laughing and can't stop. We laugh until we run out of breath, our cheeks wet, our jaws aching.

That evening, I cross one of the items off my to-do list.

33
Marsibil – *Friday, 25 November 1977*

'Aren't you going to get in?'

Instead of heading home, we'd come to the Hot Stream. Steam rose from the surface and hung in the still air, lending the valley an eerie atmosphere. Despite my drunken state, I managed to tear off my clothes, swaying precariously all the while, and teeter over the icy stones to lower myself into the deliciously hot water. I lay back until I was up to my neck, the stream enveloping me in its warm embrace.

Gústi watched from the bank. 'I don't know, Marsí, it's bloody freezing.'

'It's colder out than in.'

Gústi thought for a second, then quickly stripped down to his underpants. He grimaced as he tiptoed over the stones, then stepped cautiously into the water.

We lay there, resting against the same rock, watching the stream curl up into the black sky.

'Málfríður told me that Dad and Stína had quarrelled; that Stína wanted to leave home because of him. Do you have any idea what they had quarrelled about?'

'Well, no, but...' Gústi's eyes became evasive.

'What? Just say it,' I told him, suddenly breathless. I didn't want to hear the answer but I had to know.

'Stína had a bruise on her cheek one day. I asked what had happened but she didn't want to say. In the end, she told me your dad had done it, then she started crying. She refused to tell me why.'

'That's impossible. You must have misunderstood.'

'It's what she said.'

'But...' I bit back a protest. Dad had never laid hands on either of us, or on Mum. He wasn't that kind of man. So why would she have accused him of hitting her if he hadn't done it?

'I've found out something else,' I said instead.

'What?'

'You remember me telling you that Stína was researching the story of the girls who were sent to the workhouse at Reykir?'

'Yes.'

'Well, I found an old photo of a girl with the address "Sætún" written on the back. If I can find her, I might be able to find the person who was responsible for taking Stína.'

'What makes you think that?'

'Stína was digging around in the story before she vanished. Somehow she got hold of some belongings one of the girls had left behind at the school, and she wanted to return them. The photo must have been among them.'

'And you think this is connected somehow to her disappearance?'

'I don't know,' I admitted, suddenly annoyed at Gústi for sounding doubtful – and probably rightly so. Why was I so sure there was a connection? I had no solid evidence. Just a photo of a girl and a tenuous link to the workhouse at Reykir. 'At least it's a new clue.'

'Maybe.'

Gústi obviously didn't want to talk about Stína. He seemed distant, and I wondered what he was thinking and whether he had decided to give up the search.

'Maybe it's not important how Stína vanished,' I went on. 'Maybe I'm just trying to find someone else to blame, to let myself off the hook.'

I clamped my mouth shut, almost biting off my tongue, shocked with myself for blurting this out. But the darkness seemed to invite confessions. I had an odd fancy that my words would barely be visible, but rise into the air and evaporate along with the steam.

'None of this is your fault, Marsí.'

'But sometimes I think I remember it,' I said in sudden anguish.

'What do you mean?'

'I don't know how to describe it. I just see the whole thing so clearly.'

'See what?'

'Stína. Dead.'

The images would appear in my mind; I would see my sister lying by the road, feel her in my arms, see her blood staining my hands.

The therapist, the first person I had confided in about this, had explained that we can create artificial memories from things we've dreamt. It was possible that I had dreamt this, my unconscious inventing a series of plausible events, and that these would rise to the surface at vulnerable moments, when all my defences were lowered, such as when I was asleep.

I wanted to believe it. Wanted to believe it was nothing but my imagination, but that didn't stop the rush of feelings that followed in the aftermath: the despair, the guilt. Ever since Stína vanished I had been trying to escape these feelings, but I had never succeeded.

'Marsí.' Gústi turned to me. 'You have to remember that it wasn't your fault.'

'OK.'

'You don't have to be so hard on yourself all the time.'

I nodded. Gústi propped himself up on an elbow to look into my face.

He reached out and brushed away a strand of hair that had loosened from my plait. For a moment I was afraid he'd move his hand to the back of my head and feel how thin my hair had become there, but instead he bent closer and kissed me on the mouth. It was no more than a featherlight touch at first, but the kiss grew gradually more insistent and deeper until I sank slowly back into the hot water, the pebbles digging into my back.

'Having a nice snog?'

We tore ourselves apart.

A group of teenagers, who couldn't have been more than fifteen or sixteen, were watching us from the bank. Two girls and three boys. One of the boys was holding a bottle, taking frequent swigs of the contents that almost certainly weren't what it said on the torn label. The girls were both in flared jeans, the boys in matching corduroy jackets. In this town, everyone had to own the same things, dress in the same uniform. But maybe that was inevitable when there was only one clothes shop.

'Mind if we join you?' asked the prettier of the two girls. 'Or is it a private party?'

'We're leaving,' I said. I scrambled to my feet, feeling exposed in my wet underwear, although little could be seen through the steam-filled darkness.

'Don't let us spoil the atmosphere,' one of the boys said. He held out the bottle. 'Want a drink?'

'No, thanks,' Gústi said.

'Hey, aren't you Ína's brother?' the other girl said. She was tall and seemed shy. Her eyes weren't as glazed as those of her companions.

'Yes.'

'I'm in the choir with her.'

'No one gives a shit about your choir, Sigga,' one of the boys said. 'Are you guys getting in or not? What about you, Maja?'

'I'm up for it.' Without further ado, the pretty girl began to strip off, shrieking as the cold air made contact with her skin.

The boys followed suit. Only Sigga remained standing, a little awkwardly, on the bank.

Gústi and I picked our way painfully over the stones and snatched up our clothes. The ground felt icy under our bare feet and the chilly air gave me goose flesh. I felt abruptly sober.

'I, er … I'm sorry about Mette,' the tall girl said as we made our way past her.

I couldn't hear Gústi's reply.

'We didn't mean to drive you away,' Maja called after us. She was sitting in the stream in her underwear, clutching the bottle, her ample breasts almost escaping from her bra. 'You're welcome to join us.'

We didn't bother to answer, just made for the car as quickly as possible and wordlessly struggled to pull on our clothes over our wet skin, before driving away.

'Why did she tell you she was sorry about Mette?' I asked, after we'd been driving for a few minutes.

'Probably because of Ína or something. I don't know. They were pissed out of their minds. Teenage drinking's becoming a real menace.'

'Is it?'

'Kids of no more than eleven or twelve are smoking and drinking these days.'

Gústi carried on talking about some article he'd read, about kids in Reykjavík hanging around outside a youth centre, children as young as ten smashed out of their skulls, and the police helpless to do anything about it as the kids' parents were drunk at home.

After a while I tuned out.

My damp clothes felt icy and I couldn't stop shivering, nor could I stop thinking about last Friday night. Had I seen Mette and Gústi talking together at the bar? Why couldn't I just ask him about it?

We parted without mentioning the kiss. I didn't meet his eye as I muttered goodbye and got out of the car.

'Where have you been?'

I hadn't immediately noticed Dad, sitting in the darkened room.

'Out,' I said.

'Where?'

'Dad, I'm a grown-up.'

'Who with?' he demanded.

Something in his tone made my heart sink. I thought about the bruise on Stína's face. The row.

'With Gústi,' I replied.

'I don't want you staying out this late.' Dad stood up, went into the kitchen and put his glass in the sink.

'OK.'

'While you're here, under my roof, you obey my rules. Understood?'

I nodded. Into my mind came the dream I'd had about Dad, the sound of a raven croaking every time he opened his mouth. What had Mum said ravens symbolised? Betrayal? Death?

'What did you say?' he asked.

'Yes. I said yes.'

'Good.' Dad stood there glowering at me. This wasn't the man who cuddled me and called me his Pipsqueak. This was a completely different person. Someone I hardly recognised.

'I'm going to bed,' I said.

Dad didn't answer, and for a moment neither of us moved; we just stood there, waiting. In the end, he was the first to back down. He went upstairs to the bedroom and shut the door behind him. After a brief pause, I heard a key turn in the lock.

I didn't even know that was possible. I knew there was a keyhole but there had never, to my knowledge, been a key in it. We didn't lock our bedroom doors in this house. Mum didn't even lock the bathroom door.

I stood in the hall for a moment, looking up the stairs. Then my gaze turned to the door to the cellar. I seemed to be drawn to it, though I had no idea why. Whenever I was caught off guard, like now, too befuddled with drink and lack of sleep to be afraid, it exerted a magnetic pull on me.

I'd taken the few steps and was turning the handle before I'd even decided to go down there. The light was on and I was at the bottom of the steps, surrounded by the dank smell. I started rummaging around in the boxes again, not searching for anything specific. What did I think I would find here? I pulled out old clothes and old crockery. Books and brochures. After rooting around for a while I came across a yellow headband among the folders containing paper dolls that we used to play with as children.

It was Stína's headband. She had bought it herself on a visit to Reykjavík. The woman in the poster in the shop window had worn a headband like it and Stína said that Audrey Hepburn had one too. I smiled at the memory of her pushing the headband over her hair, checking it in the mirror, then deciding impulsively that this was what she was going to buy with her birthday money.

The blood began to throb in my head as my heartrate shot up. I had a vivid image of Stína putting on the headband as she was getting ready to go out the evening she disappeared.

'Is it too yellow?' she had asked.

'No, it suits you,' I'd replied, and it was no lie. Most things suited Stína and the headband had framed her face like a halo.

Feeling sick, I hurried upstairs to my room, taking the headband with me. There I laid it on the windowsill and sat in bed, hugging my knees and staring at it. Outside, the darkness was so black that I could see nothing but my own reflection in the glass, a vague impression of myself. I switched off the lamp on my bedside table and the darkness outside seemed less intense. Then I lay back, still staring at the headband in the gloom.

Slowly the realisation dawned on me: what was it doing here if Stína had been wearing it on the evening she disappeared?

I couldn't follow this train of thought to the end; I didn't dare.

Didn't want to know. It only filled me with sadness. It would be best to stop searching now, as my parents kept insisting. Perhaps the truth wasn't that desirable after all. Perhaps it wouldn't be in my interests to receive answers.

I hadn't expected to be able to sleep in this state but my eyelids started to droop and drowsiness stole over me. I heard the bell's insistent jangling.

I dreamt about hens, heard them squawking as they pecked at me with their sharp beaks. Saw my skin tearing, wounds opening up, the bright-red blood trickling down over my body. I was aware of the pain but couldn't move; all I could do was watch helplessly. Then Bossy, Dad's favourite, was there, her red comb flapping, her eyes pink and vacant as she started on my face, tearing out my hair, pecking at my cheek. And still I lay there, paralysed. Only when she went for my eyes were my limbs suddenly released from their spell. Sitting up, I caught her with firm hands, took hold of her neck and wrung it.

There was a snap and her squawking ceased.

34
Kristín – *Autumn 1967*

One day I run into Halldóra at the shop.

'How are you getting on with your applications for colleges abroad?' she asks cheerfully.

'Oh…' I say. 'I haven't actually started yet.'

The smile leaves Halldóra's face. 'Really, why not?'

I shrug, blushing as if I've done something wrong.

'You surprise me, Stína. I thought you were keen to go to art school abroad as soon as possible.'

'That's still the plan. I just thought it wasn't that urgent yet as I've still got to take my school-leaving exams.'

'I see,' Halldóra says. 'As a matter of fact, I was hoping I'd bump into you. I wanted to draw your attention to the evening courses at the Icelandic College of Arts and Crafts, in case you were thinking of going to sixth-form college in Reykjavík first.'

I nod, even more sheepishly. I feel I've let her down. I've always been a favourite of Halldóra's, and during the last school year she kept telling me about various colleges abroad that I'd be eligible to apply to.

'You know, some of the art schools in London don't require you to finish your school-leaving exams first. I think it would be enough for you to do a term or two at the College of Arts and Crafts in Reykjavík and get good references from there. Of course, I'm prepared to write a reference for you too.' She raises her eyebrows. 'That's to say, if you're still interested.'

'Of course.' I nod vehemently.

'Well then, Stína, I recommend that you get on with filling in the application forms as soon as possible. The competition overseas is stiff, but you have talent and I'm happy to help you. Ívar was pleased with your progress too, and naturally he'd give you a reference.'

'Would he?'

'Yes. You know it was at his request that you were allowed to take part in the evening classes. He spotted your talent while he was observing my lessons; had a chance to see how you worked and to examine your pictures. He was extremely pleased when you decided to attend.'

'Honestly?' I say. This is news to me. When Ívar and I first met on the course he couldn't even remember my name, so it seems unlikely to have been him who requested that I should be allowed to attend, but the thought gives me a warm feeling.

'Yes, he was very pleased with your progress,' Halldóra says.

'The classes were fantastic,' I reply.

'That's good to hear.' Halldóra picks up her shopping basket again. 'By the way, was Jón Ingi able to help you?'

'Jón Ingi?'

'You had some questions about Reykir.'

'Oh, yes. No, he … he was unavailable.' I still haven't done what Ívar asked me to, though it's been months now.

'Ah.' Halldóra looks thoughtful for a moment. 'After we talked, it occurred to me that you should have a chat with Áslaug from Litla-Brú. Her farm's right up at the head of the valley. It's a bit of a drive away, but she worked at Reykir in those days.'

'Do you think she might have kept in touch with any of the girls who were sent there?'

'I don't know.' Halldóra regards me with that penetrating gaze she adopts when she's teaching. 'Think about what I said. Get stuck into those applications. If you're serious about studying art, you need to pull your finger out.'

'Of course,' I say, and my face is hot as I part from her.

Autumn arrives, heralded by the first leaves turning vivid shades of brown, yellow and red. Then one day it blows a gale and all the leaves are swept away. Only the skeletons of the trees remain, and after that the sun doesn't pierce the lowering clouds for weeks. The days grow shorter, darkness settles over our little town earlier and earlier with every passing day, and Mum lights up our house with candles. Most evenings I sit over my sketchpad, practising.

One evening Málfríður, Guðrún, Gústi and I all end up at Café Hvítá.

'Do you believe in love at first sight?' Málfríður asks. Ever since we sat down she's been hinting that there's someone she fancies but she's being all mysterious and won't tell us who he is.

Guðrún says yes and I say no.

'I don't think it's common but it can happen,' Guðrún says.

I grin. 'After all, you've been in love with the same boy ever since our first year at school.'

'Don't,' Guðrún whispers. She's always been oversensitive on this subject, so I refrain from saying any more, though I notice out of the corner of my eye that Gústi is keeping his head down. It's no secret to him who the object of Guðrún's affections is, but the fact he's never done anything about it tells me that he doesn't return her feelings.

'How was it for you with Elvar?' Málfríður asks. 'Was it love at first sight?'

'I don't know,' I mutter.

The truth is that I've been avoiding Elvar recently. I made up my mind a while ago to end the relationship but I've been too much of a coward to go through with it.

'Anyway, I'm glad you're still with him,' Málfríður says. 'At first I was afraid it would only be a quick fling.'

'Why were you afraid of that?' I ask.

'Because Elvar isn't how you think. He's a sensitive soul, and when he loves something, he doesn't let it go.'

'How do you mean?' I ask.

Málfríður shrugs but doesn't elaborate.

'Oh, you two are so cute together,' Guðrún says. 'I'm so happy for you, Stína.'

I nod but I can feel Gústi giving me a hard stare.

'A little bird told me you'd sealed your relationship a while back.' Málfríður winks at me. 'It's about time you were a proper member of the family.'

'Really?' Guðrún asks, her eyes round. 'Is that true?'

I mutter something inaudible, my gaze on the window. Since I didn't tell the girls that Elvar and I had slept together, I can only assume he must have let something slip to his sister.

'What was it like?' Guðrún asks.

'Can we stop talking about it?' I say.

The truth is I was drunk and angry the first time we slept together, and remember little about it. Once we'd started, though, there was no reason to stop, and the next few times were better than the first. I was more compos mentis, at least. We have a good time, but there are no fireworks. Elvar's a considerate lover who's always asking if everything's OK, if he's hurting me, if it feels good.

When I look at Gústi, I see that he's picking angrily at the skin of his knuckles.

The next day I meet Elvar and pluck up the courage at last to tell him how I feel.

'What do you mean?' Elvar isn't angry but I feel absolutely awful when I see how hurt he is. He's sensitive, as Málfríður said, and I know he doesn't want to end things.

'I'm not ready to be in a relationship yet,' I say.

'I see.' He shoves his hands in his pockets, his gaze fixed on my face.

'I'm sorry.'

'Don't apologise, Stína. You can't help how you feel.'

'It's not that...' I begin, then stop myself. Why lie? Why pretend this is something it isn't?

'I'll see you around, then.' Elvar gives me a pale smile before walking away, head down, shoulders hunched, hands still in his pockets.

For some reason tears start pouring down my cheeks. I cry all the way home, but that evening I cross another item off my to-do list and feel a little better. At least that's one more problem dealt with.

35
Marsibil – *Saturday, 26 November 1977*

We walked to school together one day during Stína's last year at the local school. I have a feeling it was in April; the weather was unusually good, the sky blue, the air windless and full of the scent of new grass and sunshine. We took off our anoraks and carried them. Dust swirled up from the gravel road as we walked.

'Why can't the weather always be like this?' Stína exclaimed.

She turned her face to the sun, her eyes closed, her face glowing in the morning rays. She continued walking with her eyes shut, not slowing her pace or once stealing a peek at what lay ahead. In retrospect, this seemed to me typical of Stína: she trusted people and she trusted the world. Trusted that she could walk along with her eyes shut and not trip over. Now, I wondered whether she might have trusted the wrong person.

I woke up this morning from a deep sleep, my head heavy, as if all the oxygen in the room had been used up. There was an uneasy feeling in the pit of my stomach, an ominous sense that something was wrong. The conviction of impending doom was so powerful that I was reluctant to get up. I had decided to go back to Reykjavík on Monday but I still had no idea what had happened to Stína. The clues I had gathered had only given rise to more questions.

At eight, I finally dragged myself out of bed. My hair felt oddly stiff and sticky to the touch, and my pillow was damp. My back was sore too, and when I twisted round to check it in the mirror I saw red scratches on my skin. In one place there was a spot of dried blood, but I couldn't see any open wounds, only a red smear up my spine.

'You look awful.'

I hadn't noticed Mum in the hall.

'It's nothing,' I said, pulling my top down.

'There's blood on your hands, Marsí.'

'I must have fallen over or something,' I said. 'I went out with Guðrún yesterday.'

'Are you sure?' Mum was still looking at me.

'I'm sure.'

'You should have a bath and wash it off.'

Mum darted into the bathroom and turned on the taps. I didn't try to object. My body felt chilled and the thought of sinking into scalding bathwater was an appealing one.

While I lay and soaked, my thoughts turned to Gústi.

If he was the man Mette had been seeing, that would upset everything. Not because of their relationship but because he had lied to me. He'd claimed he didn't know Mette. Of course, concealing a relationship didn't automatically make someone a murderer – there was a world of difference between the two – but lying about it afterwards was another matter and infinitely more suspicious.

Gústi had taken the road where Mette was found the evening she died. He could have encountered her after giving me a lift home. But that would mean he had written the note to me, which just didn't add up. However hard I tried to convince myself that it was a real possibility, my imagination failed me. This was Gústi, for Christ's sake. I knew Gústi.

But therein lay the problem: the person who had taken Stína was almost certainly someone I knew.

I lay in the tub, my head ready to explode with the strain of wrestling with these thoughts. I kept vacillating: one moment I saw the whole thing clearly, and the next I was shaking my head over the absurdity of it all.

By the time I got out of the bath, I'd come to the conclusion that I must be overthinking the comment the girl had made by the Hot Stream last night. Perhaps it was normal in this town for people to give each other their condolences. Perhaps everyone was commiserating with everyone else because the Danish girl had been one of them – common property, part of the local scene.

But I knew this was bullshit.

Mum insisted on washing my clothes and stripped the sheets off my bed too. When I got out of the bath, I found a pile of folded clothes awaiting me: jeans and a top I'd left behind ten years ago. They were far too loose on me now, but I found a belt in my wardrobe so at least my jeans wouldn't fall down. Then I ran my hands through my hair. It never got a chance to grow properly and had become so thin at the back that I had to wear it in a pony-tail to disguise the bald patches.

I had just finished tying back my hair when I was brought up short. It had dawned on me what had caused the niggling sense that something was wrong. The headband was missing from the windowsill.

I lifted up the duvet, shook the pillow and peered under the bed. Then I checked the gap between the bed and the wall to see if the headband could have got trapped there, and looked under the desk and bookcase. It was no good: the headband had gone.

'Did you take something from my room?' I asked Mum.

'Only the sheets.' Mum was busy in the kitchen. The oven was on and the smell of freshly baked bread spread through the house.

'Nothing else?'

'Of course not. Why do you ask?'

'I've lost something.'

'What?'

I was silent. I didn't want to tell her I'd found the headband Stína had been wearing the evening she vanished. Because what did the fact I'd found it in our cellar imply?

'Oh, never mind.' I sat down.

'How are you feeling, by the way?' Mum poured me a cup of coffee. 'Did the bath help?'

'Yes.'

'I've made some buns,' she said, scooping the fresh, delicious-smelling rolls out of the oven and putting them on the table.

I took one, tore it open and spread it with butter.

Mum nibbled at hers, pinching off pieces like a little squirrel. Now that her nail polish had chipped off, I could see how dull and yellow her nails were. Her fingers were bony, the skin thin and wrinkled on the backs of her hands, the veins bulging. I felt an impulse to reach out and take her hand as I used to as a little girl. Mum always used to lead us by the hand when we went into town, a daughter on either side.

Seeing me watching her, Mum smiled. 'Go on, eat up, Marsí.'

I bit into the fresh bread, savouring the melted butter.

'Where's Dad?' I asked.

'He had to go to work early. Oh, bother. He asked me to feed the hens and I completely forgot.' Mum got to her feet, but I gestured at her to sit down again.

'They'll survive,' I said. 'Don't worry. I'll do it, just as soon as I've finished breakfast.'

'Oh, thank you, Marsí, dear.'

I chewed on another mouthful of bread for a moment.

'Mum, do you remember Stína's yellow headband?' I tried to keep my tone casual. 'The one she chose for her birthday present?'

'Yes, I think so.'

'Do you know where it is?'

'No, dear. I haven't a clue. In her room, I expect. We haven't thrown anything away. Why do you ask?'

'Oh, it doesn't matter.' Maybe I had dreamt it. That had to be the explanation.

Back when I was in therapy, I was advised to apply reason when I wasn't sure whether something had happened or not. If it seemed too unbelievable to be true, then it almost certainly wasn't.

My therapist taught me many things I hadn't been aware of before. He told me I was punishing myself by pulling out my hair; that it was my way of banishing negative feelings. I was abusing my body with alcohol and sex for the same reason. I had laughed when he brought up sex and assured him that I was perfectly in control of who I went to bed with; I did it for fun. But he had narrowed his eyes at this: 'Are you sure you're perfectly in control, Marsibil? Are you sure you're having fun?'

I was sure, but afterwards I began to have my doubts about everything I thought I remembered. Had this or that really happened or had I been imagining things?

The worst part about having no control was how it began to have an impact on everything I did. I was so plagued with doubt and uncertainty that I couldn't trust anything. Applying reason only worked to a point. We humans are irrational by nature, forever behaving in unexpected ways.

That was where my problems had begun.

36

It was lunchtime and a delicious smell of waffles carried out on to the street from Jón Ingi's house. I could almost taste them as I knocked on the door.

After a short interval, it was answered by a small, older woman with short hair.

'I'm looking for Jón Ingi,' I explained.

'Oh, yes. Come in, come in,' she said warmly. 'Jón's in the sitting room.'

The house was carpeted and brown throughout, every room wallpapered in a different pattern. The furniture was large and solid, every surface covered in books and photographs. The radio was blasting out the weather forecast at full volume.

'Jón, dear,' the woman said, as we entered the sitting room. 'There's a young lady here to see you.'

The thick curtains were pulled back, allowing the sun to illuminate the man sitting in an armchair, reading a paper and smoking a pipe. He was tall and heavy with it, his big belly straining at the buttons of his white shirt. His hair, or what was left of it, was streaked with grey and so was his beard, which was thin, with irregular bare patches.

He looked up from his newspaper, though not before he had read to the end of his sentence, and inspected me. 'And you are?'

'Marsibil Karvelsdóttir,' I said. 'My parents are Nína and Karvel. They own Fjarðaregg.'

The couple exchanged what appeared to be meaningful looks before the woman backed out of the room. Jón gestured at me wordlessly to take a seat.

'What do you want, Marsibil?' he said, enunciating my name with apparent distaste.

I had a vision of myself from the outside, sitting in that room, delving into long-forgotten events. A girl who couldn't let go of the past, who couldn't move on. Coming here had been a mistake. The sun was shining in my eyes and I could feel myself beginning to cook in my jumper, but I tried, nevertheless, to compose my features and sit up straight.

'I'm looking into the disappearance of my sister, Kristín Karvelsdóttir. At the time she went missing, she was working on a project about the teenage girls who were sent to the workhouse at Reykir. She wanted to talk to someone who knew a lot about the topic and I thought … I gather she was intending to speak to you.'

Jón regarded me for a long moment. I fought the temptation to fill the silence.

'She did come and see me,' he said at last. 'She stood on my doorstep, expecting me to help her.'

'What with?'

'As you say, she wanted to know about the workhouse at Reykir. She said she was trying to get in touch with one of the girls who had been sent there and thought I might be able to help her.'

'Were you able to?'

'I could have done. After all, it's my area of expertise. The Second World War, that's to say.' Jón proceeded to relight his pipe in a leisurely manner, then blew smoke into the air between us. He stared at me through the grey clouds. 'Do you know who I am, Marsibil? Have you any idea?'

'Yes,' I replied uncertainly. 'You're a historian.'

'Quite. But that's not all. I'm also a father.' He reached for a framed photograph on the table beside his chair and studied it for a moment. 'I have five children. All girls. Here – you can see them all.'

I examined the posed studio photo, the family all dressed up in their best clothes.

'This is my youngest daughter, Sólveig,' Jón said. 'A clever, diligent girl. Harmless, kind-hearted. Which is not something that could be said of your sister.'

I felt a shiver run down my spine and put the photo aside. It hit me where this conversation was leading: Sunny Solla.

'I remember Sólveig.'

'She was in the same class as your sister.' Jón was still staring at me, but now I perceived the emotion burning behind his eyes.

'I had no idea,' I whispered. 'I didn't know Stína had…'

'I hope you're not like her,' Jón said after a heavy silence. 'I had no interest in helping your sister at the time. Not after what she did to my Solla.'

His hostility was almost palpable. It was obvious that Stína wouldn't have got any information out of him. Realising that my visit was futile, I stood up to leave, but Jón stopped me.

'Your sister wanted information. The names of the girls. Apparently she'd found some personal items belonging to one of them and wanted to return them.' He sighed. 'Perhaps I was too lenient. I had no wish to help your sister, but in spite of myself I suggested she talk to Kristrún Hallsdóttir.'

When I looked at him enquiringly, he explained that she was the matron formerly in charge of the workhouse at Reykir, and was still alive.

'I gather she's very frail these days, but you can talk to her. I don't know if your sister ever did, but if anyone knows the names of the girls it would be her.'

I thanked him and was preparing to make a quick getaway when I was struck by an idea. 'Has anyone else approached you with the same request?'

'No,' he said curtly.

'But could…' I began, then became aware of a bustle outside the room. Jón shot a glance towards the kitchen.

'You should go,' he said.

I could hardly get out of there fast enough.

When I reached my car, I saw a face in the kitchen window. The woman was watching me and although I couldn't see her clearly, I thought her expression radiated anger. Next moment she had jerked the curtains across the window.

The question I had been intending to ask Jón Ingi was based on a sudden hunch I had about Mette. I had no reason to believe she might have been investigating the history of the girls at Reykir too, but the workhouse was the only link I could establish between her and Stína, apart from their fate, of course. Was it conceivable that they had both discovered something that wouldn't stand the light of day?

I didn't know what to think.

And I couldn't work out how all this could possibly relate to my penpal. Perhaps I wasn't thinking straight because I was so desperate for Stína's disappearance to be unconnected to him. No further letters had arrived and I was left wondering what the point of the last two had been. Did the person who wrote them merely want to remind me of his existence, or was he warning me?

When I got home, I laid the letters from my penpal on my bed and read them again. Mette had been strangled and left lying by the road along with a note to me, and although the message didn't contain any explicit threats, the knowledge that Mette had been murdered had given the message a hideous new significance.

We've known each other so long.

I wished I had the second note in front of me so I could compare it to the previous letter. The note had been different, though not entirely. For one thing, it had been written in capital letters, like a shout.

What did he mean? That we had known each other a long time through our correspondence, or in some other way? Did the person who wrote the letters want to frighten me? If so, why now? What could have compelled him to pick up a pen and send me a letter after ten years of silence?

Brákarhlíð, the old people's home in Borgarnes, was a two-storey building on the road leading into town from the south. It was still in the process of being extended, since it had become obvious as soon as it opened a few years back that there weren't enough places for all those who wanted one. When I said I'd like to speak to Kristrún, the friendly woman at reception asked if we were related. I said no, but that we used to work together.

'Oh, yes?' the woman said, clearly a little puzzled by the age difference. 'That's nice. Where was this?'

Immediately regretting my lie, I said actually it was my mother who had worked with her.

'At the sewing workshop?' she asked.

Relieved, I seized the life raft she offered and nodded. 'Right, at the sewing workshop. I often used to accompany my mother to work when I was young.'

'Hang on. I'll check whether Kristrún's still in the coffee lounge.'

It turned out that Kristrún was back in her room, which was on the first floor and had a view of the sea.

'Kristrún, you've got a visitor,' the woman announced. 'I'll leave you two alone, but call me if there's any problem.'

Before I could ask what kind of problem she meant, the woman had gone.

Kristrún regarded me balefully, then demanded in a gruff voice: 'Who are you?'

'My name's Marsibil,' I said.

The old woman's thin lips tightened. She didn't throw me out, though I sensed that she wouldn't need much of an excuse to do so. Deciding there was no point beating about the bush, I brought out the old black-and-white snapshot of the girl and the two little boys.

'I'm here because I found this at Reykir, and I believe the girl was at the workhouse there during the war. I know you were in charge of the place, so it occurred to me you might be able to tell me who she is.'

Kristrún looked from me to the picture. Her eyes were yellowish and watery, the rims drooping, revealing the pink skin inside.

When she didn't answer, I tried again. 'I know it's a long time ago—'

'Reykjavík,' Kristrún said. 'The girl was from Reykjavík. Poor. No father.'

'Do you remember her name?'

Kristrún's nostrils flared slightly and her lips moved, but I couldn't catch a word.

'Sorry, what did you say?'

'I said she was no better than she ought to be.'

'In what sense?'

'She was in the family way when she arrived,' Kristrún said. 'Couldn't deny that she was a promiscuous little slut.'

'She was pregnant?'

'Yes. And it was starting to show.'

That might explain why the girl had departed from Reykir in a hurry, leaving her belongings behind. 'Do you know what happened to her?'

'She left after the baby was born.'

'She had the baby at Reykir?'

'Indeed, she did. He was given away, sent to another part of the country.'

'Do you know where?'

'No.' Kristrún smacked her lips several times. Then she laughed, or rather snorted. 'After that she fancied herself as an actress.'

'Really?' For a moment I was pleased for her sake. It must mean she hadn't been broken by her experiences at the workhouse but had followed her dreams and gone on the stage.

'She appeared in a play,' the old woman continued. 'And no one knew what she'd done. Called herself Nína and put on all sorts of airs, but I knew … I knew what she was. Nothing but a Yankee whore.'

The oxygen had drained from the room. The air grew thick and stale; I couldn't breathe. Remotely I heard Kristrún telling me to go. When I didn't react, she raised her voice and screeched at me to get out. Even then, I couldn't move until the member of staff who had shown me in returned and took me by the arm.

37
Kristín – *Autumn 1967*

One day I steal Dad's car and drive to the head of the valley, making for the farm of Litla-Brú. Although I don't have a licence yet, I know how to drive, and there's little likelihood of being stopped by the police on this lonely stretch of road. I need to do this alone and the risk is worth it.

At the farm, the door is answered by a teenage boy, and when I ask for Áslaug, he directs me to the byre. It's raining outside and the path is wet and muddy. I wonder whether to knock at the door or march straight in, but it seems a bit odd to knock at the door of a cowshed, so in the end I just step inside.

I'm met by a pungent reek of cows. I've always liked the smell, unlike Málfríður, who gags every time she enters a byre.

I walk across the concrete floor to the stalls, each of which contains a cow, mooing and bellowing in competition with the others, but I can't see any sign of a person. Only when I call out a greeting does a head pop up from one of the stalls.

The woman has shortish hair, tied back under a headscarf, and a dark-brown knitted *lopapeysa* jumper with rolled-up sleeves.

'My name's Kristín,' I announce. 'I'm looking for Áslaug.'

The woman says she's Áslaug and asks what she can do for me.

'I'm doing a school project on the history of the Old Doctor's House at Reykir,' I say, stepping carefully to avoid the worst of the muck on the floor, and arriving beside the woman. 'I'm focusing on the period when there was a workhouse for girls there during the war.'

It was the explanation I had come up with on the way here. After all, you could describe finding the girl and returning her belongings as a sort of project I've taken on – at a stretch.

'And what makes you think I would know anything about that?' Áslaug asks.

When I explain that Halldóra suggested I talk to her, Áslaug nods slowly. I'm sensing a definite reluctance. It's like she's trying to make up her mind whether to talk to me or not.

'Will my name be mentioned?' she asks after a pause.

'Not if you don't want it to be.'

'What about the project? Will it be made public?'

'No,' I say. 'It's only for school.'

'All right, then.' Áslaug wipes her brow with her sleeve and beckons me to follow her.

We walk back to the house and enter by a side door that takes us through a storeroom and laundry. Áslaug kicks off her dirty boots and washes her hands thoroughly with soap. The byre smell is still noticeable, but a little fainter now. When we enter the kitchen, I take a seat at the table, and Áslaug offers me coffee but I ask for a glass of water instead.

Áslaug makes a coffee for herself, and while it's brewing we exchange a few bits of chitchat. Only when she sits down opposite me with her cup, does she return to the subject of Reykir.

She was only seventeen when she got the job at the workhouse, she tells me. 'My mother worked in the canteen and I used to help her after school. I couldn't wait to see the wicked girls from the city who'd been going with soldiers. I was a bit nervous about meeting them but excited too. I thought they'd be tough, worldly little madams, not afraid of anything; the type who would give people lip and make trouble. I was ready for anything, so it was a bit of a shock when they finally arrived and I saw how young they were – no older than me, and no different either. Of course, some of them wore make-up and fancy clothes, but most just seemed scared and miserable. I felt so sorry for them. I won't go into any details, but let's just say life at the workhouse was hard, which is why I went out of my way to be friendly to them, I suppose. It can't have been easy to be sent to the countryside, far from their homes, particularly in the circumstances. At the time – and maybe still today – people judged them very harshly. They were seen as a big social problem. I still think about them often. I wonder what it can have been like for them going home again afterwards. What kind of welcome did they get?'

'Did you keep up with any of them after they'd left?' I ask.

'No, not really.'

'And do you think there's any chance of finding out any of their names?'

'Maybe. But I don't know if that would be wise. I doubt they'd want to be found.'

'So you don't think they'd be willing to talk about their time at the school, then?'

'I can't imagine they'd want to. You have to understand the way people used to talk about them in those days. And still do. They were called ugly names – branded as whores. I heard they even had to undergo medical examinations of their private parts to see whether they'd had sex with soldiers.'

I can feel my face growing hot with embarrassment at the thought.

Áslaug notices. 'They were only children, no older than you – younger, some of them – yet they were treated like criminals.' Her look is intense. She's clearly still disturbed by what she witnessed. 'I very much doubt any of them will want to rake up the memories, wherever they are now.'

Áslaug sounds vehement as she says this. It's clear she doesn't want me to track them down – she wants to protect them. And I realise that if I'm to have a chance of getting any information out of her about the girl I'm looking for, I'll have to give her the real reason I'm here. I'll have to admit to her that I was lying.

'There is no project,' I blurt out. 'I made that up.'

Áslaug looks at me with raised eyebrows, as if she doesn't know quite how to react. 'Why are you here, then?' she asks.

I tell her the truth, or as close to the truth as I can get without mentioning Ívar. 'I took an evening class at the Old Doctor's House and found something that I believe used to belong to one of the girls. A shoebox of things that must have been left behind. I shouldn't have been in the room where I found it – that's why I lied. I didn't want anyone to know.'

Áslaug pauses before replying, taking a long sip of her coffee to give herself time to think and staring out of the window for a moment.

'Why do you believe it belonged to one of the girls at the workhouse?'

'Because of what was inside it,' I reply.

'And what was that?'

'Drawings and letters,' I say. 'A photo with *1943* written on the back. And a brooch with a rose on it.'

Áslaug's expression instantly changes and for a split second she looks at me, wide-eyed. Then she appears to catch herself, and averts her eyes, focusing on her cup once again.

'I don't want to distress her,' I say. 'I just want to return her belongings. I thought maybe she had to leave in a hurry and accidentally forgot them.'

Áslaug is nursing her coffee mug. She has a crease between her eyebrows that has deepened as we've been talking.

'I stayed in touch with one of the girls,' she says in a low voice. 'Her situation was different from the others. She was younger, only fourteen, and I could see straight away that being sent to the school wasn't the only problem she had. She kept her distance from the others, and never said a word. It wasn't a good place for her to be. Sometimes, as a punishment, the girls were locked in the cellar and...'

Áslaug falls silent and stares unseeingly into the middle distance for a while. I notice that her eyes are wet. She wipes her cheeks, almost angrily, before continuing.

'I've blamed myself so often for not having done something. That girl … it was like the matron had it in for her especially. She was always scolding her and mocking her. I don't know why, because the girl was pretty and very talented. She drew these wonderful pictures…'

'I've seen them,' I say quietly. Ever since I first saw the girl's drawings, I've felt a strong bond between us. That's why I have this compelling need to find her.

'You're right, she did have to leave in a hurry,' Áslaug continues, shifting her gaze back to me. 'She came to see me in the middle of the night, knocked on the door of my room, clutching her stomach. I was shocked at the sight of her: she was so pale and drenched in sweat. I thought she must be terribly ill. She kept clutching her stomach and crying. Then I realised what was happening. She gave birth to a baby boy that night. Can you believe it? She'd been pregnant when she arrived at the school but had managed to keep it hidden for months, right up until the child was born.'

'But she was so young,' I say.

Áslaug nods. 'I don't know why I find the memory so upsetting. Because she's doing well nowadays: she's got a family and a husband and lives not far away. She even tried to make it as an actress when she was younger.'

'Where did you say she lives?'

'I'd rather not betray her, if I can put it like that. I doubt she wants anyone to know she was at Reykir. Don't write about this in your project, will you? I don't want anything too personal to come out – about where she lives or anything like that. I do believe it's important for people to know what those poor girls had to suffer, though.'

'Right…' My voice seems to be coming from a great distance, and I can hardly stammer out a word. I'm still trying to come to terms with the significance of what I've just learnt.

'The boy was sent for adoption by a family out east. A couple from Sætún. They were eager to have him but…' Áslaug hesitates. 'But she was inconsolable. She was. She'd already given him a name. She called him Bergur. When the couple came to take her baby away, the staff had to forcibly restrain her.'

The name doesn't ring any bells at first. I'm so shocked and disorientated by what I've learnt that it's not until I'm on my way home that it occurs to me why the name Bergur is familiar.

38
Marsibil – *Saturday, 26 November 1977*

I wasn't aware of anything except the road in front of me. My brain was frantically occupied in trying to piece together the evidence I had gathered.

In the end, I stopped the car by the side of the road and took out the old photo. Now I realised who the girl resembled: she was a mixture of me and Stína. She was our mother more than thirty years ago.

Mum and I were more alike than I'd realised. If I compared photos of us at the same age, it was obvious that I was my mother's daughter. Although she was fair and I was dark, we had the same mouth, and there was something similar about our features and the shape of our heads.

It was deeply disconcerting to realise that I knew so little about someone I'd been close to all my life. I thought I was familiar with Mum's story, but when I tried to recall the details, they turned out to be very thin on the ground. My maternal grandmother had died when Mum was in her teens, after which she'd been forced to fend for herself. She had younger brothers but didn't know what had happened to them. Then she'd got a job in the theatre, met Dad and moved here.

Such a simple story, only a few sentences. Of course, it should have been obvious to me that Mum's story was much more complicated than that. Mum, who was always either up in the clouds or sunk deep in depression. So brittle and sad. I had come up with childishly simple explanations for her behaviour: that she was upset because of Dad or because of something Stína or I had done.

How must Mum have felt when she was packed off to Reykir? And what had awaited her on her return home?

From what I could gather, her time at the workhouse must have been terrible, and, as if that wasn't bad enough, Mum had been pregnant and forced to give up her baby. Had the photo of a baby I had found in our family album been of that little boy? Of a brother I didn't know I had?

Then my mind returned to the headband that had vanished from my room and the way Mum reacted every time I mentioned Stína. The fact she was so against my asking questions about her disappearance.

I didn't know if Stína had uncovered this story, but, even if she had, surely it couldn't have had any bearing on what happened to her. Mum would never have harmed her, would she? Her temper may have been erratic at times but she would never have laid hands on us or done anything to hurt us. Never. Not deliberately, at least.

So why was I finding it so hard to convince myself of this?

While I was driving to Gústi's house, words like 'accident' and 'authority' kept echoing in my head. I saw images of my mother plunging the baby under water; tickling me mercilessly; weeping in her room. Saw her washing me, scrubbing me with a flannel so hard that my skin burned. My dreams kept spilling over into reality until I turned up the car radio as loud as it would go in a vain attempt to block them out.

At Gústi's house, his sister Ína told me he was in the garage. As I approached, I saw the door was open and that Gústi was bending over an upturned bicycle. His hands were dark with oil and he had a black streak on his chin.

'How's things, Marsí?' he said when he saw me. He straightened up, grabbed a rag and wiped his hands.

I had been waiting impatiently to talk to him all the way here, but now that it came to the point, I didn't know how much to reveal, so I didn't say anything.

'Is everything OK?' Gústi came towards me. 'Has something happened?'

'What if what happened to Stína was an accident?' I blurted out at last.

'Is that what you think?'

'What if it was just an innocent accident that was never intended to happen, and exposing it won't make things any better?'

'Well, at least you would know,' Gústi pointed out. 'I thought that's what you wanted.'

'What if knowing is worse than not knowing?'

'Has something happened?' Gústi asked again.

Biting my lower lip, I shook my head.

'So what makes you think it was an accident?' he asked. 'Have you discovered something?'

'I'm not sure.'

'What?' He took a step closer, and I saw that his fist had tightened around the spanner he was holding. 'Marsí, what have you found out?'

'It … it's nothing,' I said. 'An accident just seems like the most rational explanation to me.'

'Oh.' Gústi's shoulders relaxed. 'It's possible, but remember that if it was an accident, it would have been a simple matter to call the police.'

'Accidents aren't always simple.'

'Well, yes, they are. Accidents are accidents – they're unintentional.'

'Not everyone sees it like that.'

'Marsí, we're in this together, aren't we? You would tell me if you'd uncovered something, wouldn't you?'

'Yes, of course.'

'Good.' Gústi brushed his sleeve across his brow. 'I'm going to jump in the shower, then we can go and get something to eat.'

'Actually, I've got to go home,' I said, backing out of the garage. 'But I'll talk to you later, OK?'

I didn't meet Gústi's eye. I was too afraid he'd see that I was lying.

Torfi didn't usually work on Saturdays but I knew he lived in a little house not far from the police station. He had been alone since his wife left him, a story my mother had been full of several years ago. Apparently his wife had decided to take a pottery course once the children no longer needed her at home and had fallen for her teacher, a Greek man who didn't speak a word of Icelandic. This didn't seem to matter, though, because they were head over heels in love and had moved to Greece together. The children were both grown up now; they had gone to university in Reykjavík and never moved back.

Torfi soon came to the door, in a T-shirt rather than his usual uniform, chewing a mouthful of food. I'd never seen him dressed so casually before.

He swallowed when he saw me and asked how I was, but I batted the question away with a flap of my hand. I was past small talk. My need for answers was like a hole in my gut.

'Why did a forensics team never come round to our house to do a proper search?' I blurted out.

'What?' He blinked in surprise and wiped some food from the corner of his mouth with a thumb. 'You mean when your sister went missing? There was no reason for them to.'

'Why did you refuse assistance from Reykjavík?' I pressed on. I felt slightly dizzy now.

'Marsibil, come in a minute.' He stepped aside to allow me to enter, but his patronising tone immediately put my back up.

'Just tell me why,' I demanded as I stepped into the hallway. 'Why was our home never properly examined?'

'Because...' Torfi scratched the back of his head. 'Marsibil, there was no reason to search your house. Stína went missing on her way home. She was last seen at her friend's place and never made it back to your house.'

'And you believe that?'

'What?'

'That she never came home?'

'What is it you're trying to say, Marsibil?' He tipped his head back a little and looked at me.

'Why were you so sure she hadn't come home?' I persisted. 'Did you just take it for granted that my parents were telling the truth?'

'We did what we believed to be the right thing at the time,' Torfi said.

'Did they ask you not to search the house?' It was a question I shouldn't have asked but I couldn't stop myself; I had to know.

Torfi eyed me for what felt like a long time. 'I've known your father since we were boys, Marsibil. Maybe I should have set that aside and called in detectives from Reykjavík to work on the investigation. Perhaps we should have done a more thorough search of your house, but there was no reason to doubt your parents' account and, according to them, Stína had never come home. Now Marsibil, I want you to sit down and explain to me what it is you're trying to achieve.' He gestured towards the living room.

My breathing was coming so fast and shallow that for a moment I thought I was going to faint in the narrow confines of the hall.

'Marsibil…'

'I have to go.'

I left without saying goodbye. Got back in the car and made a desperate attempt to focus my woolly thoughts and make sense of things. Perhaps there was nothing suspicious about the fact my father had asked Torfi to spare our house. If my parents were sure that Stína hadn't come home after she went to Málfríður's, there would have been no need.

But a number of things were troubling me.

The yellow headband I found in the cellar that had vanished from my windowsill this morning; my parents' determination to block all my attempts to ask questions about Stína; the fact that Mum had a past I'd known nothing about; and the new, darker side of Dad that I had witnessed last night. All this evidence had built up into something so overwhelming that it was impossible now for me to go back to Reykjavík and pretend nothing had happened.

39
Kristín – *October 1967*

There's no time to lose as Marsí will be back from school any minute. As soon as I get home, I run up to her room and push back the picture frame over her bed, but the letter has gone.

For a moment I stand there stock still, my mind running through all the possibilities. Where else might Marsí hide a letter?

When we were small, we used to steal sweets or biscuits to have as midnight feasts. In those days we always hid them in the same place, under our pillows. I lift up Marsí's pillow but there's nothing there. Of course, we're no longer little girls who hide things in such obvious places.

Then I notice the shape of something inside the pillowcase and when I touch it, there's a crackling of paper. Quick as a flash, I slip my hand inside the pillowcase and draw out an envelope.

It's a letter addressed to me, which gives me a moment's confusion. Has Marsí been writing to a boy in my name? I turn it over and see that the sender's name on the back is Bergur, just as I remembered. Judging by the address, he lives in the east, like the couple Áslaug said had adopted Mum's baby, though he doesn't live on a farm called Sætún but on another one near Höfn í Hornafirði.

Downstairs, I hear the sound of the front door opening and recognise the thud as Marsí drops her school bag. In frantic haste, I return the letter to its hiding place and dart out of the room, narrowly missing Marsí. She says hello, eyeing me suspiciously for a moment before going into her room. Relieved at having got away with it, I head down to the kitchen to get myself a drink.

Perhaps it's a coincidence. Just because the boy Marsí is corresponding with has the same name and lives out east, that doesn't mean he's the same one. Bergur's a common enough name; there must be plenty of people called that in the east of Iceland.

I sit down and lean my elbows on the kitchen table. Then I take out the old photo of the girl and scribble down the name of the couple's farm on the back: *Sætún*. The baby boy born at Reykir was called Bergur and sent to Sætún. It's confirmation of what I'd suspected.

The girl in the photo must be my mother.

Áslaug spoke of an actress who lived nearby and I don't know many actresses in this part of the country apart from Mum.

'If you go into my room again, I'll…' hisses an icy voice behind me.

Before I know what's happening, Marsí is looming over me, her eyes black with fury, her fists clenched.

'You'll what?' I ask, shaken by her rage.

'You'll regret it.' She storms off and I hear the door of her room slamming.

During the night I'm woken by a noise. Usually, I try to ignore this kind of disturbance and go back to sleep, but this time there's a quality to it that drives me out of bed.

The moment my bare feet touch the floor, I feel something soft brushing against my toes. Bending down, I pick up what turns out to be a hank of hair from the floor by my bed. It's a sizeable hank, too long to be mine.

Stealthily, I open my door and creep out to see what's going on. There's no one in the kitchen, and it's not until my eyes have adjusted to the gloom that I see what's on the floor – the big kitchen scissors, with more tufts of hair scattered around them.

Then a chilly draught from the laundry tells me that the back door must be open. When I go to close it, I see a figure standing in the garden, uncannily still, staring in the direction of the wood, her sweep of long hair now reduced to a few straggling, hacked-off tufts.

'You've got to do something,' I tell Dad the next day. 'She could hurt herself. She had the scissors, for Christ's sake. What if she'd cut herself?'

'I know, Stína. You needn't worry.'

Dad and I are the only ones at home. He's standing in front of the bathroom mirror, shaving, the lower part of his face covered in white foam.

'Perhaps we should lock the bedroom door.'

'Lock the door?' He carefully scrapes the razor over the left side of his jaw, leaving a clear stripe in the foam.

'Only so she … she can't go outside.' Or into my room, I think.

My mind keeps coming back to what might have happened when she was standing over me with the scissors. What might someone be capable of in their sleep that they wouldn't do normally? How far might they go? I used to think there was some kind of common sense governing a sleeper's behaviour, but recently I've discovered that this is not necessarily the case. People can do things in their sleep that they would never do when awake, and the thought frightens me more than I dare to show.

'Don't start on that nonsense again, Stína,' Dad says. 'We can't lock her in. Anyway, I usually hear when she gets out of bed.'

'You didn't last night,' I point out. 'And look what happened.'

But Dad is adamant. I can feel my frustration mounting. He was out all day yesterday. And I'm such a coward that I haven't breathed a word about what I witnessed between him and Alda, although it was months ago now. How can he be so pigheaded? Doesn't he give a damn about his family?

'Where were you yesterday?' I ask in a level voice.

'Yesterday?' Dad rinses his razor in the sink. 'I was working.'

'Right.'

He's watching me in the mirror, glowering at me with his dark eyes.

'I know about you,' I say, unable to keep a tremor out of my voice. 'I know about you and … and *her*. I saw you.'

For a beat, Dad remains perfectly still, then he resumes his shaving. 'Whatever it was you saw, Stína, you must have been mistaken.'

I'm no longer sad, I'm angry. So furious that I want to snatch the razor and slash him with it.

Does he really think I'm that stupid?

For the first time since I went to see Áslaug yesterday, the two girls merge into a single person; the girl in the photo who was sent away to the workhouse and my beautiful, fragile mother. I've never felt I understood Mum. I used to look up to her when I was younger but, at the same time, I would catch myself thinking she was weak, over-sensitive. There used to be days, weeks even, when she was in no fit state to look after us. I don't mean that she didn't feed us, but she had no love or affection to spare. She wasn't a mother but a frustrated actress who raged about the fact we were holding her back. As the elder sister, I did my best to protect Marsí from the fallout. I was the one who comforted her and gave her the affection our mother wasn't capable of showing. But now, in the light of what I've learnt, this resentment I built up against Mum has fizzled out.

'I know about Mum,' I say.

Dad rinses the razor and turns. 'What about your mother?'

'I know she was one of those girls who was sent away to the workhouse. You're a bastard to do this to her after all she's been—'

Wham.

My cheek is stinging. But worse than the pain is the shock, and for a second I'm paralysed, struggling to understand what just happened.

Dad hit me.

Not lightly but with the full force of his broad hand.

He says something, but I rush out without listening. I flee the house – into the garden, then into the wood where my knees give way beneath me and I sprawl on the cold earth.

40
Marsibil – *Saturday, 26 November 1977*

The house was filled with the savoury smell of roasting chicken.

'Marsí, is that you?' Mum called from the kitchen when I came in. 'Supper's nearly ready.'

I felt my gorge rising and did my best to swallow.

Mum called out again, but instead of answering I made a beeline for the cellar door.

It was as if the lightbulb understood the urgency. It clicked on instantly for once, shedding a yellowish glow around the room. This time I plunged down the steps without a moment's hesitation.

At the bottom, I stood there, taking stock. The air smelt of mildew but I was getting used to it. There were the streaks on the wall that I had run a moistened finger over as a child; the streaks Stína and I had believed were our grandfather's blood but were probably just a combination of damp and dirt.

Up against one wall was the stack of cardboard boxes I had been rummaging in last night when I found the headband.

Lifting one down, I began to pull out the contents, chucking them aside without paying them any particular attention. Once the first box was empty, I started on the next.

'What's going on, Marsí?' I heard Mum calling from the top of the stairs, but I didn't answer.

The second box contained nothing of interest, only old crockery. No yellow headband – but then it was unlikely it would have been put back in the same place. I did find a sketchpad, though, which I opened and leafed through. The sketches were of houses and landscapes, all drawn in pencil, using soft, muted strokes. I recognised our house, the wood and the view up the fjord, and there was another building that looked familiar. It resembled the Old Doctor's House at Reykir. Then there was a portrait of an old woman with weary eyes. At the bottom were my mother's initials: J.H.S.

Stína had inherited her artistic talent from our mother. I now remembered how, when we were young, we used to pester Mum to do drawings for us: cats, horses, rabbits. We would watch in breathless wonder as, with a few, apparently random strokes of the pencil, the images we had asked for would materialise on the paper.

The third box was full of files, which I carried closer to the light to read. The envelope on top immediately caught my attention as my own name was written on the front. Tearing it open, I saw that it was a report by the therapist I had gone to see not long after Stína went missing.

Patient name: Marsibil Karvelsdóttir
Date: 14 February 1968
Age: 15 years and 9 months

Marsibil came to see me after her parents became concerned
about certain changes they had observed in her behaviour.

I stuffed the sheet of paper back in the envelope without reading any further. I had no desire to be reminded of my juvenile problems. Yet I was aware of a tickling in my throat, as though the memory of that time was triggering the old physical symptoms. Those were the years when I had started plucking out the hair on the back of my head. At first it was only single strands, just a slight twinge as the hair tore out by the root. Then I started pulling out several at once, yanking out whole clumps, unable to stop myself. I would experience first pain, then relief. It felt as though I could temporarily extract all my pain, and it had worked. It worked until Mum caught sight of the bald patch on the back of my head. It was then that she took the big kitchen scissors and cut off my hair to shoulder length.

I don't know when I started eating the hair.

It was probably soon after I started pulling it out. I wasn't conscious of it at first, but one night I woke up to find a clump of hair stuck in my throat, and began to cough and retch. That was the feeling that overtook me now, as if there was trapped hair tickling the back of my throat. I tried to swallow but it didn't work, only made the irritation worse.

'Marsí, what are you doing?' Mum was on the top step now.

I straightened up. 'Where's Stína's headband?'

'Oh, Marsí.' Then I heard Mum calling Dad's name, as if for help.

I gulped again in an attempt to get rid of the tickling sensation, then continued digging in the boxes.

After rooting around some more, I came across several pages that had been torn from a notebook. I recognised my sister's writing. These must be the missing pages that had been ripped out of Stína's diary. Upstairs I heard Mum calling Dad's name again. Any minute now they would be down here, insisting that I stop my search. Hands trembling with urgency, I held the pages up to the light.

Each page contained a few lines of text: *I've started locking my bedroom door*, she had written on one. *I don't want to wake up again and find her standing over me*. On the next page she described how she had woken up when someone took hold of the door handle and kept shaking it. *She's not herself when she's asleep, but someone I'm afraid of. She really frightens me*. Every single page was devoted to Stína's anxiety about what Mum got up to in her sleep. It was what they all had in common, I realised. And according to Stína's descriptions, Mum's sleepwalking was much worse than I remembered.

It must have been my parents who had removed these passages from the diary.

From the top of the stairs, Mum asked if everything was all right.

It wasn't. It was so far from being all right. Nothing was all right anymore. The tickling in my throat intensified and I couldn't get rid of it however much I coughed and cleared my throat and clawed at my neck.

All that time when I believed Dad had been looking for Stína, what had he really been up to? Could he have been making sure that there were no holes in the investigation and that no one would find any clues that pointed to my parents? To Mum?

'What on earth are you doing, Marsibil?' Mum had finally climbed down the stairs now.

I threw down the loose pages and reached for the next box. I was about to open it when I spotted something odd about the wall that up to now had been hidden by the boxes. It looked as if a frame had been cut into the wall.

Shoving the box aside, I ran my hands over the surface. It was wood, not concrete like the rest.

'*Marsibil*.' Mum's voice was sharp. 'Stop that.'

'What's behind here, Mum?' When I tried tapping the board, it emitted a hollow sound. It was a door. There must be a storage space behind it that I had never known existed.

'Marsibil, don't—'

I banged hard on the door and that was all it took. It opened inwards to reveal a poky space.

Stína's yellow headband was lying on the floor, as if someone had chucked it in there in a hurry. I squeezed inside and picked it up. Then I climbed back out again and turned to Mum.

'What happened to Stína, Mum? Why can't you tell me the truth?'

I thought I'd be blinded by rage but instead I felt so weak that my legs gave way and I crumpled to the floor. All my strength had deserted me and I stared mutely at Mum, waiting. Waiting to hear the last thing on earth I wanted to hear.

'My darling.' Mum reached out to touch me, but I flinched away.

'Just tell me the truth,' I said, my voice threadbare with exhaustion. 'I know everything, Mum. I know why you're so … I know you were sent to the workhouse, that you were pregnant.'

Mum didn't move; her face was frozen.

'I remember when we were young how … how unhappy you were. I remember you walking in your sleep. Stína was afraid of you. She wrote about it in her diary.'

'No.' Mum shook her head. 'No, Marsí.'

'I know it was an accident,' I said. 'I know you didn't mean to hurt her.'

A tear ran down Mum's cheek, and with a sickening jolt it came home to me that it was true. All this time my parents had known what had happened to Stína but hadn't said a word. Just kept quiet and let me suffer.

'Where is she?' I whispered hoarsely. 'Is Stína still here?'

For a moment there was dead silence in the cellar. Then a tiny movement confirmed that my worst fears were true.

Almost imperceptibly, Mum nodded.

41
Kristín – *Winter 1967*

It's not a noise that wakes me so much as a presence, sensed through my sleep. Yet when I sit up, I find myself alone in my room. I wait for my eyes to adjust to the darkness, trying to work out if something is different, wrong. All seems peaceful; there's no sound of the wind outside and, for once, the house itself is quiet. Yet I can't rid myself of the impression that someone has been standing in my room, watching me sleep.

Wide awake now, I get out of bed and pad softly downstairs to the kitchen. After running the tap for a while, I fill a glass with water and drink it in one go. As I'm putting the glass down, I become aware of a familiar musty smell and see that the cellar door is standing ajar.

I tend to forget the cellar's there. We don't use it much, except as a storeroom for all kinds of junk from my grandparents' time that Mum and Dad can't be bothered to sort out. The door is kept locked as Dad doesn't want us messing about down there, which means that someone must have opened it now.

I try the light switch but nothing happens; the bulb must have blown. My childish fear of the cellar raises its head but I dismiss it impatiently. I'm not a child any longer. Gústi says that darkness doesn't exist as such, it's just an absence of light, but standing here, peering into the blackness below, it feels all too real – almost palpable.

I pick my way down the steps, my breathing suddenly shallow, the blood booming in my ears.

'Hello?' I whisper.

No answer.

Either Mum or Dad must have opened the cellar door yesterday and forgotten to lock it again. Our house is subject to odd draughts and if this door isn't locked, it has a tendency to open of its own accord.

I'm halfway back up the stairs when I hear what sounds like rustling.

I stiffen, then turn.

My eyes have grown accustomed to the darkness now and I can

see faintly in the light spilling down from the kitchen. Summoning up my courage, I descend the stairs again, more purposefully this time, until I'm standing on the bottom step. It could simply have been a mouse scurrying between the boxes. As I dither, unsure whether to investigate or return to the kitchen, I become aware of a different sound – not rustling but what could almost be breathing.

Then there's a sniff. I strain my eyes into the darkness.

I start violently when I make out the shape of a figure sitting on the floor, hugging its knees. I choke back a scream and it emerges as a moan.

'Come along,' I say, forcing myself to speak calmly and bending down to take her hand to lead her back up to bed.

Before I know what's happening, my hand is gripped and jerked. It happens so fast that I don't have time to react and go crashing to the floor. Next moment my hair is being savagely pulled, a blow lands on my cheek and I let out a scream. Another blow hits me in the stomach, a third on the breast.

I yell at her to stop, but the pinching and clawing goes on, and it's only when Dad comes running down the stairs and tears her off me that I can break free.

'What did I tell you?' Dad hisses at me. 'Don't try to wake her when she's in this state.'

'But I didn't mean to … I wasn't…' I can't catch my breath to finish the sentence. Dad's not listening. He lifts her in his arms and carries her up the stairs.

I'm left alone in the cellar, with something wet trickling down my forehead, but instead of moving I just lie there, shellshocked, until all is quiet again.

42
Marsibil – *Saturday, 26 November 1977*

We both jumped as a bloodcurdling scream tore through the silence. For a split second we stared at each other, and I was surprised to see alarm in my mother's eyes. I'd been expecting something different – shame or guilt, perhaps – but, no, Mum was afraid. She turned and raced up the stairs.

The screaming was coming from outside. We left by the back door and found Dad in the garden, standing in front of the hencoop, wrestling with the padlock on the fence.

'What's going on?' Mum asked. But then her face dropped and she stared dumbly at something in the run.

I didn't immediately join them, fighting the compulsion to go back down to the cellar, in the hope of finding more things that had belonged to my sister. I wanted a proper explanation from Mum, but more than anything I had a desperate need to hear from her that the whole thing was a misunderstanding.

What could Mum have meant when she said that Stína was still here?

I glanced around the garden, at the bare branches of the trees stirring in the wind. I could sense Stína's presence, but then I'd always felt that. Her presence was all-pervasive in our house.

Mum and Dad had both turned and were staring at me, their expressions unreadable. When I joined them by the hencoop, I saw what was wrong.

They were all dead, lying on the ground, bloodstained feathers everywhere, sticking to the fence and the side of the henhouse. Most of their necks were wrenched back at odd angles. It looked as if something had entered the cage – a fox or mink – and gone berserk.

Dad opened the door of the run and lifted out Bossy's limp corpse, holding her as tenderly as he would a newborn baby. Then he turned on me, an accusing, reproachful look in his eyes.

'But … but … it wasn't me. I didn't do this,' I protested. I had a confused, guilty feeling. I'd forgotten to feed them. But that couldn't have led to this. My mouth felt sandpaper dry, I could barely swallow, and the irritation was still there in my throat.

'The cage was locked, Marsibil,' Dad said. 'The key was indoors.'

'But a fox could have got in. It could have gnawed a hole or…'

'I can't see any hole,' Dad said. 'And foxes don't wring hens' necks.'

'I didn't do it,' I whispered again, but now my words sounded like a question. Last night's dream rose to my mind. I heard again the snapping of the hens' necks. The ground seemed to be moving in waves.

'Then who did?'

I simply shook my head, then watched helplessly as my parents carried the dead hen to the house. Neither of them gave me a backward look. As if they couldn't bear the sight of me. As if I disgusted them.

I was left behind in the garden, staring dumbly into the cage. There were little brown feathers all over the place, as if the birds had been involved in a frantic struggle before their necks were broken. My gaze was caught by something else, fluttering in the breeze. I ducked inside the run to take a closer look.

It was hair. Dark hair, snagged on the fence. I freed it and compared it to my own. The colour was identical.

My head swam and I had to lean against the coop. A cold gust of wind blew into my face and for a moment I couldn't breathe. My eyes stung, they were burning behind their lids. Suddenly my body crumpled and slid down the fence until I was sitting on the gravel inside the cage.

Scenes started flashing before my mind's eye, horrible scenes I didn't want to see. Me grasping the hens by their necks. Stína lying in the snow. The click of a neck breaking. Blonde hair wet with blood.

I squeezed my eyes tight shut, trying to put a stop to the flow of images.

Then I began to heave.

This time I didn't stop retching until something came up. I coughed and coughed until I had spat out the thing that had been stuck in my throat – a slimy clump of hair.

43
Kristín – *Winter 1967*

The sound of hammering.

I'm reading in my room when I hear it coming from the landing. For the last few days I haven't left the house, reluctant to let anyone see my battered face. Dad didn't ask any questions when I begged him to ring the school and tell them I was ill. Worst of all, though, are the big, black bruises on my body. My upper right arm is aching too, which makes it hard to get comfortable.

On the landing, I see that Dad has put up a stepladder in front of Marsí's bedroom door and is banging in a nail over the lintel.

'What are you doing?'

'It's for her own good,' he says.

I go down to the kitchen, where Mum is humming as she makes pancakes. She's experiencing one of her good phases, constantly humming, a bottomless well of stories that we've all heard countless times before.

'Are you hungry, my darling?' she asks. 'These are nearly ready.'

'Where's Marsí?'

'At school, of course,' Mum says.

The days have blended seamlessly into one another while I've been stuck at home, making it hard to keep track of whether it's the weekend or a school day, but I suppose it must be Monday.

'Marsí's always in her room these days, scribbling away.' Mum takes the frying pan off the stove and wipes her hands on her apron. 'I saw her take a letter to the post the other day, and she's always waiting on tenterhooks for the postman to arrive. I reckon she's got a penpal.'

'Good for her,' I say, too tired to think about Bergur and the possible implications if he is who I think he is.

'Yes,' Mum says. 'It is good for her. Your sister doesn't have many friends, so getting to know someone this way is a positive thing.'

I roll up a pancake and have just taken the first bite when I hear a bell ringing.

Mum and I both go out into the hall. Dad is standing outside Marsí's room, repeatedly opening and shutting the door. Over the top he has nailed a small piece of wood from which he's hung a piece of string with a bell on the end.

He seems quite pleased with himself. 'There. Now we'll be able to hear if her door opens in the night.'

The bell's tone is loud and clear. I don't know whether to laugh or cry. I suspect this bell is going to keep us all awake at night, just like her nocturnal wanderings. But at least now I'll have some warning when Marsí walks in her sleep.

44
Marsibil – *Saturday, 26 November 1977*

Dad came to get me and led me by the hand back to the house. Bossy's body was nowhere to be seen, but I couldn't get her squawking out of my ears. And I couldn't stop trembling. I shook like a leaf in the wind, however hard I tried to control my muscles.

'Pipsqueak,' Dad said, his voice gentle now. 'Let us explain.'

I sat down and closed my eyes, wishing with all my heart that I had never come home. That I had left things alone and stayed in the comfortable bubble I had created for myself in Reykjavík, far removed from everything here.

When I opened my eyes again, Mum had placed an envelope with my name on it in front of me. It was the same envelope I had found in the cellar, which contained the therapist's report I'd decided not to read.

'Why are you giving me this?' I asked.

'Read it,' Dad said. 'It'll explain…'

I took out the sheet of paper and began to read it under the watchful eyes of my parents.

Patient name: Marsibil Karvelsdóttir
Date: 14 February 1968
Age: 15 years and 9 months

Marsibil came to see me after her parents became concerned about certain changes they had observed in her behaviour. For some time she has shown signs of serious mental disturbance, stress and anxiety. As evidence of this, her parents point both to her sleep disorder and to the fact that Marsibil has taken to tearing out her hair. Her mother has noticed that she tends to cough and retch a lot in the mornings. Once, she threw up and her vomit turned out to be full of hair, which leads to the suspicion that Marsibil is eating the hair she has pulled out.

Marsibil's sleep disorder is having a serious impact on her life. She has been known to nod off during her daily activities, only to start awake, screaming or crying. Marsibil has a long history of sleep disturbances, including frequent episodes of sleepwalking as a child, a pattern of behaviour that has intensified during her adolescence. Her mother reports having struggled with bouts of sleepwalking herself some years ago, and it should be noted that the condition can run in families. But the mother believes Marsibil's nocturnal activities represent a far more serious problem. Not only has it proved impossible to wake her during these episodes but she has also reacted with violence on occasion. According to her parents, the following day Marsibil has no memory of what happened during the night.

'I don't want to read any more,' I said, shoving away the report.

It was bullshit. There was nothing wrong with me. It wasn't me who was ill but Mum. She was the one who used to walk in her sleep when we were young; who drank too much, took pills and was subject to fits of weeping. I had occasionally walked in my sleep as a child, but it wasn't serious. Nothing like what was described in that report.

Dad took the paper and returned it to the envelope. 'Pipsqueak, there's something you need to know. Something your mother and I haven't told you.'

The world seemed to dissolve in a mist. I blinked several times but couldn't make out my father's features, only his vague outline.

'Do you remember when you were little and used to walk in your sleep? We would find you all over the house – in the bathroom, the sitting room, sometimes even the storeroom. You used to roam around, sometimes standing in one spot for a long time, at other times heading off somewhere. We were worried about you but you never seemed to come to any harm.'

'But that was when I was very young,' I pointed out. I hadn't walked in my sleep since then. It was Mum. She was the one Dad had always had to worry about.

'The thing is, the problem became a lot worse when you entered your teens. The doctors assured us it would wear off with age, but it showed no signs of getting better. Quite the reverse. The worst – or perhaps the best – part was that you didn't seem to remember anything. You slept so soundly in spite of your nighttime wanderings that it was impossible to wake you. Your mother and I were at our wits' end, especially after the business with the car.'

'The car?'

'Once you actually got in the car and set off down the drive. Luckily, you didn't get far because you veered off into the garden. Your sister found you lying beside the car next morning. Nobody had heard a thing in the night. We were extremely worried about you after that. Another time, Stína found you in the cellar and tried to wake you, but you lashed out at her.'

'No...' I whispered.

'After that, we hung a bell over your door at night so we would always have a warning when you left your room.'

'But it was Mum,' I groaned, ignoring the distant jangling of a bell. 'It was Mum who walked in her sleep. I mean, I know I did it myself a few times, but Mum was much worse. I found the pages from Stína's diary: she was terrified of her.'

'These pages.' Dad now laid the pages torn from the diary in front of me. 'Stína was talking about *you*, Marsí. She was scared of what you might do. We were all worried about you.'

Quickly scanning the pages again, it dawned on me belatedly that Stína had never mentioned Mum. I had simply taken it for granted that she was talking about her in the diary.

'You never remembered anything about it afterwards,' Mum said. 'Usually, we just led you back to bed. And you went on sleeping and woke up next morning as if nothing had happened. We didn't want to tell you in case it made you anxious and stopped you being able to get to sleep at night.'

'But I would know if I'd done something bad in my sleep,' I argued. 'I would know.'

'Marsí, you must have been aware on some level.'

'Don't you remember the bell we hung above your door?' Dad asked.

'And you must remember sometimes waking up to find you weren't in your bed?' Mum added.

I rubbed my head.

It's true that when I lived at Nátthagi, I had sometimes woken up in strange places, but only a handful of times. It hadn't happened since I'd moved to Reykjavík.

That bloody bell. I remembered the bell, all right. Remembered it jangling in the night, permeating my dreams. At the time, I had asked Dad what it was for, and I could still recall him smiling and saying it was just to make sure we didn't go wandering about in the night. He'd talked as if it was no big deal, just a minor precaution.

'We've been trying to protect you, Marsí,' Dad said now. 'That evening, I … I don't know what happened or why. Your mother and I … Well, to be honest we'd had too much to drink. You know what it was like in those days.'

I nodded, knowing full well what they had been like then – and still were.

'Anyway, I went to check on you late that evening but you weren't in your room. The car had gone too and we were terribly worried because of what had happened the last time. I went out to look for you but didn't get far before the car reappeared with you behind the wheel. When you got out, I noticed that you were in a strange state. I wasn't sure if you were sleepwalking, but your mother and I took you indoors, led you up to your room and put you to bed. It was only then that I noticed there was blood on your clothes. I tried to ask you about it but you didn't answer, so I got in the car myself and started driving in the direction you'd come from, and then I saw ... I saw something on the side of the road.

'We knew it was an accident. You'd tried to stop the bleeding; you'd taken her coat off. We didn't know what to do, Marsí. We could have rung the police and admitted everything but we didn't want to do that to you. You had never been able to remember what you did when you walked in your sleep and we wanted things to stay like that. Not for you to have to live forever with the burden on your conscience that you'd...'

That I'd killed Stína.

Unable to control myself, I broke into loud, anguished sobbing.

Dad rubbed his brow. 'I blame myself, Marsí. I found you in the kitchen earlier that evening and I suspect you'd drunk out of one of the glasses. Is that possible?' When I nodded dazedly, he buried his face in his hands. After a pause, he looked up at me again. 'We were partying that evening and I'm ashamed to say it but ... but I wasn't a good husband in those days. I needed to go out and your mother was very drunk. She could stay up all night when she was in that sort of mood, so I put a sleeping pill in her drink. I'm guessing it was her glass you finished and that the drug had a bad effect on you.'

All these years I had been puzzled about how I could have fallen asleep that evening when I was so excited about meeting Bergur. I could still recall the strange drowsiness that had come over me when I went back up to my room to wait for a chance to sneak out.

'Why did you need to go out?' I asked. Even in my shocked state, I picked up on this discordant element.

'I...' Dad hesitated.

Mum shook her head. 'Just tell her,' she said.

'I was having an affair with Alda at the time. It's over now – it's been over for years. But Stína was furious with me about it in the weeks before she died.'

'Was that what you quarrelled about?'

Dad nodded. 'After Stína vanished, I put a stop to it. I'd begun to remind myself of my own father: drinking too much, avoiding problems. Reacting with anger and violence.'

'You hit her,' I said.

Dad nodded again, then bent his head and his shoulders began to shake. Mum laid a hand on his back.

I was too numb to feel anything now. I couldn't be furious at them. Anger would change nothing. Stína would still be gone.

'What became of her body?'

Mum took over the story. 'We went and fetched her. It was too late to save her. Far too late.' For a while Mum appeared to be wrestling with tears as well. 'We buried her in the garden. Not straight away, but as soon as we got the chance. I washed you, washed the sheets, then put you back to bed. It wasn't your fault and, whatever happened, we just wanted you to forget about it.'

'You have to understand that it was an accident,' Dad said. 'You didn't know what you were doing. And we couldn't risk the police coming to take you away. We'd already lost one daughter and we were determined not to lose the other. We decided that it was for the best.'

'If only you hadn't come home and insisted on digging around,' Mum said. 'We tried to stop you but you've always been so stubborn. I should have known that asking you to leave it alone wouldn't do any good.'

It was all too much. I felt suffocated, crushed under the weight of what they were telling me.

That must be why I had blocked out the memories – they were too much to bear.

I closed my eyes tightly but I couldn't shut out the scenes that rose to my mind one after the other as though I was finally piecing together a dream that had faded from my memory. I remembered the car, remembered my bloodstained clothes, remembered standing in the bathtub while my mother scrubbed at me with a flannel, repeating over and over 'we've got to get you clean'.

||

'It is forgetting, not remembering, that is the essence of what makes us human. To make sense of the world, we must filter it.'

—Joshua Foer

45

Marsibil – *Monday, 28 November 1977*

The fjord was a dazzling white when I drove home two days later. It had snowed, and the River Hvítá ran dark between white banks. In the home field of one farm I noticed an old bathtub, leaning at an angle, not unlike the bathtub in my dreams.

I thought I had created memories from my dreams; it hadn't occurred to me that the opposite could be true: that my memories had been converted into dreams.

As a child, it had taken me a long time to realise that I walked in my sleep. I would wake up with dirty feet and soil in my bed, and invent rational explanations for the fact: I must have forgotten to wash the evening before or not been thorough enough. It's only human to seek a rational solution, even if it's not always correct.

The night after my return to Reykjavík, I was woken by the barking of a dog. My feet were freezing and the wind was whipping my hair. I looked around me, my heart pounding, and began to shake as the realisation sank in that I wasn't in my bed but standing outside, on the wet lawn in the communal garden of my block.

'Are you all right?' An old woman had opened the back door of one of the ground-floor flats and was watching me, clutching her dressing gown tight against the gale.

'Yes,' I said, and hurried inside.

My door was wide open, and I searched every inch of my flat before I was reassured that no one had entered it while I was outside. It was three in the morning.

After this incident, I put a padlock on the door and every night I hid the key in a locked drawer and the key to the drawer at the back of my wardrobe, inside a knotted sock. But this precaution turned out to be unnecessary, as I couldn't get to sleep at all for fear of what might happen.

For fear of what I might do.

When the first shock and mental turmoil following my parents' revelation began to subside and I was able to think coherently, it struck me that one mystery remained: I still had no idea who had sent me the letters. One evening, I was trying to distract myself with a book, but the letters refused to leave my mind, so I put the book down, and went over to the window.

So far, the winter had been mild in Reykjavík. The tarmac was grey, the grass withered, and there was no snow to mask the ugliness. I suppose I was so exhausted after my visit home that I hadn't given any thought to the letters in my first days back. But now I could no longer ignore them. I took them out of my bag and began to look through them again.

It was tempting to try to forget about the whole business. Not that I would ever be capable of forgetting what had happened: the ground had been knocked from under my feet. It was my fault that Stína had gone; discovering the identity of my penpal would do nothing to alter the fact. And yes, Mette's murder remained unsolved and some unknown person had sent me those letters, but all this held no power to frighten me anymore. I didn't have the energy to be afraid, and perhaps, too, I felt subconsciously that I deserved whatever might happen to me.

When my fingers strayed to the back of my head, found a lock of hair and began to tug, I didn't even try to stop them. That night I left the door unlocked, sat down on the sofa and waited.

46
Kristín – *Winter 1967*

Every night I start up at the sound of the bell, even when it isn't ringing. Since the incident in the cellar, I've been constantly on edge; the fear that something else might happen to me keeps me awake all night. The bell was supposed to give me peace of mind but it's had completely the opposite effect; I'm permanently on the alert, convinced I can hear the jangling, even when I'm awake.

Although the bruises are fading now, I still find it hard to be around Marsí. She doesn't remember a thing, and I can't decide whether that's good or bad. Dad behaves as if the bell will solve the problem and, it's true, he did manage to intervene once. The bell rang and he was able to leap up in time to lead Marsí back to bed.

But it'll never last.

Of course, Marsí knows that she has a tendency to walk in her sleep and she knows what the bell's for, but none of us has told her specifically what she does or how often it happens. She believes her sleepwalking is innocent, even funny. But mostly she finds the subject too embarrassing to talk about, which means she never asks any questions about it. She doesn't want to know what she gets up to, and although I'm dying to tell her, I don't suppose it would make any difference. We've learnt from experience that when Marsí's happy, her sleepwalking tails off, but as soon as she's agitated or upset, it steps up again and becomes a real menace. In the last few months, the situation has got totally out of hand and I think I know why.

One day, while Marsí's at school, I go into her room and start searching. It takes me ages but in the end I find her letters secreted between the pages of some old exercise books. If Bergur is the person I think he is, I need to know what kind of relationship they have. I need to work out if he's the reason for Marsí's disturbed state of mind.

I'm chilled as I read the first letter. The situation is much worse than I thought. Not only has she been using my name but she's been pretending to be older than she is. And their letters are intimate. He writes to her in an affectionate, heartfelt manner, pretending they have a special connection. I read all the letters I've found, and end up disgusted – by the way he expresses himself, the way he manipulates Marsí's feelings, telling her things he no doubt believes she wants to hear. But he never mentions Reykir. It's not until the last letter that he says he would like them to meet because there's something he needs to tell her.

I just pray that she hasn't arranged to meet him. Surely she can't be stupid enough to agree to meet a boy she knows nothing about?

It turns out I'm wrong.

At the bottom of the pile is a letter written by Marsí that she hasn't yet sent. In it, she suggests a time and place and says she'll be there, waiting for him. Marsí is planning to meet a complete stranger without letting me or our parents know.

I tuck the letters back between the pages of the exercise books and leave the room.

No doubt Marsí thinks she's very grown up and that she knows exactly what she's doing. But one thing is certain: there is no chance that I am going to let her meet this boy alone. I'll be there to watch, regardless of how furious it makes her.

47
Marsibil – *Wednesday, 7 December 1977*

I was just setting off home from the shop when I heard someone calling my name. I had lost my job at the printer's, which didn't come as much of a surprise since I hadn't been to work for weeks – I'd lied to my parents about taking holiday; I just hadn't turned up. Now I mostly spent my days going for long walks during which I tried, and failed, to push away intrusive thoughts about the past.

It took me a while to recognise the man, though his face looked familiar. He was wearing a brown coat and a scarf wound tightly round his neck. He jogged across the road towards me, and only then did I twig that it was the journalist I had met back in Síða. What a coincidence to run into him here.

'How are things? Back in Reykjavík, I see, and you never even said goodbye.'

'It was time,' I said.

'I know what you mean,' he replied cheerfully. 'Towns like that have a way of taking it out of you.'

'What about you? Still writing?'

He affected not to notice my coldness. 'Regrettably, no. It turned out there wasn't much of a story.'

'Oh.'

'Though I have to admit it's still bugging me,' he went on. 'The mystery. I mean, no one literally vanishes, do they?' When I didn't answer, he added: 'What about you? Have you abandoned the search for answers?'

'I made up my mind to stop dwelling on the past. What's done is done.' I pictured Stína's grave in our garden, marked only by the tree my parents had planted there. The laburnum that put forth fountains of golden blossom in summer. I couldn't imagine a tree more appropriate for Stína.

'That's probably wise.' He shoved his hands in his coat pockets. 'Look, Marsibil. Could we maybe meet up at a café – tomorrow, for example? Or whenever you're free.'

'What for?'

'Are you always this suspicious?' He sighed, then smiled. 'It's only a cup of coffee. And a piece of cake, if we're lucky. I won't bring up your sister if you don't want me to.'

'OK, but I don't want to go to a café,' I said. 'You can come round to my place.'

As it happened, my flat was a pigsty, but I couldn't face the thought of being surrounded by people. Although I had no faith in his promise not to bring up Stína, I was curious to know what he wanted.

'Sounds good,' he said, and I gave him my address, writing it down in the little notepad he pulled out of his pocket.

As we were saying goodbye, it began to snow. We both looked heavenwards and watched the tiny white grains falling from the sky like flour from a sieve. I smiled and it dawned on me that this was the first time in many days that I had done so.

'Oh no,' he said. 'I can't stand snow.'

'I love it. It makes everything so beautiful.'

'You think so? No, it'll be all grey and ugly before you know it. Mark my words.'

I watched him walk away, long coat flapping, arms swinging back and forth. Striding rapidly, as if in a hurry.

What on earth did he want?

He hadn't tried it on at any point or shown anything beyond a friendly interest in me. Usually men were pushier, but then maybe my standards were a bit skewed. Hitherto, my only dealings with the opposite sex had involved copious amounts of alcohol, which wasn't really compatible with good manners. Ever since the age of fourteen I had been used to boys thinking it was acceptable to paw and lunge at me. Maybe normal, nice guys were reticent like this. Or maybe he really did simply want to be my friend.

48
Kristín – *Friday, 17 November 1967*

When the day comes round, I'm full of trepidation, as I haven't a clue how Marsí will react when I turn up uninvited to her date with her penpal. It's pouring outside, but I feel as if I'm suffocating indoors, so I grab my raincoat and go out. There's a strong smell of wet earth in the wood behind our house.

When Marsí and I were young we used to lie on the ground here and look up at the fir trees, letting ourselves daydream. Back then, I thought I would be a different person when I grew up. But now, as I lie down on the carpet of pine needles and gaze up at the branches, I feel that despite everything that has changed, I'm still exactly the same.

Eyes closed, I feel the droplets pricking my face and running into my mouth so I can taste the rain. I'm so tired. Tired of this town and these people. Tired of every day being exactly the same. With every passing moment, the feeling has been growing more insistent inside me that I want to get away. Or rather, that I have to get away. I'm not sure I can take much more of this place.

I'm so lost in thought that I don't hear the approaching footsteps and jump at the sound of a voice.

'Stína. Is everything OK?' It's Gústi. There's a worried expression on his face and it occurs to me how odd I must look.

I sit up and wipe the rain from my cheeks.

'Yes, fine,' I say, with a miserable attempt at a laugh.

Gústi sits down on the damp ground beside me. 'What's up?'

I try to talk but the words won't come and hot tears begin to mingle with the cold rain on my face. Gústi puts an arm round my shoulders and strokes my back as I lean against him.

'What's wrong?' he asks again after a while.

'Oh, it's just…' I free myself from his embrace, wipe my cheeks and laugh, successfully this time.

'You look like you had a black eye,' he says.

'Oh, it's nothing,' I say, trying to hide the yellowing bruise, but Gústi pulls my hand away.

'What happened?'

'I just … I was having a row with Dad and I fell and…'

'Stína, did your dad do this?'

'He didn't mean to,' I say hurriedly. 'It was an accident.'

'He hit you by accident?'

'Well…' I say. 'Oh, it was nothing. I don't want to talk about it. Can we just drop the subject?'

'All right,' Gústi says, but I can see he's finding it hard.

'When did everything get so complicated?' I ask.

'I've never thought things are particularly complicated,' he says.

'Really?'

He shakes his head and then, without warning, he bends over and kisses me. I'm so startled that it takes me several seconds to grasp what's happening, but the moment I do, I pull away.

'Sorry,' Gústi says. 'I shouldn't have done that.'

I could rebuke him or act offended, but when our eyes meet and I see the mortified expression on his face, I burst out laughing; I can't help myself.

Gústi doesn't know how to react at first, then he starts laughing too.

'Sorry again,' he says, when we have finally caught our breath.

'OK,' I say. 'It's OK.'

'We're friends, aren't we?'

'Yes, of course.' Suddenly remembering the camera in the pocket of my raincoat, I fish it out. I want to remember this moment, to fix it on film.

'Come on,' I say.

'What?'

'Just come on. I want a picture of us.'

'I'll take it,' Gústi says, leaning towards me.

'You need to hold it a little higher,' I say as he holds the camera awkwardly at arm's length, attempting to aim it in our direction, then clicks the button.

'Oh, do you think I got us? I can take another one.'

'No, I'm sure it'll be perfect.' I take the camera back and return it to my pocket. 'I promise to show it to you when I've developed the film.'

After a minute or two, Gústi stands up, holds out his hand and helps me to my feet. On the way back, we chat about work and school – anything but the kiss we shared. There's no need. We both know it didn't mean anything.

But as we're saying goodbye, Gústi stops me. 'Stína, I…'

'Yes?'

He hesitates, then shakes his head. 'No, nothing. I look forward to seeing the photo.'

'I'll hurry up and develop the film,' I promise, and we say goodbye.

As I watch him disappear from sight, I start to wonder if we really did interpret that kiss the same way.

In the end, I go back indoors, telling myself that it doesn't matter anymore. I'm leaving. Next week, I'll talk to Halldóra and get her to help me send a portfolio of my drawings to the art school she mentioned in London. I sit down with my sketchbook and start drawing eyes, over and over again. This time, I draw Gústi's eyes and I'm so absorbed in my task that I don't notice Marsí until she's right beside me.

'Whose eyes are those?' she asks.

'No one in particular,' I say and put down my pencil.

When I sit back and appraise the drawing, the eyes aren't the way I'd intended at all. They do look like Gústi's but their expression is sad, and despite all my efforts to retouch them, the sadness remains. In the end, I give up and put the sketchbook back in the drawer.

49
Marsibil – *Wednesday, 7 December 1977*

Something had been nagging at my mind all day but I couldn't work out what it was. Not until I opened the shoebox of letters from my penpal again and reread them.

It was the business of the snow.

Einar had said he hated snow – it was so quick to get grey and ugly. No doubt it was a common attitude, but it just so happened that my penpal had written: *I can't stand snow. It turns so grey and ugly before you know it.* The wording was almost exactly the same as Einar had used. But perhaps I was reading too much into it. Hadn't Gústi said something similar? And probably lots of other people too, if I stopped to think about it.

I collected up the letters and was about to put them back in the box when I noticed a piece of paper at the bottom, a cutting from *The Week* with my advertisement on it. I vividly remembered cutting out the page and keeping it, thrilled by the sight of my name in print. Now I took out the yellowing paper, ran my fingers over the print and read my advertisement.

Dear Week!
Many thanks for a great magazine.
I would like to be penpals with boys or girls aged thirteen to sixteen.
I myself am fifteen. My hobbies are art and films.
Best wishes
Kristín Karvelsdóttir

That's where it all began, I thought, and wasn't sure quite how I felt about it now. I vividly recalled the excitement of seeing my letter in the paper. The eager anticipation to find out who would reply to it.

I took out a match, lit it and held the flame to the paper. One corner had caught and started to blacken when my eye fell on another advertisement below mine. Dropping the paper, I beat the flame until it went out.

Below my letter was one from a boy called Helgi Hrafn, also advertising for a penpal. But it wasn't his name that caught my attention – it was his address.

The boy lived at Sætún near Höfn í Hornafirði.

Sætún was the address Stína had written on the back of the old photo of our mother.

The triumph was like a warm feeling in my chest. A connection at last; a solid lead I could follow up. But then I was immediately overcome by uncertainty. What did it all mean? Why had Stína written that address on the photo of Mum ten years ago?

I already knew what had happened to Stína, yet now I had found a word that linked my advertisement for a penpal to Stína and my mother. But I simply couldn't figure out how they were connected.

I gnawed at my nails to keep my hands occupied, so they wouldn't start tearing out my hair again. After racking my brain over this puzzle for a while, I decided to look Helgi Hrafn up in the telephone directory, starting with the Höfn í Hornafirði area.

I was in luck. There was a man with that name still living there. I dialled his number, my heart booming in my ears, the sweat pooling under my arms.

A young woman answered and I asked for Helgi Hrafn.

'No, sorry, he's out,' the woman said. 'Would you like me to give him a message to call you back?'

Heart beating wildly, I gave her my name and phone number.

50

Kristín – *Friday, 17 November 1967*

'Did Guðrún find you?' Mum asks when I go back indoors.

'No, when?'

'She came round a little while ago, looking for you,' Mum says. 'I told her you'd gone for a walk.'

'I didn't see her,' I say. 'But I'll give her a call later.'

I loathe phoning Guðrún's house because I can't bear the thought of speaking to Alda, but, thank goodness, it's Guðrún who answers this time.

'Hi, it's Stína,' I say. 'I hear you came round.'

'I looked for you,' she replies, 'but couldn't see you anywhere, so I went home.'

'I see,' I say, then invite her to go round to Málfríður's with me. Málfríður rang earlier today, saying we have to watch a film that's being shown on TV this evening; a Hitchcock film about a woman who marries a man who turns out to be a murderer.

'That sounds horrible,' Guðrún says, and laughs. 'What time shall I come over?'

The moment I've hung up, I wonder if I've been a bit hasty. Málfríður might not want Guðrún there. But when I call Málfríður, in one of her bewildering changes of heart, she couldn't be nicer and says it's no problem for Guðrún to come too. I hear her father saying something in the background, then Málfríður adds that we're both invited to supper.

Guðrún and I head over to Málfríður's together and are greeted by her father.

'Don't you look pretty this evening, Stína,' he says. 'I like your hair.' Yet another of those comments that make me squirm. It doesn't feel right for a man in his fifties to be constantly praising the appearance of his daughter's sixteen-year-old friend. Would he talk to Málfríður like that?

'Thanks,' I say, anyway.

'Málfríður's upstairs. Supper will be ready shortly. We'll call you.'

We hurry upstairs, and of course the very first person I see is Elvar. I've avoided going round to Málfríður's place since I broke up with him, but this evening I have no choice: I needed an excuse to leave the house so I can carry out my plan.

Elvar stops dead and our eyes meet briefly before he averts his gaze. It's a few weeks since we split up and I thought he'd have got over it by now, but clearly he's still hurt.

He doesn't say hello, just gives me a pale smile.

Over supper, the glances continue. He lowers his gaze every time I catch him watching me and doesn't seem to have any appetite, just pokes at his food with his fork.

'Have you done something different to your hair, Stína?' Málfríður's father asks.

'Well, I asked the hairdresser to cut it a bit shorter,' I say.

'It really suits you,' he says.

Feeling his gaze on me, I try to concentrate on chewing a mouthful of meat.

'This is very good,' I say, when I've finally swallowed it.

'Thank you, Stína. Do eat up. You're so slim and boys like to have something to grab hold of, you know.'

This is supposed to be a joke and is accompanied by a creepy laugh that I find excruciatingly embarrassing. Desperate, I turn to Guðrún, in the hope that she can lighten the atmosphere. She cottons on immediately and starts asking him questions about being a vicar.

Somehow we get through the meal and, finally, to my relief we're allowed to leave the table and take our plates through to the sink.

The film starts at nine. I can only watch the first half an hour or so, though I don't mention this to the girls when we sit down. As soon as it begins, Elvar comes in and seats himself on the sofa without saying a word. I do my best to focus on the film. Cary Grant appears on screen in the role of the charming Johnnie and Joan Fontaine plays the wealthy Lina. They fall in love and elope, in spite of the objections raised by Lina's father. Then gradually Lina begins to suspect that Johnnie is not what he seems and that he is planning to murder her to get his hands on her fortune.

It's so gripping that I long to know how it's going to end, but when I check my watch, I see that I'm going to be late. Reluctantly, I get to my feet.

'I have to go,' I announce.

'Now?' Guðrún looks at me in astonishment. 'Don't you want a lift with me afterwards? Mum's collecting me.'

'No, stay and finish the film. The weather's dry now; I can walk home.'

'Are you sure?'

'Positive.'

I need to be on foot if I'm to keep an eye on my sister and see whether someone arrives by car to pick her up. I've no idea what on earth I'm going to do at that point, though. I can hardly jump out and forbid her to go with him, but what other choice do I have?

Málfríður is so absorbed in the film that she barely glances up when I say goodbye, but Elvar is no longer watching the screen. He stares at me, his brown eyes unusually dark in the dimly lit room.

51
Marsibil – *Thursday, 8 December 1977*

'I was very interested in what you had to say about Reykir and the girls who were sent there,' Einar said, the next day.

We were sitting in my kitchen, drinking coffee. I had aired the place and tidied up, if shoving all the mess out of sight into cupboards counted as tidying. Even so, I noticed his gaze lingering on the grimy kitchen units.

'Were you?' I said distractedly.

All day I had been waiting for the call from Helgi Hrafn, jumping at the slightest noise, but the big grey telephone had sat silent on its table.

Einar was still talking. 'I went to see the old schoolhouse and discovered that about fifteen girls had been housed there. The youngest was only fourteen. It was run as a workhouse for a very short time, not even a year, but I've heard that conditions were harsh. For one thing, the windows were nailed shut.'

I sipped my coffee, struggling to show any interest.

'It could make for a decent article,' Einar continued. 'Of course, it would be best if one of the former residents could be persuaded to talk to me.'

'I don't think they will,' I said. 'Judging by what you say, it must have been a terrible experience. I doubt any of them will want to rake it up.'

'No, but—'

'And what if their families know nothing about it? What if they don't want their secret to be exposed? Do you journalists ever stop to think about that?'

'Perhaps you're right.' Einar took a mouthful of coffee, keeping his gaze fixed on me. 'You look tired.'

'I haven't been sleeping well.'

The truth was that I had barely slept for several days now and my eyes were twitching with exhaustion. The only times I'd dropped off were on the bus. I'd spent hours on board, sleeping through several circuits of the town, before eventually getting out at the same stop as I had got on. During these naps, I had my recurring dreams about Mum and the baby. Dad sometimes put in an appearance too, croaking like a raven. Apart from that, I had been wide awake for days, my body in overdrive, and I couldn't get my heartbeat to slow down.

'There are pills that can help with that,' Einar said.

'It's not a problem.'

He carried on talking, seemingly unfazed by my offhand replies.

When the phone rang, I jumped so badly that I spilt my coffee. Ignoring the mess, I hurried into the sitting room.

'Hello,' said a voice, sounding rather uncertain. 'Is that Marsibil?'

'Yes, speaking.'

Einar appeared in the hall and mouthed 'toilet' at me. I pointed in the direction of the bathroom.

'My name's Helgi. My wife told me you'd been trying to get hold of me.'

'That's right,' I said, and came straight to the point, feeling slightly breathless. 'You used to live at Sætún near Höfn í Hornafirði.'

'Yes, I did. I'm sorry, but who did you say you were?'

'Excuse me,' I said. 'This may sound odd but I found the address on the back of a photograph and I wondered if you knew a woman called Jónína?'

'No, I don't believe so.'

'What about Kristín Karvelsdóttir?'

'Kristín Karvelsdóttir?' The man sounded as if he recognised the name, but then a lot of people did after all the news reports about her disappearance. He didn't appear to have made the connection, though, and, after a moment's thought, said he didn't know her. 'What's this regarding?'

'Nothing. Nothing at all.' I closed my eyes briefly, trying to think.

'Well, if there's nothing else…'

'What about the name Bergur?' I tried.

'Bergur,' he said. 'No, unless … my brother sometimes went by that name.'

My pulse began to quicken.

'Could it be him you're looking for?' Helgi asked.

'Maybe,' I said. 'But what do you mean he sometimes went by that name?'

'Well, it was the name he was given at birth. He was adopted and our parents christened him Einar. But he sometimes liked to go by Bergur when we were younger.' Helgi chuckled, but I couldn't move. 'Hello? Are you still there?'

I put down the receiver without saying goodbye.

In the bathroom, I heard Einar washing his hands.

52

When the bathroom door opened and Einar emerged, I was still standing, rooted to the spot, by the phone.

Einar clocked instantly that something was wrong. 'Is everything OK, Marsibil?'

'It was you,' I said, my voice emerging in a whisper. 'You sent the letters.'

Einar's habitual ironic smile was wiped off his face in an instant. He stared at me for a long moment, his green-flecked eyes penetrating and hard. Finally he looked away. 'It's not like you think.'

I should have been angry but instead I was numb. Until, that is, I closed my eyes and pictured Mette lying by the road with a red mark round her neck.

Einar had been at the bar the evening Mette was murdered. He'd come to Síða to meet me, but when I refused to go with him that evening he had decided to send me a message.

'Why?' I said. 'I … I don't understand…'

'Marsibil, I just wanted to get to know you.' He took a step closer.

'Don't come near me.' My voice didn't sound as firm as I'd have liked. Suddenly, I was like a petrified mouse and could feel myself starting to tremble.

Einar stopped. 'Do you know how old I am, Marsibil?'

'How's that relevant?'

Finally, here I was, face to face with my penpal, with the living incarnation of the man whose appearance I had wondered about all these years. Even through my sluggish thoughts, it occurred to me that Einar knew far more about me than he had let on. I had told him all about myself in those letters, poured my heart out to him – and much more. Thought about him obsessively for months, wondering where he was and what he was doing. I had believed myself in love with him.

The thought made me sick to the stomach.

'I'm thirty-four,' Einar said. 'Born in 1943.'

'You said in your letters that you were only a year older than me.'

The whole thing had been a lie. I hadn't been talking to a sixteen-year-old boy but a man ten years older than me. Twenty-four to my fourteen.

'I never meant to deceive you all that time.' Einar took another step towards me, and I backed instinctively away, bumping into a chair.

'Get out,' I whispered. 'Please, get out.'

'Marsibil,' Einar said sternly. 'Listen to me.'

But I had no interest in listening to him anymore. Glancing around for a weapon to use in self-defence, I could see nothing but a candlestick on the windowsill.

'I want you to leave,' I said, making ready to grab it.

Einar eyed me for a long moment, his jaw clenched and that same hard look in his eye.

'Look, Marsibil, I admit I wrote the letters, but it was only as a way of getting to know your family.'

'My family?'

'That's what I'm trying to tell you. I was born in 1943 and adopted at birth by a couple from Höfn í Hornafirði. I never knew my mother and had no idea who she was until years later. My parents told me the whole story when I turned eighteen; who my mother was, and that she'd been very young when she got pregnant by a British soldier. I had no interest in finding her at first. But then…'

'You're lying,' I said, but suddenly I wasn't sure. How could he know all this if he was lying?

'Did you know I was at art school?' Einar asked.

I shook my head.

'It looks like both Stína and I inherited the talent from our mother. You know, before I went into journalism, I wanted to become an artist. So I went to art school and that's where I met Ívar.'

'Who's Ívar?'

'He was a student at art school and … let's just say we became good friends. When he told me he'd got a teaching position in the countryside near Reykir, I asked him to let me know if he ever encountered you or Kristín. I had discovered your names after reading an article about our mother. I'd wanted to know more about her, so spent some time at the library, researching her career. And in the end Ívar came across Kristín. At the school. He was very taken with her; he said she wasn't just talented but bright and spirited too, so I wanted to get to know her myself, but I had no idea how to go about it. Then later Ívar was invited back to teach evening classes at Reykir and it occurred to us – or rather to me – that he could put Kristín on the trail.'

'On the trail? What do you mean?'

'The only thing I owned that had belonged to my birth mother was a shoebox containing a few of her belongings that my parents had given me on my eighteenth birthday. They said I could trace her but I'd never been interested in doing so because I was perfectly happy as I was.'

'What was in the box?'

'Pictures drawn by my mother, a brooch and a photo of her.'

'Stína wanted to return it to its owner.' I recalled my conversation with Halldóra.

Einar nodded. 'It was my idea that Ívar should give Kristín my box and see if she could work it out for herself. It occurred to me that if she showed the box to her mother, her mother would either tell her about me or else keep quiet. Either way, my mother could get in touch with me if she wanted to and I wouldn't have to make the decision myself.' Einar smiled wistfully. 'But she never did get in touch.'

His words took a while to sink in. I felt as if a whole lifetime was passing as I stood there, my scrambled brain trying to comprehend what Einar was telling me.

'But you wrote the letters,' I repeated.

'Yes, that was me,' Einar said. 'One day my little brother decided to advertise for a penpal, like a lot of kids his age. He was only eleven at the time and was very excited when his letter was published in *The Week*. You can't imagine how astonished I was when I spotted Kristín's name on the same page. I guessed at once that it was her since the patronymic was so unusual: Karvelsdóttir. I just … I had to write to her. And she wrote back. I didn't want her to be able to find me, so I used the name Bergur and sent the letters from my grandparents' house. Maybe I was hoping my mother would see the name she had given me and be moved to tell you two about me. It was never supposed to be more than a few letters. I just wanted to know how she was. And I was curious about you two.'

'Why didn't you just tell the truth?'

He snorted. 'And say what? "Hi, I'm your twenty-four-year-old brother who you never knew existed. How are you doing?"'

'No, but you pretended to be somebody completely different. You lied to me.'

'Well, if it comes to that, you lied too.'

'Yes, but that was different.'

'Was it? It was never supposed to go that far, Marsibil, but I felt sorry for you. I wanted to help you.'

'We'd planned to meet.'

'Yes, but not straight away. I know I talked about meeting up but it was you who decided the date and time, Marsí. I was on the other side of the country. How the hell was I supposed to get there? Anyway, I was worried when I got your letter and realised how far things had gone – that you'd developed feelings for me. Or rather that Stína was developing feelings for me. Of course, as far as I knew it was Stína I was exchanging letters with.' He ran his hands through his hair. 'Then I saw the news about her disappearance; that Stína had vanished the very evening she'd arranged to meet me. And I was scared. Shit scared. That's why I didn't send any more letters. I mean, why would I have? The girl I'd been writing to was dead, so what would have been the point of sending more letters?'

It was true. How was he supposed to have known that it was me, not Stína, who was writing to him? Foolishly, I had never even stopped to consider this.

'But what about the letters that arrived recently? You addressed them to me.'

'I sent you one letter. I'm a journalist, Marsibil, and I became very interested in the mystery of what happened to Stína. Understandably. I thought I knew her so well, then she vanished in the very place she'd suggested we meet. Surely you can understand that I blamed myself and felt I'd played an indirect role in her disappearance? So I started investigating the case, went to visit Síða a couple of times, and reread the letters again and again, trying to work out what could have happened. Then gradually it dawned on me that it wasn't her who had written those letters to me: it was you.'

'How could you possibly have guessed?'

'I started talking to people on the pretext that I was writing an article – people who'd known your sister. They all described Stína as open and vivacious.'

'And me as sullen and withdrawn?' I chipped in.

'No. No, but as quieter and … and a bit gauche. Everyone said Stína had been good at drawing and in one of your letters you had mentioned that your sister was a brilliant artist whereas you had no talent at all.' He smiled. 'I realised that you must have written the letters, Marsí. I don't know why you chose to use Stína's name but I don't need to know. I was still interested in her disappearance and wanted to speak to you, but you always refused. I tried ringing many times but you always hung up the moment you heard I was a journalist. The reason I was calling wasn't just to write an article but to get to know you again in different circumstances. When that didn't work, I decided to write you a letter.'

'And where was I supposed to send the reply to? You didn't even give me an address.'

'I didn't want you to reply,' Einar said. 'I just wanted you to … I don't know, talk to me. I was planning to follow up my letter by knocking on your door a few days later, to explain everything, but by then you'd gone.'

'You followed me,' I said. 'You followed me all the way to Síða. Were you watching me?'

'No,' Einar burst out, louder than necessary. 'No, of course I wasn't. But when I came here and you turned out not to be at home, I guessed where you'd probably gone. It was ten years since Stína's disappearance, so I seized the opportunity and headed to Síða too.'

I rubbed my forehead, trying to take in what he'd told me. Could I trust this man? Was he telling the truth?

'What about Mette?' I asked, feeling suddenly sick with fear. 'You killed her.'

'Mette? Are you talking about the Danish girl who died of exposure?'

'She was strangled and you left a note for me on her body.'

'Was she strangled?' Einar stared at me incredulously. When I made no move to explain, his shoulders sagged and he took a step backwards.

'If you want me to go, I'll go,' he said. 'But I only sent you one letter and that was to this address. I didn't know Mette and I never left any note with her, and I swear on my life that I've never murdered anybody.'

53
Kristín – *Friday, 17 November 1967*

Outside, the night sky has clouded over, and before I have walked far, a few plump snowflakes begin to fall. I look up and smile. If there's one thing I love about this time of year it's the snow. It settles like a beautiful white shawl over the mountains, making everything look so Christmassy.

The streets are still clear, though, and it's a windless night. I'm not cold, as I took care to put on my warmest anorak and comfortable shoes before coming out this evening. It's only half an hour's walk, which means I should be home in good time. That's if I don't run into Marsí waiting beside the road for her penpal.

I stride along at a brisk pace, afraid of missing her, and cover the distance faster than anticipated.

Marsí told him to meet her by the bridge, so when I get there, I come to a halt. Marsí doesn't seem to have arrived yet and I wonder if I should hide or wait out in the open and speak to her when she turns up.

I haven't been standing there long before the chill starts to penetrate to my bones. I zip my anorak up to the neck and peer at my surroundings. The snow is falling in soft flurries and the darkness is pierced only by the distant lights from town and a few scattered farms.

Oh, perhaps this is pointless, I think to myself after a while. There's nobody here but me and not a single car has passed me since I left Málfríður's house. Perhaps I missed them, or Marsí belatedly came to her senses and realised what a bad idea this is.

Nevertheless, I linger for several more minutes, stamping my feet and trying to shiver myself to warmth, before finally giving up. But just as I've made up my mind to set off home, I see the outlines of a figure in the distance. Someone is walking towards me, getting rapidly closer. It can't possibly be Marsí because the person is coming from the wrong direction; not from our house but from the same way I came myself.

From town.

54
Marsibil – *Friday, 23 December 1977*

The wind had blown the snow into little drifts against the window. It was 23 December, St Thorlákur's Mass, and I was sitting in the kitchen at Nátthagi, warming my hands on a cup of tea, my eyes resting on the bare, windswept branches of the laburnum in the garden. Dad was fiddling with the thermostat to work out why it was so chilly in the house, a creamy rice pudding was simmering on the stove, and Mum was hanging up washing.

Dad had rung me every day to make sure I would come home for Christmas.

'It would mean so much to your mother and me, Pipsqueak,' he had said, adding: 'We haven't touched so much as a drop since you left.'

I didn't want to go home, but the only alternative was to spend Christmas alone, brooding on my misery.

Einar had tried repeatedly to get in touch but I wasn't ready to talk to him. I didn't know how far to trust him or what kind of relationship we would have, or whether I wanted any kind of relationship at all. He had said it was up to me.

I wondered what Mum would say if she knew about Einar. She must think sometimes about the child she gave up, and she had been visibly shaken when I showed her the photo of the baby she had at least got to hold before he was wrenched from her arms. Perhaps she would be relieved to know that his life was good, or perhaps she wouldn't want to be reminded of his existence.

Either way, instead of coming to a decision, I had buried myself in books, escaping into other lives and worlds. They gave me respite from my own unbearable thoughts, a rest from having to think at all. A rest from obsessing over who could have sent that last note.

'Do you want to come into town with me this morning, Marsibil?' Mum asked. 'I still need a few things for this evening.'

'Yes, I'm up for that. I just need to put some clothes on.' I deposited my cup in the sink and went up to my room.

Once I was dressed, I examined myself in the mirror.

My face was as pallid as ever and my lips were white and chapped, dried out by the frost. When I opened the desk drawer in search of lipsalve, I came across the envelope of photographs. Sitting down on the bed, I took them out and studied again the last existing pictures of Stína. The blurred shot of her with the headless boy in the corduroy jacket. Hadn't she been wearing those clothes the day she vanished? The red anorak, brown trousers and yellow hairband? Málfríður had been adamant that the boy wasn't Elvar, so who could it have been?

My gaze fell on the window as I put the pictures away again. The laburnum was waving agitatedly in the wind, as if Stína had an urgent message for me. As if she was calling me, summoning me to come to her.

'Marsí,' Mum called. 'Are you ready?'

'Coming.'

'You look nice,' Mum said, when I left my room.

'Thanks,' I said. 'You too.'

Mum looked better than she had in a long time. Her eyes were clearer, her skin brighter. She said she hadn't had a drink since I left, and I believed her. She seemed happier. During the short drive into town, I covertly studied her. She was beautiful today with the winter sun shining on her face and lighting up her hair. Like a child, I had never stopped to consider her as anything other than my mother. How could I have failed to realise that she'd had a life before Stína and I came along? That she'd been a little girl once, just like us?

I had been aware of the fact without really understanding it. But I wanted to understand. I longed to ask her about her time at Reykir but was afraid of her reaction.

Once we had parked in front of the Co-op, Mum turned to me.

'Right,' she said.

'Mum,' I said quickly. 'What was it like at the workhouse? You needn't tell me if you'd rather not, but I thought you might want to talk about it.'

Mum's smile vanished. She was silent for a while, then said in a controlled voice: 'I was only fourteen when I was sent there and, to be honest, I don't recall much about it. Though I do remember my room. It had a beautiful view. I remember...' A shadow crossed her face and she closed her eyes for a moment.

'You don't have to talk about it,' I said.

'It's just...' Mum sighed. 'It's hard. The main thing I remember is missing my mother. We weren't allowed visitors and any letters we sent home were censored, so that was quite difficult. I was lonely there.'

'I can understand that,' I said, and watched as Mum smiled, cheering herself up in that inimitable way she had. I'd always regarded Mum as fragile and vulnerable, but now I recognised that she had her own form of resilience, which consisted of a talent for survival. She was always creating happy moments for herself, whether it was by losing herself in reminiscences about the theatre or putting on a record and dolling herself up.

As we got out of the car, I wondered if she'd been conscious of the fact that the whole time she was talking, she had been stroking her stomach.

'I just need to pop round to Alfreð's, then we can go home,' Mum said, once we were back in the car after our shopping trip.

Ever since I was a child, we've taken small gifts round to Gústi's family at Christmas: biscuits, candles, chocolates, that sort of thing. Subconsciously, I must have guessed that we would go there this time too, which is why I had agreed to accompany Mum. I had only seen Gústi once briefly since we kissed in the Hot Stream, but the kiss had been constantly in my thoughts.

It had been a good kiss.

Alfreð had a drying-up cloth slung over his shoulder and the house was fragrant with cooking smells. 'Oh, how nice to see you both. Happy Christmas!'

'We've brought you some chocolates,' Mum said, holding out the box we'd just purchased at the shop.

'Thank you so much. Come in, come in,' he said. 'Ína, love, put on some fresh coffee. Chuck the old stuff down the sink.'

'Oh, no, please don't go to any trouble for our sake,' Mum said from habit, then seated herself on the sofa as Ína went to make more coffee.

I looked around for Gústi, but he was nowhere to be seen.

'Everything ready for tomorrow?' Alfreð asked, sitting down with us.

'Yes, as ready as it will ever be,' Mum replied. 'We don't need much.'

'I heard on the radio that we're in for a storm later.'

'Are we?'

'Apparently they're expecting rising temperatures, rain and gale-force winds,' Alfreð continued. 'Not that it'll make any difference to us. Curling up indoors with a book is the best way to spend Christmas.'

'Yes, that's true,' Mum said. 'Maybe it means we'll get to enjoy Marsibil's company a little longer.'

'Let's wait and see.' I glanced at the clock. If Gústi wasn't here, there was no reason to stick around.

Then, as Ína came in with the coffee, the front door opened.

'That'll be Gústi,' Alfreð said. 'He popped out to buy flour for the white sauce.'

I heard Gústi stamping on the mat in the entrance hall, then he appeared, his hair ruffled by his woollen hat, his cheeks bright red with the cold. His eyes opened a little wider when he saw me, and I couldn't prevent a smile from springing to my lips.

'Gústi's got exciting news,' Alfreð said. 'He's applied to go to college in Reykjavík next autumn.'

'Is that so?' Mum asked, shooting a glance at me.

'Yes,' Gústi replied. 'I think it's time to leave the nest.'

'What are you going to study?' Mum asked.

'I'm going to the tech to study to be an electrician.'

'What fun,' Mum said.

'Before we know it, he'll be taking over Jonni's shop,' Alfreð said.

'Oh, Dad. That's a family business – I'd never be able to take it over. But who knows? Maybe I'll start my own business.'

'No one can accuse you of lacking ambition.' Alfreð slapped his thigh. 'Coffee for everyone?'

'Not for me, thanks,' I said. 'Actually, I was hoping to…' I caught Gústi's eye. 'Could we…?'

'Sure,' Gústi said. 'Right, we'll just…'

Without looking at our respective parents, we went into Gústi's room and shut the door.

I knew exactly what Mum was thinking but I didn't care. I had to know what it meant for us. Was Gústi moving to Reykjavík for my sake or had I ceased to matter to him? Did I want to matter to him?

'So, what did you want to talk about?' He sat down on the bed, watching me with those grey-blue eyes of his.

I sensed myself growing hot under his gaze and felt an urgent compulsion to try that kiss again, to see if it was as tender as I remembered.

Gústi, seeing my embarrassment, laughed. He patted the bed beside him. 'You can sit down, you know. I won't bite.'

I perched beside him and before I could say a word, Gústi bent and kissed me again, so gently and tentatively that it drove me crazy. I wanted to get closer, to feel his body against mine. Our thoughts were obviously running along the same lines because we both moved closer simultaneously, our mouths colliding so hard that one of my teeth cut into Gústi's upper lip.

He made a rueful face and sucked at it.

'Sorry, I didn't mean to…' I said, flustered.

'It's OK.' Gústi smiled, his gaze travelling from my eyes down to my lips. When he kissed me again the clumsiness had gone and our movements were in sync, as they had been weeks ago in the Hot Stream.

Then, without warning, he drew away. There was a small frown on his face now.

'What's wrong?' I said. 'Why—?'

'You just upped and left, Marsí,' he said without looking at me. 'You didn't even say goodbye. I came round to see you and your mother told me you'd gone.'

'Sorry, I wasn't in a good place.' I had driven home in frantic haste, desperate to flee the situation. It was all my fault. I was damaged, no good. No one would ever love me.

'I tried calling but you never picked up.'

My phone had rung several times after I first got home but I had been incapable of moving, incapable of talking to anyone. I didn't deserve such happiness. My sister was dead because of me. And I was barely alive. That night I had taken two lives – mine as well as hers.

'Marsí,' Gústi said. 'I want to see you when I move to Reykjavík.'

I gazed into his beautiful eyes, wishing passionately that I could unburden myself to him but knowing I couldn't. I would never be able to.

So I said the only thing I felt I could say. Haltingly, in mumbled phrases, my eyes on the floor, I told him I couldn't see him anymore.

Gústi shrank back. 'Why not?'

'Because I'm not who you think I am.'

Gústi laughed. 'Marsí, I've known you since you were a little girl. I know exactly who you are.'

He stroked a lock of hair back from my face and I flinched. The wounded look in his eyes when I shook my head turned my stomach upside down, but I had made up my mind.

'No,' I said. 'You don't.'

Mum called me from the hall, and I stood up quickly.

'Coming.' I hastily tidied my hair and clothes, but Mum would hardly fail to notice my flushed cheeks.

'Are you going back to Reykjavík straight after Christmas?' Gústi asked.

'Yes.' I turned, then added. 'It won't work, Gústi. I'm sorry. You deserve better.'

I left the room before he could answer.

'Did you manage to have your chat?' Mum whispered as she was putting her coat on.

'Mm.' I ignored her meaningful grin.

My coat was hanging in the hall cupboard, which was crammed so full of outdoor clothes that it took me a moment to spot it. Finally, I found it next to a brown corduroy jacket. It was a man's jacket, too small for Alfreð and probably too small for Gústi these days. But I dimly recalled him wearing it when he was younger.

Gústi came out while I was putting on my coat and stood a couple of steps behind his father. He had tidied his hair and the colour had faded from his cheeks. His expression was bleak when he met my eye.

'Happy Christmas,' he said.

'Happy Christmas,' I replied and hurried out to the car with Mum.

As we were driving away, I suddenly realised why the jacket had looked so familiar: it was identical to the one worn by the headless boy in Stína's photo.

55
Monday, 26 December 1977

There were any number of ways to disappear. Plenty of places here in the countryside where the earth could quite literally swallow you up: hot springs and deep fissures in the lava fields that would be impossible to search. I couldn't stop thinking about how good it would be to disappear, to cease to exist. I didn't believe in heaven or hell but there was solace in the thought of oblivion.

On 25 December, I took Dad's razor and shaved off all my hair. There were only tufts of it left on the back of my head as it was. My hands must have been frantically busy in my sleep as I had woken up to a tangle of loose hair on my pillow.

'Oh my God, what have you done?' Mum clapped her hands over her mouth when she saw me and her eyes filled with tears.

I examined myself in the mirror. You could see the shape of my skull, and my eyes appeared conspicuously deep and dark in my exposed face.

'I think I look good like this,' I told her.

Mum's lips puckered and she turned and vanished into the kitchen.

I smiled at myself in the mirror. That was one problem solved.

On the third day of Christmas, the gale finally died down and I decided to go home the following morning. Christmas had passed in a haze of over-indulgence in food and books. My parents studiously avoided alcohol, while I retired to my room with a bottle and took nips from it at night as the rain poured down outside and the house creaked and groaned in the storm. Every day, I braved the weather to go out in the garden and stand under the laburnum tree to commune with Stína. In a curious sense, I didn't feel as lonely as before, yet my strongest wish was to fetch a spade and dig myself a grave beside her.

Gústi hadn't phoned and I determinedly pushed him out of my mind. There had been something going on between him and Stína, and I neither could nor would be a substitute for her. Everything he had said to me appeared now in a different light. It wasn't me he wanted but another Stína. Why hadn't he admitted that he was the headless boy in the photo? And if he had lied about that, what else had he lied to me about? I was hurt, but my pain faded into insignificance in the face of the wider implications.

'Shall we read the Christmas cards now?' Mum asked, the evening before my departure. 'We completely forgot to do it on the twenty-fourth.'

I sat down on the sofa and Mum picked up the wooden box of Christmas cards. I felt drowsy, almost numb. I'd only managed to scrape a few hours' sleep over the past few nights and when I did drop off, my dreams were all of being chased by ravens and hens. I was constantly running away, and although I knew what the ravens symbolised, I had no idea what the hens did.

Mum made a puzzled sound when I asked. 'Dreaming about hens? I have no idea, Marsí.'

'But ravens mean death, don't they?'

'Sometimes.' Mum carefully opened one of the envelopes with a letter knife. 'If they circle overhead that means death or betrayal, but the croaking of ravens usually means grief.'

I thought about my dream of Dad croaking like a raven. So it had symbolised grief, not betrayal. Although I wasn't superstitious like Mum, lately I had caught myself trying to interpret all my dreams. Perhaps after all we were more alike than I was willing to admit to myself.

'Ah, this is from the couple at Gröf,' Mum said. '"We wish you a

Merry Christmas and a Happy New Year." They don't mention Mette, but I suppose that's understandable. The poor things. And here's one from Ninna and Jonni. Apparently they're thinking of selling up. Had you heard?'

Mum's chatter was a comfortable burbling in the background, like a radio playing at a low volume. I ummed and ahhed and smiled in the right places, accepting the cards from her, then putting them in a pile.

'And here's one saying "Happy New Year and warmest wishes".'

Mum passed me the card. On the front was an angel surrounded by flowers and garlands and inside I read the greeting again. Those warmest wishes – from a name I knew only too well. Mum prattled on, oblivious. A card from Alfreð, from the grocer, from Dilla and Haffi, and Mummi and Lína. 1 no longer took in anything she was saying.

'Where are you going?' Mum asked when I got to my feet.

'Just out for a breather,' I said.

'Oh … well, I suppose we can take a little break. But don't be too long,' she called after me.

56

Kristín – *Friday, 17 November 1967*

The figure's outlines grow clearer as it approaches through the gently falling snow and I am relieved, if surprised, to see who it is.

'Where are you off to?' Guðrún asks when she's within speaking distance.

'What are you doing here?' I ask in return.

'I was worried about you.'

'There was no need to be,' I say, adding: 'I'm just looking out for Marsí.'

'Is she on her way?'

'I think so.' I hesitate, then decide there's no harm in confiding in her. When she comes to a halt in front of me, I tell her what I've discovered about Marsí's penpal and the fact she has an assignation with him here this evening.

Guðrún wrinkles her brow. 'What are you planning to do about it?'

'She's only fourteen; she shouldn't be meeting strange boys late at night.'

'So you're worried about her?'

'Yes, I—' But some quality in Guðrún's voice makes me break off. 'Is everything all right, Guðrún?'

'Why shouldn't it be?' she asks. Then she shrugs and looks at her feet. 'Anyway, why would you care if it wasn't?'

For a moment or two, I assume she's joking, but then I see her expression. I recognise that look. It's the same expression she wore when we were children and I accidentally broke her favourite figurine, a little china fairy with wings that her father had bought her on a trip abroad. She had slapped my face and I had burst into tears. Instead of comforting me, Guðrún's mother Alda had stroked her hair and said to me angrily: 'You mustn't break things that don't belong to you, Stína.' I was so ashamed that I never told my parents what had happened.

'Do you even know where I was in the summer, Stína?' Guðrún asks now.

'You were on holiday,' I say, puzzled at the turn the conversation has taken. 'At a summer cabin down south.'

'I was down south but I wasn't on holiday, and I wasn't at any bloody summer cabin.'

'But Guðrún hon, I don't know—'

'Don't "Guðrún *hon*" me.'

'What's the matter with you?' I see that she's fighting back tears now, so I take a breath, control myself and say, as calmly as I can: 'You can talk to me.'

'Can I?' she says on a sob. 'Can I talk to you, Stína?'

'Of course. Always. We've been friends since we were tiny.'

With that, Guðrún finally breaks down and starts crying. But when I step closer to comfort her, she shakes her head.

'Do you remember the party back in the spring?' she says through her sobs.

'Which party?'

'You know the party I'm talking about.'

'Do I?' I ask.

'You abandoned me. You made me drink all that alcohol, and I only did it to please you because I was so upset. So wretched,' she says, wiping away her tears. 'Then you abandoned me.'

'I'm sorry,' I whisper, and put a hand on Guðrún's arm, but she shakes it off.

'Leave me alone, Stína. Don't try to comfort me. I don't want any comfort from you.'

'I know. I'm sorry, Guðrún.' I feel a gnawing sense of guilt, because the truth is that I abandoned her deliberately. I looked at her lying there on the sofa and felt too angry to help her.

'When I woke up next morning, I … I…' She's sobbing so violently now that the words are unintelligible.

'Guðrún, love. I had no idea…' I'm so upset that I'm feeling quite weepy myself. 'Did something happen?'

There's a long pause before Guðrún speaks – as if she has to control herself before she can tell me.

'I wasn't sure at first,' she says in a quiet voice. 'But then I didn't get my period when it was due and Mum took me to the doctor.' Her face grows hard again. 'That's why I was away all summer. That's why we went to Reykjavík. To … to make it disappear.'

I raise a hand to my mouth, then instinctively put my arm around my friend. She endures my hug but doesn't return it, and I sense that she's no longer crying.

'I fooled myself into believing you were fond of me,' she says in a low voice. 'That everything could go back to being like it used to be.'

'But Guðrún, I had no idea.'

'That you cared about me. That I mattered to you.'

'You *do* matter to me,' I say, but she doesn't seem to be listening.

'I don't matter.' Her voice is toneless, devoid of emotion. 'I don't even matter to Mum. All she can think about is meeting your dad, who makes her all these promises. Whereas you – all you have to do is click your fingers and you can have anything and anyone you want. But no one wants me.'

'That's not true.'

'Then I saw you two today,' Guðrún continues.

'Who?'

'I saw you and Gústi. In spite of everything you know, in spite of everything I've told you.' Her voice is no longer choked with tears but cold and steely.

Guðrún has always been in love with Gústi, ever since we started school. I've listened to her talking endlessly about how kind, helpful, funny and nice Gústi is. And I've tried, without her knowledge, to say positive things about her to him, but I think he sees her more as a friend than anything else. Quite apart from which, I've only ever regarded him as a friend myself. Today's kiss was a foolish impulse at a vulnerable moment, and I can't believe the bad luck that Guðrún happened to spot us just then.

'Guðrún, it wasn't like you think—'

A sharp pain in my stomach makes me break off. I feel a burning sensation, but can't work out why until I look down and see that Guðrún is holding something – something that appears to be sticking into me.

Guðrún jerks back her hand and I stare aghast at the knife. She seems as horrified as I must look. As if suddenly waking up to what she's done, she starts crying again.

'I'm sorry,' she whispers. 'I'm sorry, Stína.'

I lurch towards her and she takes a step backwards.

I try to beg her to wait, to help me. She needs to fetch somebody, I think, but my thoughts are becoming increasingly sluggish, confused by the searing agony in my stomach. I can no longer speak for the pain.

'Sorry,' Guðrún whispers again, then turns and runs away.

I crumple on to the cold gravel, then roll on to my back. I try to breathe through the agony. My vest feels soaking wet and I hardly dare think about what that means. Someone will find me soon –

they're bound to. I just need to hang on for a little while longer and someone will come.

I close my eyes.

And when I open them again, the pain has almost gone. I feel much better. It's going to be all right.

Everything is turning white around me. The snowflakes are tumbling down from the sky now and settling on me like a quilt. So beautiful. So warm.

Then I see a blinding glare heading my way and what feels like moments later a face looms over me. I smile: I'm safe now.

'Marsí, I knew you'd come.'

57
Marsibil – *Monday, 26 December 1977*

Half an hour later I was standing at the front door of the red house in the middle of town. Guðrún answered my knock and seemed pleased to see me.

'Marsí, how are you? Do you want to come in?'

'Hi, Marsibil. Happy Christmas.' Guðrún's mother also came to the door. She was wearing a pretty shawl with a violet-and-brown pattern on it.

'I won't stop,' I said. 'I just wanted to say goodbye.'

'Are you leaving straight away?' Alda asked.

'Yes, I need to get home.' I smiled. 'Could we maybe go for a quick walk, Guðrún?'

Guðrún regards me for a moment or two, then grabs her jacket. 'Of course we can. I won't be long, Mum.'

'You're not dressed warmly enough, Guðrún dear,' Alda said. 'Here, take my shawl to wrap round your neck.'

Guðrún took the shawl with the violet pattern and we set out into the darkness, in silence at first. She was pressing so close to me as she walked that I could smell her floral perfume, such a heady, unnatural scent in the freezing air that I felt momentarily light-headed.

'Is everything OK? You seem a bit down,' Guðrún said.

'I'm fine,' I replied.

'Are you still thinking about the Stína business?'

I shook my head.

'Oh, what then? Man trouble?'

When I didn't immediately reply, Guðrún apparently took this as assent and nudged me playfully.

'You can talk to me, Marsí. I've always been able to keep a secret. Mum says I'm a good listener, and I think she's right. Anyway, I like it when people feel they can talk to me, and I promise you I never tell.'

It's true, it was good talking to Guðrún, I'd always found her someone I could turn to for help. Always known exactly what to expect from her.

'OK, there is someone,' I said.

'I knew it. So what's the problem?'

'I suppose I'm the problem. I'm too damaged.'

'Don't be silly. Is it someone in Reykjavík?'

'No.'

'Someone from here?' Guðrún raises her eyebrows when I nod. 'Have you known him long?'

'Ever since I was a child.'

'I see,' Guðrún said. 'You must know him pretty well if you've known him all that time.' I nodded, and Guðrún tittered. 'Come on, Marsí, spill the beans.'

'It's Gústi.'

Guðrún's lips form a small 'o'. 'You know, I once saw Gústi and Stína together. They were kissing in the wood behind your house. I should have guessed what was going on, but Stína never said a word. She claimed they were just friends.'

We had gone beyond the outskirts of the town now, past the house where Gústi lived with his family. Neither of us had spoken for a while. The sky was so overcast that only the odd star managed to shine through the clouds and the moon was hidden, making it even darker out here than usual.

Guðrún stopped and turned to me. 'Marsí, why aren't you saying anything? I hope I haven't upset you by telling you about Gústi and Stína.'

I shook my head calmly. 'No, I'm not upset.'

The Christmas card was in my pocket. I took it out and handed it to Guðrún.

'What's this?' she asked.

'Mum and I were reading our Christmas cards earlier and I happened to notice the sign-off at the bottom.' I watched Guðrún's reaction as she peered at the card, but her face remained impassive, so I went on. 'When Mette's body was found, she had a note to me with her, which had the same sign-off: *Warmest wishes*. Unusual, if you think about it. Most people just say "best wishes" or "season's greetings".'

Guðrún continued to study the card for a while, then tossed it casually on the ground and carried on talking as if I hadn't spoken.

'I caught them in a clinch in the wood behind your house. We were best friends – or at least we were until Málfríður came along – and she knew I'd been in love with Gústi ever since we were little girls, yet in spite of that she thought it was OK to take him away from me. Like everything else.'

I stared at Guðrún, trying to read her mind. Her manner had changed in a way that I couldn't understand. 'Like everything else?' I asked. 'How do you mean?'

'Stína was always so bossy. So domineering. Everything revolved around her and what she wanted to do. She always got special treatment because everyone thought she was so unique and talented, but the fact is, she used people. She used her teachers, her friends and me. She even used you, Marsí. Were you aware of that?'

'How do you mean?'

'She was always pretending she had to go home because you were going through a rough patch. Saying she was worried about you because of this penpal you were writing to.'

My heart leaped into my throat and I had to step backwards. 'She … she knew about that?'

'Of course she did. She used to read your letters and have a good laugh about them.' Gone was the nice old Guðrún; there was no trace of kindness or sympathy in her voice now.

'You're lying,' I said, feeling hot despite the chill air.

'She was always making fun of you. Always telling us how crazy you were, walking in your sleep and waking up in different places around the house. And she joked to everyone about how innocent and naïve you were, in love with a penpal you'd never even met.'

So Stína really had known about the letters and told Guðrún about them. I didn't believe she had laughed at me, though. Stína wasn't spiteful.

I shook my head, trying to put on a show of indifference, but it must have been unconvincing because Guðrún smiled.

'That's why she left early that evening,' Guðrún went on. 'She told me she'd read your letter arranging to meet this boy and she wanted to make sure you were OK. "She doesn't know what she's doing," Stína told me. She saw you as a little kid.'

'She was looking out for me?' The lump in my throat was making it hard to speak. Here, at last, was the explanation of why Stína had gone home early that evening: she was looking out for me.

'Yes, she went to make sure you were OK,' Guðrún said.

I swallowed the lump in my throat and tried to marshal my thoughts. I still couldn't understand how it all fitted together; why Guðrún was suddenly being so hard and vindictive.

'Guðrún, did you write the note that was found on Mette?'

'I had to send you a warning.'

'Why?'

'Because I didn't want you to go the same way as Stína.'

The world seemed to darken before my eyes, and for a moment I was sure I must be dreaming. 'What on earth do you mean?'

'Oh, you must be able to work it out, Marsí,' Guðrún said, a note of irritation entering her voice. 'When Stína left Málfríður's house that evening, I followed her.'

'But ... but that's impossible. Málfríður said you'd been with her the whole time.'

Guðrún laughed. 'Málfríður lied for me. You see, she knew I had something on her that she didn't want to get out. Do you remember the Icelandic teacher, Þór? The good-looking one? Well, he'd been messing around with Málfríður and didn't want his wife to find out. I caught them kissing in the classroom once, and Málfríður made me promise not to tell anyone. She was so frightened I'd give away her secret that she kept on lying for me, even after she heard that Stína had disappeared. I must say I was quite surprised about that. But I suppose that's how it is with some lies. Once you've started, it's hard to stop and take them back, because then everything else you say loses its credibility. Sometimes it's just easier to keep going.'

'I don't understand…'

'You don't understand how your sister treated people. The people who stuck by her through thick and thin. I was always there for Stína, but she was ungrateful. She threw me away like a broken toy.' Guðrún breathed out hard through her nose, then said through gritted teeth: 'It was time to teach her a lesson. Show her that she couldn't always have everything she wanted.'

I stared at Guðrún, and for a moment I couldn't speak.

'What … what did you do to her?' I stammered.

'What did *I* do to her?' Guðrún was suddenly shouting. 'How about what *she* did to me? Don't you care about that at all?'

'Just because Stína wasn't always a good friend to you, that—'

'A good friend?' Guðrún snorted. 'You haven't a clue what your sister was like. Did you know that she deliberately got me drunk at a party, then left me there, at the house of a boy we didn't even know, and let him do what he wanted to me? That I got pregnant when I was only sixteen and had to go away for the whole summer to have … to get rid of it.' The corners of her mouth twitched down as if she was about to burst into tears again.

'That's not true,' I whispered. 'Stína would never—'

I flinched at a sudden pain in my cheek and it took me a second or two to work out what had happened.

I put a hand to my face. Guðrún had slapped me as if I was a naughty child. I couldn't believe it, despite my stinging cheek. I'd known Guðrún since we were little; she'd been like a second sister to me. Always so kind and good, a little shy, but fun and mischievous.

'Not true? Are you calling me a liar?' Guðrún tugged her mother's shawl from around her neck. 'Stína abandoned me there out of revenge. Like it was my fault your dad was having an affair with my mother. And the worst part is that I forgave her. I didn't want to lose her so I forgave her. I didn't even tell her about my terrible summer and all I'd had to go through because of her.' Guðrún sniffed. 'You're just the same, you two. You don't care about anyone else.'

'What on earth have *I* done?'

'Ever since you came back to town, he hasn't had eyes for anyone but you.' Guðrún's fists were clenched round the ends of the shawl as she came towards me. 'I forgave Stína, though I shouldn't have, but then she went too far, and when I saw them there in the wood, I couldn't take anymore.'

'Is this about Gústi?'

'First it was Stína, then that Mette, and now you. He won't have eyes for me as long as there are girls like you in town. I'm just waiting for him to see me, don't you understand? That's what everybody wants, isn't it? To be *seen*.'

I retreated a few steps, pinching myself hard on the arm, but I didn't wake up.

'Gústi and I had finally become close. He even told me I was the only decent girl in this town. Then Mette turned up, all young and pretty, and wouldn't leave him alone. But the very evening I dealt with her, you had to pop up, so I sent you a warning.'

'You're saying you actually killed Mette and ... and Stína?' Even with the facts laid out before me, I couldn't believe it. It was too insane. I must be dreaming.

'It's been tormenting me, you know?' Guðrún looked almost thoughtful now. Strangely calm. 'Wondering all this time what happened to Stína. I mean, I killed her that evening. Or I thought I had. After I'd stabbed her, I fled, but her body was never found. I've sometimes thought she must have survived and deliberately done a disappearing act. That would be typical of her, don't you think? Like we said when we were talking about her, Marsí. Do you remember what a good time we had at the bar?'

When I didn't answer, Guðrún sighed.

'I don't suppose we'll ever find out what actually became of Stína.' She shrugged and pouted her lips, like she was talking about a lost toy. 'But you know, I was genuinely hoping you'd leave, Marsí.' She gave me a small smile. 'I really didn't want to have to hurt you.'

Guðrún swung the shawl over my head, and before I could react, she jerked at it, pulling me off balance so I toppled towards her. As I tried to recover, she smashed her fist down on the back of my head. I was knocked to the ground, landing on my face. When I tried to scramble up, I felt a heavy weight on top of me. Guðrún was kneeling, one knee pressing down on my back. The gravel cut into my hands as I resisted, but she was unusually strong. Or perhaps I was unusually weak.

I felt the soft fabric of the shawl tightening around my throat.

'This shawl is made of silk,' Guðrún said, her voice strained with the effort. 'Did you know that silk's actually a very strong material? Difficult to tear. I used it on Mette too; it only took a few minutes. Not that she fought back; she was too drunk. That's why I offered her a lift home. She was a bit upset about Gústi too, you know. He'd said he'd drive her home but he disappeared as soon as he saw you. She was terribly disappointed. This is a much neater method than the one I used on Stína. Knives are so messy – too much blood.'

Guðrún tightened her grip and a rattling noise escaped my throat. My sight was clouding over now and I could see tiny dots everywhere, as if it was snowing black flakes. My fingers clutched convulsively at the gravel on the road and I felt the grit under my fingernails.

'If only you'd stayed in Reykjavík, where you belong. You needn't have come back, Marsí. Then everything would have been all right. Then—'

Guðrún was abruptly silenced as a handful of gravel caught her full in the face. Her grip momentarily slackened, which was all I needed to be able to twist round on to my back. I shoved her off me, grabbed a big stone and slammed it down with all my strength on her head.

'What are you…?' she exclaimed in astonishment, clasping her head as if she couldn't believe I had hit her.

I didn't wait for her to get her bearings but hit her again, and this time she went down.

There were so many things I wanted to say to her as she lay there on the ground, a bleeding gash on her forehead. I wanted to bring home to her what she'd done to me and my family. Make her understand that for a decade I had blamed myself for Stína's disappearance, that my parents were no more than empty husks, that our home was nothing but an echo of the past. I wanted her to feel pain, wanted her to experience the same grief and loss as I had.

But I knew it was pointless.

That's why I didn't think, didn't say a word, just brought the stone down again and again on her head until a deep dent had formed there.

58

When it was over, the stone fell from my loosened fingers.

I sat down beside Guðrún's body and wept. Wept so hard that my body convulsed and my face contorted in a grimace.

Eventually, I calmed down, and as I wiped away my tears, I experienced a feeling I hadn't had for a long time: relief. There were no thoughts racing through my head anymore. There was nothing left to say. It was over.

The door opened as I was walking up the drive. Mum stood there in her nightie, looking like an angel in blue.

'Marsí love, what…?' She raised a hand to her mouth. 'The state of you.'

Dad appeared in the doorway beside her. When he saw me, he ran out in his socks to meet me and led me inside. I had no strength left to explain anything. All I could say was Guðrún's name.

'What happened?' Mum asked, holding me from the other side. 'Where is Guðrún?'

I looked behind me, towards the road. They must have asked me more questions and spoken to each other about me but I didn't respond. I was too numb to understand or take in what was happening around me.

The next thing I remembered was Mum leading me into the bathroom. She made me stand in the tub as she undressed me, taking each piece of clothing in turn and placing it in a black bin bag.

'There, there,' she said soothingly, as if comforting a small child.

Then she took the shower head and began to wash me. Using a flannel and soap, she rubbed my body with firm strokes. I closed my eyes, suddenly unable to remember what I was doing there. I must have been dreaming. It was the same dream I'd had many times before: of standing in a bathtub while Mum washed me.

'What are you doing?' I asked.

'Nothing, Marsí love. We just need to wash you,' Mum said. 'We've got to get you clean.'

My memories were slipping away from me but I squeezed my eyes shut, forcing myself to hold on to them. This time I wasn't going to push it all away. I wanted to remember what had happened, however painful it was. But perhaps it wasn't so painful, after all. Perhaps I had done the right thing. For Stína.

After the bath, Mum put me to bed and tucked the duvet around me. She stroked my face with her fingers, closing her eyes and humming a lullaby. Sleep came quickly – heavy, longed-for sleep – but even through my drowsiness I heard the sounds coming from the garden.

Sitting bolt upright, I looked out of the window.

The moon had come out from behind the clouds and cast a dim light on Dad, who was labouring away in the quiet night, digging a hole in the garden near the henhouse. Beside him was a black bin bag, the size of a human body.

I smiled to myself in the certain knowledge that everything was going to be all right. The soothing sound of the spade followed me into my sleep which, for once in my life, was dreamless.

ACKNOWLEDGEMENTS

If you look for Hvítársíða in Borgarfjörður on a map you will find a sparsely populated rural area stretching along the banks of the river Hvítá (which means 'White River'), but you won't find a town there. I made up the town in this novel for several reasons, one of which was that I wanted the freedom to shape the setting exactly to the story's needs, without tying it to any real place or people. That gave me room to explore difficult themes without pointing fingers at an existing community. If you want to explore the setting of the story, however, I do recommend you go to Hvítársíða anyway and enjoy the beautiful views of mountains and glaciers, and the steam rising from the earth. It's easy to imagine secrets hiding in the mist.

All that said, this story is inspired by something very real – the so called 'situation girls' here in Iceland. The situation girls were mostly teenagers accused of having relationships with soldiers during WWII. Many were labeled as morally deviant and sent to a state-run institution at Kleppjárnsreykir in 1942–1943. There the girls were placed under strict controls, simply for defying social norms. It's a dark chapter in Icelandic history, in which young women were punished more for what others perceived they had done than for any actual wrongdoing. While the events in this book are fictional, the stories of those girls have stayed with me. However, I chose not to focus directly on what happened to them – I don't feel it's my place to tell that story. Instead, I wanted to explore the aftermath of what they went through, and how that kind of trauma can echo through a person's life.

Writing a book is never just about typing words. It's about conversations, encouragement, coffee (so much coffee), and people who keep believing in you even when you're staring at the screen wondering if you should throw the book in the bin just before the deadline.

Thank you to the brilliant team at Orenda: Karen, West, and everyone who touches my manuscripts with your magic – I'm so grateful. And my books wouldn't be able to travel very far if not for my translator, Vicky Cribb, whose work continues to amaze me.

To my agent, David Headley – thank you for always cheering me on and for making sure these stories reach readers far beyond Iceland. The journey has been wild and wonderful, and I know we'll keep finding more reasons to celebrate.

Thank you to my Icelandic publishers at Veröld, for being the first ones to meet every new book and for doing so with excitement and encouragement (and, let's be honest, a little bit of healthy fear while we wait for the reviews).

To my family – thank you for keeping me grounded and for always being there. Thanks for the daily dose of perspective, noise and joy. You make life better, even when it's a bit chaotic.

And finally, to you, the reader – thank you for choosing to spend your time with my story. There are thousands of books out there, and the fact that you have picked up mine means more than you know. Every message, review, recommendation, or quiet moment spent with one of my characters, keeps this whole strange, wonderful writing life going. I'm endlessly grateful – and always writing for you.

Eager to read the explosive finale to the Forbidden Iceland series?

Preorder
THE LAST TENANT
By Eva Björg Ægisdóttir
Translated by Victoria Cribb

The multi-award-winning, international bestselling Forbidden Iceland series continues...

When the skeletons of a young woman and a baby are uncovered on a long-abandoned farm in Hvalfjörður, it is clear they were buried years apart. West Iceland CID begins to investigate the disturbing discovery, aware that someone has gone to great lengths to keep the past hidden.

In Akranes, Karitas, a young single mother seeking a new start, settles in with her four-year-old son and rents a basement flat from an eccentric landlord. A cautious sense of happiness returns when she meets the boy next door.

But when news breaks that a local girl has been murdered, Karitas must decide who she can trust, knowing that one wrong choice could place her and her child in danger.

Detective Elma is drawn into the case, forced to navigate long-hidden family secrets to understand a killer's motive, while trying to hold together her increasingly troubled relationship with Sævar.

Dark, atmospheric and rich with psychological suspense, *The Last Tenant* confirms Eva Björg Ægisdóttir as one of Iceland's finest crime writers, as a meticulous investigation and a series of unsettling discoveries draw a close-knit community towards a reckoning no one can escape...

OUT SEPTEMBER 2026
Scan here: